SANCTUARY

SANCTUARY

A NOVEL

Translated from the Italian by
Howard Curtis and Katherine Gregor

Luca D'Andrea

HARPER

An Imprint of HarperCollins*Publishers*

First published in Italian as *Lissy* by Einaudi/Stile Libero, Turin, 2017.

First published in Great Britain in 2019 by MacLehose Press, an imprint of Quercus, a Hachette UK Company.

HarperCollins books may be purchased for educational, business, or sales promotional use. For information, please email the Special Markets Department at SPsales@harpercollins.com.

FIRST U.S. EDITION

Library of Congress Cataloging-in-Publication Data has been applied for.

ISBN 978-0-06-289700-8 (pbk.)
ISBN 978-0-06-297212-5 (library edition)

20 21 22 23 24 LSC 10 9 8 7 6 5 4 3 2 1

SANCTUARY

1

"Sweet Lissy, little Lissy."

2

Two light knocks and these words: *Nibble, nibble, little mouse! Who is nibbling at my house?*

Marlene, twenty-two years old, one metre sixty, maybe a little more, eyes a melancholy blue, a beauty spot at the edge of her smile, undoubtedly beautiful and undoubtedly scared, looked at her reflection in the steel of the safe and felt stupid. Metal, not gingerbread like in the fairy tale. And not a witch in sight.

It's only fear, she told herself, that's all it is.

She relaxed her shoulders, held her breath the way her father did before he squeezed the trigger of his rifle, emptied her lungs and focused again. There were no such things as witches. The fairy tales lied. Only life mattered, and Marlene was about to change hers forever.

The combination was easy to remember. One. Three. Two. Then four. A flick of the wrist, then another four. Done. So simple that Marlene's hands moved as if automatically. She took hold of the steel handle, pulled it down and gritted her teeth.

A treasure.

Wads of banknotes stacked up like firewood for the *Stube*. A pistol, a box of ammunition and a velvet pouch. Under the box was a notebook worth more than all that money multiplied a hundred-fold. There was blood, and maybe also a couple of life sentences, preserved within its crumpled pages: an endless list of creditors and debtors, friends and friends of friends, all in Herr Wegener's small, wiry, slanting hand. Marlene didn't give it a second glance. She didn't care about the pistol, the box of ammunition or the bundles of banknotes. The velvet pouch, though, made her hands sweat. She knew what it contained, knew its power, and was *terrified* of it.

Hers was not a simple theft.

Let's not mince our words. The name for what the young woman was doing, with her heart in her mouth, was *treason*. Marlene Wegener, *née* Taufer, lawful wedded wife of Robert Wegener, the man they all doffed their hats to, a man with a forty-year career of contraband, intimidation, violence and murder. No one messed with a man like Wegener. No one even dared call him by his first name. To everybody, Robert Wegener was *Herr* Wegener.

Even to her. To Marlene. His wife.

Get a move on, time's flying.

And yet, perhaps because the ticking of the clock was turning anxiety to panic from one tick to the next, when Marlene opened the velvet case, the fairy tale once again prevailed over reality and her eyes met the deep, terrible, dark-blue eyes of tiny, angular creatures.

Kobolds.

It even struck her as obvious. Kobolds loved metal, cold and death: the safe, the pistol, the money, the notebook.

A perfect nest.

The kobolds reacted fiercely against the intrusion. They drained the room of light, trapped Marlene in their cruel little eyes, and turned her into such a savage essence of hatred that the pouch almost slipped from her fingers.

That brought her back to the present, to the wide-open safe, the villa on the River Passer.

In other words, to reality.

The velvet pouch was filled with sapphires. Pressed carbon which, through a trick of physics, has learned to sparkle like a star. Herr Wegener's entire fortune – or near enough – clutched in her hand. But no witch and no kobolds. Because, Marlene told herself again, there were no such things as witches or kobolds, whereas these precious stones were not only real, they were the key to her new life. As long as she stopped wasting time and got out of here.

Without giving the world of fairy tales another thought, and without even considering the consequences of what she had just set in motion, Marlene tied the pouch, hid it in the inside pocket of her padded jacket, locked the safe, put the painting back to hide it, straightened up, flicked back a strand of hair that was about to fall into her eyes and left the bedroom.

She walked along the corridor, down one flight of stairs, across the living room, through the hall with its excess of mirrors and down the outside steps. The night greeted her with a light northerly wind.

She did not stop.

She got into the grey Fiat 130 and drove away. The villa disappearing in the rearview mirror. The passing street lamps. The gold wedding ring thrown out of the window without a trace of regret. The sleeping town. The scrapyard. A brief halt and, thanks to an envelope stuffed with money, the Fiat 130 became a cream Mercedes W114 with new number plates, papers all in order, brand-new tyres and a full tank.

Then, without so much as a farewell thought, she was off again, heading west.

Apart from the first snowflakes, everything was going according to plan. At least until the roadblock a few kilometres from Mals. A real pain in the neck.

At the end of a series of bends she had just started along, Marlene glimpsed a van, its rotating beacon switched off, and a couple of carabinieri who looked as if they were freezing to death. Or falling asleep. Or maybe slyly waiting for someone or something.

Herr Wegener had eyes and ears everywhere. Even among officers of the law.

So: Should she try her luck or change route?

If it had not been for the fear and the tension, Marlene might still have been able to protect her plan from unforeseen occurrences like this. But the tension, the fear and the increasingly heavy snow made her brake, reverse and turn onto a back road, setting off a new chain of events.

The back road led her to another, even narrower, winding one, which went through a sleeping village and brought her to a cross-roads (left or right? heads or tails?), then further on, with the snow piling up around her, layer upon layer.

And when the car started to skid, the young woman with the beauty spot at the edge of her smile decided to carry on anyway, with one eye on the road, which kept climbing, and one on the map – on which, needless to say, this stretch wasn't marked. Damn them and their useless maps!

That wasn't true.

The map may not have been precise – none of them were. But inaccurate? It was 1974, and by 1974 man had already left his prints in the dust of the moon, so a map could hardly be inaccurate. Marlene should have just pulled over, switched on the light inside the car, taken a couple of deep breaths and checked. Things would have turned out differently.

But Marlene did not stop.

Her anxiety was now compounded by the incredulous realisation that she was well and truly lost.

Step on it, but *gently*, she told herself. Keep going. The road will take you somewhere sooner or later. A village, a shelter, a lay-by. She would even have been happy if the road had widened enough to let her do a U-turn, drive back the way she had come, and brave the checkpoint: anything, just to put a stop to this new, remorseless sequence of events and take back control of her own fate.

It was not to be.

Maybe it was the snow, maybe she couldn't take her eyes off the map, but suddenly Marlene felt the Mercedes lose traction, swerve abruptly to the left, spin around and . . . *take off*.

It was terrifying: the headlights sweeping the blackness, the swirls of dark snow, the gaping precipice, the tree trunks, motionless and in perfect focus.

The impact was violent, the explosion of pain stifled by the screech of ripped metal. Yes, this time it really was an infernal lament, all too similar to the creaking of the witch's door.

Marlene cried out the name of God. And as the black, nameless mountain loomed over her, her cry turned into a gasp. The last thing she invoked, though, was love. Love, which had driven her to betray the most dangerous man she'd ever met. Love, which had a name.

"Klaus."

Marlene's last word before the darkness.

3

It was nearly dawn, but had it not been for the clock, nobody would have noticed. The snowfall had turned into a blizzard. No light outside, only white mist.

No light inside the room, either. The crystal chandelier seemed not to illuminate anything, merely to draw a shapeless patch on the floor.

Staring at it for too long was likely to bring on horrible thoughts. Both the man and the woman avoided doing that.

It looked too much like a bloodstain.

Apart from the ticking of the grandfather clock and their breathing, there was silence.

The woman was sitting in an armchair, as stiff as a tin soldier, hands clasped on her clenched thighs, features frozen in a grimace that made her look ten years older. She was wearing a kind of uniform, with a knee-length skirt and a white apron, and her hair was gathered in a plait. But for her scowling (or frightened?) expression, she would have been beautiful.

Her name was Helene, and she had been the housekeeper at the villa on the Passer for more than five years. She hadn't bitten her nails for at least twice as long. That was one of the first lessons she had been taught at the home economics school in Brixen where she had learned the basics of the job. A good housekeeper's hands, her teachers had said, are her calling card. They must be perfect. Always clean and well cared for. At the start, not biting her nails had been almost as hard as giving up smoking, but then she had got used to it.

For years, it hadn't even occurred to her to go back to her bad old habit.

Until the screaming had started.

What kind of man could let out such screams?

It had taken her no more than a moment to relapse. She had bitten, she had nibbled, and when her teeth had sunk into the raw flesh, she had dropped her hands back down to her lap and twisted her apron nervously.

Then she had started again.

Hands. Mouth. Nails. Teeth. A small pang of pain. Apron.

And then all over again.

Helene had exchanged just one look with the man who stood leaning against the large fireplace nobody ever used. A single look, but it said all there was to say.

His name was Moritz. Early thirties, rings like bruises under his eyes and an automatic in a holster concealed by the jacket of his dark suit. Usually he looked wonderful in that suit. He had paid a fortune for it, but it had been worth it. That was what he would tell himself as he looked in the mirror in the morning and knotted his tie or gave his brilliantined hair a final touch, and it was confirmed by the looks the women he passed in town gave him.

Now, though, in this dawn, with or without his dark suit, Moritz would have felt as twisted and ungainly as a scarecrow. Because, when he had caught his reflection in Helene's eyes, he had glimpsed something that had terrified him. An expression like so many he had seen since he had become a member of Herr Wegener's circle. The expression of a victim.

And that was not good.

Not good at all, because Moritz was a simple man who divided the world with the toss of a coin. Victim or executioner? One metre ninety, over ninety kilos, and with a natural tendency to violence, Moritz had never experienced a victim's fear. Until the moment he had seen himself reflected in Helene's eyes and he, too, had wondered: What kind of human being can let out such screams? And how long can he keep it up before he goes completely mad? But also: What's going to happen to *us*?

That was why he had stopped looking at Helene. Or at the stain on the floor.

Too many questions, far too many questions.

Moritz hated questions. Because you couldn't break a question's nose. You couldn't fire a bullet into a question's heart (and one into its head, just to be safe) and silence it forever. Questions were like those persistent, disgusting insects with their big, hungry, relentless jaws that could cause even the strongest castle to come crumbling down.

Silence. Moritz wished there could be silence.

He wished he could ignore the screams and disappear for a few minutes. Just long enough to chase away the bad thoughts. He wished he could go out into the garden for a smoke. Or else have a small glass of brandy.

But orders were orders. For someone like Moritz, orders cut the heads off question marks. They marked the boundary between what you could do and what was forbidden.

Orders made everything much simpler, and he was a simple man. They also made disobedience much more exciting. And to be completely honest, that was what had got him into trouble.

So Moritz stood there, motionless and stiff in his dark suit, leaning against the unlit fireplace. Listening to the screams and feeling the weight of the automatic dragging him down to the ground, to the shapeless stain on the floor.

Helene, on the other hand, had a more complex view of the world. Things were not just black and white, obedience and transgression, victims and executioners. There was a whole sea of greys to navigate. It didn't take much to turn an order into a suggestion, and suggestions weren't traps, they always offered a way out. Her duty, for example, was to the villa, not to her employer. The villa and her employer were two separate things.

That was a way out.

When she decided she had had enough of the screams, Helene stood up abruptly and left the room, as silent as a ghost.

4

It was dawn now. He did not so much see it as feel it in his bones. He could not have done otherwise. The windows overlooking the garden were shut. A single lamp, broken but still working, lit up the disordered room. Wardrobes flung open, drawers pulled out, blankets and clothes ripped, an infinite number of papers, items of jewellery, paintings and books (except for one) on the floor, innocent victims of his rage.

In the middle of the room, all stucco and velvet curtains with gold trimmings, Herr Wegener sat on the unmade bed, aware that if he did not stop screaming and start thinking in a lucid, rational manner, every conquest that had led him to be what he was would turn into a heap of shit, a monument to wasted effort.

His self-control was something he had boasted about for years. His steady nerves, his composure, had led him to rule over what he had secretly dubbed "the Empire." An Empire ready to make the big leap – this was the plan, anyway – the leap that would allow him to go from being a man to whom people took off their hats to a man in whose presence they were obliged to *genuflect.*

In that icy dawn, however hard he tried to regain self-control, it remained an illusion.

This was because Wegener could not bring himself to believe what his steady nerves, his composure, were telling him. That there could be one explanation and one only: Marlene.

Impossible. Marlene would never betray him. Marlene was his wife. Marlene was the woman he loved. Above all, Marlene was a *woman*, and it was unheard of for a woman to screw over someone like him. Or maybe yes, maybe there were women in the world capable of doing something as daring as that, but Wegener was certain Marlene did not belong to that category. Not even as a joke.

The steady nerves, the composure, disagreed. They kept repeating it over and over.

It was her, it was her. Marlene.

The steady nerves, the composure, had proof. For example, there was no sign of a break-in at the villa, not on any of the doors or windows. He had checked them himself. No sign of forced entry. Nobody had come in or gone out. Which meant that whoever had committed the burglary had the keys, knew the layout, was familiar with the routines of the house.

Another incriminating piece of evidence: the day and time of the theft.

Friday night. The night Wegener would take the Fulvia Coupé, leave Merano with his right-hand man, Georg, and go to a dive in Appiano where, *every Friday night*, he would meet up with his men.

There they would talk about new markets, new strategies, problems that needed solving. He would get the latest gossip, the latest hearsay, the latest tips. Sometimes, new faces would be introduced, so that he could take a look at them and decide what to do with them.

Do you want a well-paid job, my boy? Have you got guts and balls? Then have a chat with Herr Wegener. He can help you.

There had been a time, early in his career, when it had actually been exciting to shake hands with these men, to watch them show off in his presence and know how easy it was to crush someone with a word or a raised eyebrow.

But now he was bored by his minions. He hated them.

All the same, this pantomime was part of his duties. His men were mostly coarse people. Brawny, ill-shaven. When they wore jackets and ties, they looked like peasants who had come down to

12

the town for Sunday Mass. As a matter of fact, many of them were, or had been, peasants. When they spoke, they used a dialect that set his teeth on edge, they ate with their mouths open and could knock back whole barrels of beer and spirits, making as much racket as a horde of trolls. And he would do the same.

He had to.

He had to speak that foul-mouthed, vulgar *dialekt*, he had to drink more than the lot of them put together, just because that was the only way these men, mistrustful by nature and by culture, could feel sure that, despite the jacket and tie, despite the Fulvia and the bodyguard by the door, despite frequently having his picture in the papers, Herr Wegener was, and would always be, someone they could trust. *One of us.*

And so, every Saturday, at about four in the morning, Wegener would return to the villa in a foul mood, nursing a hangover and stinking of cheap cigarettes and alcohol. It was a smell that not even a long shower could remove, a smell he didn't like to inflict on Marlene. That was why, just one night a week, he slept in one of the guest rooms rather than next to his wife. In fact, on this damned Saturday morning, if he hadn't needed to get the black notebook out of the safe in order to add some more names, he would not have noticed Marlene's disappearance until late in the morning.

So: No forced entry.

So: Friday night.

Weren't two clues enough? The steady nerves, the composure, were ready to provide others . . .

Let's consider the sapphires.

The thief (or thieves) had left almost twenty million lire in cash and as much in foreign currencies. He (or they) had stolen only the sapphires. Only them. Nobody knew about the sapphires. Nobody except Georg and Marlene.

Georg had been up all night watching over him, just as, right now, he was at the door of the villa, smoking and looking for any trace left by the thieves. Georg was always supervised. Wegener knew who he saw and what they talked about. He could remove him from the list of suspects. Who else was there?

Marlene, obviously.

It wasn't true, Wegener objected. There were others who knew.

Not much of a defence.

Of course, the Consortium knew about the sapphires. But the members of the Consortium had no reason to steal them, since they were the very people to whom he was supposed to be delivering the dark velvet pouch. Why go to the trouble of stealing something that already belonged to you? That would be a stupid move. And he didn't think the members of the Consortium were stupid, did he?

No, of course not.

That left Marlene.

Marlene, Marlene, *Marlene*.

So he still didn't want to believe it? Alright, but the clues did not stop there. There were more.

The car.

The grey Fiat 130 was missing, the car Herr Wegener had given Marlene after persuading her to take her test, because a boss's woman has to be a modern woman, fashionably dressed and able to drive. If Clyde had had to escape in the middle of a shoot-out, he wouldn't have called a taxi: it would have been Bonnie who'd have floored the accelerator, dodging the bullets. Besides, *dammit*, this was the '70s, not the Stone Age.

The Fiat was not there.

Why would the thieves have stolen it?

And last but not least, the most irrefutable evidence of all. The thing that drove him insane.

The book was missing. That book. *Her* book. The tales of the Brothers Grimm. The only thing Marlene had brought with her from her parents' house to her husband's. An old edition with a damaged cover and the title page missing. Marlene never let it out of her sight. It was her lucky charm, she would say. It drove away nightmares. That was why she kept it on her bedside table.

Where had the damned book gone?

Herr Wegener had looked everywhere. He had turned the room upside down, even ripped open the pillowcases and mattress cover. Because if he found the book, then the accusations against Marlene would fall away and he would know what to do. He would know what orders to give and who to give them to. He would drag every single bastard on his payroll out of bed and launch them on a manhunt until he had recovered his sapphires, and then he would take great pleasure in slaughtering the son of a bitch who had dared to make a fool of him.

But the book had vanished. Along with the Fiat and the sapphires.

And Marlene.

She wasn't here. Nobody had seen her.

But Marlene would never have . . .

And so it would begin again.

In Herr Wegener's mind, logic and feeling collided terrifyingly. The blood rushed to his head and he felt an irrepressible desire to scream until his vocal cords snapped, a need so pressing that he couldn't control it.

That was what he found even more unbearable than the theft, than Marlene's betrayal: that safe, wide open like a sneer, mocking him.

And so he screamed. At Marlene. At the safe. And, above all, at himself.

And as he screamed, it was not only Moritz, standing next to the unlit fireplace, but also Helene, who had taken refuge in the kitchen, and Georg, back inside now to shake off the snow and warm himself, who wondered what kind of a man could let out such screams.

The combination to the safe. That was the answer.

5

The combination.

One, three, two. Double four. As in 13 February 1944.

In 1944, Wegener was twelve and not yet Herr Wegener. No man in his right mind would have called that skinny little brat "Herr."

Actually, his surname did not even have a second "e." Back then, Wegener was Robert *Wegner*, like his father, Paul *Wegner*.

Paul Wegner (without an "e") had joined the Wehrmacht as a volunteer. He had not even had time to write his wife and son a letter before the war swallowed him up. A grenade had fallen in the German lines, and Paul had instinctively thrown himself on it, saving the lives of his platoon.

It was the *Standartenführer* of the barracks at St. Leonhard in Passeier who broke the news to the skinny boy and his grief-stricken mother. He was a good-looking man, that *Standartenführer*. A smooth face, intelligent blue eyes. An elegant black uniform that instilled fear and respect, with the two silver lightning flashes of the S.S. Beautiful, glossy, knee-high boots.

While the guard of honour stood to attention, the *Standartenführer* gave Robert's mother a letter and a freshly ironed flag and Robert a little box engraved with an eagle and a swastika.

The boy was not wearing shoes, only rags tied with string. He felt ashamed, but he was used to it. They were poor, there was nothing you could do about that. Inside the box was an Iron Cross.

The boy read out the letter because his mother was illiterate. In it, his father's name had been misspelled, with an extra "e." The boy checked the back of the Iron Cross. It was the same there, too: Weg-e-ner instead of Wegner.

Neither he nor his mother pointed out the mistake: the mother because she had too many tears to shed, and the boy because he recalled the last words his father had spoken as he had boarded the train that would carry him away to die like an idiot. "If you do the right thing nine times, it'll bring you nothing but sorrow. The tenth time, you'll understand why you did it. And you'll be glad."

He hated him for those words, and hate, he had discovered, was a powerful form of self-control.

That was why the barefoot little boy's voice did not shake as he read the letter of commendation in front of those strangers, and it was thanks to that hate that he did not cry when the *Standartenführer* shook his hand.

You're the son of a hero, the officer said, you must be proud of him.

No, his father wasn't a hero, just an idiot. A *dead* idiot. What could be more stupid than that?

He did not say that. He nodded, thanked the officer and squeezed the Iron Cross so hard that the metal cut into his skin and drew blood. Only his mother noticed, but she said nothing.

His mother never said anything. All she knew was how to cry and pray. Cry and pray. Nothing else. And what about him? He was clutching the Iron Cross. And staring at the *Standartenführer*'s boots.

They must be really warm.

It was thanks to the Iron Cross that early on the afternoon of 13 February 1944 the sentries let him through, and it was only because of that Iron Cross that the *Standartenführer* motioned him to an armchair and held out a small piece of chocolate.

"It's Belgian," he said. "The best in the world."

He spoke a beautiful, melodious German. Not the guttural *dialekt* Robert used with his friends and relatives. It was as sweet as honey to his ears. He wished the *Standartenführer* would never stop talking. Instead, there was only that offer and a wary reaction to his silence.

The chocolate was there, between them, suspended over the desk.

"No, thank you."

The *Standartenführer* was taken aback. "Don't you like chocolate, *liebes Kind*?"

Child.

He wasn't a child. Not anymore.

Hate was added to hate.

And it was hate that gave him the strength to reply, looking the officer straight in the eye, as men do. "Of course I like it, but I have enough already."

And he showed him a dark, heavy bar, twice – no, three times – the size of the one the *Standartenführer* had offered him. "The Bogeyman gave it to me," he said after a brief pause.

"The Bogeyman?" The *Standartenführer* laughed. "There's no such thing."

"Yes, there is. I saw him. He's big and black."

The boy showed the officer the words in block capitals on the back of the chocolate bar: U.S. ARMY FIELD RATION D.

The *Standartenführer* opened his eyes wide.

The *Standartenführer* blinked.

The *Standartenführer* smiled.

"You're a good boy."

6

That was what he was. A good boy.

His father had left him nothing except bare feet and the mountains. The mountains, he had told him, give us water, food and wisdom. Everything you need in order to live. And mountains are the only thing money can never buy. They're there for everybody.

Another stupid idea worthy of a corpse. Try asking a mountain for a pair of boots as warm as the *Standartenführer*'s and see what you get.

Nothing. That's what you get.

Yet it was in the mountains, surrounded by bushes, firs, ash trees and hidden paths, that the skinny boy spent his days.

Depending on the season, he would pick blackberries, mushrooms, chestnuts, walnuts, set traps for birds or plunder their nests. Every so often, he would manage to catch a squirrel.

His mother forbade him from using his father's rifle, otherwise the boy would have been able to get hares, deer, even the odd stag. But his mother hated weapons, and so they were reduced to living off the charity of the Reich or off the crops from the barren fields his father had ploughed from morning till night before he went off to cover himself in glory.

Idiot.

On one of those paths, at dawn on 13 February 1944, with the Iron Cross in his pocket (not even he knew why he kept carrying it around), the skinny boy had met the Bogeyman. He had popped out of nowhere, suddenly.

A rustle in the brambles, and there he was.

The Bogeyman had pointed a sub-machine gun at him, his camouflage clothing all muddy, and that face with its broad nose and skin as black as charcoal, blacker than the boy had ever seen. He did not know there were men that colour, so he had burst out laughing.

It was that laugh that had stopped the American from squeezing the trigger and mowing him down.

The Bogeyman lowered his weapon and let out a whistle, then laughed along with him. Three more men emerged from the undergrowth. There was a Stars and Stripes painted on the helmet of one of them, a short guy with a thin moustache and rabbit teeth.

Americans.

In other words: the enemy.

That was something the teacher at school, on the rare occasions Robert attended, kept repeating. Enemies, enemies everywhere. Especially the Jews and the Americans. The Americans were half-Jews anyway. But the Jews and the Americans were not the only ones. The list of bad people was a long one. For instance, his father had died trying to drive away the Reich's other great adversary: the Bolsheviks.

Then there was the matter of the Italians.

Ever since the Italian flag had been replaced by the swastika, about six months earlier, the teacher in the black shirt who had forbidden him to speak German had been replaced by a *Lehrer* who not only encouraged them to use their mother tongue but had added "Italian traitors" to the list.

Italians were evil, they were traitors and liars.

And what about him? Was he German, as the *Lehrer* said, or Italian, as the teacher in the black shirt had maintained?

What a mess!

Anyway, nobody had ever told him that Americans, or at least some of them, had that funny-coloured skin. Or maybe Robert had skipped that class. School is the least of your concerns when your belly's empty and your feet are always frozen.

The Americans talked among themselves while the boy studied them. He knew it: they were deciding his fate. A bullet in the forehead and bury him in the brambles? Well, maybe that was the Wegners' destiny. Like father, like son. Both idiots.

Only, Robert had forgotten that he was no longer a Wegner.

The name on the Iron Cross was Weg-e-ner, and that extra vowel must have brought his wretched surname a bit of luck, because the four Americans decided that the boy would live.

One of them took a little book from his rucksack, leafed through it and started muttering a few words in German.

Were there any Germans nearby?

Robert pointed his thumb at his chest. "I'm German. Italian, too. But German."

They shook their heads: No, bad Germans, with weapons.

"Ra-ta-ta-tat," the Bogeyman said, pointing his index finger at the tree trunks and miming the firing of a gun.

Robert laughed. He was nice, this Bogeyman.

"There aren't any soldiers. Not here."

They had a map, but the boy had never learned to use one. He only knew where he was because his father had shown him the hidden paths in the woods and mountains, but he would never be able to point them out on a map. All those lines, those silly names.

"No."

The four of them shrugged, as if they had expected nothing different.

A safe place, they asked. To sleep. They put their palms together, pressed them against their tilted faces and made snoring noises.

The Bogeyman was good fun. Maybe even Jews were that much fun, but Robert had never met any. The S.S. had kicked down their doors and flung them onto trains like the ones for cattle. That was what his father had told him one evening. Good people who had vanished overnight.

"Really?"

"They say they get taken to camps where—"

"Shhh, you're frightening the boy."

"Of course I know a safe place."

They did not understand what he was saying.

The boy knew only one word in English and was happy to utter it.

"Yes."

They followed him, walking in single file, stooped, their sub-machine guns at the ready. Four American commandos who had landed by parachute miles from their intended destination, behind enemy lines, and a boy whose bare feet sank into the February snow as he tried to ignore the biting cold.

Less than an hour's walk away, his father had built a shack, hidden by the branches of a fir tree. It wasn't much bigger than a dog kennel, but it had a door, a kind of fireplace and a few blankets.

It was shelter.

When they got there, the Americans smiled gratefully, patted him on the back and rubbed their hands on his head (they would have liked to ruffle his hair but, beneath the woollen beret, Robert's head was completely shaved, for fear of lice), and the Bogeyman gave him a kind of chocolate brick.

He'd never seen so much chocolate in his life.

U.S. ARMY FIELD RATION D.

"Bravo bambino," the Bogeyman said, having glanced at his comrade's vocabulary book.

Then he smiled and said in English, "Good boy."

7

One. Three. Two. Double four.

All he had to do was get a squad together and follow that strange skinny boy to the shelter. A few shots, and the Bogeyman was dead. Eyes rolled back, mouth wide open, frizzy hair smeared with blood.

The *Standartenführer* put his gun back in its holster and looked at the boy, who stood beside him, unfazed by the slaughter.

"Chocolate is for children. You're not a child." He gestured, and one of the soldiers started pulling the boots off the corpse of the American with the rabbit teeth.

"You're as strong as Siegfried and as cunning as . . ." The *Standartenführer* lifted his index finger to his chin, searching for inspiration. ". . . as an elf? No." He shook his head, annoyed with himself. "No, not an elf. What do you call those . . . ?"

"Sir?"

The soldier handed him the boots. The *Standartenführer* tested the soles. They were soft and sturdy. He handed them to the boy.

A gift.

13 February 1944: the boy accepted it. It cost him no effort.

"These will be much more useful to you than a piece of chocolate, don't you think, my little . . ." Inspiration came at last. The *Standartenführer* smiled, delighted with his own wit. "My little *Kobold*?"

That was it: *Kobold*.

Just like in the fairy tales, Marlene had said when Wegener (in love? Yes, in love) had told her the story. *Kobold*. Like the cruel creatures who lived in metal and in the ground. With blue eyes that turned the light into the essence of hatred and terror. Marlene knew about the *Standartenführer*, she knew about Kobold. But she did not know everything. She did not know about the *Standartenführer*'s gift.

The boots.

Boots so warm that Robert could barely hold back his tears.

"Who's Siegfried?"

"Don't you know?"

Robert shook his head.

The *Standartenführer* took him outside. Night had fallen by now, but the boy's feet were warm. The officer took off the gold watch he wore on his wrist and showed him the engraving on the case: a knight holding a spear.

"This is Siegfried. A true Aryan. The greatest hero of them all. He climbed a mountain and killed a dragon."

"There's no such thing as dragons."

The *Standartenführer* smiled. "Not anymore. But in the past? Who knows? The Bogeyman was real enough, you showed him to me. He ended up just like the dragon. And kobolds? I thought they were a legend, but now I've got one right in front of me."

He touched the boy's forehead with his index finger and smiled, then went back to barking orders at his men.

The nickname stuck.

"Informer Kobold" was what it said on the *Standartenführer*'s dispatches. Not "Robert Weg-e-ner," just "Informer Kobold." Robert Wegener could be tracked down and killed. But Kobold? It was impossible to kill a Kobold.

The boy had been a great discovery of the *Standartenführer*'s. Kobold had talent. He was clever. He knew the most hidden paths and mountain passes. He was a skinny boy with strange boots and nobody paid any attention to him. And so he would listen and take note. Who sold bread on the black market, who was trying to evade conscription, who was hiding weapons or tuning in to forbidden radio stations.

Shortly before Christmas 1944, Kobold changed sides. The Americans, the British and the partisans had broken through; and the Reich was on the verge of surrender.

In 1945, the war came to an end, but hunger didn't. Kobold learned that, for those who are born barefoot, war never ends. So he carried on with his activities.

Men fleeing south and goods going north.

After a while, there were no more fleeing men, but there was still hunger. By now, Kobold had grown stronger. He was barefoot no longer, he carried a gun concealed in his jacket and could eat with no risk of running into debt, but he was under no illusions.

There was still a war on.

Over a new word now: respect.

Kobold wanted people to take off their hats to him as he walked past, the way they used to do with the *Standartenführer*. He wanted men like his father to whisper warnings to their children and cross the street. He hated these men. They weren't heroes. They were wretched cowards. In a word: idiots.

Kobold realised he needed to enlist help, but knew that fully grown men would never agree to be ordered about by a teenager. So he roped in barefoot boys whose eyes were shiny with hunger. He taught them discipline, obedience and perseverance. Not violence, because these callow youths had learned that a long time ago.

It worked. It worked really well. The volume of business increased, and Kobold decided it was time to use more reliable methods of transport than strong backs or bicycles. He acquired a van, then a couple of lorries, which grew to five, six, ten. It was never enough.

Kobold wanted more.

He realised that if he wanted to expand his business, he would have to study, and he did. Mathematics, economics. But not only that. He discovered that he enjoyed reading. Especially history books and biographies of famous people. He found them enthralling.

He read a lot and learned a lot.

About the same year his future wife was born, 1952, Kobold, nineteen now and already with quite a reputation in some quarters, was approached by an accountant looking for easy money.

He didn't beat about the bush. Now was a good time, he said. Italy needed to get back on its feet, and the State turned a blind eye to anyone who helped money circulate. But soon this fun would come to an end, and the State would revert to its old role as a damned watchdog.

And when that happened, the dog would bite him.

In order to avoid this, you had to learn to stroke it. That's where he came in, he said. In exchange for a small slice of the proceeds, he would set up dummy companies (for which he would have to pay his taxes like an upright citizen, which amused Kobold greatly), put figureheads in charge of them and make sure the accounts were open and aboveboard.

Kobold approved of this plan.

His activities prospered.

When the wave of terrorism came, job offers increased to astonishing levels, but Kobold turned them all down. No TNT. No weapons. He had learned that the watchdog could be tamed in just about every way, except one.

Violence. The State was jealous of its own power.

It was alright to get rid of someone by tossing him into the Passer or the Adige. Fights were fine, so was knifing somebody in the dark. Even setting competitors' warehouses on fire was tolerated, as was the occasional shoot-out – but terrorism? That was going too far.

Kobold also refused proposals to move men from one side of the border to the other. That was something he had not done for a long time, for decades, and he had never told anyone the real reason.

Not even Marlene. Some secrets had to remain secret. For his good and for hers. It all went way back.

To September 1945.

The last fugitive Kobold had agreed to help was the *Standartenführer*. He had a long beard and was emaciated, unrecognisable without his uniform, a shadow of the man who had offered him Belgian chocolate. The best in the world.

"Kobold," he'd said to him in a trembling voice, "you have to get me out of here."

There was no need to ask him why. The newspapers were full of pictures of what the Jews, the Americans, the British and the Russians were doing to former S.S. officers.

Kobold had led him to the woods of the Ulten Valley, telling him they would meet up with "patriots" there who would get him out of Italy and then put him on a ship to Argentina, where he would be able to make a new life for himself, or else plot to revive the defunct Reich.

It was a lie.

Once they had reached the middle of the forest, Kobold had taken out his revolver, made the *Standartenführer* kneel amid the roots of a yew tree, pinned his father's Iron Cross to his chest and shot him in the forehead.

He had turned the body over with his foot, slipped off the gold watch and put it on his own wrist. He had returned to Merano before dawn and, that same morning, had made his mother change his surname from Wegner to Wegener.

He still wore the gold watch.

It had never missed a second.

8

He was sitting in the *Stube*, his wide-brimmed black hat next to him on the wooden bench, his broad forehead furrowed. His sparse grey hair was cut short. Every so often, he would sigh and run the palm of his hand over the back of his neck.

He had spread a threadbare linen cloth, frayed at the edges, on the table. Carefully, because waste was an insult to work, he had emptied the contents of a small wooden box onto the small table-cloth. A cascade of small black seeds.

With the help of his thumb and a tablespoon, squinting in the light of the oil lamp, the hollow-cheeked man examined them one by one, then dropped them into a cotton pouch the size of a packet of cigarettes.

A pan was simmering on the stove.

The man's name was Simon Keller, and his father, *Voter* Luis, had been a *Kräutermandl*. Many people owed their lives to *Voter* Luis. There wasn't a single herb, berry or root in the whole of South Tyrol whose properties *Voter* Luis had not known.

Voter Luis had been a father, a *Kräutermandl* and, above all, a man of faith. He knew that life was like the warmth of the Föhn wind, an illusion, and had made sure his knowledge would not die with him. *Voter* Luis could read and write. He had read a lot and written a lot. His notes were Simon Keller's most prized possession.

After the *maso*, of course.

Simon Keller had learned from him the secrets of the herbs and the mountains, and the knowledge of the ancients who had lived there.

The ancients were a mystery. Why had they chosen to live in such rugged terrain, perched high over the valley, above the forest, clinging to pastures that were as steep and sterile as overhanging rocks, so close to the sky that they might be blinded by it? And when had they arrived there?

At the time of the Flood, Voter Luis would say, *the waters rose and they came up here to escape His wrath.* Voter Luis always had an answer to his son's questions. He was a man of faith.

Simon Keller didn't know how long ago the Flood had taken place, just as he did not know who the ancient peoples really were, but thanks to *Voter* Luis he knew that there were herbs for sleeping, soothing toothache, making blood coagulate and keeping pain under control. The seeds, small and dark as fleas, which he was in the process of selecting belonged to that extraordinary category.

They were poppy seeds, from which you could extract opium to drive away pain.

It was incredible that such power could be contained in these almost invisible grains. As *Voter* Luis used to say, "The world teems with miracles and mysteries."

Like his father, and his father before him, Simon Keller was a *Bau'r.*

A *Bau'r* was a peasant but also a *Kräutermandl*, a hunter, a woodsman, a cook, a carpenter, a farmer, a doctor, sometimes an athlete and even a priest. *Above all*, a priest. Without faith, you could die of loneliness and silence up here. Faith filled the blank spaces of the long, endless winters with answers.

A *Bau'r* was the lord of the mountain.

It was right at the foot of the mountain that Keller had found the young woman. It had been pure chance. Or perhaps fate. Keller did not usually stray so far from his *maso*. There was no point. But a sky that promised the first blizzard of the season had compelled him to go down the mountain to retrieve the traps he used for obtaining fresh meat during the winter. The task had taken him all afternoon and well past sunset, until, cold and tired, he had decided to return home.

He had seen her on his way back. Motionless in the crumpled Mercedes. He had thought it unlikely there was any hope for her. It was not uncommon in these parts, in winter especially, to come across dead bodies. Most had died from exposure: smugglers, poachers, travellers. Keller never refused them a blessing and a prayer. That was the reason he had come down the slope. But much to his surprise, the young woman was alive. He had dropped his traps and done what he could to help her.

He had pulled her out of the car, rubbed her body to bring back the circulation, heaved her over his shoulder and carried her up to the *maso*. There, by the light of a candle, he had checked the reaction of her pupils, washed her injuries with soap and stitched the worst cut, the one on her forehead, and bandaged it in linen strips he had first boiled in water. Then he had given her an infusion to alleviate the pain.

Once she was awake, the young woman would ask a whole lot of questions (Where am I? Who are you? What happened?), and that worried him. *Voter* Luis had composed magnificent sermons. He had a way with words. Simon Keller did not. *Voter* Luis knew how to stir people's hearts, while Simon approached them only when he had to, when he needed to sell what little surplus he produced and buy what he could not make himself. He hoped he could at least reassure her that here she was safe. There was food, wood for the *Stube*, opium for the pain and a large number of Bibles upon which to meditate.

After weighing the pouch, Keller replaced the leftover poppy in the wooden box, folded the cloth in four and put it in a drawer whose brass handle had been darkened by time. The box went on a shelf.

From the sideboard he took out a ceramic cup (chipped and

cracked, but the best he owned), blew on it and placed it on the table. He bent over the fireplace, lifted the pan with a rag so as not to burn his fingers and poured the boiling water into the cup. He immersed the pouch with the poppy in it and stared at the colours the infusion was taking on.

There were no clocks in the *maso*. All you needed to determine the time of day was the sun. Keller had learned patience from an early age. "Time," *Voter* Luis would say, "belongs to the stars, not to men. What are you in comparison with the stars, my son? They were shining when Terah begat Abraham and they will still be shining when you are long forgotten. The stars own time, while men are crushed by it. Not being able to wait is a sin of arrogance."

Keller waited until the infusion was ready.

Oil for the lamp was expensive, and he turned it off. He could move around his *maso* in the dark without fear of tripping over. This was his home. He was born here.

People said that sooner or later there would be electricity even in the highest *masi*, but he did not believe it. He would not even be able to buy a generator, as others had done, because he would never be able to afford one. Generators and fuel cost too much. Besides, why light up the night when the night was made for sleeping?

He went upstairs. He did not knock, there was no point. The young woman was unconscious and would not wake up until tomorrow. He put the cup down on the bedside table next to a candle stub, which he lit with a match.

By the light of the flame, he studied the young woman's features. She was in pain, and he felt sorry for her. Pain, though, as *Voter* Luis had taught him, was a good sign. It meant the heart was still beating.

Was the beating of the heart not a miracle full of mystery? Indeed it was.

Keller lifted the young woman into a sitting position, holding the pillows behind her back and head with his left hand. With his right, he poured the hot infusion between her lips in such a way that she would swallow it by reflex, in small sips. Gradually, her face relaxed. Keller was glad.

When he had emptied the cup, he pulled the blankets back over the young woman and studied her face.

Especially that peculiar beauty spot.

"The world is a sign of His existence, and He conceals signs in the world for men of faith to see. The world teems with signs, miracles and mysteries."

Especially mysteries. Yes, indeed.

He stood up and checked that the window was firmly shut. Beneath it, he had put dried moss to stop the cold draught coming in. Not that it made much difference, he was sorry to see. Outside, the blizzard was still wailing.

In Simon Keller's mind, there was only silence.

9

The man with the goatee was waiting.

The parking lot of the scrapyard was deserted, and he was alone, his only company two crows circling gloomily over heaps of demolished cars.

He was smoking one MS after the other. He would light them, take a couple of drags then toss them far away. Heedless of the snow and the wind, he stood there in full sight, shivering, smoking and smiling.

He was happy. He found the circling of the crows appropriate.

He was waiting.

The man with the goatee was plagued by a recurring nightmare. He did not have it every night or he would have gone mad, but often enough for him to be certain it would follow him until the day he died.

In the nightmare he was a child again and had done something very naughty. It did not matter what exactly. That was a detail that changed each time. He had done something naughty, and to escape his parents' wrath he was hiding in their bedroom wardrobe. Once he had closed the doors, he discovered to his horror that he was naked, stark naked and trapped, since in the meantime he could hear the room filling with voices, footsteps, words.

As the voices gradually increased in volume, he started groping in the dark, searching for something to cover himself with, panic pressing on his bladder, until his hands found a soft, warm piece of cloth: a blanket. He immediately crawled under it, aware of the air diminishing, the heat increasing and the discomfort in his bladder turning to pain. His certainty grew that somebody would fling open the wardrobe doors and tear the blanket off him just when he was no longer able to hold it in. The crowd would see him, stark naked and soiled with piss. He clenched his teeth, bit his lips and held on.

When the urge to urinate became unbearable, the man with the goatee, knowing that he was asleep next to his wife in his bed at home, did everything he could to wake up. Hard as he tried, though, he could not. All he could do was tremble, hold on and hope that, just this once, the nightmare would change.

It never did.

His bladder relaxed, the wardrobe was flung open, the blanket was snatched away and the crowd pointed at him, shouting and laughing in disgust.

The final image – before, bathed in sweat, his heart pounding, he started biting his pillow to stop himself from waking his wife with his cries – was the face of the man who had exposed him in front of everybody. The face of Herr Wegener.

You did not need a psychiatrist to interpret this nightmare. It summed up the whole life of the man with the goatee: Captain Giacomo Carbone.

As a boy he had been skinny, with deep-set, elusive eyes. At seventeen, he smoked German cigarettes and was terrified of being drafted. He was very bright and had found a way to be useful to the Germans without having to face lead and shrapnel on the front line. Just like Kobold.

By spying, informing, *collaborating*.

Unlike Kobold, though, Carbone had insisted on wearing a balaclava. That was why the *Standartenführer* showed contempt towards him and called him a coward. Still, his cowardice had saved his life during the post-war reprisals.

Carbone remembered that time well. He had spent months living off the charity of a distant relative, shut up in a loft, smoking and waiting for someone to discover him and put a bullet in his chest. But that hadn't happened.

When he heard that the *Standartenführer*'s body had been discovered in the woods in the Ulten Valley, he felt reborn. The secret of Carbone, the coward in the balaclava, had died with the S.S. man, while he himself had survived. Life was smiling on him.

He began to show himself in public again.

He finished school, and on a damp, rainy day enlisted in the carabinieri. He passed the officer's exam at his first attempt. And since he spoke German, his superiors posted him to Bolzano, in South Tyrol. There, he met a girl called Isabella who knew nothing of his past as a collaborator. He grew a goatee to impress her. He worked hard at his new job and got ahead. He was transferred from Bolzano to Brixen, then to Brenner and finally to Merano. On the banks of the Passer, he proposed to Isabella, and they started making preparations for their wedding. Two days before the big occasion, Kobold knocked at his door.

Kobold knew.

It was bad luck, pure and simple. Kobold had seen him just once without a balaclava, at the Alpini barracks in Bolzano, but that was enough. Kobold had a prodigious memory, and as the skilled hunter he was he had waited until Carbone had a lot to lose before making his move. He had not said much.

"You're my dog now."

And he had put him on a leash.

That was the night Carbone first had the nightmare about the blanket and the wardrobe.

Being the dog of someone like Herr Wegener also had its advantages. Wegener not only knew when to tug on your collar, he also knew when to reward you.

Backhanders, complimentary tickets to events Isabella wouldn't have missed for the world, incredible discounts from car and household appliance dealers.

In return, Wegener asked him for tip-offs, the odd confidential file concealed between the pages of a newspaper, maybe also to turn a blind eye to certain lorries travelling to Switzerland through the Passeier Valley. What he wanted most was information.

Carbone kept having the same nightmare. He had had it for decades now, at least once a week. Always the same: the wardrobe, the blanket, the people pointing at him.

The shame.

Wegener had sentenced him to a state of never forgetting. That was why Carbone hated him.

Today, though, Giacomo Carbone, now a captain, felt light. He finally knew how to rid himself of that nightmare once and for all. He was not chain-smoking because he was nervous, but because he could not wait to tug at his leash one last time.

The crows flew away. The snow continued to fall.

Carbone had almost finished the packet of MS when Herr Wegener arrived.

His eyes were bloodshot. He looked like someone who has had a sleepless night. There were no hellos. Carbone motioned Wegener to follow him. He led him into a shed. There, removing a canvas cover, he showed him a grey Fiat 130.

"Is this it?"

No answer. Wegener's expression said it all.

Carbone smiled. "Didn't you know women are bitches? You have to keep them on a leash."

He had prepared that line while waiting.

Herr Wegener did not react. So much the better. Carbone had no desire to get into a fight. He would be all too tempted to take out his gun and shoot the son of a bitch. Why risk losing everything so close to the finishing line?

Freedom.

He loved the sound of that word.

"It wasn't hard to find. The model, the colour, the licence number. The description of your wife was useful but not really necessary."

"Who?"

"The guy who owns this place."

"He . . ."

Carbone shook his head. "The poor devil shat his pants as soon as he heard who the car belonged to."

"And . . . ?"

"He came of his own accord. I didn't even have to call him in."

Clutching his hat in his hands, the owner of the scrapyard had also handed over a wad of banknotes. It was the money Signora Wegener had paid for the changeover, he had said. The Fiat 130 for a Mercedes. The money was safe in one of Carbone's drawers, and he had no intention of returning it to its rightful owner. Let's call it a tip.

"How?"

"How what?"

"How did Marlene know where to find him?"

"You can't be married to a pastry cook and not know who in the neighbourhood has a sweet tooth."

Herr Wegener took a step towards him. "I don't like your tone."

Carbone ignored the threat. "A Mercedes W114. An excellent car. Solid. Cream finish. The number plate is on this piece of paper. I've already issued a description to my people. It has a very good engine, you can drive it quite a distance."

"Did she say where she was headed?"

Carbone looked into his eyes, enjoying every ounce of embarrassment, terror and anger he saw in them, and allowed himself one final dig. "You think you married a stupid woman?"

Wegener turned and left.

Carbone lit an MS and smoked it all, down to the filter, really savouring it.

He came out of the scrapyard and got into the car waiting for him at the corner of the street with its engine running. He ordered the driver to return to the carabinieri station.

He smiled. He had one last thing to do before he was a free man again. Make a telephone call.

10

It was a short call, lasting under three minutes. Carbone knew how to keep things brief. It was a job requirement. He left out all interpretation, anything personal, giving nothing but the facts.

When the call was over, Carbone gathered his subordinates and bought them a round of Fernets. It was only mid-morning and they were all on duty, but an exception to the rule could do no harm.

His men did not need to be asked twice. They did not often see Captain Carbone in a good mood. Besides, with all this snow, there was not a lot for them to do except twiddle their thumbs and catch up with paperwork. And nobody liked paperwork.

Far better to have a glass of Fernet.

"To the Consortium!" Carbone said, raising his glass, fully aware of the men's puzzled looks. None of them had the slightest idea what the Consortium was.

Carbone could not blame them. Not many people knew about the Consortium, and the few who did had the good sense to keep their mouths shut. Even fewer were stupid enough to consider doing business with the Consortium. As stupid as Herr Wegener.

Poor, poor Kobold.

He refilled the glasses.

"To letting dogs loose!"

This time, they understood – or thought they did. Carbone did not care much either way.

"To freedom!"

Glasses clinked. The men laughed with him.

11

Room 12.

Herr Wegener could not get it out of his mind. He had thought about it while he was questioning Georg, Moritz and Helene for the second time (no unusual behaviour on Marlene's part, no meetings with anyone, nothing at all outside her normal routine) and also while he was on the telephone, giving orders to his subordinates and all those who were in his debt one way or another.

Room 12.

Room 12 of the corps.

He had thought about it while he was in the Lancia H.F., being driven by Georg to the scrapyard to speak to Carbone. He had done nothing but think about Room 12 even after talking to Carbone (he hadn't liked the captain's tone) and had thought about it again while issuing new orders and circulating new information on the telephone, taking note of those who'd been unable to conceal their pleasure. The big boss screwed by his wife. Brilliant.

Go ahead. Laugh.

Even now, it was the only thing Wegener could think about, as he walked up to the door of a boutique on one of the ritziest streets in Merano. Old Mother Frost, it was called. He owned it. Or rather, it had been Wegener's wedding present to Marlene. Old Mother Frost, just like in the Grimm fairy tale.

She had picked the name.

Herr Wegener did not think it was appropriate for a shop specialising in evening and wedding gowns, but Marlene liked it (that damned book of hers again), and since it was a gift, Wegener had not insisted.

In any case, the name had not put off the customers. Quite the contrary. The place was as busy as an assembly line. Despite the financial crisis, which pushed up the price of petrol every day and made even Sunday a day when people walked everywhere, and despite the growing hordes of the unemployed, you still needed to join a long waiting list and spend a fortune if you wanted to buy a wedding dress from Old Mother Frost. The first time Herr Wegener looked at the account books, he had been astonished.

Actually, the purpose of the gift, at least at first, had been to provide his wife with a career, an aim, and stop her turning into one of those harpies that powerful men ferried from one party to another, increasingly embittered and increasingly at risk of being seduced by the first stud who came their way.

But although buying the shop had turned out to be an astute business move, Herr Wegener never liked setting foot inside Old Mother Frost. Because he would see Gabriel there. He hated him. Gabriel Kerschbaumer, the dress designer, was worse than a migraine. With his affected manner and snobbish expression, Gabriel could make him feel worse than a piece of shit on the sole of one of those leather moccasins of his, the kind only a queer would wear. And he probably was a queer, even though Herr Wegener had noticed the power of his charm on female customers, in spite of the fact that he was bald – or perhaps because of it. They said he looked like an ageing, more refined Yul Brynner.

Still, he thought, at least a queer wouldn't flirt with his wife.

Marlene was beautiful, truly beautiful, with those deep blue eyes and that raven hair of hers. Herr Wegener was aware of all the heads she turned at parties and even when they were simply taking a walk along the Passer Promenade.

He had ambivalent feelings about the looks she received. On the one hand, he was pleased. Being envied made you strong. Marlene was like a jewel, the living proof of his greatness. Beautiful women were drawn to rich, powerful men. Their beauty was like a slap in the face to the poor and the wretched.

And the idiots.

On the other hand, when it came down to it Herr Wegener was a man, and like all men he was prone to that petty feeling called jealousy.

All the same, until today, Wegener had never considered the possibility of Marlene being attracted to another man. Not only because he was certain she really loved him, but because he was not just any man, he was Herr Wegener. No one in his right mind would make a pass at his wife.

And yet . . .

There was the Fiat 130 swapped for a Mercedes, the opened safe, the missing sapphires, the book of Grimm fairy tales, the carefully laid plan of someone who knew she could never turn back and had therefore taken with her whatever was necessary to start over again from scratch.

And there was only one reason a woman would want to start over again, wasn't there?

Concentrate. You need evidence. What you're thinking is just *fantasy.* Imagination. Or, worse still, fear. And fear is pointless. Think about Room 12. Think about hatred. Think about Gabriel. The filthy queer. You hate him, don't you? Hating helps.

Use it.

He opened the door.

There he was. Gabriel. Upright as a pole, shirtsleeves rolled up, a needle between his lips, glasses pushed down to the tip of his nose.

Wegener had considered firing him more than once, but at almost seventy, Gabriel Kerschbaumer was probably the best dress designer in South Tyrol. In fact, if it hadn't been for his lack of ambition (Gabriel considered himself an *artist*, and artists do not need such vulgar stuff as money), he could have held his own with the best Paris couturiers and made a fortune. That was another reason Wegener kept him at arm's length. But not today. Today, he needed him.

When Gabriel saw Herr Wegener walk in, he went up to greet him. Herr Wegener grabbed him by the elbow and led him to the back room: a rough gesture that startled the five little seamstresses busy embroidering pearls on a veil as diaphanous as a spider's web – although infinitely more expensive – and sent them running off as fast as their legs could carry them.

"We have to talk."

"At your service, Herr Wegener."

"Where's Marlene?"

"She didn't come in today. Has she got the flu?"

Wegener shook his head. "I'm asking the questions."

"I beg your pardon?"

That nasal voice! That pretentious way of speaking!

Wegener massaged his temples.

"Have you noticed her behaving strangely?"

"Marlene?"

Wegener yanked him by the collar of his shirt. "Don't play games, Gabriel. Not with me. Not today."

Gabriel looked him up and down. Wegener did not relax his grip.

"Marlene's an artist. Artists always have their heads in the clouds."

That spiel again!

When Herr Wegener had given Marlene the boutique, he had thought of her as a "hostess," definitely not as a dressmaker. He had pictured her entertaining well-to-do women, offering them coffee or sparkling wine, gossiping about who was sleeping with whom (and incidentally, who was Marlene sleeping with?), then arranging to meet up for a dull evening at the theatre.

43

He certainly had not bought the shop to see his wife turn into one of those seamstresses who fled when he was around. And yet that was precisely what had happened.

Marlene had started to *sew*.

When he protested, she had replied that she enjoyed the work, that she was happy sitting in the back room, tacking bodices and trains, and had no intention of stopping. That had been the end of the discussion. Wegener suspected, though, that it had been Gabriel who had put ideas of being an artist into his wife's head. Probably to get the better of him.

When he had mentioned this to Gabriel, the queer had replied that Marlene had talent. It was a gift, he had said. He'd even shown him some of his wife's creations, which cost practically their weight in gold.

She was the person most in demand at Old Mother Frost. After Gabriel, naturally.

Hatred.

Hatred is the last resource, and Wegener clung to it.

"Do artists bleed like everyone else?"

"If you ask me specific questions, Herr Wegener, I'll do my best to answer accordingly."

"Did Marlene mention that she was going away? A holiday perhaps?"

"No."

"Has she been . . ." Herr Wegener paused and looked straight into Gabriel's impassive eyes. "Shall we say, more *artistic* than usual?"

"Perhaps she's been a little absent-minded. You see that dress? She had to redo the lace hem twice. Strange for someone as skilled as Marlene."

Herr Wegener pointed to the dummy on which the dress was displayed. "Is that *artistic*?"

"You'd call it merchandise, Herr Wegener. I call it art."

Herr Wegener grabbed a pair of scissors and cut the dress to shreds. "Now I also think it's art."

"That dress has to be ready in three days' time. It's traditional for the bride to arrive late at the ceremony, but the dress must be delivered on time. And that's not a tradition, it's a rule of the market."

He was quite unfazed, the son of a bitch!

Herr Wegener put the scissors to his throat. "I'm asking you one last time. Did you notice anything unusual about Marlene? Was she ... seeing someone? Had she altered her habits in any way, or—"

"Why are you asking me?" Gabriel snapped, upset more by the tone of his voice than the proximity of the scissors to his Adam's apple. "Weren't you having her followed?"

Taken aback, Herr Wegener lowered the scissors.

"How did *you* know?"

"Everybody knew. Marlene told us. One day, Clara, one of the staff, saw a man following your wife. She didn't like the look of him, so she told me and I immediately mentioned it to Marlene. She told me not to worry, that the man was one of your ... associates. Her exact words were" – Gabriel clicked his tongue – "'My husband is concerned about me. End of story.'"

End of story.

He had never heard her use that expression. Who had she learned it from?

End of story.

Furious, Herr Wegener had again thought about Room 12.

12

Room 12 was simple. You went in alive and came out dead.

That's if you were a bandit or criminal of any kind. Or even if you were just suspected of being one. If, however, you were Kobold, you went in frightened and came out stronger. Because Kobold was a fast learner. The *Standartenführer* always said so. The skinny little boy with a quick mind and nerves of steel.

A pure Aryan.

Once, the *Standartenführer* had even gone so far as to express regret that it wasn't Kobold who bore his surname rather than his own son, an incompetent young man who, far from being covered in the glory of war, was stuck behind a desk in Frankfurt. Kobold had felt happy. Flattered, even.

Encouraged by Kobold's talents, the *Standartenführer* had started teaching him between missions. What Kobold hated was lessons in theory. Reading out loud from *Mein Kampf* and other books that went on about esoteric orders of knighthood and rambled on about superior and inferior races. Kobold would memorise everything, then, standing rigidly to attention, recite it all like a good little parrot and receive praise with a fake smile.

As far as Kobold was concerned, all those words were rubbish. It was not about Jews and Aryans. The world was divided into two categories.

Those who owned shoes and those who walked around barefoot.

Of course, he could never express these opinions openly, or the *Standartenführer* would carry on hammering nonsense into his head instead of moving on to the lessons he enjoyed most. Or maybe even have him shot.

The best lessons were the practical ones. They were less boring and more useful. Guerrilla techniques taken from the most recent manuals of the Waffen-S.S., the *Führer*'s elite troops. Infiltration and exfiltration. Camouflage, map reading and using a compass. Methods for extracting information through interrogation.

And then there was Room 12 of the Alpini Army Corps in Bolzano, a gloomy building some called the Place of Evil.

There the *Standartenführer* would show him how to tear out fingernails, dislocate joints and strike the soles of the feet in an economical, effective way. In Room 12, Kobold learned not to be afraid of pain.

Pain was not the worst thing that could happen. The worst was *waiting* for the pain.

That was why Herr Wegener had left Moritz alone for so long. Locked in the tool shed of the villa by the Passer, in the bitter cold, with the shadows growing longer until they merged into the darkness of the night, and his consciousness crying out for an end to it all.

Moritz had had a task to perform. An important task. Following Marlene and telling Herr Wegener of anything unusual in her behaviour, anyone she met, whether or not by chance, which customers gave her one look too many or blatantly flirted with her. And he had to do it without being seen.

If Marlene had noticed she was being followed, Moritz should have informed him. He would have got a tongue lashing, maybe a couple of cracked ribs, nothing more.

But now . . .

13

Moritz was terrified. He sat on the floor, his head between his knees. He looked up at Wegener and began stuttering an apology. "I made a mistake . . ."

"Only one?" Herr Wegener said mockingly.

Moritz corrected himself. "Many, many mistakes, *too many*, Herr Wegener, and I don't know how to apologise . . ."

Wegener took the automatic from his belt. "If you say the word 'apologise' one more time, I'll put a bullet through your head. Marlene saw you. Did you realise that?"

It was pointless lying. "Yes."

"When?"

"A couple of days ago."

"Are you sure?"

"Maybe a week."

"And you didn't say anything to me."

"I wanted to be sure, sir. I didn't want you to . . ."

"Get any strange ideas?"

"I don't know anything about the burglary, sir. It was an oversight on my part. I was distracted. Your wife . . . I'm as surprised as you are."

"So you also think it was Marlene?"

Moritz swallowed a couple of times.

Wegener began pacing up and down the shed. Three steps forward, then an about-turn. "Tell me about your distraction."

"It was because of the boredom. Frau Wegener always did the

same thing every day. She'd go to work, break for lunch at one o'clock and be back by two. Then at six o'clock she'd go home. Sometimes she'd have coffee in the café next to the boutique with Herr Kerschbaumer and the other employees. Everything was very regular. Always the same route to work and back. Never a deviation."

"She never met anyone?"

"I'd have told you."

"You'd have reported it."

"Of course, sir."

Herr Wegener brought his face close to Moritz's. "And how the fuck do you expect me to *believe* you?" he barked.

"I give you my word, I—"

Herr Wegener grabbed him by the hair, forced him down onto his hands and knees and banged his forehead on the concrete floor, once, twice, three times, until he drew blood. A lot of blood.

Wegener let go of him. Moritz put his hands to his forehead and rolled his eyes.

"Does it hurt?"

"I deserve it."

Wegener took the safety catch off the gun and pointed it at him. Moritz stretched out his hands. "Please . . ."

"What's the name of your distraction?"

Moritz replied quickly.

Too quickly.

"There's nobody, there's—"

Herr Wegener fired.

The bullet hit Moritz in the ankle. Georg stuck his head around the door of the shed, took a quick look and vanished. Moritz was curled in a foetal position, screaming. Wegener pressed the barrel of the gun to his temple.

"My teacher used to say that shooting isn't a good method for obtaining information. A gunshot wound reduces the thinking process to nothing and renders a person unable to cooperate. I don't agree. I think a bullet can produce miracles. Do you want to know how a bullet can turn into a miracle?"

"Yes, sir," Moritz replied, his face drained of blood, dripping with sweat and tears. "How?"

"You'll tell me the truth, and I'll be satisfied. Georg will take you to a doctor, and you'll have a two-week holiday. When you get back, we'll shake hands. You'll limp for the rest of your life, but it's better to limp than be dead. And if that's not a miracle, then what the hell is?"

"Helene."

"The housekeeper?"

"We . . ."

Of course. It was obvious. The housekeeper was an attractive woman. With a little make-up, she would be more than attractive. Wegener could picture the whole thing: the intimacy that comes from working side by side, the exchange of glances, the touch of hands, a stolen kiss.

Then something more daring.

Man is programmed to keep raising the stakes. And it's also in his nature to get bored once passion has waned. The sex becomes less steamy, the craving turns into a habit, then a bother. And so you get an idea for rekindling your desire: break up the endless hours of surveillance with the thrill of a secret meeting. Danger is the most powerful of aphrodisiacs.

Oh, yes, Wegener could picture it.

He almost didn't hear the gunshot.

14

He found Helene at her usual place, in the villa's kitchens. She was sitting by the stove, leafing through a book, a cheap novel with a black-and-white cover. She leaped to her feet as soon as she saw him, her index finger wedged in the pages as a bookmark. She was pale and tense, but did her best to smile at him.

Wegener did not respond to the greeting. He walked up to her without a word, still wearing his coat, the corners of his mouth drooping.

When Helene noticed the revolver Wegener held at his side, she understood and tried to run away, but it was too late. Wegener grabbed her by her blonde plait and pushed her to the ground. She collapsed, winded by the impact.

Wegener sent the book flying with a kick, again seized Helene by the plait, which had come loose, forced her to kneel before him and pressed the automatic to her forehead.

"Right now, Georg is chopping your boyfriend to pieces. Small pieces, because the trout in the Passer are snobs and don't chew with their mouths open. He won't be long. Do you know what that means?"

She knew.

"It was his idea," she said. "Moritz's. I was getting tired of it. It was boring and never lasted long . . ." She sniffed and stared at him with cold eyes. "He wasn't much of a lover."

Wegener smiled. He liked coldness in a woman. It was a rare commodity.

"Did he ever tell you anything about Marlene?"

"No."

"And did you see anything?"

Helene bit her lip.

"Georg's nearly done," Wegener said. "He'll be here soon."

"It was only an impression."

Helene was thinking hard. She did know something, something that put her at risk of also being eaten by the trout. She was weighing the pros and cons. Should she talk and risk being killed, or keep quiet and end up like Moritz anyway?

There was only one way to tip the scales in the right direction, Wegener thought. He had learned that in Room 12. It was to keep silent. He said nothing.

Helene bowed her head. "She had someone else."

The hand holding the revolver trembled. Herr Wegener's voice did not. "Do you know who?"

Helene shook her head. "It's just a guess."

Herr Wegener struck her across the face with the butt of his weapon. She fell onto her side, sobbing.

"It was three weeks ago, sir. I was tidying up your study. Marlene was on the phone. I don't think she knew I was there." She spat blood and saliva, then hastened to say, "In fact, I'm *sure* she didn't see me or hear me. She was speaking softly and twisting the telephone cord around her finger, like this . . ."

She twisted her hair between her index and middle finger, mimicking the gesture.

"What was she saying?"

"She was speaking softly. All I heard was a name."

"What name?"

Helene stared at him. "You're going to kill me after I tell you."

"The name."

"Klaus."

Herr Wegener lowered the revolver and tucked it into his belt. He turned, went over to a large fridge humming a small distance away, opened the door and took out a bottle.

Vodka. He liked it ice cold.

"I don't know any Klaus."

"It's not for you to know him, sir."

It was a sharp reply. Herr Wegener poured vodka into two metal cups.

"Get up. Drink."

Helene obeyed. Her face was a mask of blood. There was a swollen open wound under her earlobe.

"You'll need stitches," Herr Wegener murmured.

"It doesn't hurt that much," she said, sipping at her vodka.

"You heard her on the phone. You heard her use the name Klaus. How can you be sure it was her"– here there was a brief hesitation – "her lover?"

Helene downed the contents of the cup in a single gulp. Liquid courage. "She was smiling when she said it."

"Is that supposed to mean something to me?"

Helene placed her fingers on her wound, lifted them to look at them, then wiped them on her apron. "There's the smile you give the postman, the one you give a stranger on the bus. There's the 'How are you today, darling?' smile. And then there's *that* smile. Every woman knows it."

Herr Wegener nodded. "The way girls smile when they're in love?"

"Yes, sir."

Helene was about to add something when Georg appeared. He took in the housekeeper's bloodstained face, the bottle of vodka, then Wegener.

Wegener ignored him.

Helene shuddered.

"Can you show me the smile, please?" Wegener said to her. "*That* smile? I'd like to understand."

"This is how she was smiling. Like this."

She had a beautiful smile. Had Marlene ever smiled at him like that? He couldn't remember.

"Carry on. I like it. Don't stop."

Helene continued to smile.

Wegener grabbed one of the knives from the rack next to the steel sink and plunged it between her shoulder blades. She stopped smiling. She tried to defend herself, kicking and punching him. Wegener pushed deeper, then twisted the blade.

Helene stopped kicking. A death rattle, then she stopped breathing, too.

Wegener left the room.

Georg remained. He took some black rubbish bags and bleach from under the sink. Luckily, the kitchen was the only room in the villa that wasn't carpeted. Removing blood from carpets was a real pain. There was always the risk you would have to throw them away.

15

She closed her eyes again immediately. She had to. She was nauseous, there was a sour taste in her mouth, a slight whistling in her ears, and her head was pounding. Only her sense of smell was intact. And that was something she could not ignore.

Soot, burnt wood, cold. The cold had a specific smell. Like ozone or lightning, but more pungent and metallic, like congealed blood.

She recognised these smells. She recognised the lumps in the mattress that dug into her back, and the texture of the blankets in which she was wrapped. They meant poverty.

Soot, poverty, cold. For a moment, Marlene was swamped with memories: cows in the shed, the stench of manure, stale polenta morning and night, her father's boots propped against the stove, her mother's face.

Her mother's face made her open her eyes wide and accept reality. Her mother had been (*crazycrazycrazy*) dead for a long time, and she didn't want to think about her. Not now. Not ever.

Even with her eyes open, it was almost impossible to distinguish reality from memory. The room in which Marlene had just woken was exactly like the one where she had spent the first years of her life. Walls covered in pine, a narrow window, a polished wardrobe, stale smoke. Even the rickety chair on which her jacket lay was almost identical to the one on which, as a child and a teenager, she had kept her clothes folded.

As soon as the sense of *déjà vu* faded, the pain came. She lifted her hands to her forehead and felt the texture of a bandage. She pressed gently. A moan escaped her lips.

She remembered.

The Mercedes skidding, the fir trees so distinct they looked fake, the crash, the blood on the steering wheel, then a series of grainy images: a man in a black hat bending over her, picking her up and heaving her over his shoulder. A man with very pale blue eyes.

As he walked through the snow he sang softly.

She could not remember the words to the lullaby, only the tone in which the man had sung them. A gentle tone.

The pain subsided.

Marlene took a closer look around. There was a candle on the bedside table, but nothing to light it with. Light barely filtered through the closed blinds on the window. She noticed that there was dry moss stuffed under the window frame: an old trick for stopping draughts. She blew gently, and her breath condensed into a small cloud.

Old tricks aren't always the best. A coherent thought at last.

Come on, you can do it.

Lifting herself from the bed and placing her feet on the floor was torture; bending down and putting on her shoes, agony. Getting up made her so dizzy; it took all her willpower to get it under control.

She had never felt so weak.

She staggered to the chair and felt her padded jacket. The pouch with the sapphires was still there, safe in the inside pocket. Thank goodness. Those gemstones were the only thing she could rely on. Marlene did not know where she was or who had brought her here. She did not even know what time it was, she realised. Her watch had stopped, and she couldn't tell the time of day by peering through the blinds. There was too much snow.

It was important to know the right time. A lot of things depended on it.

But first, she had to get out of here.

She opened the door.

"Anybody there?"

No answer.

She risked a few steps in the dark.

"Anyone there?" she said again in a louder voice.

Still no answer.

She saw a staircase and a glow of warm light coming from below.

Once again, that sense of *déjà vu*. But no recollection, no dream. There was a simple explanation. A fork, she told herself, is a fork, even at the North Pole. A fork consists of a handle for holding and prongs for skewing. A *maso* consisted of a barn, a water fountain, racks for brown bread, a room for smoking speck (you need three things to make speck, her father always said: salt, smoke and clean air), an outside toilet, a shed for the animals, a cellar for storing wine and oil and – the most important room – the *Stube*.

A *maso* would always be a *maso*, even at the North Pole.

She went down the creaking stairs, making sure she held firm to the banisters. At the bottom was the *Stube*, exactly as she had expected it to be. A table with a bench against the wall and a couple of rickety chairs. A sturdy larchwood door almost hidden under the stairs, which probably led to the cellar where wine and oil were stored. Different timber to break up the monotony of the pinewood walls. A large, soot-darkened pot simmering on the fire.

Seen one, seen them all.

Or almost.

The mess and filth of this *Stube* provided further proof that, no, she wasn't dreaming. And it wasn't a memory either. Not even when times were bad had Mamma allowed so much dirt to accumulate. Whenever Mamma lost her mind she would do nothing but clean, clean then clean some more.

But Mamma was dead, and Marlene didn't want to think about her. *Ever again.*

Instead, she focused on the stuffed animals strewn all over the room: on the mantelpiece, the shelves, on top of the cupboards. They were not trophies to flatter a hunter's vanity. They had a specific name: *Vulpendingen*. Marlene had heard of them but had never actually seen one. There were about twenty here.

A *Vulpendingen* was a joke. A non-existent animal, stuffed by assembling random pieces of game, with the sole purpose of surprising the viewer and having a laugh. The ones heaped up around her were seriously amazing.

A fox with a chough's wings and a bushy, glossy squirrel's tail. A grouse with a stone marten's head and the tiny wings of a wren. A wolf's head with bat wings instead of ears. That one must be quite old, Marlene thought. Wolves and bears had been extinct for almost a century in South Tyrol.

She went closer and touched its muzzle. In the warmth of the *Stube*, the wolf seemed almost to be breathing.

She kept stroking it while her eyes searched for a clock. There was always a clock in a *Stube*. A clock and a calendar.

Seen one, seen them all.

So they had to be there, hanging on the wall somewhere. Except that she couldn't find them.

Once again, this *maso* was different.

Shit.

It was important to know what time it was. She had calculated a narrow window for her escape. Moreover, depending on the time, she would be able to tell what Wegener was doing, work out who he was in the process of "interrogating" and the information he would be obtaining.

The scrapyard? Moritz? *Or worse?*

In order to work it out, though, she needed a clock, and in this *Stube* there were *Vulpendingen*, plus a hundred or so statuettes of animals carved in wood – a goat, an eagle, a bull, a wolf, squirrels in various poses, a whole litter of sows and smiling piglets and a large ibex with a broken horn thrown in a corner next to the firewood – but no clocks.

She took her fingers off the wolf's muzzle and went to the window, which was merely a tiny rectangular hole designed to prevent the heat from escaping. The pane was encrusted with ice, and it was almost impossible to see outside. It was definitely still snowing.

Bad news. It meant she was stuck in this place, waiting. While Herr Wegener had all the time he needed to pursue leads, gather clues and . . .

The thought that Klaus might be in danger made her feel faint.

"Shit," she whispered, tears of frustration stinging her eyes. "Shit, shit, *sh*—"

The sound of the latch made her jump. The door of the *maso* opened, and, along with a flurry of icy needles, a man dressed in black came in.

The man seemed surprised to see her up and about. He was holding two large metal buckets.

It was easy for Marlene to work out what he had been doing outside in spite of the blizzard. The smell was unmistakable. He had been feeding his pigs.

Marlene smiled at him, and he nodded in return. He stamped hard on the floor with his boots, twice with his left foot and twice with his right, to shake off the snow. He came forward, put the buckets by the door, removed his greatcoat and hung it on a metal hook next to a rifle. Marlene recognised it: a ten-bore. Her father had one like it for poaching. Illegal, but hunger is hunger. A roebuck could feed a family of three for a week. Two weeks, even, if you were careful.

End of any ethical dilemma.

The man examined her a moment longer with those piercing blue eyes of his.

He was a *Bau'r*. He must have been sixty or so, but it was always difficult to guess a *Bau'r*'s age. The hard work, the wind, the freezing winters and scorching summers made their faces enigmatic and as hard as bark. This *Bau'r* was tall and appeared to be strong. That was natural, too. A *Bau'r* seldom showed signs of weakness. Just like the trees they resembled, they lived frugally and dropped dead suddenly. A *Bau'r* couldn't afford protracted death agonies.

The man closed the door and spoke.

16

"I didn't think you'd be up until tomorrow," he said, surprise in his voice. "I'm glad. You're strong for a city girl."

The clothes. The nail polish. The Mercedes.

City girl.

Marlene did not contradict him. But although she had deceived herself over the past four years that she was a city girl, it was not true. City girls could walk around in jeans and look like queens. They could drive because it was natural to do so. It was girls from the mountains, more accustomed to shovelling shit, who had to spend hours picking out clothes that would conceal how inexperienced they were. They were the ones who felt challenged whenever they sat down behind the wheel of a car, not city girls. But the *Bau'r* had no way of knowing that. Just as he had no way of knowing that Marlene hated this nail polish and these clothes because they made her feel like a fraud (not to mention a filthy whore). No, despite the nail polish, the clothes and the Mercedes, Marlene was not and never would be a city girl.

Nor had she ever felt truly strong. Not even for a minute, in all the twenty-two years of her life.

Strong? Like hell she was.

She smiled, though, grateful to be called that, because she knew that in *Bau'r* language, "strong" was a compliment, maybe the greatest. To a city girl, the word would have conjured up an uncouth country lass with legs as solid as an ox's and a sour expression on her face. She would have preferred to be described as "beautiful," or "charming," or, better still, "sexy." She might even have taken offence. But the man by the door wasn't just any man. He was a *Bau'r*.

And Marlene, like all mountain girls accustomed to shovelling shit, had been trained from an early age to be aware of subtle nuances in language and to perform verbal minuets that, to an outsider, might sound ridiculous.

That was why she smiled.

Marlene knew that when a woman was called "strong" by a *Bau'r* ("What does a good *Bäuerin* need to do, Daddy?" "Sew, not eat too much and grit her teeth"), the word took on a meaning in comparison with which the adjectives "sexy," "charming" and "beautiful" might as well hide their faces in shame.

"Thank you for your kind words," she replied, bowing her head slightly and adopting the respectful tone due to someone whose face had more lines than one's own. "And I'll always be in your debt because without your help I'd be dead. You saved my life. My name is Marlene. Marlene Taufer."

Taufer was her maiden name. Saying it out loud lent a tad more warmth to her smile.

The man took her hand and held it in both of his. They were as rough as granite, but his grip was gentle, almost as if he were afraid of hurting her: a consideration that only a mountain girl could fully appreciate.

"My name is Simon Keller," the *Bau'r* said. "You don't have to thank me. No, really. Thank *Voter* Luis. He taught me everything I know. I gave you the poppy because you were in pain, but it was *Voter* Luis, years ago, who showed me what to do. I stitched up your wound, and that's another thing I learned from him."

He pointed at her forehead, which was wrapped in a bandage, and said, "There are no mirrors in the *maso*, but I don't think it'll leave a scar. Your skin is like a child's. A few years from now, nothing will show."

A scar?

Marlene turned pale and instinctively raised her hand to the bandage.

What will Klaus think when he sees my face patched up like Frankenstein's? Will I give him nightmares, or will he love me anyway? What if—

Stop it! The stupid reaction of a stupid city girl.

"Scars don't matter. I'm alive. That's the most important thing, Simon Keller." Marlene let go of his hand, dropped her voice and, although she suspected she already knew the answer, asked, "*Voter* Luis is no longer with us, am I right?"

"Yes, you are."

"Then I shall make it my duty to thank him in my prayers."

Keller seemed pleased. "*Voter* Luis was a man of faith. It will make him happy."

The minuet was over. They continued to stare at each other for a few seconds longer. It was the *Bau'r* who put an end to the awkwardness. He cleared his throat, took a chair, moved it close to the fireplace and motioned to her to sit down. Marlene obeyed, but only after Simon Keller had sat down on the bench, with his back to the wall. It was one of the unwritten rules of *maso* life. Even if the *Bau'r* said "please," it was an order, not a request. The *Bau'r* would choose the prayer before the meal, slice the speck and pour wine for his guests. The *Bau'r* was the first to sit down in his own home.

Home? A *maso* was hard work and a curse. It was the legacy of centuries of stubbornness and perseverance, a refuge from the elements, a safe fortress in a landscape of icy death. The *maso* was a self-sufficient world regulated by age-old mechanisms. Only a city girl would call it a home.

"Is there a *Bäuerin* I can thank?"

"Only a man could bear to live surrounded by all this mess, don't you think?" Keller replied in an amused tone. "The fact is, I never married, because even when I was young, women didn't want to be *Bäuerinnen* anymore, just like men don't want to be *Bau'rn* these days. Things were already starting to change then, and as usual women saw it a long time before us men did. But it's fine by me. I have all I need."

"Doesn't the solitude get you down? It takes great strength to bear that."

Mountain grammar: a question concealing a compliment.

Keller's chest swelled with pride. "This was my father's *maso* and his father's before him. It's been in the family for centuries. The date 1333 is carved into one of the beams in the pigsty, but *Voter* Luis used to say it was older than that. It's been destroyed many times, and the Kellers have always rebuilt it, more solid than before. The *maso* has always protected the Keller family, and the Keller family has always taken care of the *maso*."

"Wise words," Marlene said.

Keller rubbed the back of his neck, which was covered in sparse grey hair. "They're *Voter* Luis' words, not mine. *Voter* Luis was a very wise man. And," he said, getting to his feet as if he had suddenly remembered something urgent, "he was better than me, not only in his words but also in his manners."

He went to the cupboard and opened its doors.

Marlene also stood up.

Keller stopped her. "You're strong, city girl, but you need to eat. Eat and restore your health."

Marlene tried to protest. "My mother didn't raise me to be rude. Let me help you."

Keller left the plates and spoons for a moment, put his hands on her shoulders, and gently forced her to sit back down. "Would your mother rather have you eat or wait on an old bear like me?"

Marlene smiled.

He was paying her a great honour. *Bau'rn* didn't serve at the table.

That was a woman's job. And what he had cooked for her was also a sign of deep respect: small, dark liver dumplings, floating in an oily broth. Liver dumplings were only prepared when there were important guests, such as the priest, the mayor, the schoolmaster. Usually, the *maso* diet was monotonous and far less nutritious: polenta, sauerkraut, black bread, speck, a little cheese.

Marlene waited for Keller to sit down and bless the meal, but he did not. He took up his spoon and started eating, so Marlene did the same. It was scorching hot, but although it looked unappetising, it tasted delicious. She did not ask for a second helping. It was Keller who refilled her bowl. Marlene emptied it.

They resumed talking only once Keller had filled his oddly shaped white meerschaum pipe with tobacco. Sated with the food, Marlene now returned to her anxieties.

"May I ask what time it is?"

"I usually feed the kids, then have dinner," Keller calculated, "but today I was a bit late, so it must be around six."

Marlene blinked. "Kids?"

Keller laughed and sucked at his pipe. "I mean my pigs. There also used to be cows, but only the kids are left now. That's what I call them. Pigs are intelligent animals. They're also very touchy and always want to eat at the same time. I try and keep them happy, otherwise they scream all night long." He let the swirls of tobacco smoke disperse through the saturated air of the *Stube*. "So, yes, I'd say it must be six o'clock. Six o'clock in the evening on the Day of Our Lord."

Marlene felt faint. "The Day of Our L—"

"Sunday."

"I've spent—"

"You slept for two days."

Two days.

17

One. Two. Three.

The captain picked up at the third ring. Wegener could hear the murmur of the television news, mixed with the evening's domestic sounds. Isabella was washing up. He could make out her voice in the background, singing a tune.

He did not say hello or give his name, but got straight to the point. "I need the villa's telephone records," he said.

"I don't like being disturbed at home."

"And I don't like your tone. The last three months. Actually, let's make it six."

The captain laughed. "Are you joking?"

"And I need them urgently."

"It's not like buying a few oranges from the greengrocer."

"I still don't like your tone."

There was a bit of bustle as the receiver was put down on a hard surface, followed by footsteps and the sound of a door closing. The clatter of dishes stopped abruptly, and so did the singing.

The captain came back to the telephone. "It would have to be signed off by a judge, which is a major hassle, not to mention risky. You're well known, somebody might notice what I'm doing, and I'd have to face questions I can't answer."

"It's not a request."

"There are prosecutors who'd trade two years of their lives for your telephone records. Have you thought of that? And what if I get caught and these records end up in the hands of one of them?"

"You're not a prosecutor. Prosecutors decide. You don't decide a fucking thing. You just have to be cleverer than they are. We're in the same boat, Carbone. If I go down . . ."

"That's outside my jurisdiction."

"I have a name. Klaus. I want to know who he is."

"You're asking me to—"

"I told you," Herr Wegener cut in. "It's not a request."

He hung up. Irritably, he rubbed his chin. The prospect of dinner made him feel nauseous, but he dialled the internal number all the same and ordered Georg to bring him a sandwich and something sweet to drink. Peach tea, iced, with a lot of sugar. He needed energy. And coffee, please. Thank you.

He had to stay awake. Alert. His men could call any minute, and he had to be ready. Except that nobody had called. Not yesterday, not today.

He walked up and down, his fists in his pockets, trying to clear his mind. The *Standartenführer* had taught him that patience was a formidable weapon. As he paced the room, he tried to follow that advice.

Georg knocked at the door, entered and put a plate of ham sandwiches, a pitcher of peach tea and a cup of coffee on the desk, then withdrew, shutting the door behind him.

As he ate, Wegener spread a detailed map of South Tyrol on the desk and studied it for the umpteenth time. He had spent the whole of Sunday on that map, racking his brain, constructing theories, and had always reached the same conclusion. Marlene did not have many options.

His instinct and his reason told him that she had fled north and not south. Marlene did not speak Italian very well, whereas in Austria or Switzerland no one would notice her accent. Austria or Switzerland. Wegener considered Switzerland, but for purely logical reasons plumped for Austria.

The Swiss border was better protected than the Austrian one.

More guards, more border posts. Marlene had no contacts who could get her across without her being subjected to a thorough check.

Or did she?

He was consumed with doubt. Was there another traitor working with her? A traitor who belonged to his organisation? Or maybe someone from outside? Perhaps this Klaus belonged to the competition. At the same time, Herr Wegener was tormented by the fact that there was no organisation from Neumarkt to Brenner, or from the Reschen Pass to the Puster, powerful enough to dare challenge him. Except for *them*.

But *they* were something else.

No, South Tyrol was his.

There were only a few mavericks, a few gangs of blowhards, hotheads of no importance, whom Herr Wegener tolerated. Had he underestimated them? Was Klaus one of these loudmouths who were all muscle and no brain? And how had he met Marlene? Where? When? How had he managed to seduce her? What had he promised her that he, Herr Wegener, could not buy her?

Did she love him?

Herr Wegener hated these questions almost as much as he hated waiting, but what he hated even more was being distracted from his thoughts. So when Georg came into his study without knocking, he let out an irritable curse.

"You have visitors, sir," Georg announced, out of breath. "They've just driven in through the gate."

"Why didn't you stop them?"

"Sir . . ." Georg was worried.

Wegener went to the window and parted the curtains. Two cars had just parked by the front steps. Two black Mercedes, the latest model. He did not recognise any of the four men who got out, two from each car, but instantly knew the breed. Bodyguards. Athletic bodies, cautious gestures. Professionals.

He did recognise the silver-haired man in the elegant charcoal coat who got out of the front car immediately afterwards, leaning on a cane. The man looked up and gave a sign of greeting.

Wegener knew who he was, who had sent him and what he wanted. The only thing he did not know, and this filled him with anger, was how *they* had found out so quickly.

The Consortium.

18

It was a rumour, a whisper.

It was gossip, the kind you come across in every workplace. The reason for the schoolmistress's prolonged one-to-one meetings with the hot-tempered headmaster. The worker who was too fond of his drink and risked having a colleague on his conscience. The good sacristan consumed by resentment. The office manager who steals. The underworld was a workplace like any other, and criminals, too, enjoyed gossip and idle chat. Only the nature of their stories was different, not the tone. They would talk about the prostitute who boasted of spending nights in a cardinal's bed, or the doctor whose shifts coincided with a rise in the mortality rate on the wards, or the magistrate who had concealed the peccadillos committed by a degenerate son.

And they would whisper about the Consortium.

Whisper and keep away from it.

Few people spoke about it openly. Fewer still wondered about its true identity. They relied on their imaginations rather than on facts. They said it was a branch of the C.I.A. or a vestige of the *Stille Hilfe*, the S.S. veterans' association, which had turned into a criminal organisation. There was talk of entire boards of directors of banks being involved, as well as members of the government and other high-ranking politicians. Why not aliens? Wegener had wondered with a sneer the first time this rumour had reached his ears.

Still, the *Standartenführer* had not believed in the Bogeyman, and Bogeymen had dismantled his Reich piece by piece, to the sound of gunfire and TNT Which meant that it was wise never to underestimate a legend. So he had begun to investigate. Especially since, so they said, the Consortium considered South Tyrol – *his* patch – a free zone to be exploited at will, without the need to ask anybody's permission. And this Wegener found intolerable.

It had taken him three years to get to the bottom of the mystery, and he had been astounded by what he had discovered. Not only did the Consortium really exist, but it wasn't a criminal organisation in the sense Herr Wegener had experienced until then. The Consortium was a fierce, living entity.

He was thrilled.

The Dragon did exist, and he wanted to ride it, but even if only half of what he had unearthed was true, what was someone like him to the Consortium? A bug, to be squashed underfoot without a second thought. For all his villa, his properties in the Dolomites, his beautiful wife, his loyal men, his weapons, his safe-deposit boxes crammed with notes in three different banks in three different countries, Herr Wegener was *nothing* compared with the Consortium.

This would have put off men more powerful and perhaps more cautious than Wegener, but for him it became a further incentive. Once he had savoured the mirage of riding the Dragon and sitting at the grown-ups' table, he had begun racking his brain for a way to make the big leap.

He decided he had to get himself noticed.

He would not go to them like a beggar asking for a handout. The Consortium would come knocking at *his* door. For that to happen, he had to impress them.

Only by biting, and biting hard, would the bug escape the sole of the shoe.

The opportunity presented itself when, after lengthy stakeouts, flattery and threats, Wegener discovered the route of an articulated lorry, a monster carrying goods of astronomical value across his territory with just two men on board. Nobody would ever have dared make a move against that mobile strongbox. The eighteen-wheeler, the men and the cargo all belonged to the Consortium. Only a madman would have thought of attacking it.

A madman, or Herr Wegener.

He assembled a small team from among his smartest henchmen. Three men armed with pistols and automatic rifles. Four, including him. He set up fake roadworks that diverted the lorry onto a road that was not much frequented. There they sprung the ambush. Pointing their pistols, handkerchiefs over their faces, like outlaws in the Wild West. There was no need to fire a shot. The two drivers were no amateurs. They knew what they had to do. They put their hands up, got out of the cabin and followed their assailants' orders without breaking a sweat. Why should they be scared? *They* weren't the dead men walking.

Before leaving, as the lorry, driven by two of his men, vanished around the bend and Georg waited for him in a Citroën with the engine running, Wegener removed the handkerchief and revealed his face in the light of the street lamps.

"Do you know who I am?"

"Yes."

"What's my name?"

"Wegener."

"*Herr* Wegener, arsehole."

"Herr Wegener."

"Report back that I have a business proposition."

The two Consortium men laughed heartily.

Look at that, a dead man walking.

But Wegener had hit the bull's eye. The faceless members of the Consortium were favourably impressed with his audacity. And so, instead of a hitman, they had sent the silver-haired man to knock at his door. A lawyer.

The lawyer did not utter a single word that could have been used in evidence. And yet he was perfectly clear. He described his employers as businessmen who did not like to waste time but who prized initiative. Initiative was the engine of the economy, and for some people the economy mattered more than anything else. What he had done, even if over the top and perhaps too theatrical, had been interpreted as a sign of *outstanding* initiative, and had led them to give him a chance to prove just what he was made of.

Hadn't this been the aim of that stunt out of a John Wayne film?

"I hate John Wayne," Herr Wegener had replied. "Tell me what I have to do."

"Apart from paying back the loan?"

"Complete with a full tank, an oil change and my sincerest apologies."

The lawyer had smiled. "Wait for instructions. Though I must warn you, it may take a long time and it won't be pleasant. You'll have to show total dedication. Beware of disappointing my clients, Herr Wegener. Beware."

19

"No, thank you."

Worry lines appeared on Keller's forehead. "It's going to hurt. Once the effect wears off. Later on."

"I can bear it," she said. "It'd be a waste otherwise. I just need to sleep, I'm alright."

Unconvinced, Keller hesitated. "I have a large supply of it."

"I'm alright. Really."

Keller put the poppy seeds back on the shelf and escorted her to the upper floor, watching her struggle up the creaking stairs, but making no comment.

"Wait," he said, once they had arrived.

He went back downstairs. Marlene heard him moving about the *Stube* and opening a door to the cellar. He came back with a hammer and nails, a couple of thin planks, an old sheet embroidered with hearts, a bucket and a container of quicklime for unpleasant smells.

Within a few minutes, without saying a word, he had built her a private toilet in the corner of the room opposite the window. He checked that the nails were in tightly, spread the sheet and nodded, pleased. "Women," he said, blushing, "don't like to be seen when they do certain things. And the outside toilet is much too cold for a city girl."

Marlene repressed a smile at the man's sense of modesty and thanked him with the respect due to him.

Keller turned his back on her and made to leave the room. He stopped at the door.

"Tomorrow," he said with a little cough, not turning around, "I think I'll go hunting in the woods. For a couple of hours, or maybe longer. But at least two hours."

Marlene looked out of the window. Darkness and blizzard.

"In all this snow?"

He cleared his throat again. "The storm will take a while to subside. You may have to stay here for a couple of days, and women don't like being dirty. Tomorrow, I'll heat some water for the tub. Then I'll go hunting, so that you can . . . You never know what you can catch, even in this weather. You need fresh meat, city girl."

He turned, looking embarrassed.

"I make the soap myself. It smells of carnations, my mother's favourite. Do you mind the smell of carnations?"

"I love it," she said reassuringly, touched by all his care.

Relieved, he bade her goodnight and closed the door gently behind him.

Marlene waited a couple of minutes and then rushed to her private toilet. Then, dressed as she was, she got in under the blankets. She was nearly asleep when the pain returned. Without the poppy infusion, it really hurt.

Marlene was angry with herself for having declined Keller's offer.

It was not only the injury to her forehead, it was the bruises all over that were clamouring for her attention, and Marlene was forced to keep tossing and turning on the uncomfortable mattress to resist the stabbing pains – the stabbing pains and the thoughts.

All things considered, her plan had been straightforward. Steal the sapphires, exchange some of them for clean identity documents and a new life with Klaus, as well as some currency (possibly dollars: dollars were accepted pretty much everywhere), get on a plane and escape to the other side of the world (any part of the world as long as it was warm: Marlene had promised herself she would never again

75

suffer the cold), then, once they were safe, *very* carefully arrange for Herr Wegener to find the remaining sapphires.

Letting him find the remaining sapphires, at least 70 per cent of them, according to her calculations, would serve a dual purpose: first, to leave a false clue for her husband's henchmen, and second, to get him to back off.

Or try to, at least.

She was dubious about the outcome, though.

There was a third reason, the one that mattered most to Marlene. The sapphires were her last connection to Wegener, a connection she could not wait to sever.

Starting from scratch meant forgetting: forgetting Wegener, forgetting *everything*.

A new life with Klaus, that was all she asked. In a warm place, with sand and sea and palm trees. She liked palm trees. The way the leaves swayed in the breeze.

That was her dream.

A new life, she thought, huddling under the blankets, exhausted, before at last falling asleep.

Despite her tiredness, Marlene had dreams. Not about sun-kissed beaches and palm trees. Not about Klaus and the future. Not even, as she had feared, about the crash.

Marlene dreamed of small, nasty, cruel creatures with blue eyes.

That night, Marlene dreamed about kobolds.

20

Small, treacherous and nasty, kobolds had blue eyes that glowed in the dark. The dark was the only thing they loved. The dark, and the soil in which they lived. Sometimes, though, the light would disturb them even there, in their burrows deep in the entrails of the earth.

The light was not brought there by heroes like Siegfried the dragon-slayer or even by kind, handsome Prince Charmings like the ones in the stories that Mamma (when she was still Mamma) would tell Marlene to get her to fall asleep.

The disturbers of the kobolds' peace, their bitterest enemies, were frail little pixies worn down by hunger, exhaustion and disease. Skinny creatures forcibly sent down cracks into mines in places with exotic names: Thailand, Burma, Kashmir.

There was a word for these pixies who were not pixies: "children." Slaves with pickaxes in their hands and crusts of bread in their pockets, although those who put them down those shafts didn't give a damn. They were only interested in the shiny blue stones, not in the pixies who brought them to the surface.

Sapphires.

Kobolds.

The kobolds had travelled a very long way to Herr Wegener's villa on the River Passer. From Burma to Hong Kong, from Hong Kong to Israel and from Israel to Merano.

Travelling made them *furious*.

Too much light.

Kobolds hated light at least as much as they loved revenge.

Revenge on the innocent and the guilty. Revenge in thousands of different ways. That was why the journey they had made had left a trail of blood in its wake.

The blood began in a mine surrounded by men whose favourite pastime was squashing mosquitoes and using the butts of their rifles to hit those children who were slower, more tired, or simply happened to be in their way.

One of them, the pixie who had dug into the rock and brought the kobolds up into the light, died with his eyes wide open in a tunnel with no oxygen, two days after handing the small stones over to his jailer, a wiry guy who, exactly one month later, got drunk and (dreaming that pixies were dancing on his throat) drowned in his own vomit.

The smuggler with rotting teeth who got the sapphires from the jailer died with his eyes open, after giving the sapphires to a shifty Chinese man in a Miles Davis T-shirt just across the border. This smuggler was on his way to the village where he had planned to spend half the money he had earned on drugs and whores when he was set upon by bandits. They searched him and took the roll of dollars, knocked him about, forced him to his knees and killed him with a shot to the back of the head from a Kalashnikov, which sounded like the laughter of the still-travelling kobolds.

The Chinese man carried the precious stones in his 4 × 4 for many kilometres through the jungle, and two weeks later, clean-shaven now and without the Miles Davis T-shirt, boarded a merchant ship bound for Hong Kong. Once there, he got on the telephone and duly reassured the relevant person. At the appointed time, a slim blonde knocked at his door, was given the pouch of sapphires and took off on a Boeing 707 to Israel.

The blonde was never to know that a homemade bomb killed the Chinese man, whose only pleasures had been making money and listening to "Kind of Blue" with the lights turned down low.

Just as she was never to know that the cutter in Tel Aviv, after working on the rough stones she had given him in a nightclub and then sending them on to Genoa, became racked with guilt about the petty life his debts had forced him into, stuffed himself full of tranquillisers and whisky, wrote a confused letter (in which apologies to his nearest and dearest alternated with visions of blue-eyed creatures eating away at his brain) then cut his wrists and died in his bath with his mouth open.

The blonde was never to know these things because, a week later, swimming off Australia's Great Barrier Reef, wondering if she'd like to have a Manhattan or something less strong, she made the acquaintance of a wonderful specimen of *Hapalochlaena lunulata*, a member of the octopus family whose body is adorned with beautiful blue rings (as brilliant as a kobold's eyes).

Fascinated, the blonde dived in order to get a better look, and the animal took fright and bit her, injecting into her thigh muscle the speciality that makes it famous among toxicologists throughout the world: tetrodotoxin, a neurotoxin that attacks the muscular system and paralyses it.

The blonde did not drown; it was the poison that killed her.

Meanwhile, the kobolds had arrived in Genoa. Had their thirst for revenge been quenched? Not in the slightest. The man who went to pick them up on Wegener's behalf and exchanged them for a heavy suitcase full of money wore a perfectly tailored suit. He was a simple man named Moritz.

Asphyxia. Lead. TNT Remorse. Poison. The kobolds' revenge.

In a thousand different ways.

Also part of their revenge were the questions planted like knives in Herr Wegener's mind as, assuming a mask of calm to conceal his terror, he let the silver-haired lawyer into the study of the villa on the River Passer and offered him his best brandy.

Which of his men had tipped off the Consortium?

Or had it been more than one?

How many had betrayed him? How many were loyal to him?

And the worst question of them all: Was he alone now? No longer barefoot, no longer a child, no longer forced to walk in his father's footsteps through the cold and ice, but alone once more?

His only certainty lay in the mocking sneer of the opened safe. No, he corrected himself, as the lawyer told him to drop any mawkishness and forced him to tell him *everything*. No, it wasn't true. There was another certainty.

His life depended on this meeting.

21

The lawyer had listened, sitting there in the study, sipping his brandy with an engrossed, almost kindly expression on his lean face.

Herr Wegener had not lied. The fact that the lawyer had come here meant that the Consortium was aware of what had happened, so it was pointless making up stories.

He had begun by telling him about the Friday-night meetings. He had described his return home, the need to disturb Marlene in order to write a few names in the black notebook. His surprise at not finding her there asleep. He had told him about the detail that had immediately alarmed him: the painting that concealed the safe hanging askew.

His frantic hands composing the combination and discovering that the safe had been raided. The missing velvet pouch. He told him about the clues he had gathered and the investigation that had ensued. The telephone calls. The orders. The certainty of Marlene's betrayal.

The wait.

"We're looking for her. All my men, without exception, have been alerted," he said, running his fingers down the crease of his trousers. "We'll find her. I can assure you of that."

The lawyer leaned forward with a benevolent look on his face. Suddenly he slapped him. "You're a fool," he said. "I'm the only thing standing between you and a bullet, Wegener."

"Everything's under control."

The lawyer's gaze had turned mocking. "Do you realise the

seriousness of what's happened? Do you even know what's been stolen from you?"

"Yes," Herr Wegener said, his cheek burning as if it were on fire.

Yes, he did now.

Those sapphires had been his trial by ordeal before the great leap. Converting his assets into precious stones. Into sapphires, to be precise. Blue, like the sky he aspired to ascend into.

Acquiring a large number of sapphires on the black market presupposed friends and contacts who could demonstrate courage, audacity and initiative. Yet this was not an ordinary money transaction, like buying shares so that you could sit on a board of directors.

The Consortium had other aims. Property could be plundered, money stolen and multiplied. Men like Wegener, on the other hand, were rare. And the hearts of men like Wegener had to be conquered.

The Consortium had no use for servants. They needed people whose ambition went even higher than the stars in the sky. That was why, just as the old feudal lords used to do, what the Consortium puppeteers asked of the candidate was a pledge. And that was what the sapphires were. A symbol of submission and a promise of freedom. Above all, proof of goodwill. It's what distinguishes the servant from the master.

And the living from the dead.

"Today," the lawyer said, "I was asked some questions, and I had to answer them."

"What kind of questions?"

"About your goodwill. I vouched for you. I went out on a limb. I shouldn't have, but I did. I said that the Herr Wegener I knew was strong, brave and unscrupulous and that he would do everything in his power to recover the sapphires. And more."

"That's very kind—"

"I haven't finished yet," the lawyer cut in.

"Sorry."

"I guaranteed that the problem would be eradicated. As soon as possible."

Wegener sat up straight. "Marlene is dead. I'll kill her with my own hands, you can be sure of that."

"When?"

"As soon as my men find her."

"How can you be certain they will?"

"You have my word."

The lawyer ran his fingers through his hair and looked him in the eyes, his face turning livid. "Don't you realise your word is worth nothing anymore?" he cried. "Until this matter is brought to a conclusion, even you are *nothing*. You're not even a human being." He pointed a finger at Wegener's face. "You're a thing. An object. You belong to the Consortium. Is that clear?"

"Yes," Wegener said, trying hard to restrain his anger.

"Are you sure?"

"Yes."

"Who does this house belong to?"

Wegener looked at his reflection in the lawyer's pale eyes. "The Consortium."

"Who do your men answer to?"

"The Consortium."

"And who do you have to thank for the fact that you're still breathing right now?"

"I get the idea," Wegener growled, punching the armrest of the sofa.

"Answer me, damn it!" the lawyer yelled, flinging his glass to the floor. "You were stupid enough to tell your wife about the sapphires! Like any little amateur. You were stupid enough to have them stolen by a two-bit whore, and you still think you're . . . just what do you think you are, Herr Wegener?"

Wegener stared at him for a long time, feeling his veins bursting with rage.

There was only one answer.

"A puppet. Of the Consortium."

"So tell me: who do you have to thank for the fact that you're still breathing?"

"The Consortium."

"That's right, the Consortium."

The lawyer took a business card from his leather wallet and placed it on the mahogany coffee table between him and Wegener. It had no name or address on it.

Only a telephone number.

When he next spoke, the lawyer's voice was once more calm and reassuring.

For a moment, Wegener felt scared.

"It's a voicemail. Leave a message. Arrange a time and place to meet. A safe place of your choice. Go there and wait. The person the voicemail belongs to might already be there, or he might keep you waiting for hours. Even days. He's very cautious. You just hang on and wait."

Wegener turned the business card over in his hand. "Who is this person?"

The lawyer stood up and buttoned his elegant jacket. "They call him the Trusted Man."

"And this man is . . . ?"

"He's not a man," the lawyer said, looking him up and down. "He's a weapon." He checked his watch and pulled a face. Then he added, "And he's also your last chance to prove to the Consortium that your goodwill can be relied on."

"Is he a hitman?"

The lawyer proffered his hand.

22

Was it night or day?

The blizzard had not let up. Marlene woke with a start, with an ache in her head and a feeling of nausea that made her gasp for a couple of minutes before she was able to slip out from under the blankets. It took her ages before she was in a state to go down into the *Stube*.

Keller had been up for a while and was smoking his pipe, watching the embers in the hearth.

Marlene smiled at him and, insisting he remain seated, asked where she could find the coffee, the coffee pot, the sugar, the cups and the teaspoons. There was no sugar, Keller said with a touch of embarrassment, and the cups were chipped, but Marlene still managed to make some strong, invigorating coffee.

"I buy it in the village," Keller explained. "Along with bananas, cartridges for my rifle and medicine for the kids."

"Bananas?"

He laughed. "I love bananas."

"And I love your *Vulpendingen*, Simon Keller," she said, clearing the cups and indicating the stuffed animals. "They're amazing. You could sell them and buy quite a few bananas with the proceeds." She laughed. "I'm sure people would queue up to buy them."

"Don't you find them scary?"

"Why should I? I think they're funny."

One in particular, which she hadn't noticed the previous evening: a marmot with large bat wings sprouting from its hindquarters. The marmot was bent forward as if about to perform a somersault, and there was something childish and gross about the whole thing that made her giggle.

"Elisabeth found them funny, too. I used to make them for her. *Voter* Luis would say I'd end up being better than him at making them. Do you know the story of the *Vulpendingen*?"

Leaving the cups in the sink, Marlene turned, puzzled. "Elisabeth?"

"My sister. She died when she was little."

"How stupid of me, I shouldn't have—"

Keller gestured with his hand. "It's alright, city girl. I loved Elisabeth, she was a beautiful child. And she was good. But many years have passed."

Marlene bit her lip. "I've been too nosey, I didn't . . ."

"So you don't want to know why the *Bau'rn* used to waste their time making *Vulpendingen*?"

"Of course I want to know."

"It's a really funny story," Keller began, filling his meerschaum pipe and lighting it. "Many years ago, South Tyrol was hunting land. There were forests – many more than there are now. The Bavarian aristocracy liked these mountains and woods, but above all they liked good beer and the fact that their women hated travelling."

A coil of smoke rose from his pipe.

"Imagine all these counts and marquises arriving in their fine carriages, with their rifles and all the rest. They'd shoot deer, they'd shoot bears and they'd drink. After a while, though, they'd start to get bored. Beer wasn't enough, and they'd hunted all there was to hunt. So they started saying: Why do we travel so many kilometres to go after the same animals we could just as easily kill in the woods behind our castles?"

"Because of their wives."

Keller slapped the table with his hand. "But they could have sent their wives away from their castles and done the same thing there as they were doing here. Don't you think?"

"I imagine so."

"A peasant heard them and realised that if the Bavarian counts stopped coming down to South Tyrol, there would be trouble. They brought a lot of money with them, they were wealthy. So he waited until they were full of beer and started telling them about a terrible creature that prowled the mountains."

"The *Vulpendingen!*" Marlene exclaimed, amused.

"A very rare creature that only left its lair on the night of the full moon. And only when the night of the full moon coincided with the day of the devil."

Marlene frowned. "What's the day of the devil?"

"Friday."

"But . . ."

"The wealthy Bavarians weren't taken in by the story either. So the peasant, who was much more cunning than them, produced one of those" – Keller pointed to the forward-leaning marmot – "and offered to be their guide. He took them all over the mountains until they were exhausted and then said, 'There it is! Shoot! Shoot!' But they could never manage to hit one. It was a real challenge, and the rumour spread. More and more noblemen arrived. And since they didn't want to look bad in front of their friends . . ."

"They started buying *Vulpendingen* in secret."

"So that they could take them back to their castles as trophies, while continuing to shower the peasants and hunters with gold."

Marlene clapped her hands. "You said *Voter* Luis had the gift of the gab, but you, Simon Keller, are his worthy son. I hadn't heard a story told so well in years."

"It's just something silly to pass the time," Keller protested. "Actually, it's time to feed the kids then put the water on to boil."

He laid down his pipe and stood up.

"I can help you, if you like," Marlene said.

Keller looked her up and down. "It's not a job for a city girl."

"But I'm not a city girl. I was born and raised in a *maso*. It was much further downhill than yours, but I can milk a cow, make butter, wring a hen's neck, and I know just how smelly pigs are."

Keller did not smile, but looked at her with his piercing eyes. "You have the hands of a city girl."

"All that was a long time ago, when I was a child. Then life took me to other places. But I remember everything my mother and father taught me."

"Pardon my insolence, but to me you're still a child. A child who needs to build up her strength."

This time, Marlene did not give in. "I learned many things in the *maso*, Simon Keller. Above all, I learned to show gratitude. Please, let me help you."

And that was how Marlene got to know the kids.

23

It was more than a wind.

The *Wehen* was a wind that gathered snow, turned it to ice and used it as a sharp weapon. Not for nothing was the word *Wehen* used as a synonym for "distress."

The *Wehen* greeted Marlene and Simon Keller.

Once out of the *Stube*, they descended the unsteady wooden staircase. It led them to ground level, which the snow had raised by at least a metre and which Marlene saw was very steep and treeless.

They walked quickly, she close behind him, hugging the wall of the *maso* and huddling as much as they could to shield themselves a little from the intensity of the storm. Halfway around the house, they paused to allow Keller to clear the icy mounds outside a small wooden door. They had arrived.

Marlene wrinkled her nose. It was very warm and *very* smelly. It's a pigsty, she reminded herself. It can't very well smell of lavender.

Her parents had kept pigs, too, and Marlene remembered their cries whenever her father bled them to death for speck and ham to sell at the market. Even if she covered her ears, those bloodcurdling screams, sounding almost human, haunted her for days. Her father noticed, and, when the time came to slaughter the pigs, he would send her to Tante Frida and Onkel Fritz to spare her nightmares.

Later, the pigs disappeared. They were too expensive and did not bring in much money. A small van spluttering exhaust fumes arrived and took them away.

From then on, her parents used the old pigsty as a hen coop, but even though they constantly poured quicklime over the place to disinfect it the stench remained.

"Wait," Keller said, going down a steep staircase until he vanished into the darkness. "I don't want you to hurt yourself."

Marlene did not have to wait long. The light came on almost immediately, along with the grunting of the pigs and blasts of a sickly sweet stench. Then she heard Keller's voice. "Come, the kids are anxious to meet you."

Nine steps down.

Marlene had thought that all *masi* were built the same way but Keller's was an exception, first because of the absence of a clock, and now because of its pigsty.

It was not so much a matter of its unplastered walls, built with big, coarsely cut stones, or the depth of the sty, or even the beams on the ceiling, so thick and dark that they also seemed to have been carved from rock.

It was the overall dimensions that were astonishing. The pigsty was *huge*.

"Look," Keller said, raising the lamp above his head to show her the inscription he had mentioned to her earlier: *1333*. "See? I wasn't lying, the *maso* is very old."

Marlene looked around, bewildered. "I've never seen a pigsty like this before."

Keller beamed. "And you've never seen such beautiful pigs, my dear."

Now that her eyes had grown accustomed to the dim light cast by the lamp, Marlene noticed that the place was divided in three. Behind her, there were the nine steps that led outside and some sacks of feed thrown against the wall. To her left and right, she could see the pigs rooting about in wooden pens. Before her stood an iron grille, the bottom rising out of the straw-covered rock floor and the top embedded in the ceiling, forming a kind of cage.

A little door was cut into the metal, fastened with a sturdy padlock. The inside of the cage was shrouded in darkness.

Seen one, seen them all? Marlene shook her head. Like hell she had.

"Meet the kids," Keller said, pouring the contents of one of the buckets into the trough in the left-hand pen. "These are the boys. See? I have to feed them first, before the girls, otherwise they start screaming. And you should hear them scream. Boys, don't be rude, say hello to our guest."

The three boars, so fat that their eyes were practically covered in lard, did not deign to give her a second glance. Marlene went closer to take a better look. They were strange. Just like the females in the other pen, the males were spotted. There were large black spots all over their bodies. This, too, was new to her.

Piebald pigs?

"Are they sick?" she asked Keller.

"A normal pink pig can't survive at such a high altitude," he explained. "The ancient peoples bred dark pigs that were stronger and could survive the cold, but they didn't provide enough meat. That was a big problem, so they decided to try cross-breeding. That's why you get the black marks. Come closer, they aren't dangerous. Allow me to introduce Franz and the Doctor. The shyer one is Kurt."

Marlene blinked. "The Doctor?"

"That's right." Keller pointed at two little dark marks around the animal's eyes. "Those are his glasses. He's a bit unfriendly, he thinks he knows more than anyone else. Kurt and Franz, on the other hand, are smugglers. Look at Kurt's paws. See how black they are up to the knee? He's wearing cowboy boots. Don't laugh, he's shy but also extremely vain, so you might hurt his feelings. Anyway, he and Franz are partners in crime. Both outlaws." He put the empty bucket down on the floor and smiled. "They smuggle cigarettes. Don't you believe me?" He took a handful of tobacco from his supply and dropped it inside the pen. The two pigs rushed to it, grunting and squealing. "They love it."

Marlene couldn't help laughing. Down here, Simon Keller seemed different. Less formal, happier. As if he were more at ease with animals than with humans. His eyes glistened like those of a child at Christmas time.

"And these are the girls," he said, turning to the pen on the right. "Mountain girls, much better behaved than their friends over there."

Indeed, when he tipped the bucket over the trough, they approached less frantically, although they did not exactly stand on ceremony.

Marlene decided to play along.

"Do these young ladies have names?"

"This one's Maria, like the mother of Our Lord. That one with the black eye is Birgit, she likes to get into scraps" – here, he jokingly mimed a punch in the face – "but she's a distinguished lady. See her well-cared-for nails? And that one's Helene, she's a bit fussy. The one over there at the back is Gertrud. She was so funny when she was born, she used to love running up and down the pen and rolling in the hay. Now she's old. See how tame she is?"

Heedless of the chatter, Gertrud had her snout in the trough, lapping up Keller's slop. She seemed focused rather than tame.

"But don't even think about letting her out. She ran away once. Really. She climbed those steps as fast as a weasel, and out she ran! Out into the mountains. I didn't think I'd ever see her again. If she'd gone into the woods, she might have found food and turned wild, but up in the mountains? There's nothing there but rock and ice. But guess who came back home three days later and still on top form?"

"Gertrud the fugitive."

"Precisely!" Keller said. "Gertrud the fugitive. She's the oldest here. I should have turned her into speck and sausages years ago, but I can't bring myself to do it. It would have been like slitting the prodigal son's throat. Not exactly the right thing to—"

A gentle jingling sound.

The pigs fell silent.

Keller broke off halfway through his sentence and turned to the grille.

To the darkness.

The jingling sounded again. A soft peal.

"Who's that?" Marlene whispered.

Not what. *Who.*

"Oh, her," Keller said. "She's my little Lissy."

24

Keller undid his greatcoat, which he had kept buttoned until now despite the stifling heat in the pigsty. Beneath it, he was wearing a canvas bag over his shoulder. A hunter's haversack. He unfastened the buckles and took out a plastic bag. It was stuffed full and looked as if it must weigh a good few kilos.

He asked Marlene to hold it. "Little Lissy is spoilt," he said. "She's a real princess, doesn't like the same food as the others."

From one of the shelves, he took a bowl the size of a basin. Marlene stared in disbelief. The bowl wasn't made of steel, but of silver. Simon rubbed it with a cloth until it shone in the light of the oil lamp. Then he took the bag from her hands and emptied its contents – a repulsive-looking gloop – into the bowl and carefully stirred it until it became a homogenous mash that reminded Marlene of slightly runny polenta. Finally he rinsed his hands in the pigs' drinking trough, dried them on his greatcoat and slapped himself on the thigh. Only then did Marlene speak.

"Lissy?" she said. She had instinctively dropped her voice.

"Like the Emperor's princess," Keller said cheerfully.

"Sissi?"

"*Lissy*," he corrected her as he approached the iron grille with the bowl in his hand. "We say Lissy, not Sissi."

Marlene had never thought about it, not even when she had seen the film. Yet the *Bau'r* was right. Sissi was Romy Schneider, all made-up and captured on celluloid. Maybe at the Habsburg court, the real princess, the one who was assassinated, was also called that.

But here, in South Tyrol, they spoke dialect. And in dialect, the diminutive "Sissi" was mangled into "Lissy."

"Lissy," Marlene repeated.

Keller put the bowl on the ground, took from his canvas bag a steel glove, the kind used by butchers to avoid hurting themselves, and put it on. He opened and closed his fist. Satisfied, he loosened the top button of his shirt, the only piece of white in his clothing, and took from around his neck a thin chain with a key at the end. He inserted it in the lock of the little door and opened it.

The door opened with a squeak (*Nibble, nibble, little mouse! Who is nibbling at my house?*) that set Marlene's teeth on edge.

Keller put the bowl with the slop inside the grille and closed the door again. The key disappeared under the shirt, the glove into the haversack and the haversack under the greatcoat.

But he had not finished yet.

From a pocket in his waistcoat, where a gentleman would have kept his watch, he took out a little bell and rang it. The sound was a twin to the jingling that had interrupted their conversation. Keller began to murmur, "Sweet Lissy, little Lissy . . ."

Suddenly, the darkness turned liquid. Marlene felt weak. She staggered backwards until she brushed against the pen with the males, but they did not react. They were silent, their snouts pointed in the direction of the metal grille.

Marlene coughed, but in vain.

"Sweet Lissy . . ."

The light from the oil lamp could no longer hold back the darkness, which spread across the walls, causing them to sway as if they were the curtains in front of a stage.

". . . Little Lissy."

The stench of pig became unbearable. Marlene felt trapped. She had to get out of there. She needed air.

"Sweet . . ."

She needed Keller to stop saying those words and ringing that little bell.

". . . Lissy."

Feeling dizzy, Marlene leaned all her weight against the pen. If she hadn't, she would have fallen to the ground.

Keller noticed. He stopped ringing the little bell and looked at her, alarmed.

The walls stopped undulating. The darkness withdrew.

"Are you alright, city girl?"

Marlene swallowed a couple of times. "I'm afraid . . . I'm not feeling well."

Keller stood up. "I'd have liked you to meet Lissy, but it'll have to be another time. My princess is shy. She doesn't like strangers. Let's go. She won't eat if we stay."

Marlene did not need to be asked twice. She clambered up the stairs to the door and threw it open.

The *Wehen*. The cold. *Air.*

She turned and saw Keller with the buckets in his right hand.

That was when Marlene's imagination ran wild.

Once again, the fairy tale overwhelmed reality.

She heard the soft, gentle jingling from the darkness at the far end of the sty. From behind the metal grille.

Keller extinguished the oil lamp. The sizzling of the flame as it went out became a white space between a *tick* and a *tock* and Marlene's imagination transformed reality into something else. It lasted for a second, maybe two. At that moment, she saw something stirring.

In the darkness.

Tick . . .

A fleeting vision out of the corner of her eye, with her mind all over the place from the heat and the stench, as the darkness guillotined the pigsty. It was like during the accident. Marlene's eyesight grew sharper and she saw (or imagined) every detail.

Lissy.

Black on black. Muzzle more than a metre from the ground. A four-hundred-kilo mass. Powerful loins quivering like bellows. A small tuft of white bristles between the ears. Two blades of pale skin that joined the eyes and the twisted tusks glistening with saliva. A rough grunt through sharp teeth.

And eyes.

Intelligent eyes.

As if Lissy knew. As if she could see through Marlene, all her lies, all her memories, her soul stripped bare.

. . . *Tock.*

The darkness. The cold. The blizzard.

Reality.

Running while lashed by the *Wehen*, the staircase with the rickety banister, the warmth of the *Stube*, Keller talking cheerfully as he warmed one large pot of water on the stove after another until he'd filled the bathtub.

A little leftover coffee to warm her bones.

Keller saying goodbye.

Carnation-scented soap.

25

On Golgotha, the cross. On Sinai, the Law. On Moriah, not one drop of Isaac's blood.

Mount Greylock showed Herman the Leviathan. Mount Ararat stopped the Ark. The Himalayas gave birth to the Buddha.

Mount Meru is the centre of the world, and the North Star watches over it. On the summit of Mount Kailash, as dark and icy as the surface of Pluto, Shiva the Destroyer dances.

Beneath a mountain with no name, Marlene met Lissy.

26

It was only later that she worked it out. A couple of hours after Keller had put his rucksack and a ten-bore rifle over his shoulder, a handful of cartridges in his pockets, his hunting knife at his belt, and vanished into the blizzard.

Marlene worked it out as she lay in the warm, fragrant water, trying to relax her aching muscles and not think about Herr Wegener. Or about Klaus.

Or about Lissy.

The only result was that all she could imagine was her husband's anger, all she could think about was Klaus and all she could wonder was why a black sow behind a grille had scared her so much.

Little Lissy. Sweet Lissy.

Little?

The animal Simon Keller kept behind that disquieting iron grille was the largest pig Marlene had ever seen.

Not to mention the fangs.

Every so often, a piglet would be born with unusual teeth. Her father had explained that there was nothing to worry about, it was just a whim of nature. As if those pigs remembered what they were before man had domesticated them. Usually, though, it was just one or two slightly crooked, slightly sharp teeth. Nothing in comparison with sweet Lissy's fangs.

Those were a boar's fangs, fangs that could rip open the most formidable hunter.

Only then did she work it out.

Lissy.

Sissi.

Both short forms of Elisabeth.

Marlene lifted a hand to her face, opened her eyes wide and stared into space. Simon Keller had named the sow after his dead sister.

Her immediate impulse was to laugh.

But she didn't.

It was the saddest thing she had ever heard.

27

He had followed the lawyer's instructions to the letter. He had called the voicemail and left a message arranging the location of the meeting: his wife's boutique, the following day.

"You'll find me there from eight in the morning."

He had not slept a wink all night and had set off bright and early, getting Georg to drive him there in the Lancia H.F. Then he had sent Georg away and prepared to wait. Old Mother Frost was empty. He had given Gabriel and the seamstresses instructions: the boutique was to close for a day. When Gabriel had protested, Wegener had slammed the receiver down on him.

Once there, he lit the stove in the back room, sat down on a chair, folded his arms and looked out through the front window.

The streets were deserted, and the snow showed no sign of easing off. How long had this damn blizzard been going on for? Three days? Four? Four. The first flakes had fallen on the night of the theft.

Four days. An eternity. Marlene could be anywhere.

That thought made him feel like a caged animal. None of his men had found a trace of her. Her or the Mercedes. The telephone records that would allow him to establish Klaus's identity were late in arriving. Carbone wasn't answering his calls.

Worse still, his men were starting to champ at the bit. The economic crisis had increased business tenfold, but without him it was hard for them to handle it all. They needed orders and instructions. Every hour wasted chasing after Marlene amounted to heaps of money being thrown away. They could not understand. They . . .

He clenched his fists.

Powerlessness. A feeling that reminded Herr Wegener of endless walks along the mountain paths, clutching the Iron Cross.

Somehow, the morning went by. Herr Wegener did not stir from the workshop. He sat by the stove, which was turned up to the maximum. He was cold, his feet especially. They were frozen and he could not warm them.

Midday went by, too.

Herr Wegener stood up just once, in order to empty his bladder and drink water from the bathroom tap. He was not hungry. He could not shake off the feeling of cold.

The afternoon drew to a close. Merano was shrouded in a fog of silence. The only sounds were those of the snow ploughs trying to stem the white madness endlessly falling from the sky.

He had been told to wait patiently, and so he waited patiently. As it got dark, the feeling of cold disappeared and at last he felt his head clear. His thoughts became specific, precise. Thoughts of death. For Marlene. For Klaus. For all the men who had betrayed him, who had mocked him for having been screwed by a woman. Carbone would be top of the list. He had been the one to inform the Consortium, Wegener was ready to swear to it. What about Georg? Was he loyal? He did not know, but he hadn't liked the look he had given him that morning before leaving. A look of pity. Or perhaps defiance? Either way, he would pay for it.

Everybody would pay. His revenge would be terrible. He would kill them and their families. He imagined a pile of corpses, a pyramid of arms and legs, with himself standing on top, laughing at the mangled bodies, as merciless as only he could be.

What about the lawyer? He, too, would die. He would have to devise something that would arouse no suspicion. An accident. A little cyanide, like the pills that S.S. officers carried in their pockets to avoid the humiliation of defeat.

Thinking about revenge dispelled his frustration. Time passed, and the number of corpses grew before his eyes.

He noticed that the fire in the stove was petering out, and he stood up to add fuel. He washed his hands and drank a little more water, then went back to sitting and staring at the door.

He dozed off.

He dreamed he was in the woods of Val d'Ultimo. The *Standartenführer* was kneeling in front of him, his father's Iron Cross pinned to his chest, his fingers intertwined behind his head.

It was a dream, not a memory, because in actual fact, the *Standartenführer* had begged him to spare his life. But in the dream, the S.S. officer was teasing him.

"Are you sure you know what you're about to do, Kobold?"

Wegener had pulled the trigger. Three times.

The shots almost made him fall off his chair.

Three more shots.

A form in the darkness beyond the shop window.

The form knocked again.

28

He had pictured him differently.

The hitmen he had met all looked contemptuous. They were predators who bore the marks of their murders. They knew it and were proud of it.

The Trusted Man was handsome. As handsome as a Hollywood actor. Warren Beatty in *Bonnie and Clyde*, Herr Wegener thought, that was who he looked like. The Trusted Man's eyes reminded him of the crucifix in the little church where his mother would take him to pray. Pure eyes with a hint of suffering, an underlying pain.

No, not suffering. Compassion. There was compassion in the Trusted Man's eyes.

They settled in the back room without a word. The Trusted Man was elegantly dressed. Jacket and tie under a knee-length woollen coat. A hat and a leather bag like the ones that doctors carry. He removed his gloves, reached his hands out towards the stove and rubbed them together.

Herr Wegener cleared his throat. "I called you because—"

The Trusted Man gestured to him to wait. He took off his coat, folded it carefully and put it on one of the tables in the back room. Then he undid the buckle of the doctor's bag, opened it wide, pulled out a spoon wrapped in a crisp white napkin and handed it to Herr Wegener.

Very carefully, he also took from the doctor's bag a tureen, the lid secured with adhesive tape. He removed the tape by slicing it with his fingernails and placed the tureen on Herr Wegener's lap.

It was still hot.

The Trusted Man removed the lid and put it on top of the stove. Then he sat down. "You've been waiting all day," he said, smiling. "Please, eat."

Wegener looked first at him, then at the contents of the tureen.

Soup. It had an inviting smell.

"What about you?" Wegener said, taken aback. "Won't you keep me company?"

"I'm the one who asks the questions. First of all, let me know what you think."

Wegener dipped the spoon in the soup.

It was delicious.

"It's good. Really good."

"Does it need more salt?"

"No, it's fine as it is."

"Are you sure? Don't be polite."

"It's excellent. No salt, thank you."

Wegener put another spoonful into his mouth.

The Trusted Man sat back in his chair and crossed his legs. "Before anything else," he said, "I need to clarify a few details. Do you mind?"

He paused, waiting for a sign. Wegener shook his head.

"The number you called doesn't exist. The people I work for don't exist. I don't exist, either. Even you don't exist. Would you like some water? Do you have a glass?"

"Through there."

The Trusted Man got up, filled a glass in the bathroom sink and came back.

"You want to negotiate a contract with me. We'll discuss my fee once the job is done. The payment will come from you, not my employers. I assume you can imagine the reason for that. There'll be no expenses or advance required. The job could last hours or years, but that wouldn't alter the price."

"What if you don't succeed?" Wegener said, wiping his lips with the napkin. He had almost emptied the tureen.

"That's never happened."

Wegener nodded.

"Naturally," the Trusted Man went on, "discretion is a given. On my part as well as yours. In order to achieve my goal, I'll need to ask you a few questions, some of an intimate nature, but just as you've never seen my face, I've never seen yours."

"Right now, I'm talking to myself."

The Trusted Man smiled graciously. "They told me you had a great sense of humour. That's a trait I like. Especially in these circumstances. It shows mettle and nerve. Good, very good."

"What else did they tell you about me?"

"That you need to make a decision," the Trusted Man said, suddenly looking serious.

"I already—"

The Trusted Man silenced him with a sigh. "Let me make things even clearer. Have you ever shot anyone?"

"Of course I have."

"Then you'll know that once the trigger has been pulled, the bullet has started on its trajectory and is irreversible. Do you know what that word means? I am that trajectory. The decision you need to make is irreversible. I want you to fully understand the gravity of what you're about to do. Forgive my bluntness, but have you ever killed anyone?"

"Yes."

"How many people?"

"One or two."

"Tell me about the first one."

Wegener stared at him.

The Trusted Man smiled. "Must I remind you that I promised discretion?"

"I killed an S.S. *Standartenführer*."

The Trusted Man studied him with those Christ-on-the-cross eyes of his. The smile vanished. He shook his head, seemingly sad. "We're not there yet. No. We're not there yet. You're not paying attention to what I'm saying."

He took the tureen from Wegener's lap and put it on top of the stove. He did the same with the spoon and the napkin. He moved his chair closer, leaned forward, his elbows on his knees, and reached his hands out to Wegener, palms upwards.

"Please."

Wegener obeyed. They sat there, faces half a metre apart, eyes locked, hands joined.

"Tell me the truth."

"That is the truth," Wegener said. "I killed him in '45, in the woods in Val d'Ultimo. I made him kneel and shot him in the back of the head. An execution."

The Trusted Man squeezed Wegener's hands in a fraternal gesture. "What I'm trying to make you understand, Herr Wegener, is that here and now we're forming a bond. A bond that's stronger than a marriage or a friendship. Do you understand? You and I are talking about killing a person. That creates a bond. The kind of bond that goes beyond the concept of Good and Evil. And do you know what's beyond Good and Evil? Truth, plain and simple. Are you with me?"

"Yes," Wegener whispered. He felt a lump in his throat. The workshop had vanished. The world had vanished. There were only the Trusted Man's words, the touch of their interlaced fingers, almost as if they were praying, and their low voices.

"Then I would like you to think about this. It's important. When was the first time you killed someone?"

Their eyes still locked. Breathing in unison.

Wegener swallowed. "The thirteenth of February, 1944."

"Who was it?"

Wegener felt a pang in his heart and a salty taste in his mouth. "A man . . ."

The seconds passed. Slowly. The salt invaded his mouth.

"A man who, instead of shooting me, gave me chocolate."

At this point, unable to stop himself, Wegener burst into tears. Bitter tears. The Trusted Man put his arms around him and held him tight. Like a friend, a brother, a saint forgiving a sinner.

"He was a good man, a . . ."

"It's alright," the Trusted Man said, cajoling him. "It's alright. It's in the past. It's alright. I'm here with you. And we've gone past it. We've gone beyond."

"He could have . . ." Wegener sobbed. "He should have . . ."

"It doesn't matter. Can you feel the force of the truth? Can you feel it now?"

"He . . . I killed him. I killed a good man, a . . ."

The Trusted Man shifted. Once more, he took him by the hands and looked at him with infinite gentleness. "Now," he whispered, "now you're ready to tell me the name. The name at the end of the trajectory. If you still want to. Do you want to?"

Wegener thought about Marlene. Marlene in a waitress's uniform, the first time he had seen her. Marlene in a wedding dress, bathed in light.

He thought about Marlene stroking his face. He thought about Marlene arching her back as he thrust into her, her lips moist and half open, filled with desire, so beautiful.

Marlene nibbling at her thumb as she turned the pages of the book of Grimm's fairy tales.

He thought about her and almost said that he had changed his mind. He almost admitted he could not go through with it, could not pull the trigger. That it wasn't fair that he should be asked to give up the one creature he had ever been able to love. That there had to be another way, a way to turn back time and make amends. But just as his lips were about to utter the word "no," he thought about Marlene opening the safe.

Marlene smiling, whispering a name that wasn't his.

Marlene betraying him.

The Consortium.

His bare feet.

His father's Iron Cross.

And he made up his mind.

"I want to."

29

Voter Luis was a highly respected man.

Like his father and his father's father, *Voter* Luis knew the Scriptures and the wisdom of the ancients. That was why people listened to him.

They preferred his words to the priest's. *Voter* Luis knew about the torments of life at high altitudes and the cruel tongue of the *Wehen*, whereas the priest clung to a Gospel these tough, weary men could not understand.

The Gospel spoke of dates and deserts, camels and fishermen. How could it provide answers when their questions were all about ice and forests?

Voter Luis seldom went down to the village. He liked the solitude of the mountains. That was where his will and his duty lay, he would say. Then he would add, with a smile, "Leave? Why would I do that? The reward for escape is always the desert. It's written in the Bible. Moses teaches us as much." *Voter* Luis was a wise man.

Simon Keller, his first child, was born on 11 January 1911. A significant date, *Voter* Luis had noted, as specific as a verse in Genesis.

Young Simon adored his father. *Voter* Luis was tall as an ash tree and just as strong. He often laughed, and he knew the names of all the plants and animals.

Whenever *Voter* Luis would take him down to the village with him, to buy tobacco, coffee and whatever else he was unable to produce himself, young Simon would burst with pride, seeing how people recognised and greeted his father. *Voter* Luis was always happy to stop and talk to them. He would impart advice, suggesting remedies for sick calves and newborn babies with runny noses. Other *Bau'rn* would often walk for hours to come and knock on the *maso* door and ask for his help. *Voter* Luis never refused anyone.

Ein guter Mensch. A good person.

Before these expeditions, his mother would make Simon put on a nice dark suit with a waistcoat, a shirt collar as white as snow and a velvet bow which, even though it tickled his chin, made him feel like a real adult, a worthy son to *Voter* Luis.

Mutti would say goodbye with a kiss and a pat on the cheek and remind him of his obligations. To bow his head to men and remove his hat when meeting a lady. Not to speak unless spoken to. To cross himself at the wayside shrines. To carry *Voter* Luis' Bible in the knapsack she herself had sewn for him. It was heavy, but it was also his most important task.

With the Bible weighing him down on his left side, Simon would become a giant.

Voter Luis owned hundreds of Bibles. All copied by hand. Some by him, others inherited from past generations of *Voter*. It was a Keller tradition.

The Keller Bibles were kept in the cellar of the *Stube*. Young Simon was not allowed down there. He longed to see this collection of wisdom, but Mutti said the cellar steps were too steep for a child and there were too many insects that could sting him and cause painful infections. *Voter* Luis regularly assured him that the day would come when he, too, would be able to go down to the cellar and admire the collection of Keller Bibles ("to drink from the wisdom of past *Voter* and take care of it" were his exact words), but first he had to grow as strong as his father.

Until he did, he would not be allowed into the cellar. He would have to wait. Everything in its own time.

Thus it was written.

Copying the Bible by hand helped wisdom grow in the heart. Like sowing a seed and waiting patiently for it to yield fruit.

Taking care of the Word did not only mean copying it – that would be nothing but a dry exercise in calligraphy – but also meditating and noting down the germs of thoughts that the verses triggered in your mind, in order to pass them on to future generations.

Every *Voter* had added reflections, altered verses, rewritten entire passages based on his own thoughts and experiences. So the Keller Bibles were full of sayings, meditations and marginal notes that made them thicker and heavier. Each of them, like those that *Voter* Luis would study in the evening after dinner, sitting there absorbed, pipe held tightly between his teeth, was divided into several volumes.

Simon could not wait to receive his first Bible from the hands of *Voter* Luis. He could already picture himself sitting at the table in the *Stube*, with the ink and the inkwell, elbow to elbow with his father, just as he had seen his grandfather, Opa Josef, do (although these were faded memories because *Voter* Luis' *Voter* had died young).

Opa Josef had also been a wise man. And a highly respected one. A man of faith, naturally.

The day finally came soon after the announcement that the war was over and that the mountain men were no longer subjects of the Emperor in Vienna, but of the King in Turin. Simon was eight years old, it was late March and the days were growing longer and lighter. It was the day his sister Elisabeth was born.

When Mutti had gone into labour, *Voter* Luis took him aside and gave him his first Bible (its blank pages rustling with promise like spring flowers) and told him that the time had come for him to prove he was a worthy son of the Kellers.

Simon heard his mother moaning and groaning for a whole night and a day. *Voter* Luis' herbs and all his efforts could do little to soothe the pain. It was not an easy birth. Once the screams and the weeping ceased, his father presented him with the new arrival.

She was a sweet, pink little thing with light skin and thick dark hair like her mother. She looked tiny in *Voter* Luis' hands.

Simon had never seen anything more beautiful. And he had never seen *Voter* Luis look so worried.

"She's like a princess," Simon said, eyes open wide.

Voter Luis burst out laughing, that same laugh that would make women in the village (even those who wore a wedding ring) turn to look at him with a gleam in their eyes. "You're right," he said. "She's as beautiful as a princess. We'll call her Elisabeth. Elisabeth Keller."

Then he showed him two little bells, each attached to a ribbon, and tied one around Simon's wrist and the other around the baby's ankle.

"She's your sister and you must always take care of her," he said. "Will you do that?"

Simon felt his chest swell with pride. He raised his bell and made it jingle.

The baby waved her arms and legs. Her little bell rang. And this made him feel as tall and strong as an ash tree.

He stroked her forehead and began to sing.

30

"Little Lissy, sweet Lissy," Keller whispered, taking out the key. "Little Lissy, sweet Lissy . . ." He opened the little door and put the silver bowl down.

And there was Lissy, huge, entirely black except for the crest of bristles and the stripes under her eyes, lying on her side in the straw, in her favourite corner. By the light of the oil lamp, her eyes shone like blades.

"Sweet Lissy, little Lissy, good Lissy . . ."

Lissy got up and came towards him. The bell jingled.

Keller giggled. "Are you hungry, sweet Lissy?"

Lissy took another step forward. She stopped a metre from him, shaking her corkscrew tail. He showed her the contents of the bowl. She bowed her head, her nostrils quivering and oozing mucus, a thread of saliva dripping from her snout as black as night, her fangs shining in the light of the oil lamp. She stood motionless.

"Eat, Lissy, little Lissy . . ."

But instead of diving into the bowl with her snout, she carried on trembling, resisting the smell of food. Keller looked at her, struggling to understand.

"What's the matter, sweet Lissy?"

Lissy was hungry. That much was obvious. Keller saw the signs of her voraciousness not just in the saliva dripping to the floor, but also in the trembling of her legs and ears. Still, Lissy kept staring at him. She was hungry, the slop was there, ready for her, and yet she wouldn't budge a centimetre. She was just looking at him. Simon had never seen a pig resist the impulse to eat for so long. Especially Lissy. Because Lissy was hungry. Lissy was always hungry.

And yet she was not eating.

Why not?

Keller tapped the silver bowl. Once again, Lissy waved her tail, annoyed by the noise, but did not lower her snout or stop staring at him. Keller stepped back, closed the little door, took out the bell from his waistcoat and rang it.

Once. Twice. Three times.

Only then did Lissy put her snout into the bowl.

Keller smiled. He switched out the light, left the pigsty and stood gazing at the mountain peaks to the east. What a miracle dawn was! Waiting for the sun's first rays to come to rest on his face, he closed his eyes, lost in meditation.

He allowed the minutes to flow and the light and warmth to relax his muscles and dispel his worries. He thought about the young woman in the carcass of the Mercedes, and about Lissy. Lissy was the seventh-born. An important number. The Lord had created the world and all its creatures in six days. On the seventh, He had rested. Then, when the world was still young, He had flooded it with waters, and so the ancients had come all the way up here. They had been brave enough to build a *maso* at such altitude. They had shown so much wisdom in doing so. Over the centuries, the *maso* had never betrayed the Kellers. Because the Kellers . . .

Keller opened his eyes wide. Cursing himself, he went back into the *Stube*.

31

It had stopped snowing. The sky was clear. Seeing it that morning, Marlene felt relieved. The world was still there. It had not vanished. Along with the relief, though, came the worry, the anxiety, the fear. Because, yes, the world was still there.

But so were the sapphires and the kobolds. Yes, the kobolds. She now understood why, faced with the open safe, she'd thought about kobolds. *Kobold*, like . . .

Wegener.

Wegener and his unquenchable thirst for power, from which she had fled.

She had wasted these days, avoiding the most urgent question of them all: What to do?

Simon Keller had promised to take her to the village. He had said there was a bus stop. Did she have enough money to buy her ticket home? Yes, of course. Please don't worry. It'll be alright.

A bus, of course.

But where to?

Unable to find an answer to this question, Marlene had started tidying up the *Stube*. The mess bothered her. She also felt guilty for having laughed (even for a second) at the *Bau'r*'s solitude. In a way, she owed him this much.

She swept the floor and dusted with a frenzy that would have scared her if she'd been able to see herself from the outside. It was the same nervous energy Mamma had had when she was no longer Mamma.

Fortunately, she was not even aware of it.

When she had finished her work, she filled the espresso pot with coffee and, when she heard Simon Keller's heavy footsteps on the steps, put it on the ring. Keller came in and hung his heavy greatcoat on the hook, next to the rifle.

She could tell at a glance that something was wrong. Keller looked upset. Marlene did not ask him why. She waited for the coffee to gurgle, then poured it into the chipped cups.

Keller sipped his coffee with an absent expression, then thanked her politely, as he always did, but his words lacked warmth. His anxious eyes kept darting from one side of the *Stube* to the other, unable to settle.

Marlene could not keep quiet any longer. "Is everything alright, Simon Keller?" she asked.

"Yes, everything's fine," he replied. Then he thought about it and shook his head. "Actually, no. There's a job to be done before we leave. It can't be put off. There's too much snow on the roof, and it needs to be shovelled off. The *maso* can withstand a lot, but it needs to be taken care of, otherwise . . . And it's going to take time. An hour or two. Too long." Keller massaged his chin. "I could show you how to get to the village by yourself, but it's a long way and it's dangerous. Six hours on foot. Maybe even seven, with all this snow."

Marlene tried to reassure him. "Then we'll leave tomorrow."

Keller shook his head firmly. "Absolutely not. No. You have a home to get back to. There are people concerned about you. It would be unfair to keep them worrying any longer just to—"

"It would be unfair for you to postpone your duties in order to help me. One more day won't make a difference."

Unless Wegener had discovered something. Unless his men were already on their way up to the *maso* to kill them both. Marlene was under no illusions. Herr Wegener's henchmen would not take pity on Simon Keller. They would kill him and set the *maso* on fire. She knew Herr Wegener and had seen what he was capable of when he was angry.

For the first time, Marlene realised that she was endangering the man who had saved her life.

"The *maso* has protected your family for centuries," she said, forcing a smile, "and for centuries—"

"—the Kellers have taken care of the *maso*," Keller said flatly, finishing her sentence.

"So there's nothing more to say. Just give me a minute to take off this apron and put my jacket on."

Keller looked at her, not understanding.

"I'm going to give you a hand," she said.

"No, it's a dangerous job," he said, getting to his feet.

Without waiting for her, he put on his greatcoat and went out. He propped the ladder against the outer wall of the *maso*, fixing it firmly in the icy snow and testing its steadiness, then climbed up to the roof, as agile as a stone marten.

Fifteen metres from the ground.

He had barely had time to look around, his shovel over his shoulder, and decide where to begin when a voice directly behind him made him jump.

It was Marlene, up on the roof with him. She was wearing her padded jacket and a woollen hat Keller had found in a cupboard and brandishing a sorghum broom. "My father used this. Not a shovel."

"You're stubborn."

Marlene did not reply. Her attention was drawn by the beauty of the surrounding mountains. Until now, her field of vision had been limited by the walls of the *maso* and the blinding whiteness of the blizzard. Now that the horizon was clear again, she reached out with her hand as if able to seize hold of the peaks, and breathed in air as pure as balm.

"It's wonderful."

Keller followed the direction of her gaze. "You've never asked me where we are," he said. It wasn't a question, but an observation.

Marlene shrugged. "Somewhere safe."

Keller smiled, dispelling some of the darkness he had brought back from the pigsty. "Beautiful words."

"Not as beautiful as this place."

"Wasn't your parents' *maso* like this?"

"It was further down, in Venosta, on the side that gets less sun. From my bedroom window, I could see tree trunks. As a child, that's all I would draw, trees and hens. My job was to feed the hens. Not too much, or the corn would run out and we'd have to kill them. We were very poor."

Keller stuck the shovel in the snow, took out his pipe, filled it and lit it. "Once," he said, "I saw an asp dancing in the moonlight and even thought I could hear it sing. Another time, I was following a white crow and found the carcass of an ibex with three horns and three eyes. But I've never seen a rich *Bau'r*."

Marlene laughed. "You're a wise man, Simon Keller."

He puffed out a cloud of smoke and smiled slyly. "If I were as wise as *Voter* Luis, I would have tied you to a chair and forced you to stay in the *Stube*."

"Didn't *Voter* Luis ever tell you women are stubborn?"

Simon laughed, too. "*Voter* Luis took that as read. Women are stubborn and inquisitive, and you're no exception. You don't ask, but I'll answer you."

One by one, he pointed out all the mountains they could see from the roof of the *maso*, starting with the nearest ones and ending with the furthest summits. He knew the name of each one and uttered it with affection if it was connected to a memory, but also with reverence in the case of peaks that instilled fear.

Most of these names meant nothing to Marlene. She had never heard of them, although some (Rabenkopf, Valvelspitze, Weisskugel and Saldurspitze) reminded her of the map on the passenger seat of the car.

And she suddenly realised where she had made her mistake. She had driven into a minor valley that led nowhere except to the huge Alpine barrier of glaciers and permanent snowfields that separated Italy from Austria. It was a mistake that might have proved fatal if it hadn't been for this man with his hard face and melancholy expression, who called his pigs "kids" because they were all he had for company. The man who had made her liver dumplings and built her her own toilet.

The man whose life she was putting at risk just by being here.

While Keller was still busy listing the names of the mountain peaks, indicating them with the stem of his meerschaum pipe, Marlene went close to him and gave him a light kiss on the cheek.

"Thank you, Simon Keller. Truly, thank you."

Keller stared at her, then turned his face away. His eyes were watery and he did not want her to see.

"I've never asked you anything, city girl," he said after a long pause. "Asking questions means expecting answers, and *Voter* Luis used to say that answers can be as painful as a viper bite. So my question isn't one you need to answer, alright? It's just something I have to say."

"Ask anything you like. I'm in your debt."

"Are you in trouble, city girl?"

Marlene lowered her eyes. "I . . ."

He turned towards her, and that was when it happened.

Perhaps it was the sun. Perhaps their joint weight. Perhaps chance. Or fate.

The snow creaked and slid down by one centimetre. A compact sheet of snow at least one metre long.

Keller dropped his shovel and flailed with his arms. The sheet shifted another five centimetres.

Marlene let out a scream. She stepped back instinctively and almost lost her balance.

The sheet fell.

Marlene saw Keller roll his eyes in surprise and fear. She heard the sound of ice shattering, losing all friction.

A solid, terrible sound.

Keller reached out to her, uttering something that could have been a curse or a request for help, and Marlene desperately tried to grab hold of his hand.

She couldn't.

One.

Two.

He fell.

32

Three days after giving birth, Mutti had developed a high fever. Four days later, she was as pale as the sheets she lay on. She did not even have the strength to feed Elisabeth. *Voter* Luis had to give the baby boiled cow's milk.

On the fifth day, since the fever hadn't receded and Mutti had become delirious ("The pigs are talking to me, Luis, they want the baby, make them stop, please, please . . ."), *Voter* Luis decided to go down to the village and fetch a doctor.

But this was no ordinary fever. It was septicaemia.

Voter Luis' herbs were as useless as his prayers and his final, desperate rush to the village in a thunderstorm that had turned the paths into rivers of mud. By the time he returned with the doctor, there was nothing for the medic to do but write the poor woman's death certificate. Another death in childbirth at a time and in a region where, sad but true, such deaths were far from unusual.

If there had been a road suitable for vehicles instead of a path, if the *maso* had not been so high up . . . then *maybe*. When he told Simon that his mother had died, *Voter* Luis held him tight. Then, together, they stacked up bundles of wood outside the *maso*. *Voter* Luis sprinkled them with herbs, sulphur and broken stones, then later, that night, he set them alight.

They produced flames Simon had never seen before: blue flames. Like the sky Mutti had flown to, *Voter* Luis explained, going down on his knees and looking him in the eyes. For centuries, he said, the Kellers had used fire to say goodbye to the souls of their dead. They had done this also when Opa Josef had died, except that Simon could not remember because he was a child lying asleep in his bed.

This blue fire, *Voter* Luis told him, pointing at the stars, was a farewell that could be seen all the way from Heaven.

The notion of Mutti looking down at him from above made Simon cry. Gently, *Voter* Luis told him that these were his last tears as a child. He was now a man (had he not already begun to copy his first Bible?), and men had to be modest about showing their feelings. Only Elisabeth was allowed to cry, he added. She was little and could do it without anybody judging her.

Then he asked Simon to pray with him.

After that, there were still good days. Every so often you could hear *Voter* Luis' laughter echo from one side of the valley to the other. Yet the fact that Simon remembered these outbursts of joy meant that something had changed in *Voter* Luis. And not just towards his son. In time, his attitude towards his daughter changed, too.

When Elisabeth began to speak her first words and toddle about the *Stube*, *Voter* Luis got into the habit of shutting himself in what young Simon called "the forbidden room," the *maso*'s cellar, with the wine, the oil and the Bibles of past *Bau'rn*, and spending hours on end there, alone.

So it was that the task of raising Elisabeth fell to Simon.

She was a beautiful child, lively, alert, who called him "Sim'l" and was always smiling. Simon did not mind playing with her. On the contrary – he enjoyed telling her stories, making her rag dolls and carving animals. He learned to make *Vulpendingen* from the carcasses of animals that *Voter* Luis hunted and was never happier than when little Lissy would clap her hands at a new creation. Elisabeth looked at Simon in the same way that he, with his velvet bow tickling his chin, had watched *Voter* Luis talking to people in the village, dispensing advice and receiving praise.

Time passed.

Voter Luis grew increasingly withdrawn, Elisabeth increasingly cheerful, along with her growing resemblance to Mutti (the same raven hair, the same dimples), and Simon Keller increasingly tall and awkward, like any other teenager.

When Simon turned thirteen and Elisabeth was five and had already learned to chase away spiteful spirits by weaving garlands for burning in the *Stube*, *Voter* Luis had the accident that changed everything.

It was harvest time, but, hard as he tried, Simon knew he was not much help to his father. Not with such a heavy sickle and on such sloping fields as the ones below the *maso*, wedged between the rocky peak of the mountain and the forest that led down to the valley. The bulk of this arduous labour rested on *Voter* Luis' shoulders.

It might have been exhaustion, or melancholy, or an angry wasp, but the blade of the sickle slipped and *Voter* Luis fell, screaming. Simon rushed to him and saw that his father's leg had been severed clean off from the shin down, the stump gushing with blood just like when the pigs were slaughtered in November.

Somehow, using his belt, *Voter* Luis managed to stop the bleeding. He told his son to run down the hill for help. Fortunately, Simon did not need to go as far as the village. On his way, he ran into the doctor coming back from another *maso* on the other side of the valley. *Voter* Luis did not die. If he had died, things would have turned out differently for Sim'l and Lissy.

Like the grain of wheat that falls to the ground, *Voter* Luis did not die.

33

The sheet of ice quivered and began to slide down. Marlene felt as if she were being sucked into the void, unable to do anything but wave her arms and scream. Her mouth open, an icy breath in her lungs, unable to cry out, she watched the edge of the roof draw closer. She considered throwing herself to the side and hoping for the best.

But she didn't.

Barely twenty centimetres from the edge, for no apparent reason, just as it had started moving, the sheet of ice stopped dead. Marlene swayed, opened her arms and held her breath. She forced herself not to close her eyes.

The ice held.

She took two hesitant steps. Panting, she paused once she had reached the ladder.

"Simon Keller?" she called out.

No answer.

Marlene turned, her back to the void, and climbed down the ladder, looking straight ahead, until she felt solid ground under her boots. Her knees gave way, and she fell in a sitting position on the snow. Only then did she venture to look.

Keller was motionless a few metres from her, his leg twisted in an unnatural, painful way, his head to one side. All around him, blood spread, staining the snow and steaming in contact with the frosty air.

His hat had rolled far away. A mound of snow had stopped it in its tracks. Otherwise, it would have ended up heaven knows where. All Marlene could think of was that hat. It was important to keep your head warm, or you could easily get flu or pneumonia. Or maybe . . .

Or maybe, a steely voice Marlene barely recognised as her own said, *you've completely lost your mind. What are you doing sitting there like that? Get up, move!*

But she didn't. She was shaking too much.

She called out Simon Keller's name. The body lying on the ground did not reply. Nor did it move. The blood kept steaming.

He's dead, Marlene thought.

He's dead.

She got up and moved unsteadily towards him, calling his name again. No reply.

Marlene bent over him.

He was breathing. He was moving his lips, muttering incomprehensible words. He was alive.

Marlene was about to grab hold of him, but she stopped as soon as her fingers came into contact with the texture of the greatcoat, which lay spread around him like the wings of a bat.

Maybe he had hit his head. Or maybe his neck was broken. If she lifted him the wrong way, she might be sentencing him to a life of paralysis. She might even kill him. She was no doctor.

There was nothing for it. She had to go down to the village. Get help, come back and . . .

And find him dead, that steely voice replied. *You can't leave him out here. He'll die of cold. Have you gone completely mad? Take him inside, into the warmth. Then you can decide what to do.*

Marlene took him by the armpits. Keller let out a heart-stopping moan.

Marlene did not let go. Whispering words of apology, she dragged him as far as the steps. The entrance to the *Stube* up there seemed as distant as the moon. And just as unreachable.

"God . . ."

This man carried you over his shoulder for hours. He saved your life. He gave you his food, his home, his protection. You made him a target. Now stop crying all over yourself.

Marlene propped Keller up against the outside wall of the *maso*. She took a deep breath and tore off her woollen hat. She wiped her sweat, unaware that she had smeared her face with Keller's blood, crouched down and put an arm around his chest. She did the same with his arm, which she put around her shoulders.

Then she *pulled*.

She felt something tense up in her back muscles, but she refused to feel the pain, refused to give in. She pulled with all her strength.

Keller weighed a ton. She would not be able to do this alone.

"You have to help me, Simon Keller," she begged. "Come on."

He reached out with his free hand and grabbed the rail.

"Good, well done."

One step. Two.

The door.

The warmth of the *Stube*.

Out of breath, Marlene laid Keller on the floor and looked around. Carrying him upstairs and putting him to bed was out of the question, as was leaving him on the floor. If the mountain won't come to Muhammad . . .

She went upstairs to Keller's bedroom and pulled off the blankets. She did the same with hers. She came back down the steps two at a time, made a makeshift bed in front of the fireplace and, with what was left of her strength, moved Keller onto it.

What now?

Clean his wounds and bandage them.

She added wood to the fire and put water on to boil. She undid the collar of Keller's greatcoat to let him breathe more easily and checked the wound. There was a nasty gash from his temple to his jaw. The edges of the skin were clean, as if cut with a scalpel. The injury seemed to be swelling as she watched.

She tore a sheet into strips, immersed them in boiling water, counted to two hundred and pulled them out with a fork. Then she counted to two hundred again before touching them with her fingertips. They were hot but not boiling.

She began carefully cleaning Keller's face. He had told her that he had cleaned the injury on her forehead with soap and it had not got infected. So using soap was fine. Better than nothing, anyway. She found his soap, dipped it in the water and cleaned the gash. Keller winced at every touch.

He opened his clouded eyes.

"Can you hear me?" Marlene said.

He nodded. "What happened?"

"You fell off the roof."

He tried to get up, but Marlene held him down.

"Keep still. Your leg—"

"I want to see."

Marlene helped him sit up. Then she pulled the blankets off.

Keller shook his head. His eyes were once again alert. "I need scissors. They're in the sideboard. Second drawer."

"Why do you need scissors?"

"You have to cut my trousers. I need to see my knee. Something's not right."

Marlene obeyed, skilfully cutting Simon's trouser leg (although Gabriel would have turned his nose up at such a rudimentary, unartistic job) and exposing his leg to the light. It was strong and covered with protruding veins. His knee was a disaster. Swollen, purple and bent thirty degrees more than usual.

Simon pushed himself forward as far as he could. "Can you hold me? I want to touch it."

128

Marlene supported his back as he checked the bruised swelling, biting his lip and grimacing at every touch.

"It's not broken. But the leg . . . It needs to be pulled and reset. You'll have to do it."

Marlene turned pale. "We need a doctor. I can't do it, I really can't. I'd only mess it up . . . You stay here in the warmth. Tell me which way to go and I'll—"

"Do you want to help me?" Keller said, looking her straight in the eyes.

"I'll run as fast as I can and—"

"You'll get lost in the woods. Or fall into a crevasse, or end up under an avalanche. You wouldn't reach the village before sunset, and you'd find yourself walking during the night, when it gets so cold that . . . No. Do you want to help me, Marlene?"

It was the first time he had called her by her name.

"Tell me what to do."

He explained, and she felt her head spin.

"It'll hurt."

He smiled. "Better me than you."

Marlene put one hand on his thigh and one on his shin.

"Come closer, you'll need to yank it. Hard. Twist it and put it back in its socket."

Marlene moved her hands closer to his knee. It was hot and throbbing. "Pull, twist and—"

"Pull, twist and put it back in its socket. You can do it."

"I—"

"Pull!" Keller said, panting.

Marlene closed her eyes, counted to three, then let go. "I can't do it. The pain—"

"We'll deal with the pain later."

Marlene's face lit up. "I can prepare the infusion. Tell me where

I can find the poppy. It'll be easier without the pain. We can—"

"And what if I fall asleep? Would you know what to do? What we have to do now is straighten the knee and then immobilise it, make a frame to keep it still. Would you be able to do that without my instructions?"

Marlene shook her head, her eyes filled with tears. "Don't ask me to do it, I beg you. I don't want to hurt you."

Keller stroked her face. Marlene felt his fingertips linger on her beauty spot.

"Are you a mountain or a city girl?"

Marlene did it.

Keller cried out.

"The poppy!" Marlene cried, seeing how red in the face he was, his veins protruding and a grimace of pain distorting his features. "Please, the poppy . . ."

Keller persuaded her to carry on. The operation was not over yet. Marlene managed to make a splint for the knee, using thick string, wire and little else – and somehow she did not scream.

Keller did, though, despite all his efforts to restrain himself. Finally, he pointed to the shelf. "Half a tablespoon."

"In boiling water?"

His face dripping with sweat, Keller replied with a smile. "It acts faster if you chew it."

34

Half a tablespoon a day.

That was the dose *Voter* Luis took to stop the pain. His stump felt the seasons, the damp, impending rain. It itched like hell.

But it wasn't for his stump that *Voter* Luis used poppy.

The pain that made him beg his son to hurry up with that *verfluachtn Monbluam* came from the part of the leg that was gone, which would send out shooting pains that turned his prayers to screams. Sometimes, they were so strong that Simon had to prepare an infusion with three times the usual dose.

Within a few weeks, *Voter* Luis started telling him to bring just the seeds. He would chew them and calm down. Tears in his eyes, he would thank him and fall asleep. Or sometimes, after the poppy, *Voter* Luis would recite passages from the Bible. Staring into space, his mind clouded over, lips moving frantically, his voice mechanical, flat, with no variations in volume.

Voter Luis started drinking. When drunk, he would curse and beat his son, though he was never quick enough or strong enough to shut that damned little girl's mouth.

One day, he tore the little bells off both of them and threw them away. The sound was driving him mad, he cried.

Sim'l found them and hid them. They became his most precious treasure, and he would shake them whenever he felt scared, whenever *Voter* Luis was drunk. The supply of wine and grappa had diminished. Whenever he drank, *Voter* Luis would turn into an unrecognisable monster.

Sim'l feared his father's rages as much as he feared snakes hiding in the long grass.

Voter Luis loaded the bulk of his work onto his son's slight shoulders, which meant that the food supplies were diminishing, too. In order to prosper, the *maso* needed a *Voter*, not a beardless boy. Despite all Sim'l's efforts, the Kellers began to experience hunger.

The days went by, all identical.

The pain. The screams. The blows.

The opium.

And the misfortunes did not end there. It was as if, with the death of Simon and Elisabeth's mother, a curse had befallen the Keller family *maso*.

The hens were decimated by buzzards. One after the other, the cows died from a mysterious illness. The barn was struck by lightning and burned to the ground. The *maso* only narrowly escaped the fire. *Voter* Luis did not bother to rebuild the barn.

There was no point, he said. We won't keep cows anymore, only pigs. Because the pig, *Voter* Luis said with a snigger, is the most sacred of animals. The pig was the clay out of which He created man.

Don't you believe me, son? he screamed, laughing.

"Look at the pig and admire His masterwork. At the dawn of time, He took the pig, blessed it and changed it. He replaced its legs with fir and yew branches. The yew is solid enough for walking, because He knew men would be travellers, and the fir tree is slender enough to provide agility but not strong enough to spare man having to build tools for his work. Too strong a man would have been arrogant, whereas work makes him humble. Man had also to speak and pray, so He squashed the pig's snout so that man's mouth could invent the alphabet and use it to sing His praises. Then, using pebbles from the streams to remind His new creation that life had emerged from water, he changed the shape of its ears. Finally, he tore the wings off an eagle and inserted them into the pig's head, to enable man to think. But for all His infinite wisdom, He forgot to remove from man the pig's hunger. That is why the eagle's wings are of no use to man. His thoughts cannot fly because hunger is a boulder that keeps him pinned to the ground. Man is His *Vulpendingen*. His damned joke."

Less than a month after uttering this terrible sermon, *Voter* Luis killed Elisabeth.

35

Elisabeth, small and sweet, still breathing as she died in Simon's arms, whispering confused words he would never forget. With fear in her eyes, unable to understand what was happening, unable to make sense of the pain. Searching for an answer that Sim'l was unable to give her.

And Sim'l could do nothing but cradle her, looking at her increasingly pale, frightful face, with that small bloodstain beside her mouth, the mouth itself forming the shape of a reproach. Why didn't you save me, Sim'l? Why don't you take this pain away? You're as tall and strong as an ash, so why can't you do anything but cradle me and whisper, cradle me and whisper? Why?

Why, Sim'l?

"It's alright, Lissy. It's alright, little Lissy. Sweet Lissy. It's alright."

Not knowing when the sun would rise.

Not knowing the reason for that blood.

Only knowing how to lie.

36

"It's alright," Keller whispered, "it's alright."

Marlene wondered how this man, who in spite of the poppy was suffering the pains of hell, could still find the strength to reassure her with kind words and a childlike smile: such a contrast with a face so hard and gaunt it made her think she was hallucinating.

"It's alright, it's alright."

"Yes, it'll be alright. Go to sleep now, please, go to sleep . . ."

Simon reached out a hand and touched her beauty spot. The way her mother used to stroke her after closing the book of Grimm fairy tales and wishing her goodnight.

Marlene took his hand in hers and said, "Forgive me, Simon Keller. Forgive me."

He did not hear her. He had fallen asleep at last.

Who was she apologising to? To him or to herself? She did not ask herself the question.

All of a sudden, the accumulated tension of all these days spent trapped by the blizzard, the anxieties of the past few weeks – planning to steal the sapphires, worrying about Klaus, about Herr Wegener, about Gabriel and all those who would suffer (or had already suffered) because of her – exploded, and Marlene burst into tears.

Her life had been nothing but a series of lies. Lies on top of other lies. She had lied to everyone. Especially to herself, and to this man, who, despite his pain and the fact that she was a stranger (and a liar at that), had not only saved her life but even now was reassuring her. This man who had fallen asleep with a childlike smile on his frost-scorched lips. This good man.

The only good man, she realised, she had ever met.

37

An inviting smell out here on the landing. At this time of night?

Perhaps it was his neighbour, Frau Gruber. Lately, she had become a little absent-minded. Old age. Now that was a depressing thought, because they were the same age. She was a widow, he a bachelor. On Sundays, Frau Gruber would invite him over for lunch and flirt a little. Maybe she had fallen in love in him. Well, why not?

They were old, but not *that* old.

Poor Frau Gruber. In all these years, she had not yet realised that no delicious titbit or languid glance would get her anywhere. It was a matter of tribes, Gabriel kept telling himself. There were two tribes: the one that liked women and the one forced into hiding.

Even so, he never declined Frau Gruber's delicious dishes. She was an outstanding cook.

Once he shut the door behind him, Gabriel forgot all about her. He was tired, dead tired. He needed a shower and a glass of sherry, though maybe not in that order.

You're getting old, he said to himself when he noticed that he had left the light on in the kitchen.

But it was not old age. It was something worse.

An intruder.

An impeccably dressed intruder with an apron tied around his waist. A man (as handsome as a Hollywood actor, Gabriel couldn't help thinking) standing there cooking.

Using *his* kitchen, *his* stove, *his* pots and pans.

The breath caught in his chest.

There was a gun on the table. A gun with a bottle-shaped thing fixed to the barrel.

A silencer.

"Good evening, Gabriel. You may have had dinner already, but please don't be ungracious. Try this and tell me what you think."

Gabriel stood rooted to the spot, unable to take his eyes off the gun.

The stranger saw where he was looking. "Don't be afraid. We're civilised people, it won't be needed."

Gabriel started shaking. Not because of the gun, but because of that gentle, melodious voice. This man as handsome as a Hollywood actor was terrifying.

"Who are you? What are you doing in my apartment?"

His voice came out as a squeak that wouldn't have intimidated a child. It happens when you get old.

"Please sit down, and I'll explain everything."

Gabriel felt the impulse to turn and run.

The stranger read his mind. "Don't," he said, and smiled.

Gabriel sat down.

"They call me the Trusted Man," the intruder said. "I have a job to do. Nothing for you to worry about." He put a pan on the table and removed the lid. "Spaghetti, with a little mountain of butter and forty-month-old Parmesan. A simple dish. I hope you don't mind, I opened one of your bottles." He poured the wine and sat down opposite him. "Do eat, please."

Old age. It was old age, or so Gabriel thought, that made him give in. Old age made you weak, fragile. Every gesture was an effort, every thought reminded him of the frailty of this body he no longer felt was his.

The flesh is weak. And the food was indeed delicious.

"Sharing a meal brings men closer, Gabriel. This is my way of asking you to trust me."

"For what?"

"Men who are close, friends who are like brothers, don't need this" – he indicated the gun – "in order to be honest with each other. We're going to have a short and, I hope, successful conversation. An intimate conversation. I'd like to know if you intend to lie."

"I don't even know what . . ."

The Trusted Man poured himself some more wine. "It's a shame to waste good wine. And it would be a shame to cause you pain. Especially as it would be hard for me to miss from where I'm sitting. I wouldn't shoot you in the heart or the head, but in the stomach, which they say is extremely painful. Not to mention the fact that, after a meal like this one, surgeons would have a hard time putting things back together. Are you scared?"

Gabriel gave a start. "Shouldn't I be?"

"Not at all. There are many people who would say that dress-making isn't an art, but then there are also many people who think Monet was a misfit obsessed with water lilies. In other words, you're an artist, and I like art. I would never hurt you. As long as I'm not obliged to. Are you going to oblige me to hurt you, or would you prefer a civilised conversation?"

"A . . . a civilised conversation, please," Gabriel stammered.

"Does that mean you trust me?"

"Partly."

"An honest answer. Thank you. My job is to find people. I'll be honest with you: I find them in order to kill them."

Gabriel turned pale. "Are you planning to—"

"No, not you. Although I do believe our conversation will end with your having a small wound. Not a physical one, naturally. Please, Gabriel, don't faint. Would you like some water?"

Gabriel nodded, and the Trusted Man brought him a glass from the sink.

"Marlene Wegener *née* Taufer. Do you know her?"

"Is it her you want to . . . "

"I've never in my whole life borne anyone a grudge, believe me. I am a weapon, Gabriel. Just as you are a hand that obeys inspiration. I have nothing against your young friend. Even so, yes, I am going to kill her."

Gabriel leaped angrily to his feet. "I've already told that son of a bitch Wegener that I have no idea where—"

"That's not the kind of information I'm interested in. I know you haven't the faintest idea where the lady in question might be, or where's she headed. Please sit down."

"I want you out of my apartment!" Gabriel cried.

The Trusted Man looked him straight in the eyes. "Please. Sit. Down."

Gabriel obeyed. "What is it you want?"

"Information. I'm interested in getting to know Marlene, seeing her through your eyes, understanding her. You're more than just a colleague to Marlene, aren't you? Can we use the word 'mentor'?"

"I would never presume . . ."

From the doctor's bag he had kept between his feet, the Trusted Man took a pair of steel pliers and put them on the table. Then he grabbed Gabriel's hand and slammed it down on the wooden surface. With the index finger of his free hand, he counted his phalanges. "Twelve. Plus the thumb. Artists' hands are precious, don't you agree? You're misinterpreting my words. That saddens me, and I apologise. Let me make myself clear. What I'm suggesting is an exchange between equals. I intend to trade your hands or, God forbid, your very life for information. I haven't lied to you and I won't lie to you. I need the information you give me to find and kill Marlene. That'll make you an accomplice to murder. I doubt you'll call the police when I'm gone, and I wouldn't advise it, but if you were to do so, I'm certain that any charge against you would immediately be dropped. The information will have been obtained from you under threat of torture and death. Even so . . ."

The Trusted Man let go of Gabriel's hand and leaned back in his chair.

"We've shared a meal and drunk the same wine, so I can assure you that, even if you're innocent in the eyes of the law, you'll have a guilty conscience. That's the wound I was referring to. So what I'm suggesting is not an exchange between information and life, but between information and conscience."

When the Trusted Man said "conscience," Gabriel heard "soul."

38

She spent all night curled up in a chair, a woollen blanket around her shoulders, watching over Keller as he slept, trying to interpret the lines on his face, fearing that his chest might stop rising and falling.

All night, watching and thinking, listening to the wind, listening to the silence turning into the sweet music of the dawn.

The first rays of the sun. The snow dripping. The timber breathing and creaking.

Marlene continued to brood even after Simon Keller had woken with a coughing fit and a moan, and she had changed the dressing on his face.

She kept thinking as she prepared his poppy infusion, while he looked on with pained, watchful eyes, as she listened to his instructions on how, what and how much to feed the pigs, and as she made Lissy's meal. Separately, since Lissy was fussy. And always hungry.

She continued to ponder as she poured the slop into the trough, illuminated by the oil lamp, as she changed the water, as Kurt and the Doctor squabbled over a half-rotting potato peeling, and as she put on the steel glove and opened the little door in the grille, absent-mindedly, even though Keller had told her to be careful with the sow.

Very careful, Marlene.

"Of course. Lissy is fierce."

"No," he had said. "She's not fierce. Lissy is hungry. That's different. You will be careful, won't you?"

"Don't worry."

But Lissy, perhaps intimidated by her presence, hid in the

shadows the whole time. Marlene only managed to get a glimpse of her crest and white stripes.

She did not call to her. She had other things on her mind.

She thought about it for a long time and reached a decision after Keller had dozed off for a second time, as she gazed at the outline of the mountains beyond the windowpane, seeing her own reflection in their quartz silence.

Those edges, those depths of light and dark, removed all doubt.

She suddenly felt something she had not experienced for years. Peace.

Reaching a decision made her feel light with relief. She would tell the truth, no matter how unpleasant, and risk showing Simon Keller who she really was.

But not right away.

First, Keller had to get better and rebuild his strength. It would be cruel to offload this burden, too, on his weakened shoulders. She would wait for him to recover, then tell him the truth. Only then would she decide on her next move. Where to go. What to do. Marlene looked up at the sky.

No clouds.

The *maso* was beautiful. She understood why Keller was so proud of it. She herself was not a Keller, and yet she felt safe between its walls.

It was a place of peace.

39

The moon in Aries. Or Taurus in Jupiter. Or perhaps Aquarius in Alpha Centauri.

His wife Isabella was crazy about astrology. She said people's fates were written in the stars. She had become a real expert in that bullshit. Every so often she would launch into lengthy explanations about the astral reasons for various events in their lives. She was Pisces (with Scorpio rising), he was Aries (with Virgo rising), and they had met when Saturn was on the cusp with Planet Fuck-Knows.

How can you make any sense of it?

Carbone not only couldn't make any sense of it, he didn't give a damn. All the same, he would listen to her. He loved her and believed this obsession would fade away, sooner or later. Besides, it could have been worse. The wife of one of his colleagues had gone crazy for exercise, and the poor guy was forced to spend Mondays, Wednesdays and Fridays in some lousy gym in Bolzano. On top of that, Carbone thought, if he did not pay her enough attention, then Sagittarius in opposition to something or other might drive her into somebody else's arms. Maybe a well-hung Taurus.

Isabella was still, in her fifties, a beautiful woman. Which was why Carbone would just keep quiet and nod, muttering only the occasional astonished "Ah."

Carbone should have called Isabella today to ask what his horoscope said. ("Aries: the stars will grant you a pleasant opportunity to piss on the heads of your opponents. Mind your cock doesn't catch cold . . .")

Carbone sneered. He did not know if he had ever been so happy in his life. He had Herr Wegener's telephone records in front of him. They had been brought to him by a guy who was almost certainly Secret Service, whom he had met during what the papers had dubbed a "terrorism emergency." Someone he could swap favours with and know he would not cause too many ripples.

The way he saw it, cultivating that kind of friendship was part of his job description. And it didn't matter if his friend had blood on his hands. In some situations, you could not afford to be choosy.

If you want peace, according to the Latin motto Carbone had learned at school, then prepare for war. And every now and again, he thought, patting the bulky stack of papers on his desk, you actually had to go to war. Not in order to destroy an opponent (although that, too, of course) but above all, as he saw it, to scare off potential enemies. As the French liked to say, *pour encourager les autres.*

Of course, you had to win the war. And win it outright. Strike a decisive blow.

Carbone stood up, opened the minibar he'd had installed in his office, and poured himself a glass of Fernet. "To *Blitzkrieg*," he said, raising his glass, before realising that the men who had coined that expression had ended up bogged down in a long war of attrition. Too bad for them. It wouldn't happen to him.

He had the ultimate weapon. A sledgehammer.

The telephone records.

Prosecutors would have given years of their lives to get their hands on these papers, he'd told Herr Wegener, although in his heart of hearts he thought he was exaggerating.

It wasn't true.

These records – which would have given any prosecutor an ulcer, since, on account of where they had come from, they could never be used in court – were a nuclear bomb.

The names of the subscribers, in black and white, underlined and carefully annotated. Businessmen above suspicion. Officers of the Treasury Police. Politicians. Prominent individuals. All of these people had had contacts with Wegener, and Carbone could now hold a gun to their heads. A wonderful, bright future was unfolding before him. He would be able to piss on all of them.

He would have to be careful, of course. They were people who could refute everything point by point, and a number on a telephone company record did not necessarily mean anything. Their phones had not been tapped. All Carbone had was numbers: he did not know the content of the calls, only that there had been contact between these people and Wegener. Still, there had been investigations based on much less than this that he had brought to a successful conclusion. Working in secret, without arousing suspicion, he would have to put together an irrefutable case, find concrete evidence – solid, bullet-proof evidence. It would involve a lot of work and a fair amount of risk. Even so, the stack of yellowing paper on his desk was pure gold.

The real cherry on this dynamite cake was the only telephone number, circled in red and with several question marks scribbled next to it, which Herr Wegener had never dialled. Not in a thousand years. Of that he was certain.

It was not a matter of instinct. It was plain, investigative logic.

Why? Because otherwise, what had happened would not have happened.

Simple.

What star sign was Wegener?

Captain Carbone sat at his desk and allowed himself a few seconds to catch his breath. He did not want to sound overexcited. Herr Wegener might . . . What? he asked himself, smiling.

Nothing.

There was nothing he could do to him.

Not anymore. Not after what he was going to tell him.

Goodbye, Kobold.

Here's your horoscope, he thought as he dialled Wegener's number. You're dead!

At the fourth ring, Wegener picked up. "Who is it?"

The man with the goatee raised the sledgehammer. "Carbone," he said.

"Go on."

Carbone paused before he struck home.

"I know who Klaus is."

40

The Trusted Man always carried a handful of telephone tokens with him. He inserted them now, one by one, into the slot in the payphone and listened to them clang as they dropped into the metal container.

He dialled his voicemail number and heard the sounds of the telephone exchange, picturing the signal travelling underground, through thousands of kilometres of cable.

The message was plain, despite the screams and tears of rage and despair.

"Klaus is my son. Marlene is pregnant. We have to meet. Stop everything. Everything."

He deleted the message, hung up and looked around. Nobody. He took a silk handkerchief from his pocket, wiped the receiver and gently put it back in its cradle. Then he folded the handkerchief.

There was no trace of emotion on his face. Just a hint of curiosity, as usual when confronted with tears. Tears were a mystery to him.

In any case, Herr Wegener's screaming and begging had had no effect on him.

"Irreversible" was a word with one meaning, and one meaning only.

41

Ensconced on a chair, with his tobacco and his pipe, one pillow behind his back and one under his knee, ready to listen.

"Moneymoneymoney," Marlene began.

Keller raised his eyebrows.

Marlene gave an apologetic smile. "There were mice in the walls of the *maso* where I was born. I could hear them squeaking all night long. They said, 'Moneymoneymoney.'"

She brushed a lock of hair from her forehead. That morning, she had carefully removed the bandage and looked at her reflection in the bottom of a steel pan. The scar was red and swollen but not inflamed. She had decided to let it breathe. Besides, it wasn't that ugly. She might as well start getting used to it.

Klaus . . .

She bit her lip.

The time had come to tell the truth: the story of Marlene and the Thieving Magpie, the mice in the wall, Wegener, Klaus, the kobolds.

She had spent the night hours searching for the right words to tell her story in a way that would make sense to the *Bau'r*.

Now, though, as he sat smoking his pipe and listening to her, events, dates and voices started getting in a hopeless jumble. She apologised.

"I don't know where else to start. The mice were my mother and father. Onkel Fritz, my mother's brother, was the Cat. As for me" – she paused briefly – "I was the Thieving Magpie."

She sighed. It was hard.

She put the book of Grimm's fairy tales on the table. "This was a gift from my mother. She would read me a story every night. My favourite was the one about Old Mother Frost. Do you know it?"

Keller nodded. "The old woman who makes it snow. Of course."

"The Taufer family had debts, the fields weren't yielding any crops, the cows weren't producing enough milk. Papa asked the banks for money, but the banks wouldn't give him any, so he was forced to beg Onkel Fritz for it. Onkel Fritz would come up to the *maso* almost every day and insist that Mamma and Papa sell the *maso*. To him, obviously. It was a small debt, but even something small can be too big when your pockets are empty. Onkel Fritz was a greedy . . ."

She broke off.

Keller completed her sentence for her. "Son of a bitch."

It was as if he had not spoken. Marlene was not there anymore. She had gone back to another time, another *maso*.

"Mamma and Papa did their best to repay the debts, but there was never enough money. At night, I would hear them whisper . . . Moneymoneymoney."

"The mice in the walls."

Marlene turned her gaze to the cover of the book. "It was the only way I could stop myself from going mad. I was scared of those voices. Whereas the mice . . ."

"Like the ones in *Cinderella*?"

"I was no Cinderella. My parents loved me. Although gradually . . ." Searching for the right words, Marlene ran her tongue over her lips; they were hard and dry. "Although gradually I disappeared. I became a ghost to them. Mamma and Papa would make lunch and dinner, ask about school, Mamma would tell me stories while Papa would try and make me laugh with his jokes, but . . ."

"They weren't themselves anymore."

Marlene looked into Keller's face. He understood. Yes, he understood everything.

150

At this point, her confession turned into an avalanche. She could not have stopped herself even if she had wanted to.

"I began stealing. I don't know why. I became the Thieving Magpie. It was perfectly clear in my mind. Almost fair. Marlene became the Thieving Magpie the same way Mamma and Papa had become the mice in the walls. I had no use for the things I stole. They were small things. I took them from school and also from the village shops on my way home. The most valuable object I stole was a little chain. I stole it from my teacher. It was strange. I liked the teacher, she was fond of me, she said I was intelligent and good at my work. But I stole it from her anyway. Naturally, she noticed."

"Did she tell your parents?"

Worse: she told Onkel Fritz, who was better known in the village than Marlene's parents. Onkel Fritz, with his beer gut, his powerful wrists and his chipped teeth. He apologised profusely and told her about his sister (who really wasn't well at all) and his brother-in-law (who was no good).

Onkel Fritz came up to the *maso* and confronted Marlene as she was raking out the cowshed, her hair gathered in a scarf. She did not hear him coming.

She just felt his hands lifting her.

And the taste of excrement after Onkel Fritz hurled her against a heap of manure.

"That's what you deserve, you stupid little bitch! Where is it?"

Onkel Fritz was shaking. And not just with anger. He seemed pleased with himself.

"Where have you hidden it?"

Marlene wiped her face in disgust. "What?"

"The necklace. Where is it?"

Marlene blushed. "Don't tell Mamma or she'll be angry. Please don't tell her, Onkel Fritz, she'll get so angry, please, Onkel Fritz, don't tell Mamma and Papa, they . . . Please, don't—"

Her head hit the manure again.

Onkel Fritz towered over her. He was tall, he was fat. And he had that glint in his eyes that terrified her to the point of madness. He was dirty, incomprehensible. Horrible.

Marlene took the little necklace from her apron pocket. Onkel Fritz snatched it from her hand.

"What were you planning to do with this? Sell it? Wear it on Sundays? Is that what you were thinking? To make yourself pretty?"

"I didn't—"

Onkel Fritz grabbed her by the back of her neck and rammed her face into the manure. "You're just a shit shoveller. A dirty shit shoveller. You were born a shit shoveller and you'll die a shit shoveller."

Marlene was sobbing. Why wasn't Papa coming to help her? Where was Mamma?

"And now say thank you."

"Onkel Fritz—"

He grabbed her roughly by the shoulder. "Say, 'Thank you.' I've taught you your place in the world. Say, 'Thank you, Onkel Fritz.'"

She lay motionless in the manure, like a broken doll, legs spread, skirt raised.

Onkel Fritz panting, huge, above her. With that look in his eyes.

"Thank you, Onkel Fritz," she muttered.

Onkel Fritz did not keep the secret. He told Mamma and Papa while she sat in a corner by the fireplace, her head down, listening to all her parents' exclamations of "Oh, my God!" and "That's impossible!" and "Shame on her!"

They didn't tell her off. They did not utter so much as a word of reproach. She simply became even more invisible.

Mamma got ill. She would spend half the day in bed, barely breathing, one arm over her eyes. The other half of the day she would spend cleaning the house. She would dust, sweep, scrub and scour, thousands and thousands of times.

Everything's dirty. Dirty. Dirty. That was what she said.

Mamma was taken to hospital. Marlene remembered her eyes staring into space as Papa and Onkel Fritz carried her to the ambulance. Where were they taking her?

"The asylum," Onkel Fritz said. "And it's all your fault. Remember that, you stupid shit shoveller."

Then he resumed whispering in her father's ear. Always the same tune. Moneymoneymoney . . .

Papa gave in. The *maso* was sold. Onkel Fritz got him a job in a sawmill in Lana. Marlene moved. At the age of sixteen, she began working as a waitress in a hotel.

Papa never took her to visit Mamma. It was not appropriate. He said Mamma was feeling better. She was recovering and would soon be back with them. But he always said it with that squeaking sound that still tormented Marlene in her dreams. "Moneymoneymoney" had become "crazycrazycrazy."

In the hotel, Marlene realised men liked her. It was not a pleasant discovery. It reminded her of the way Onkel Fritz had looked at her. The glances. The furtive touches. The half-uttered words. The men, drunk, offering her money to talk to her in private. She had never considered her body as something desirable. And yet the attention was undeniable.

It opened her eyes.

She realised why some of the girls who worked in the hotel could afford particular clothes, particular jewellery, particular "treats," as they called them.

One of the waitresses, Brigitte, taught her how to wear make-up, how to accentuate her face – a face like a nineteenth-century lady's – and turn it into a trap for shitheads, as she called the hotel's guests. Shitheads with money.

Moneymoneymoney.

The mice had gone. Papa would fall asleep, exhausted, straight after dinner, and Mamma never returned home. Yet their squeaking haunted Marlene night and day, night and day.

Brigitte told her: you've got to be clever.

The Thieving Magpie was clever, but . . .

She resisted.

Naturally, in order to scrape together a few more tips, she would put into practice what Brigitte had taught her. A smile and a slightly shorter skirt than permitted, but nothing else. That was how they all started, Brigitte said one night, showing her a little diamond ring, a gift from one of her "admirers."

A smile and a short skirt, and the rest followed naturally.

"But if you want my advice, Marlene my dear, you should make up your mind. One of these days, your skin won't be as smooth as it is now, and your breasts will start to sag. Not to mention this . . ." Brigitte patted herself on the behind. "Men like a bit of flesh, otherwise they wouldn't know where to put their paws, but when it gets too big they start complaining. If you want to make money, now's the time."

No, Marlene told herself, not her. She would never do that. Not for *moneymoneymoney*. To do that would mean going *crazycrazycrazy*. Never, she swore.

The very next day, she met Herr Wegener.

He was twenty years older than her, self-confident and handsome. He dressed impeccably. And he had done nothing but stare at her all through his dinner.

The courtship. The invitations declined, not out of calculation, but rather through disbelief: how could such a rich man be interested in a shit shoveller like her? His good manners. His fine words. The flowers. The first kiss.

"It won't last," Brigitte said. "Take as much money from him as you can before he tires of you. And trust me, he will."

But Herr Wegener did not tire of her. He asked her to marry him.

"I went to the hospital. Mamma had become as small and shrivelled as a prune. I told her about the wedding. I told her I was happy. And do you know what she said?"

Keller shook his head.

"She looked at my new dress, my polished nails, my hairdo and spat on the floor. She called me a whore. 'You filthy whore,' she said. I burst into tears."

Keller reached out his hand to stroke hers, but Marlene pulled it away.

The truth. The whole truth.

"I even cried at my wedding. Don't all brides do that? They're happy, they're overcome with emotion. Do you know why I was crying? Because my father was there to walk me to the altar. In that suit of his." Marlene blinked, and her face grew hard. "The shit-shoveller suit. I was ashamed of him, his hands, his fingernails. I was ashamed of the stench of poverty he carried around with him. I invited Onkel Fritz to the wedding, too. I didn't have to. He'd stolen my parents' *maso*, driven my mother crazy, and . . ." Marlene shrugged. "I wanted him to suffer. I wanted him to see the champagne, the clothes, my husband's money, which was my money, too, now that I was his wife. I was rich. He was nothing but a shit shoveller. And he always would be, whereas I . . ."

She was rich.

A new life, with new rules. And new whispers.

Marlene was bright, she always had been. Even during the courtship, she had realised that Wegener was not the simple businessman he liked people to believe he was. Brigitte's glances told her. The men her future husband met with told her. The deference with which people approached him. Wegener was a criminal.

He himself confided in her one evening over dinner, a few weeks after the wedding. He told her about the war. About his childhood amid the paths. He told her about his empire. He outlined his

155

plans for the future. He spoke of his ascent into the Consortium.

He said there was nothing to fear, that he loved her and would protect her.

He took her hands and asked if she could forgive him for having kept her in the dark. She loved him, so of course (*moneymoneymoney*) she could.

And so she had become his (*crazycrazycrazy*) accomplice. Until . . .

Marlene put her hands in her lap.

"Until I found out about Klaus. Our son."

Keller's eyes opened wide in astonishment. "You're pregnant?"

"When I found out, I realised that . . . that I had to get out of there. I didn't want Klaus to become another Herr Wegener. It was wrong." Marlene took the velvet pouch from her pocket. "I stole these. I ran away. But then . . ."

"You had the accident. And here you are."

Marlene nodded. She had run out of tears and out of words. Her head was spinning. "The truth, Simon Keller, is that you saved the life of a thief and a liar."

Keller put his pipe on the table and took her hands in his. "It's you who've just given me a gift. A great gift."

Gently, he touched the beauty spot on her cheek.

He allowed himself to think of a word he had been toying with for a long time.

Redemption.

Marlene emptied the contents of the velvet pouch onto the damaged boards of the table.

The sapphires.

Keller looked at them in silence.

"Shiny stones are worth a lot. They drive men mad." He counted five, then put them aside. "These are enough to give you a future. The others," he said, putting them back into the velvet pouch, "we'll return to their rightful owner."

156

"My husband is a dangerous man, a killer, a—"

"Leave it to me to persuade him. No man is too cruel to grant a second chance."

"No, you mustn't. You—"

"But first, you must do something for me. *Voter* Luis always said that you become a man when you put on your father's clothes. What you see are his clothes. His trousers, his shirt. I need you to make me a new suit. You said you're a seamstress. I have some fabric. It's old but strong. Can you do it?"

"I . . ."

"Can you?"

Marlene nodded. "I don't know about the hat, though . . ."

Keller smiled. "In that case, it'll still be *Voter* Luis'. It's fine. I like it. It's a good, sturdy hat. And it's right that I should remember."

"Your father?"

Keller stared at her for a long time before answering. "The man I killed."

42

In despair – beyond despair – Herr Wegener was yelling orders. Making telephone calls. Yelling more orders. Two, three, a hundred times. But nobody had seen the Trusted Man.

Warren Beatty? *Who?* The actor?

Had the boss had too much to drink?

He had lost his mind. Because of a woman. His wife.

Isn't that what always happens?

Herr Wegener promised a reward of millions for the head of the Trusted Man. Millions to anyone who could put him in touch with him.

Nobody came forward.

Captain Carbone was trying to soften him up. The lawyer would not answer his calls. Wegener had reached the point where he got down on his knees and prayed. Take my life, God. Mine and not my son's. Not Klaus's. My son, Lord. I beg you.

The crucifix remained silent to his requests.

So Wegener grabbed the telephone. He was furious. No more requests, no more promises. Orders. Orders his men understood immediately.

Revenge. Reprisals.

Death.

43

There was not much light in the *Stube*, but Marlene was a skilled seamstress. An artist, Gabriel liked to say. Marlene had never believed it, but she was flattered a man of such refinement and such undeniable talent should call her that.

She had spent the happiest hours of her marriage to Herr Wegener in the workshop of the boutique: chatting with the other seamstresses and learning the tricks of the trade from Gabriel, caressing the fabrics brought by the wholesalers and choosing the best, transforming the fruits of her imagination and the new brides' requests into fine garments.

Wegener had never understood it, but, bent over the work benches, her brow furrowed, her eyes sometimes watering with fatigue, Marlene had felt free.

The *Stube* of a *maso*, though, was not a workshop for wealthy snobs. A *Bau'r*'s clothes did not have to be artistic, she reminded herself. They had to be sturdy. The seams had to hold, the cloth cut in such a way as not to impair movement, the buttons sewn on with a double thread.

Even so, the result was not without elegance.

Marlene pricked a finger and raised it to her lips.

Keller's fabric was old, but it was of excellent quality. He had brought it up from the cellar – he had not allowed Marlene to go down with him and help him carry it up to the *Stube*. She wondered where he had got it. She wondered *when*.

Maybe it had been his Mutti's? A *Bäuerin* was also a seamstress. That and a million other things.

Keller had told her how his mother had died giving birth to his sister. He had also told her about *Voter* Luis' madness, how he had turned from a man of faith into a monster, how afraid he, Simon, had been of his father's silence and his father's rages. A monster who had killed his own daughter.

Elisabeth. Little Lissy.

He told her how he had sat up with her until dawn, rocking her dead body in his arms.

Little Lissy . . . Sweet Lissy.

He told her, with the extinguished pipe between his lips and a vacant stare in his eyes, how one day he had gone into his father's bedroom to find his dark, severe clothes.

And do what had to be done.

"I put on his clothes. These clothes. And I cut his throat while he slept. I should have made him suffer. Should have filled him with terror, the way he'd filled little Lissy with terror. But that would have been revenge, and revenge isn't worthy of a man of faith. Pity, though, is. I acted out of pity. He was still my father, and before he lost his mind he'd been a great man."

Marlene looked at Keller's gnarled hands spread open on the table: the damaged knuckles, the scars, the dark spots on the frost-bitten skin.

A killer's hands.

"Do I scare you, Marlene?"

Marlene had not replied immediately. She had looked at those hands and thought of the torment he must have felt, having to watch over his little sister's body. She thought of those years of fear and terror, years of such extreme solitude that it was impossible to see an end to it.

No, Keller's hands were not a killer's hands.

"It wasn't murder," she said. "It was justice."

44

There was only the candle flame. If you looked into it, you could see miracles and mysteries. Men and women writhing in pain behind the façade of a hotel. In the wind howling outside, you could hear the echoes of their screams.

Alone in the villa, surrounded by snow-covered vineyards, Herr Wegener smiled. It was a beautiful sound. As beautiful as the acrid stench of petrol that reached his nostrils, making them sting.

Four twenty-litre jerry cans standing by the door. It rushed to your head like the best champagne in his cellar. Wegener could see Georg standing guard. He was waiting with him.

Indoors, by the light of the candle, Herr Wegener was seething with hatred.

You can't be the baker's wife and not know who in the neighbourhood has a sweet tooth. That was what Carbone had said. God, how he hated that son of a bitch.

He hated everything and everybody. And soon this hatred would turn into slaughter. Because Carbone was right – he was the baker. The local cake lovers had no secrets from him. They were all in his notebook.

Names, addresses. Meeting places.

The hotel. A bullet marked its location on the map spread open on the table. The candle flame produced an infernal glow, caressing the brass.

Bullets with hollow tips. A few grams of concentrated death.

In Wegener's head, it was a perfect plan. The motivation was as clear as daylight. Revenge. He would strike in such a way that it would be impossible to ignore him. A show of strength to attract the Consortium's attention.

To force them to call the Trusted Man back.

On the map were the words GRAND HOTEL STEINHOF. Wegener read them as "casino." An illegal casino that belonged to the Consortium. Useful for scraping together a bit of money, but not just that.

The Consortium had no need of money. How much could it possibly rake in from an illegal gambling house, even such a high-class one? A mere trifle for an organisation whose takings would be the envy of quite a few puppet regimes in Africa. This casino had a different purpose, a much more forward-looking one.

Nobody played *watten* or *briscola* or any other silly card games there. There were no cheap cigarettes or stale wine. They played blackjack and poker.

It was a different world.

You entered from a well-lit street in Merano and ended up amid the blinding lights of Las Vegas. Behind the façade of the Grand Hotel, there were roulette wheels, beautiful long-legged blondes from northern and eastern Europe, cocaine on silver trays.

Nobody swore, nobody cursed. Patrons accepted their losses with a smile and toasted the croupier. It was a classy place for classy people. Why complain about a bad hand or the whims of a little ball? Just being there already meant you were a winner.

You weren't admitted to this casino with a tip or a wink. You received a formal invitation in silver lettering on thick paper. *We request the honour of your presence . . .* A place for the elite. Security was 100-per-cent guaranteed, since the purpose of the casino, not far from the racetrack and located one floor below the lobby of one of the town's best-known hotels, was to facilitate meetings, handshakes, agreements, friendships.

Handshakes were the source of the Consortium's power. Money was the result.

"We request the honour of your presence," Wegener said out loud, the candle flame reflected in his eyes.

He had thought of everything. Two cars blocking the road. An act that cried: "Big trouble ahead." It wouldn't just be revenge, it would be a show. A show to prove to the Consortium that here, on *his* territory, the master of ceremonies was Herr Wegener.

Seven men. He had chosen them with care. The toughest he had, veterans of robberies and ambushes. The weapons were ready on the table. Black, glossy and perfectly oiled. Czech-manufactured Škorpion machine pistols. Barrels filed, magazines full. Selectors on automatic. To one side, semi-automatics, with a small bag of Benzedrine next to them. White, amphetamine-based capsules to give his henchmen a kick. The same drug that fighter pilots used, or soldiers in the jungle. He wanted them bloodthirsty.

It would be another Vietnam, the likes of which no one around here had ever seen.

That was the plan.

Phase one: arrive and get rid of the guards, men with holsters under their arms who patrolled the entrance discreetly and professionally.

How many times had Herr Wegener smiled at these men, with Marlene in an evening dress on his arm? And how many times had he won and lost in that room filled with velvet and glittering with gold?

Too bad for them. They must be given no time to beg for mercy.

Phase two: burst in. Seven masked men and one showing his face. Him. The spectacle required a director and a star. He would be both. And then would come the slaughter. Spray the casino with lead. Men in dinner suits, long-legged whores, waiters, croupiers: he wanted them all dead.

All of them.

Phase three: the jerrycans of petrol. Over the gambling tables, the sofas, the ornamental plants, behind the bar. And then strike a match and unleash hell. He could already see the bodies writhing in the candle flame and hear their screams as he listened to the wind.

Two knocks at the door.

Georg.

"Sir . . ."

That one word was enough. Wegener understood.

45

Wegener ordered Georg to wait outside in the car, with the engine running. Georg nodded and left. The squeak of the door hinges set Wegener's teeth on edge.

With an angry gesture, he swept the map off the table. The hollow-tipped bullet bounced off the wall, and the Benzedrine capsules were scattered across the floor.

Wegener put his hands over his ears. The wind no longer sang of revenge and reprisals. Now it was telling a different story, a story of scorched earth. He could not bear it.

He knew how certain things went. He could imagine them. Someone approaches you and offers to buy you a beer. He asks you how things are going. Then he whispers a piece of advice in your ear. *Ulysses never made it back to Ithaca*, he says. *The Cyclops feasted on his flesh. Did you know that? The rest is nothing but lies.*

Then he smiles, and you know what he means. You realise he's giving you an opportunity.

So you quickly nod, quit your stool and go home to pack. The man who offered you a drink is the Cyclops. You owe it to fate that you're alive. And you can't spit in the face of fate.

"Fuck Wegener, and fuck his wife."

Run while there's still time.

Wegener pressed his fists to his ears.

He could not stop thinking about it.

His men. The seven men he had chosen for their ruthlessness and determination. All it had taken was a murmur from the Consortium and they'd bolted, leaving him alone and defenceless.

What did it mean? He knew perfectly well, but couldn't admit it to himself.

And he could not stop imagining it.

A persuasive voice on the telephone. *Siegfried never pierced the Dragon's chest with a spear. The Dragon is too powerful. Do you want to end up like him? You're an intelligent person. You have a family. You have friends. Do you really want to lose everything? And for what? For someone like Wegener? Don't you know Wegener's finished?*

So when you put the receiver down, you feel that life is wonderful, you feel how sweet the air coming into your lungs tastes. You feel the desire to make love to your wife, to hug your children, to joke with your old friends. And you don't give a fuck about Wegener. It's his life. His revenge, his downfall. Why stand up to the Dragon?

Scorched earth. That was what the Consortium had done. The weapons, the petrol, the drugs: all in vain. There would be no bursting in. No hotel on fire. No slaughter.

Herr Wegener swallowed a couple of times. Once more he recognised the taste of humiliation. He stood up, but his legs gave way and he was forced to sit down again.

46

Simon Keller had told Marlene about Lissy and *Voter* Luis, but he had left many things unsaid. Because even though the story of Lissy, Sim'l and *Voter* Luis was as simple as a circle traced in the snow, that circle had the shape of mystery and miracle.

And Keller had kept quiet about both.

47

Voter Luis had sketched the beginning of this swarm of mysteries and miracles at nightfall, while Sim'l and Lissy were hunched over their dinners.

The children ate slowly, focusing on every spoonful of soup, which, as usual, was meagre and flavourless. Salt and oil had run out a long time ago, and the *maso*'s vegetable garden yielded only bland potatoes and bitter herbs.

All at once, *Voter* Luis, who had not eaten and was just watching them, arms crossed, stood up, supporting himself with his crutch, took a bag full of pungent-smelling powder, opened it and threw a pinch into the fire. Blue flames flared up, much to Elisabeth's astonishment and young Sim'l's concern.

Voter Luis put the bag away, took up his hunting knife, bowed his head and recited in a whisper, "And if thy right eye offend thee, pluck it out and cast it from thee; for it is profitable for thee that one of thy members should perish, and not that thy whole body be cast into hell."

Sim'l understood immediately.

He understood that bereavement had become an unbearable torment, a hell for *Voter* Luis. A man of faith should have found comfort in the thought of his beloved sitting in the presence of the Father, but *Voter* Luis could only wallow in grief.

Sim'l at last understood why *Voter* Luis could not look his daughter in the face, why he could not play with her, why he would punish her for a trifle, why he kept saying that she was nothing but a useless extra mouth to feed.

In being born, Lissy had killed Mutti and trapped *Voter* Luis in a spiral of despair that neither opium nor alcohol nor the Word could break.

Sim'l understood too late that Lissy was the eye that caused him to sin.

Voter Luis raised the knife and plunged it into his daughter. A single thrust, straight to the chest. He drew out the blade and went into his bedroom, leaving Sim'l in tears, rocking his dying little sister, trying to comfort her.

Little Lissy could comprehend neither her death nor her dying. With what was left of her strength, a single drop of blood marring her emaciated face, she pointed anxiously at her soup bowl and whispered as her soul was already on its way to heaven:

"I haven't finished, Sim'l. I'm hungry. Keep it for me. I'm so hungry . . ."

Then, just before leaving him, Lissy transfixed him with that terrible look that seemed to be asking, "Why? Why, Sim'l? Why didn't you save me?"

Sweet Lissy. Little Lissy. It's alright. It's . . .

The following day, *Voter* Luis buried the body and burned Lissy's clothes and toys on a wretched bonfire outside the *maso*. Sad flames that were not blue.

Those had already been lit.

From that moment on, it was as though Elisabeth had never existed, and *Voter* Luis resumed his usual activities. Drinking too much and chewing poppy seeds, shut up in the cellar.

All that was left of Lissy was a memory and two little bells hidden in Sim'l's mattress.

Now it was Sim'l's turn to drown in his own personal hell. Because without Lissy, he did not know if he would ever feel as tall and strong as an ash tree. Because he had been unable to stop his father.

Naturally, he wrote: it was his duty. He copied the Word, although the Word did not provide the comfort he was hoping for. And after he had finished his first Bible, *Voter* Luis pulled him by the arm and shut him in the cellar.

"It's time you saw the Kellers' work."

In the dark, for the first time in the presence of the Bibles of past *Voter*, those severe volumes that seemed to whisper their terrible wisdom, Simon felt his bladder relax and his trousers become wet.

Voter Luis left him there for two nights, without food or water, to pray, hallucinate and tremble. He thought over and over again about Lissy's face and her final words until, terrified and blinded by hunger and thirst, he was struck by a sudden intuition – *Voter* Luis would have called it a revelation – and was swallowed by the darkness of despair.

When, on the morning of the third day, *Voter* Luis opened the door to let him out, Sim'l almost didn't notice. Because there was something worse than his feelings of guilt over not saving Lissy. The Scriptures left no room for doubt: the sins of the father would be visited upon the children.

That meant that in the eyes of the Lord, it was he who had killed sweet little Lissy.

48

The days went by. The months. The years.

All identical. Working in the fields. *Voter* Luis' sudden outbursts of anger. The Word of the Bible, the sense of guilt. Lissy's blood staining his hands. The hardship, the loneliness, the hunting.

The sleepless nights. The fear of damnation.

Finally, one morning, a sow was born. She was small and lively, but she was not like the others. She was special.

She had a black spot under her left eye, just like the drop of blood on Elisabeth's cheek. The one Simon dreamt about every night.

His back covered in sores from *Voter* Luis' lashes, Simon bent over the sow, took her in his arms and began rocking her and singing softly.

Sweet Lissy. Little Lissy.

That was when he heard the Voice. The Voice was inside his head, and at the same time it was all around him.

Simon nodded the whole time the Voice spoke to him. He stroked the sow one last time, went back to the *maso*, climbed the steps to his father's bedroom and, as *Voter* Luis, drunk and dishevelled, slept, he put on his clothes.

Here I am, he thought as he adjusted the large hat over his forehead.

Then he cut *Voter* Luis' throat.

When the man had drawn his last breath, Simon dragged the body outside and buried it next to his mother. Since *Voter* Luis had been a good father and a man of faith before losing his mind, he lit the Kellers' blue flames and prayed for him.

After he had finished, he went back home, found the two little bells and took them to the pigsty. He tied one around the sow's neck and held the other one tight in his fist. He spent the night there, singing to her.

Little Lissy, sweet Lissy.

He slept and did not have nightmares.

The next day, though, he woke in a state of anguish. Wearing *Voter* Luis' clothes did not make him a real *Voter*. What if someone asked after his father? What would he reply? Would he have to run away? Leave the *maso*? The prospect left him with a sense of dread, deep in his gut. He had no idea what the world outside was like, apart from the village. There were times he even doubted the existence of anything beyond the mountains.

In his dismay, he asked the Voice for help, but the Voice kept silent.

He did not run away. And nobody came up to the *maso* to ask after *Voter* Luis. When he took a chance, went down the mountain and announced his father's death in the village, people expressed their condolences but nothing else. Somehow, he kept going.

He wasn't a *Voter*, but he was a Keller; he could scythe hay, dig for potatoes, shoot a deer, cure meat and stop wholesalers from cheating him with their scales when he sold them his produce.

Anything he had not learned directly from *Voter* Luis he found in his notes, and anything *Voter* Luis had not transcribed he discovered in the Bibles of past *Voter*. Through study, he became a good *Kräutermandl*.

The only joy of his day was filling the sow's trough. Lissy was hungry, and he fed her. A perfect circle (though without mysteries or miracles) that brought him a little serenity.

The sow with the spot under her eye grew to adulthood, and Keller mated her with boars he bought at fairs. Each time, Lissy would give birth to a litter which would die within a few weeks.

Each time, Keller would grieve, but no remedy suggested by past *Voter* seemed to have any effect on the sow.

Lissy started ageing faster than normal. Simon assumed there was something wrong with her blood. Anxiety came back into his heart. What would become of him without Lissy? He shuddered at the thought of her death.

The day Lissy, by now half blind, turned seven, as Keller stood pointing his rifle at a fox's lair, he heard the Voice again.

It hadn't happened since his father's death, and he had started to think it had never existed. But seven years after *Voter* Luis' death, the Voice returned.

It pointed him to a thick, wild part of the woods, where young Sim'l had fired a rifle for the first time. That was an important place, the Voice explained. He was to bring the sow here, set her free and go back home without turning back. The sow would find her way back on her own, pregnant. Her line, the Voice promised, would continue. A new Lissy would be born.

He would not be alone. He would never be alone again. It was a promise.

The Bibles of past *Voter* disagreed on many points, but all urged obedience, and so Keller, who was a man of faith, obeyed. He tied a rope around Lissy, dragged her into the forest and set her free. Then he left, his heart swollen with worry.

And even though this was madness – *Voter* Luis used to say there were no wild pigs or boars in the area (but had *Voter* Luis really uttered those words? Sometimes Keller's mind was such a muddle . . .) – he discovered that the Voice had not lied to him.

His faith was rewarded.

Lissy returned, her body scratched, her trotters covered in mud, her teeth chipped as though she had fought a pack of wolves – but pregnant. Three months, three weeks and three days later, as is the norm for pigs, Lissy gave birth to a female. Another Lissy. With more spots, larger, hungrier. And more intelligent. Because, the Voice explained, she was more like her father than her mother.

When the old Lissy died, Keller lit a funeral pyre with blue flames in her honour and, barely holding back his tears, read out a passage from his Bible: "One generation passeth away, and another generation cometh, but Lissy abideth forever."

From that day on, the Voice was always with him. It would urge him not to lose heart whenever anguish seemed about to crush him, and would make him laugh whenever he needed to. It would dictate new, dazzling versions of the Scriptures that filled him with inspiration. It would suggest ways to make the winters pass more quickly, carving wooden toys or putting together increasingly imaginative *Vulpendingen*. One day, as Keller was feeding Lissy her slop, the Voice made a request that alarmed him. His initial reaction was to shake his head and try to ignore it. In other words, he convinced himself he had misheard.

In time, the Voice grew more insistent and, fearful of such vehemence, Keller accused it of mocking him. It should stop now. This constant buzzing prevented him from concentrating on his duties as a *Bau'r*. The Voice burst out laughing. And it began to pester him, night and day, relentlessly.

The Voice changed.

It became deep, hard as flint stones scratching against one another, making his teeth vibrate and his gums bleed. Keller resorted to every available means to silence it. This was impossible, he discovered. Even blocking his ears with beeswax or eating handfuls of poppy seeds was no use.

Screaming like the *Wehen*, the Voice told him that he had to do it for Lissy, that it was his duty to obey, because he was both a man of faith and a murderer seeking redemption. Or had he forgotten that? Keller's hands were stained with Lissy's blood. The damnation of hellfire awaited him. Or did he doubt the Word of the Bible as well as the Voice? Did he not understand that Lissy was hungry and that it was up to him to feed her?

Having asked this final question, the Voice disappeared. At first, it was a welcome relief. Simon was able to sleep and rest. He looked after the *maso*, Lissy and the other pigs in the sty. He carved more animals and went hunting.

But without the Voice, the *maso* was an empty shell, the mountain a desolate heap of stones. He began to find the solitude oppressive. The fire in the *Stube* reminded him of Lissy's face. No, he thought, the Voice was not a consequence of madness. The Voice was mystery and miracle. And he was a man of faith. He believed in miracles and mysteries. He stopped doubting, and the Voice returned.

The solitude vanished.

Keller complied with the Voice's request. Not just once, but always. He did whatever the Voice asked whenever it commanded him. He began to kill. Killing made him feel one step closer to redemption.

But that was not the reason he killed.

He killed in order to satisfy Lissy's hunger. And Lissy was always hungry.

49

By a strange quirk of fate, it was Herr Wegener who had given him Carbone's number.

Carbone told him that, in among the villa's telephone records, he had found the number of a gynaecologist in Merano. And putting two and two together . . .

At first, when the Trusted Man explained the reason for his visit, the gynaecologist (a white moustache, a bald pate between two tufts of curly hair) lost his temper.

How dare he waste his time?

The Trusted Man made him change his mind. It did not take long.

The doctor remembered Marlene, who, as far as he knew, was called Brigitte Egger, since that was how she had introduced herself to him. A very beautiful woman, and very happily pregnant. She had even confided over the telephone the name she had decided to give the baby.

"Don't tell me. Klaus."

"How did you know?"

"The trout in the Passer told me. Do you have anything else for me, Doctor?"

He had to insist a little, but not too much.

The doctor handed him Marlene's file. The state of her pregnancy (everything normal) and her destination (a clinic in Switzerland).

Pregnancy. Theft. Escape. Clinic.

Marlene had bought herself a safe haven, the Trusted Man

thought. Not a bad idea. Nobody knew she was pregnant. Nobody would think of looking for her in a clinic.

Having left the surgery, the Trusted Man made a call. Pretending to be the gynaecologist, he asked after his patient. He used the name Marlene had used to sign the doctor's papers: Brigitte Egger.

The Trusted Man had no idea who this Brigitte was – a relative? a friend? a made-up name? – but took note of it for any future investigations. Best not to neglect anything.

Frau Egger had not shown up at the clinic yet. Perhaps something had happened to her? The Trusted Man reassured the secretary that everything was alright.

He said goodbye, wiped the receiver with a silk handkerchief and hung up.

Something had happened. But what?

There were still a few pieces of the puzzle missing. For example, the gynaecologist had sworn over and over again that he had nothing to do with the clinic. Even Carbone had never heard of it. So either it was chance (except that the Trusted Man had long ago stopped believing in chance) or Marlene had an accomplice. Or, if not exactly an accomplice, then someone with enough money and connections to help her one way or another.

Who and why?

Finding out would take him a step closer to his target. And so he set off for Switzerland.

Most of the roads had been cleared, but snow ploughs were still operating on some stretches, and the Trusted Man had to wait, listening to dull music on the car radio. It was a tiring journey, from Merano to Val Venosta, the Reschen Pass, the Swiss cantons.

He stopped just once, to refill, and chatted with the petrol station attendant about the rapid rise in the cost of petrol.

"It's because of the financial crisis."

"They say it'll be over soon."

"Do you really believe that?"

Nobody believed it. They had a good laugh.

When the Trusted Man took out his stuffed wallet, the attendant stopped being polite.

Despite exceeding the speed limit – something he rarely did – the Trusted Man got to the clinic just seconds before it closed its doors to visitors. He politely persuaded the woman at reception to let him in. He only needed a few minutes. It was an important matter.

"*Extremely* important, you understand?"

Now, sitting and leafing through a magazine, he was doing just what would have been expected from a man like him: discreetly checking the watch that protruded from his sleeve cuff as he turned the pages.

He was not reading the articles but admiring the photographs, fascinated by how casually they would skip from the picture of a little girl burned by napalm to an advertisement for a personal hygiene product. Then he grew bored with this game and passed the time thinking about does and vixens.

Wegener, Carbone and even Gabriel the dress designer had formed the wrong opinion of Marlene. All described her in more or less the same terms: a frightened doe who had gone crazy. Now that he possessed more information, he had a more precise portrait of Marlene.

This was not the whim of a young woman who had suddenly come into money, but the actions of a mother trying to protect her own cub (from what? from Wegener's money?). The more the Trusted Man thought about it, the more convinced he was that their description had been misleading.

Marlene was no doe. She was a vixen.

And hunting a vixen required cunning, time and patience. Vixens have sharp teeth and are far-sighted. They can smell danger several kilometres away.

Hunting a vixen was—

"I'm Doctor Zimmerman."

The Trusted Man stood up and shook hands with a short man wearing tortoiseshell glasses that made him look like a know-it-all sixth-form pupil.

"If you'd like to follow me . . ."

The doctor's office had walnut panelling and smelled of pipe tobacco. The Trusted Man wasted no time. He placed Marlene's file, which he had purloined from the gynaecologist with the moustache, on the desk.

"Your wife?"

"I only want to know who paid for the room."

"Didn't she?"

"Just tell me who paid. It wasn't Frau . . . Egger, since at the time the booking was made, it would have been – how shall I put it? – impossible for her to raise the required sum without prompting questions."

Zimmerman crossed his legs and tapped his front teeth with his index finger. "Are you from the police? Is the young lady a criminal?"

"No."

"Are you a relative?"

"No."

The doctor got to his feet. "In that case, you're wasting my time and yours. Our clinic is well known for its privacy rules. Have a good evening."

Had he not been hunting a vixen, the Trusted Man would have tried to reason with this skinny man with the thick, myopic lenses, but he was tired, and Dr. Zimmerman's tone was getting on his nerves.

He took a pair of steel pliers from his leather bag. Not a tureen of soup or a portion of spicy chicken wings – one of his specialities – but a pair of steel pliers and a plastic bag containing ice and three fingers: index, middle and ring finger. The ice had partly melted and pink-coloured water had formed at the bottom of the bag.

"I was sorry to cut them off. They belonged to an artist. Art is one of the few things of any value in this world. I see you have a beautiful reproduction of "Les Demoiselles d'Avignon." Picasso is too violent for my taste, but I suppose you must have chosen it because you, too, like art. Don't you think there's something unique about artists?"

The colour had drained from Zimmerman's face. "You . . ." he began, then stopped when he saw the Trusted Man start to screw the silencer onto the barrel of his gun.

"Unfortunately," the Trusted Man continued, "you are not an artist. For all your fine qualifications, you're not even a real doctor. Doctors are useful. But you're not an artist or a doctor. What do you do for a living? You administer. You're a bureaucrat."

The Trusted Man pointed the gun at the little man's head. Then he lowered the barrel to his stomach.

"How many bureaucrats are there in the world?"

50

Herr Wegener's shoes were lined, warm and elegant. He had had them made to measure by a craftsman in Florence, who had put his mark on them with a red-hot iron, just like in the Middle Ages. He had paid an arm and a leg for them. Inside them, his feet were dry.

Wegener was no longer skin and bones. He was a fully fledged man. Over forty-two years old, not twelve. And he was about to become a father. The thought of it made him dizzy. Father: it was like the beginning of a prayer the words of which he had forgotten years ago.

And yet, sitting in the silver-haired lawyer's office, he felt as if he were still twelve, still barefoot, hungry and alone. And, what was worse, still defenceless.

"The Trusted Man can't be stopped."

"Marlene is . . ."

"Nobody can stop him."

". . . pregnant."

The lawyer looked away. He plucked a cigarette from the drawer and brought a large, bull-shaped lighter close to it, the flame emerging from the animal's nostrils. "I understand," was his only comment.

"She's expecting a child. My son. If he kills her—"

"The Trusted Man—"

"—he'd be killing my son."

"—has never made a mistake. Never."

Wegener would not give up. "There must be a way of communicating with him."

"The voicemail."

"Apart from the voicemail."

The lawyer was about to respond, but Wegener continued, swallowing his words, hunched forward, his hands clutching the edge of the desk like a castaway.

"The contract doesn't necessarily have to be annulled. That's not what I'm asking. The contract will remain valid. He just has to find her and hand her over to me. Postpone the date of her death. Wait until she gives birth, then kill her. If it's a question of money, I'll pay."

Irritably, the lawyer crushed his barely smoked cigarette in a crystal ashtray. "Even the Consortium can't stop the Trusted Man. You don't understand. The man won't stop until he's fulfilled the contract. That's the way he works."

"I'm just asking him to make an exception . . ."

The lawyer pushed a button, and one of his bodyguards looked into the room.

"Trust me, Wegener, it's for the best. This child" – he gave him a pitying look – "wouldn't be any good for a man like you. It would distract you from your duties."

"My—"

"Remember the reason you're still alive."

Wegener did not offer his hand, but stood up and left.

As soon as Georg saw him come out, he started the engine of the Mercedes.

Wegener did not speak once during the ride. As soon as he got back to the villa on the Passer, he shut himself in his bedroom, took the 9-mm automatic out of his belt and put it down on the mattress. Then he threw open the window and let the cold air rush into the room. He sat down on the edge of the bed and started thinking.

About an empty chair and a bowl of soup, a long, long time ago.

51

Too many, Zimmerman had to admit. Truly, too many. The world was full of bureaucrats. Half the passengers on any scheduled bus spent half their lives dealing with official stamps, permits needing signatures, paperwork. The other half consisted of people who would have been only too happy to hang them from the first available tree.

It did not take Zimmerman long to work out how much he was worth in the grand scheme of things. It's easy to replace a bureaucrat, even one as scrupulous as he was.

And so he immediately came up with a name. The question had hardly been uttered when there it was. Zimmerman even wrote it down on a sheet of letter-headed paper, in block capitals to be sure it was legible.

Lorenz Gasser.

The man who had paid Marlene's expenses in advance. The Vixen's accomplice. A name that did not mean anything to the Trusted Man.

This is going to take time, he thought as he inserted the tokens into the payphone, one by one.

There were other files in his doctor's bag – the results of the last few days' research and of Carbone's tips – that needed careful study. They were bound to yield something. Or else he would find another way.

That was how it always was.

There were three messages on the voicemail. All of them were from Herr Wegener, begging him to annul the contract or suspend the operation until after his son was born.

The last message was just a long, exhausting sigh that ended with a sob cut off by the sound of the line being disconnected.

The Trusted Man cleaned the receiver with his silk handkerchief, hung up and left the telephone box.

The air was heavy with damp. It was probably going to start snowing again.

Lorenz Gasser, he thought.

52

They had always been poor, since before the war.

The only luxury item in the Wegner (no *e*) household was a chair, a wedding present carved by one of the best craftsmen in the Passeier Valley. There were flower patterns on the back, and at the top a heart had been carved out, through which, when his father was sitting there, weary but cheerful, young Robert could see his shirt.

But the luxury lay not in the carving, but in the upholstery, which was red.

That chair, at the head of the table, was the only one they owned that was upholstered. His mother was truly obsessed with the seat cushion in its red covering. Once, over dinner, his father had suddenly burst out laughing (Herr Wegener couldn't remember why, only that his father had thrown back his head, a full glass of wine in his hand, spilling some of it on his shirt) and some spots of wine had ended up on the red material. His mother had gone crazy.

Literally.

She had screamed, her eyes bursting from their sockets, practically throwing her husband off the chair, pushing him and hitting him with the cloth she had started using to rub and rub, terrified because, as is well known, wine stains are hard to remove.

Thinking back on it, it was the only time he had ever seen her truly angry.

From then on, that otherwise quiet, shy woman had made her husband put a white cloth on the seat cushion whenever he sat down. It had made both father and son snigger, but in secret.

There was nothing funny about the cushion on the luxury chair. They both knew it, and that was why it was impossible to restrain their hilarity. Young Robert enjoyed this complicity. Sometimes, when his mother had her back turned, his father would give him a little smile and pretend to tip the contents of his glass over himself, and young Robert could barely stop himself from laughing. He shared a secret with his father.

Then war broke out, and the war changed everything.

Now, years later, Wegener understood why his mother had been so obsessed with that chair and its wretched upholstery. That cushion was a symbol, the symbol of something which even they, for all their poverty, had been able to obtain.

Well-being.

It must not be damaged, it must not get dirty. Not a breadcrumb, not a single spot. Because – although this was something Wegener understood only many years later – the red cushion represented the hope of a better future.

This was what Wegener was thinking about, with his head in his hands and the automatic lying on the bed.

About the upholstered chair, that day long ago. His father already on the train taking him to the front. His mother crying all afternoon, lying on the bed with the door locked, while he wandered around the house, in a daze.

When the clock struck seven, young Robert decided to make dinner. Eating something would do them both good.

He took the cold soup and put it to warm on the stove, sliced some cheese, laid the table and, when the soup was ready, poured it into the bowls. He went upstairs, stopped outside the bedroom, called his mother, who replied in a small, thin voice, and went back down and sat at the table.

His mother was not long in coming. Her face was pale and her eyes red. She smiled when she saw the table already laid, and she made to caress him, or maybe stroke his cheek, the way she did when she wanted to show her approval.

But then her gesture froze in mid-air.

Her face turned red and the veins on her neck protruded. Tears pooled in the corners of her eyes. Tears of anger. The caress turned into a slap.

She did not give him any explanation.

She sat down, muttered a prayer, crossed herself and started eating. Only then did Robert understand. He had laid the table for three. Three bowls, three pieces of cheese, three spoons.

He sat there for a long time, staring at his father's empty chair. His mother told him to hurry up, the soup was getting cold. He ate, tasting tears instead of the food, staring at the empty chair, frightened to death. And by the time he had finished the soup, cleared the table and washed up, his fear had changed to anger. The same anger that had made him wander for hours on end along his father's hidden paths.

In the bedroom of the villa by the Passer, as he felt the icy cold penetrate his bones, Herr Wegener realised that on that distant day, young Robert had understood the meaning of a terrible word. The worst of all. Not "war," not "death." Not even "grief."

He had understood the meaning of the word "irreversible."

The empty chair. As irreversible as the trajectory of the train that had taken his father to the Russian steppes. As irreversible as the trajectory of a bullet.

Even so, for the third time within the past few hours, he picked up the telephone, which felt as heavy as lead. He dialled the number, heard mechanical noises, rustling.

Were he able to explain about the empty chair, he thought, the Trusted Man would understand. If he could make him feel as if he were in the same vice he himself was now in, then everything would change. He had merciful eyes, the Trusted Man.

The weapon.

But weapons were innocent. Weapons didn't fire of their own accord.

That was what "irreversible" meant. He had been the one to say, "I want it." He had been the one who had pulled the trigger.

He let out a moan that was also a sigh and a sob.

At that moment, the connection was cut.

53

Even though the *Stube* was lit, the icy cold scraped at her bones. But it was not the cold that was making Marlene shiver.

"Have you got everything?"

Keller smiled.

She pointed at his knee. "Maybe it'd be best to wait a few more days."

He smiled again and stamped his boot on the floor. The wood-and-wire casing that kept the dislocated joint firm creaked.

"I think I'd better come with you," Marlene insisted.

Keller checked that his greatcoat was done up under his throat. The wound on his face had healed.

"You're not obliged to do this, Simon Keller," Marlene went on, her voice cracking. "Please think again."

Keller put on his gloves, kissed her on the head and went out.

The landscape was a glistening abyss of snow and darkness. He heaved his holdall over his shoulder and went down the wooden steps. At the bottom, he attached the snowshoes to his feet, tested their grip on the blanket of snow and turned to Marlene, who was looking down at him from the top of the steps, arms folded to shield herself from the cold, face streaked with tears.

Keller raised his hand in farewell, and Marlene did the same.

Limping, he set off.

Marlene did not close the door until his dark shape was swallowed up by the slope.

Dawn.

Were it not for his knee, and the wood-and-wire casing that imprisoned it, making every movement awkward, he would have been much quicker. He was familiar with the paths and could find them even when they were hidden under the snow.

After walking for six hours, Keller reached the point where the cream-coloured Mercedes had left the road. The place where their paths had crossed. If it weren't for his memory and his eyes, accustomed to recognising trees as though they were old friends, he would not have noticed it. The Mercedes was in the ditch at the side of the road, buried under at least three metres of snow. Nobody would see it. The girl was safe, at least until the spring.

Keller massaged the thigh of his injured leg. His knee would never be the same again. The ligaments were torn. He would have to use a stick for the rest of his life, like a cripple. When that kind of thing happened to animals, there was nothing to do but put them down. The thought made him smile. He tried to take a step, tested his knee's resistance by carefully shifting his weight.

It hurt.

He took off his gloves. His hands were so numb that he clenched his fists a few times to get the circulation going. He undid his greatcoat and took a linen pouch from one of the pockets. He smiled. Marlene had embroidered his initials on it.

He slid a few poppy seeds out of the pouch, calculating half a tablespoon. On second thoughts, he added a few more. Just to be on the safe side.

He chewed them slowly.

Midday.

Keller sat in a bus that was puffing and chugging under its load of *Bau'rn*, worried-looking holidaymakers, layabouts with alcohol-reddened cheeks and women in headscarves. There were also a couple of kids looking around, turning their heads here and there like owls perched on a branch.

On the seat next to him, a little girl sat on her mother's lap, staring at him, her fingers in her mouth, snot coming out of her nostrils. Her mother, a tall, slim woman, was asleep with her forehead against the window, snoring softly.

Keller had his black hat on his lap and his holdall tight between his shins. Each time the bus jolted, pain shot up his leg. He could not find a comfortable position. He tried not to think about it and just concentrate on the surrounding landscape.

The road wound halfway up the mountain. Every now and then, Keller would catch sight of a *maso*, high up. More often, there were tiny clusters of houses gathered snugly around long, pointed belfries. The bus would stop long enough to allow passengers to get on or off. The same expressions, the same faces. There was not much traffic despite the time of day. Partly it was the snow, he heard two men saying three rows away, but mainly it was the economic crisis. What with unemployment and rising taxes, how many people could afford the luxury of travelling by car?

The bus stopped for the umpteenth time, braking suddenly and waking the little girl's mother with a start. Whispering gently, the woman wiped her daughter's face. She looked up at Keller in embarrassment, as if he had caught her red-handed neglecting her duties as a mother and, judging by her clothes, as a *Bäuerin*. What was a *Bäuerin* doing on her own, on a bus?

Maybe times were changing, Keller thought. Then he took a closer look at the little girl's face and understood. She had a fever. She was ill. Her mother was probably taking her to see a specialist. That was why she had left the shelter of the *maso*. Many things were changing, but the mountains were not among them.

The engine rumbled. There were still kilometres of snow and deserted roads to go. His leg was hurting. It was as though he had a red-hot iron stuck under his kneecap. He chewed some more poppy.

"Opa?" the little girl stammered.

Keller smiled. *Opa*: Grandpa. Nobody had ever called him that.

"What's that?" the little girl asked, pointing at the pouch of poppy seeds.

"It's my medicine."

"Is it nice?"

"It's medicine. It's not supposed to be nice."

"Are you ill, Opa?"

"Don't be rude to the gentleman, Anna," her mother cut in.

"Anna," Keller said. "What a beautiful name."

"Thank you," her mother replied for her. "Please excuse her. She's little and she wants to know everything."

The woman was young, not much more than twenty. A girl, in Keller's eyes.

Opa. Grandpa.

"That's a sign of intelligence," he said. "An intelligent child is a precious gift."

The woman blushed, uncomfortable speaking to a stranger, uncomfortable receiving compliments.

"Are you better now, Opa?"

"Much better, little Anna."

The girl smiled.

Keller bent forward and untied the strings of his holdall. He spread it open with his hands until he found what he was looking for. He knew it was there.

"A tribute to a polite little girl," he said, handing her a wooden figurine.

"You shouldn't . . ."

But the little girl had already grabbed her new toy, eyes wide open and glistening with joy.

"It's just a pastime. I have dozens of them in my *maso*."

"What do you say, Anna?"

"Thank you, Opa."

Slipping out of her mother's arms, the little girl shifted closer to Keller and kissed him on the cheek. He was as surprised by this as the young woman.

"Did you see, Mamma?" the little girl said, beaming. "Opa gave me a little pig."

56

Evening. No darkness. Lights everywhere. Sleet.

Merano.

The little girl and her mother had got off a few stops earlier. They had said goodbye and thanked him profusely. The bus had set off again. A thousand stops on a journey that never seemed to end. Keller had dozed off.

He had been woken by the driver's voice announcing the end of the journey.

Trying not to put too much weight on his injured leg, Keller got off the bus and looked around. There were far too many lights.

He was used to just one colour at this time of day: black. Black seemed to have been banished from Merano. He told himself he was in a town now. Towns had different rules.

In the mountains, black meant safety. Black attracted the rays of the sun and, with them, heat. Black in the midst of a snowdrift could save your life.

White was the colour of mourning. When a local *Bau'r* was to be buried, people went down the mountain in a long procession to the small village church. Everybody came, it was a sign of respect. At funerals, women did not wear black headscarves, they wore white ones. Death was the colour of innocence.

He walked, doing his best not to collide with the passers-by, who all seemed to be in a rush, their heads down. There were cars (not many, admittedly, but far more than he was used to seeing) whizzing past, splashing the pavements with slush-blackened snow, as well as the odd motorcycle, traffic lights, brightly lit shop windows displaying merchandise that bewildered him.

He could not fathom men's fashions. Why did they wear jackets like that in the winter? Didn't they freeze to death? And those moccasins. They would not even withstand an April shower. And how could people afford these prices?

As for the women's clothes shops, they made him avert his eyes. He remembered the glances *Voter* Luis gave Mutti, glances charged with desire. He also remembered how she would blush with embarrassment and, above all, with pleasure.

Mutti was beautiful, and Elisabeth would have been beautiful, too, with that raven hair of hers and those long legs that made you think of a spider. He would sometimes call her his little spider. But why show off so casually what was meant to stay hidden?

A man does not desire what he can see, only what he imagines.

Maybe, he thought, what his eyes were seeing was not about seduction. Maybe there was something else hidden behind these lights, these shop windows, these strong, pungent smells.

In his final years, *Voter* Luis kept saying that Death loved the mountains. It loved them the way you love a game that is fixed from the start. An exhausting fight for survival from which no one emerged the winner. No one except Death.

"Death loves mirrors. The world is its mirror. That's why it's written in Ecclesiastes that all is vanity. Vanity is the same as death."

Maybe that was what the blinding lights and garish clothes were trying to do. Not to seduce, like the furs and feathers of animals in the mating season. On the contrary, they were trying to push life away, scare it off. And escape death.

Because death sought life. If you wanted to escape the former, then you had to frighten away the latter.

He carried on walking, deep in thought.

Merano.

"Town," as *Voter* Luis called it.

The pain in his leg was just a minor nuisance. The heating in the bus, the poppy, maybe little Anna's kiss, had all had their effect.

Not far from the bus station, on a square where some children were having a snowball fight, making a happy racket, there was a café. Inside, it was crowded. Women drinking steaming cups of coffee and eating slices of strudel with cream. Men underlining their words with emphatic gestures over glasses of spirits. The café also had a couple of small metal tables outside, along with some uncomfortable chairs. Keller sat down at one of the tables.

Whenever *Voter* Luis went into town (you could count these occasions on the fingers of one hand), he would always bring back two slices of *Sachertorte*, one for his wife, one for his son. Keller had not had any for years. He thought of Lissy, who had never got her slice of *Sachertorte*, and that made him a little sad.

He took a small package and a tin container out of his holdall and put them down on the table. Inside the package was the meal Marlene had prepared for him. Simon folded the napkin and was about to bite into the hard bread and speck when, to the words of a song ("Where is my happy ending?" a mawkish voice whined), a waiter came out of the café and approached him in an irritable, aggressive manner.

"You can't eat here, old man. Go away."

"I'd like a slice of *Sachertorte*."

"Are you deaf? You have to leave."

Keller put a couple of banknotes on the table. "I can pay. I'd like a slice of *Sachertorte*. No cream."

"You're scaring away the customers, you'd better leave. I don't want your wretched money."

Keller gave him a long stare, then put his hunting knife on the table next to the banknotes. "And I don't need any cutlery."

The waiter looked at him, then at the knife and withdrew. When he flung open the door, the background music had changed: a deep, gravelly voice was singing words that made Keller smile. "*Um Elf'e kommen die Wölfe, um Elf'e kommen die Wölfe, um Elfe kommen die Wölfe, um Zwölf'e bricht das Gewölbe.*"

The door closed. Keller took a couple of bites of the bread. All the customers in the café were now staring at him. A strange old man, tall and sturdy, with a hat on his head and a greatcoat as black as a raven's wings, nibbling at the bread with precise, methodical bites, heedless of the waiter's chiding. Heedless, too, of the café's fat owner, who was nodding and turning red as the waiter explained the situation to him with broad gestures.

"You have to leave."

Without waiting for a reply, the owner slapped Keller. The sandwich fell onto the dirty snow. Keller picked it up, then got to his feet. He smiled.

"I can pay. I just want a slice of *Sachertorte*. To see if it's as good as I remember it."

The owner put a hand on his shoulder. It was heavy. He squeezed, hard. "Just take your shit and go. I have a rifle behind the counter, and it's loaded."

Keller moved his face close to the owner's and let out a squeal, just like a pig who knows he's about to be slaughtered, although without losing his smile. That was what terrified the owner: the smile. His knees gave way, and Keller held him up.

"A slice of *Sachertorte*. Thank you."

He got it. Two slices, in fact. He ate one of them. It wasn't as good as he remembered. Too sweet. He wrapped the other slice in the cotton cloth.

After a final sip from his thermos, he stood up. Marlene had given him very specific directions to Herr Wegener's villa. Outside the town, by the river. An hour from the centre. He had time to look in a few shop windows.

With that strange Charlie Chaplin gait of his, he resumed his walk.

197

57

Gun loaded. Safety off.

Herr Wegener was alone, sitting on the bed he had shared with Marlene. The quilt in a heap in a corner, her pillow still redolent of her perfume. The 9-mm automatic, black and heavy, on his knees.

The window was wide open, and the breeze stirring the velvet curtains brought in sprays of sleet that melted on the carpet. Wegener felt the same way they did. Lost, weak, dying.

He wished he had the Iron Cross with him. Holding it tight in his fist might have brought him some comfort, but he had pinned it to the chest of a cruel man.

He had been regretting that for hours, remembering the moment when his father, his hands on his knees, his breath smelling of tobacco and coffee, his eyes filled with infinite sadness, had uttered the words that, years later, had prompted him to pick up the automatic, turn off the safety catch and cock the weapon.

"If you do the right thing nine times, it'll bring you nothing but sorrow. The tenth time, you'll understand why you did it. And you'll be glad you did."

Little Robert had not grasped the meaning of those words: he had been too innocent, too scared of that uniformed man who looked like his father but could not possibly be him, so pale and with such short hair. Kobold, who had little use for innocence and was blinded by hatred, had refused to understand them. Wegener, by now too tired to feel any hatred or fear, understood them as he watched the snow melting on the carpet.

His father had made the right choice. He had made an irreversible decision: to save his wife and son.

His father had not joined up in order to be a hero, or for ideological reasons, or because he was stupid, as Kobold had told himself so many times that he had ended up believing it.

His father was a peasant, the son of peasants. A man who, every time he shot a deer or a pheasant, would whisper a prayer, asking forgiveness of the spirit of the creature whose life he had taken to satisfy their hunger.

His father was a good man.

Kobold had mangled the surname of this son of peasants, just so that he could forget him. He would sooner have had the *Standartenführer*'s name. At present, Wegener wondered which of them had been the true hero: the S.S. colonel or the peasant with the wistful smile. Siegfried, who had taught the barefoot child to hate, or the peasant who had gone to his death in order to make the right choice?

Wegener took off his shoes, one after the other, then his socks. Barefoot, he stood up and walked to the window. The crisp air made him shiver. He took a handful of snow from the windowsill, went back to the bed and sat down again. He dropped the snow on the floor and trod on it.

"Teach me, Papa," he murmured. "Teach me to be brave."

To make the right choice.

He picked up the automatic. The gun was loaded and the safety catch was off. If he put it to his temple, it would all be over. He had heard that a bullet in the brain was not painful. It was like blowing a lightbulb. Game over.

The Consortium would have proof of his cowardice, but the sapphires would fall in value and the wrong would be righted. Maybe the Trusted Man would be called back and the order to kill Marlene (and Klaus) revoked. Then they would take everything.

The empire would be plundered.

The empire?

Wegener could see it clearly now, this empire of his. Illegal gambling dens, third-rate hotels for clandestine trysts, a handful of prostitutes to exploit, then throw away, smugglers with no future, drunks who acted tough. His *empire*, Wegener thought, was worth less than the snow now melting at his feet. It had never been anything but a dream, the illusion of a hungry child wandering through the woods.

Nine times out of ten . . .

"What is the right choice, Papa?" he asked the silent villa.

The villa did not answer. His father did not answer.

Nor did the man at the door.

Wegener saw first the shadow, then the man.

He thought: the *Standartenführer* was wrong. The Bogeyman does exist. He was not a soldier, the wretched son of a wretch, like his father. The man at the door was tall, with blue eyes, and was staring at him. He was holding a knife, and his hands were dripping with blood.

He was certainly not here to bring him chocolate.

All the same, Wegener smiled.

58

Lorenz Gasser.

It was three in the morning. Lying on his bed in a cheap hotel, the Trusted Man rubbed his chin with satisfaction. It was all in a black-and-white photograph. A newspaper cutting.

For the Trusted Man, research was part of the process. Whenever he drew up a contract with an important person (and he had dealt with more influential people than Herr Wegener), the first thing he did was look for information about him, more than about the target. Getting to know the predator was more useful than going straight for the prey. Why do some men prefer hunting deer to fly fishing? Find out and you'll know where to find the deer as well as the trout.

A man was all he wanted. The rest was just flesh and illusion.

And here he was.

Lorenz Gasser. The Vixen's accomplice.

The piece of paper the Trusted Man was triumphantly holding was part of one of the files he kept in his doctor's bag. A newspaper cutting stolen from a library archive. Newspapers were an excellent source of information, especially about men with heavy burdens on their conscience.

Sometimes they did not even know they had a conscience. They slept like children, these men. And yet something inside them drove them to seek atonement.

There was vanity in atonement, because powerful men liked to see themselves reflected in other people's eyes. There was no difference between contrition and wallowing in one's own sins. Rich men like Wegener called this vanity "charity." And that was precisely the subject of the article in the newspaper. A charity ball.

Christmas 1972. Illustrious guests. Wreaths. An over-decorated tree. Gifts for the underprivileged. In the photograph were Marlene and Herr Wegener. He was in a dinner suit. She looked stunning, hair gathered in a perfect chignon, her daring neckline brazenly displaying the flower of her youth. Was it surprising that all eyes were on the couple?

They were the embodiment of everyone's dreams: rich, attractive, happy. But the slender little man, only half of him in frame, wasn't staring at Marlene with admiration or even desire, but with *yearning*.

The slender little man had a name. It was there under the picture. The list of guests in the article was a long one. In fact, the piece was mostly made up of names, almost as if the reporter were afraid of leaving someone out. The slender little man was a big cheese in import–export. His name was the same as the one Dr. Zimmerman had written on that sheet of letter-headed paper.

Lorenz Gasser.

It was just a matter of finding him. That would not be difficult.

It was against the rules, but the Trusted Man was only too happy with this discovery. Besides, he was tired, and it was cold outside. He did not feel like getting up, getting dressed and going out just for a telephone call. He picked up the receiver and dialled the number.

A woman answered.

"Isabella, sorry to bother you. May I speak to your husband?"

59

A car hooted its horn, and Keller woke with a start. He had spent the night in the entrance hall of an apartment building, wrapped in his greatcoat, his holdall under his arm.

It was not yet daylight, and his knee was throbbing. Pain radiated down to his ankle and up to his groin. He tried to shake off the chill of a night spent without shelter. His back was so stiff, it took him a while to get back on his feet.

It had stopped snowing, and the temperature was some way below zero.

He felt his knee. It was swollen again. A knee like this, he thought, will never heal.

A handful of poppy seeds.

No, two would be better.

He filled his meerschaum pipe and leaned back against the wall, watching the few cars in the street and waiting for the poppy to take effect.

As he smoked, he smiled.

He had not felt this well for decades. For the first time since hearing the Voice, Keller dared to think about redemption. Killing Herr Wegener had been like making up for a mistake he had made many years earlier.

Not saving little Elisabeth.

It was as if he had somehow gone back in time and the paths of the present and the past had crossed, allowing him to protect, if not Lissy, then at least Marlene and the life she carried in her womb, by killing the man who was threatening her.

Miracle and mystery.

Maybe that was how it had been. Or maybe not.

Maybe it was the opium that made him think so. Or maybe not.

Keller heaved the holdall onto his shoulder and set off, limping, towards the bus station.

60

Funny how his calling Carbone's wife by her first name had made the captain act so quickly and efficiently. Less than half an hour later, he called back with the details of Lorenz Gasser, the slim little man in the newspaper cutting. He was slightly breathless. The Trusted Man thanked him kindly and asked him to convey his regards and apologies to Isabella. This scared Carbone even more.

The Trusted Man wiped the receiver, made his bed and paid the bill, leaving a tip that was neither too small nor too showy. He treated himself to a coffee at a service station and drove for the rest of the night. No Reschen Pass this time. He was heading east.

He crossed the Swiss–Austrian border and drove down to Brenner from there, stopped to stretch his legs and empty his bladder, had another coffee and a stale croissant while a drunk lorry driver rattled on about the end of the world and nuclear apocalypse to a sleepy barman and reached Brixen at around eight in the morning.

Finding the slim little man's house was child's play. It was a villa surrounded by a garden on the northern outskirts of the town. The Trusted Man forced the outside gate open and rang the doorbell. The door was opened by a sleepy man. Skinny, with just a few hairs on his head and protruding front teeth. The kind of man who thinks he is cleverer than anybody else. A ferret. So this was the Vixen's accomplice.

Lorenz Gasser.

"May I come in?"

The ferret did not object, merely glancing absently at the gun the Trusted Man was pointing at him, as if being threatened with death were a habitual occurrence.

He invited him to sit down.

The Trusted Man indicated a door through which the pounding of a shower could be heard. "Who's there?"

"A friend."

"Might this friend be a problem?"

"She's a whore. High class. Costs me a hundred and fifty thousand lire a night. I know her. She'll be in there for ages."

The Trusted Man crossed his legs. "Marlene Taufer."

Gasser rubbed his hands together. "I figured as much. Did Wegener send you?"

"One could say that."

"Or one could say the Consortium sent you."

"One could."

"Do you mind if I smoke?"

"You don't look scared."

"Why should I be? It's business. You want information, and I'm willing to give it to you. Free of charge. It's your lucky day."

"Let's hope it's your lucky day, too."

Gasser winced at this remark. "Marlene called me a couple of weeks ago. I can check my diary, if you like. I write everything down. I'm meticulous. She needed a favour. A favour Wegener knew nothing about."

"How did you meet her?"

"She's Wegener's wife, isn't she?" Gasser said, almost annoyed by the unnecessary question. "That son of a bitch drags her around with him like a trophy. 'Let me introduce you to my lovely wife . . .' At least I have the decency to keep whores in their place."

"Is Marlene a whore?"

Gasser displayed his nicotine-stained teeth. "By the way, you haven't told me your name."

"I'm the only entry missing from your diary, Herr Gasser."

"Are you asking me if I screwed that airhead Marlene?"

"I'm wondering what the nature of the exchange was."

A clucking laugh. "As a matter of fact, I did hope I might at first. Screw her every which way, if you know what I mean. And fuck that bastard. Just for the sake of . . . You must be wondering why I hate him so much."

"Envy. Pride. Frustrated ambition. Does it really matter? Time's flying, and by the time that shower's over you'll have a bullet in your head. Make it brief and no one will get hurt. Maybe."

The ferret licked his lips. "Marlene asks me a favour. She knows my professional field: insurance, banking. Insurance for private clinics. Merchant banks. I'm her man. I suppose she must have found my number in Wegener's notebook. We meet. I'm hoping for a good fuck, but what little Marlene offers me is even better, trust me."

"Sapphires," the Trusted Man said.

"Take a look around, my new friend with no name. Do you think I need money?"

"A hundred and fifty thousand a night is a substantial sum."

Gasser looked at him. "We both know what those sapphires represent."

"You tell me."

"The Consortium. Wegener wants to be a part of it."

"And so you agree because you know that this way Marlene will sabotage her husband's plans."

Gasser applauded.

"Give me the details."

"Could you put that away?"

The Trusted Man indulged him. The gun disappeared into the holster under his jacket.

"Marlene was supposed to get to the Reschen Pass between three and nine in the morning. During that time, she would meet a border guard who owes me a couple of favours and who would let her through with no fuss. Then she would go to the clinic. You know about the clinic?"

"Zimmerman."

"Terrible character, but efficient. I hope you didn't kill him."

"No."

"I paid in advance, out of my own pocket, to make sure the operation went according to plan. I was supposed to go there to pay my respects and conclude the exchange. I would convert Wegener's sapphires into dollars and new identity documents. Taking a reasonable commission. Fifteen per cent, if you want to know. Plus one sapphire. As a keepsake, let's say."

"Marlene trusted you."

Gasser grimaced. "You forget what a crook Wegener is. Marlene didn't come to me because of my pretty face, but because she was aware of the friction between me and her husband."

"Something went wrong."

The ferret absent-mindedly scratched a shin protruding from his pyjamas. "Marlene disappeared."

"Before the border."

"My man didn't see her. Not that day, not the following days."

The Trusted Man allowed himself a moment's reflection. Marlene had disappeared somewhere between Merano and the Reschen Pass. That narrowed the hunting ground. Vinschgau. The Passeier Valley. The Ulten Valley. And all the surrounding valleys. Not exactly a tiny area, but not the Wild West either.

He stood up.

"Are you leaving?"

Funny how such a shrewd operator had not picked up on such an important detail, the Trusted Man thought as he shook the ferret's hand. In sabotaging Wegener, Lorenz Gasser had hindered the Consortium's plans.

The Trusted Man was shaking hands with a dead man.

61

He had reached his destination.

The bus swerved just before completing its journey, and Keller, who had stood up early to get to the folding doors, had to hold on tight to stop himself from falling. Pain shot up from his knee, making him clench his teeth. The driver looked at him in the rearview mirror, as if daring him to complain about his driving. Keller got off.

There were a few people at the stop. Some meeting passengers, others saying goodbye.

Keller breathed in the ice-cold air and sat down on the church steps. He chewed on what was left of the hard bread prepared by Marlene and emptied the tin flask.

The bread tasted like the best thing he had ever eaten. Even so, the night he had spent in the open had left its mark. His knee demanded respite. He doubled the dose of poppy seeds.

He could not get the tune heard in the café in Merano out of his head. He hummed it until he felt the seeds flow through his veins in a warm wave. He stood up and took a few tentative steps towards the mountains. As he reached the square, halfway between the general store and a couple of houses, his knee gave out without warning and he collapsed to the ground.

A little boy popped his head around a door, stuck a finger in his mouth and closed the door immediately.

Keller ran his gloved hand over his face and cursed himself. With some difficulty, he got back on his feet.

The little boy came out, wearing a scarf, heavy boots and an open padded jacket. He said nothing, just stared at him.

"You should zip that jacket up. You'll catch cold."

The little boy ran away.

Once out of the village, Keller put on the snowshoes, took a little more poppy and set off.

62

He put in the telephone tokens.

There was a message. No begging this time, no lamentations or threats. It wasn't Herr Wegener's voice the Trusted Man found on his voicemail. It was Carbone asking him to call the villa. He sounded breathless.

"Wegener's dead," he said succinctly. "He's been murdered."

Five rings. A stranger picked up.

"Could you put me through to Captain Carbone, please?"

"Who's speaking?"

"Right away."

"I must have your name."

"Carbone, please."

Something about his tone persuaded the man at the other end to obey.

There was some bustling, then the captain's voice. He sounded hesitant. "Is that you?"

"When?"

"They found him half an hour ago. I thought it best to call you."

The Trusted Man glanced at his watch. It was just before four. He calculated the time it would take him to get there. "Don't touch *anything.*"

He hung up, walked back to his car and headed for Merano. It was dusk, and he turned on the headlights.

It was only after several kilometres that he realised he had not wiped the telephone receiver. The realisation filled him with sadness.

63

Dusk at the *maso*.

Marlene had spent the night, the previous day and the night after Keller's departure in such a heightened state of anxiety that she had eaten practically nothing. She had slept fitfully, curled up by the window, waiting. She had fed the pigs (though Lissy had not come out) and done a lot of thinking.

About Klaus, whom she could feel throbbing inside her so strongly.

About what she would tell him of the mystery of his birth, the theft and her escape in the night.

Above all, about what to tell him of the man in dark clothes who, the moment he came in through the front door of the *maso*, his face drained of colour, took his holdall off his shoulder and, with a smile, put a crumpled package down on the table in the *Stube*.

"It's for the two of you."

A slice of *Sachertorte*, a bit squashed but still in one piece. Marlene's eyes filled with tears.

"It's good," Keller said, sitting down on the bench. "A bit too sweet, though."

"I didn't think I'd ever see you again."

"Why ever not?" Keller said, stuffing tobacco into his pipe. "He's a reasonable man."

Marlene blinked. "Reasonable?"

"We talked. He understood. He's a good man. He wishes you well in your new life."

Marlene felt her legs give way beneath her. She did not so much sit down as sink. "I can't . . ."

"You can't believe it?"

"He . . ."

Keller looked at her with his piercing eyes. "Or is it just that you don't *want* to believe it?"

That was indeed the crux of the matter.

Herr Wegener, the Herr Wegener she knew, had never given anybody a second chance. Giving someone a second chance, he would say, was like shooting yourself in the foot. And yet Simon Keller was right here in front of her, alive. He had brought her a slice of *Sachertorte*. If Herr Wegener had not agreed to the exchange, then Moritz would be here instead of Keller or else Georg. Or Wegener in person. Not with a slice of cake but a gun.

Unless . . .

Marlene looked up at Keller, who was smoking his meerschaum pipe and studying her.

A *murder*.

Like the killing of *Voter* Luis. Not murder. Justice.

Could killing Herr Wegener be considered another act of justice?

"What's that nice smell?" Keller said.

Marlene stood up. "Barley soup. I hope it's good."

It was.

They ate, and after the meal Marlene prepared poppy tea. Keller accepted it gratefully. They laughed and joked the whole time while having dinner. Keller told her about the shop windows, the dummies dressed in clothes that had left him speechless, and Marlene laughed with him at his naivety – although the correct word was "innocence."

Murder. *Two* murders.

Justice.

Revenge.

Could an innocent man be guilty? That was a question she could

213

not answer. Because the question itself was wrong. The right question had been asked by Simon Keller: "Or is it just that you don't *want* to believe it?"

That was the crux of the matter. Either you had faith or you didn't. There were no half-measures.

Marlene split the slice of cake in two, but Keller declined.

He just had a glass of spirits to warm his bones. He did not offer her any. Pregnant women were not supposed to drink alcohol. Marlene could allow herself beer, but only stout, and only while breastfeeding. It was written in one of the old Bibles. Stout helped women produce milk.

Keller seemed happy and excited. "I have some money," he suddenly said. "It's not much, but I can give it to you."

"I could never accept."

"It's not for you. It's for your son."

"You've already done so much for us."

"You don't like accepting money, I can understand that." Keller touched the shirt Marlene had made for him. "Then let's just call it payment. I've never had such nice clothes. Nicer than the ones in town. It costs a lot to raise a child. Modern children are even more of a commitment. That's the way it is. They need toys. A feather bed with cotton sheets. An apartment with electricity and central heating. Breathing chimney smoke isn't good for them. And books. Lots of books. Children must read a lot. And they need medicines and . . ." He broke off with a sigh and smiled. "All that costs a great deal."

Marlene placed a hand on her belly. You couldn't see it yet but she could feel herself growing a little bigger every day. Maybe I won't call you Klaus, she thought.

"Simon's a beautiful name," she said.

64

Keller still had his clothes on. He had been so exhausted, he hadn't had the energy to take them off. He had only removed his boots and undone the top button of his white shirt.

He was lying on the bed, beneath the blankets, eyes closed, jaw clenched. The poppy was starting to take effect. He could feel his muscles relax. The pain was easing off.

Marlene's words had touched him deeply. In the dark, he pictured her child's face. A little boy with his mother's blue eyes and his father's strong-willed chin. And, of course, the beauty spot.

Half asleep, Keller smiled. Of course, the beauty spot: identical to the bloodstain on Elisabeth's face. The beginning and end of the mystery-filled circle that was his life. One that started with Elisabeth's blood and ended with Wegener's.

And so: redemption.

He imagined taking the little boy by the hand. A beautiful, lively child with scores of questions demanding answers. Why do marmots sleep so long? And what do they dream about all winter? He pictured taking him sledging. Teaching him about herbs: devil's claw, willow bark, larch bark. Watching him rolling around in the snow and doing somersaults. Buying wool and learning to knit in order to give him a scarf as a gift.

Keller drifted closer to sleep.

Obviously, a child couldn't live up here, in the *maso*. It was too cold, too solitary. He would get ill. Besides, it was important for children to go to school. He himself had never been. *Voter* Luis had taught him to read, write and do sums, but those were different times. Education was essential. Moreover, it was important for children to learn to be with others. Life took place in towns these days, side by side with other people. It was important to get used to that. Marlene's son might even go to university. Become a doctor, who could say?

The boy could come and see him in the summer, during the holidays. Why not? In the summer, the air was clean and good for the lungs. The smog in towns was harmful to children and made them weak. Spending time in the fields would strengthen him. Plus, the nights up here were not as stiflingly hot as they were down there.

The little girl on the bus had called him *Opa*. Grandpa. *Opa* Simon: he liked the sound of it. He imagined the boy calling him *Opa*.

He imagined buying a couple of hens and a cow. Top-quality eggs for breakfast and milk and sugar to help the boy grow healthy. Yes, it was a good idea.

His heart was at peace.

For him, it was a strange feeling.

Shortly before the darkness wrapped itself around him like a soothing blanket, just as his mind was plunging into oblivion, he heard the Voice. It was teasing him.

Do you really believe that a new outfit can change anything?

65

The villa was all lit up.

The carabiniere by the door had never felt so cold in his life. He wasn't used to it and doubted he ever would he. He hated the cold, and he was in a foul mood. He had been here for ages. Surely the captain should have finished by now. Instead of which, Carbone had sent away the officers who were supposed to remove the body and had ensconced himself in the villa as if he never meant to come out again. He had said he needed to think. When the examining magistrate had asked him to let him get on with his work, he had hurled insults at him. Furious, the magistrate had left.

The young carabiniere had been serving under Carbone for almost a year and, all things considered, he thought he was a good chief. He did not demand any more from his men than he was willing to do himself. If work ran over, he would immediately take the heaviest tasks upon himself and would be the last one to go home.

There were rumours about the captain, that he was in cahoots with some shifty characters, and a couple of times the young carabiniere had actually seen odd individuals go into his office, people who were clearly Secret Service. Still, the young man did not believe most of these rumours. Besides, Carbone not only always enquired after his parents, he had never refused him leave.

But tonight Carbone looked scared. He had given orders that made no sense and had even been rude to the examining magistrate.

The car drew up, almost splashing the young carabiniere with melted snow and mud. He stepped forward to protest. The man who got out looked like an actor. A Hollywood actor, though he could not remember the name.

Somebody famous, anyway.

66

The stench of stale cigarette smoke in the air, and, beneath it, the smell of blood.

The Trusted Man looked down at Wegener, lying on his back on the floor. He was puzzled by the expression on his face. He saw fear in it (and who wasn't afraid when faced with death?), but there was something else. He stood there for a long time, thinking, while the pale young carabiniere stood at the door and Carbone smoked one cigarette after the other.

The Trusted Man got down on one knee, taking care to avoid the pool of congealed blood. Wegener had not even tried to defend himself. The gun lay there, loaded and with the safety catch off. He could have used it, could have reacted. But he had not done so.

The Trusted Man stood up. He tried to picture the dynamics of the murder.

Georg, Wegener's bodyguard, had been killed in the garden. The carabinieri had found his body in the snow-covered bushes. He had not died immediately, but had evidently taken a while to bleed to death. A rushed job, Captain Carbone said. The Trusted Man disagreed.

Whoever had killed Georg had sliced his jugular with a single cut. The blade must have been big and sharp, at least thirty centimetres long, something like a hunting knife. The killer had not been hasty, he had been thorough. He had come in through the front door, gone up the stairs and into Wegener's bedroom. A tall, well-built man. There was a footprint in the pool of blood. A size forty-five mountain boot.

Not a vixen. Not a ferret. Something larger.

The Trusted Man went to the bookshelf, pulled out a couple of volumes of the Treccani Encyclopaedia and put them on the floor. Then he took the young carabiniere by the arm and made him stand in front of him, about an arm's length away.

He stood up on the books. "How tall are you?"

The young carabiniere looked first at the Trusted Man, then at Carbone, who signalled to him to answer.

"One metre seventy-five."

More or less the same as Wegener.

The Trusted Man added two more volumes of the encyclopaedia and once again stepped up onto the pile. Now he was towering over the carabiniere. He reached down, took a ballpoint pen from the pocket of his uniform and quickly ran it under the carabiniere's throat.

The young man jerked back.

"Keep still."

"You—"

"Do as you're told."

The carabiniere got back into position.

The Trusted Man added one more volume and repeated the action. The young carabiniere held his breath when he felt the point of the pen dragged across his Adam's apple.

"Thank you. You can go."

Relieved, the carabiniere took his pen and left the room.

"Our friend," the Trusted Man said, "is no doe. She's a vixen with many friends: a ferret and now . . . this is a different animal."

Carbone studied the Trusted Man's face intently. "What are you talking about?"

"A wolf. I think it was a wolf."

The captain took a step back. "Can't you see he's been stabbed? Do you really think a wolf could have . . ."

The Trusted Man smiled. "I know, there are no wolves in South Tyrol."

"And you know wolves can't stab."

"Ah, but this is a special wolf. One metre ninety, I think. Strong, with a firm hand. It's a clean cut. No second thoughts, no hesitation. An irreversible act."

"Maybe a Consortium man," Carbone said in a low voice.

"In that case, why didn't he use a gun?"

Carbone shrugged. "Strange business, don't you think?"

"Why didn't Wegener defend himself?"

"He was taken by surprise."

The Trusted Man pointed to the space between the body and the door. "Six metres. The gun was loaded and the safety catch was off. Even if the killer had started running, Wegener would have had plenty of time to fill him with lead."

Carbone lit his umpteenth cigarette and shook his head. "None of this makes any sense."

"Have you looked at him carefully?"

"I was here for three hours before you deigned to arrive," the captain snapped back.

"Look into his eyes. What do you see?"

"Fear. Death. Nothing. What do you expect to see in the eyes of a corpse?"

"Relief. Wegener had been expecting death for a long time."

This startled the captain. "You think he knew the killer?"

"Not the killer. Death."

"That doesn't make any sense. Wegener was a son of a bitch, and believe me, there'll be a lot of us celebrating."

The Trusted Man jabbed two fingers at Carbone's chest. "I had a connection with this man, don't you understand that? A very strong connection. There are some things I won't allow you to say in my presence."

Carbone let the cigarette slip from his fingers.

The Trusted Man was upset. The veins on his neck stood out, and he looked pale and drawn.

Good God, the captain thought, it's as if an actual friend of his has died.

"Wegener's death changes nothing," the Trusted Man said. "Until I tell you otherwise, you'll continue to report to me and me alone. Is that clear?"

Captain Carbone had been involved in five separate shootouts. He had once been grazed by a bullet. He had trampled over guilty and innocent men alike. He had lied to magistrates and to his own conscience. He had never experienced such terror before. "Of course."

"Marlene is still out there. Somewhere. I know it. And she's scared."

"How can you tell?"

"If she's behind this, it means she's scared. And if she's scared it means she knows she can be found. She's still out there."

"Where?"

"It's never a matter of where. Trust me, it's merely a matter of when."

67

One week. Seven days of keeping the *maso* tidy, making clothes for Simon Keller, preparing meals, feeding the pigs. Breathing. It was as if Marlene had been living in limbo up till now. It was not just the mountain air, it was Keller's words.

For the first time in her life, Marlene was not thinking of the past and was not worrying about the future. She was living in the present, the here and now. Her major concern was giving the pigs the correct mix of feed, preparing the wood for the stove and the infusions to ease Simon Keller's pain. Making sure he got enough rest. Telling him off, gently, when he went out hunting. Then, she thought, once he had regained his strength, she would ask him to take her to the village, say goodbye to him (goodbye, not farewell) and see what fate had in store for her.

Marlene was no fool. She knew Simon Keller had lied to her, she knew he had killed Wegener. That was the only reason the two of them – the three of them, actually – were still alive.

God alone knew what was going on in town. She pictured carabinieri and police drinking a toast to her husband's death and doing the absolute minimum to bring his killer to justice. Wegener had been hated, and men who are hated seldom receive justice. She imagined Georg and Moritz swiping gold and valuables from the villa on the Passer to sell on the black market. And no doubt looking for new employers to whom they could offer their talent for violence.

The cars auctioned off. The villa sold. The boutique, too.

What about Gabriel? She tried to picture him happy. She was fond of him.

Wegener had died the way he had lived: violently. And in killing him, Simon Keller had not just protected her and her child. He had saved an untold number of her husband's future victims. Was that crazy?

No, it was *right*.

She kept repeating it to herself every day. It was not a murder, it was justice. It was not wrong, it was right. Marlene was sick and tired of feeling she was in the wrong.

And she remained happy all week.

68

Not Keller, though. No, he was unwell. Very unwell.

He did his best to stop Marlene from noticing. He made jokes, expressed delight at the sunshine outside and stood as still as a scarecrow as the young woman with blue eyes (and the beauty spot at the end of her smile) measured his neck, chest and arms for new clothes. Later, once the night took control of his thoughts, and hiding them became more painful than the vice around his knee, he smoked his meerschaum pipe, looking blissful and praising the cook for a delicious dinner.

It was all a lie.

Keller kept hearing the Voice. It was ever more insistent. In the dark, its call was so loud that it drowned out every other thought. As he lay curled up in bed, his hands over his ears, trembling, it would make him dribble like a baby. When the Voice started screaming, he would put his trouser belt between his teeth and bite down on it to stop himself from crying out. He did not want Marlene to hear.

The Voice would insult him, flatter him, threaten him.

Sometimes it would whisper.

Of course, it was asking for just one thing, always the same thing. Blood.

It was his duty, the Voice kept saying, his duty to kill. The Voice never said it explicitly, but Keller knew perfectly well whose lives had to be cut short.

Marlene. And the child she was carrying.

That would never happen. He would never do it. He couldn't do it. It wasn't right. He didn't *want* to. In shedding Wegener's blood, he had closed the circle, and now he had plans, hopes.

The Voice would not let him go.

During that week's anguish-filled nights, Keller clung to the image of a boy with Marlene's blue eyes and his father's chin. He wanted to see him grow healthy, strong, sturdy. He would teach him about herbs, build him a sledge. They would look at the starry sky together, and he would tell him that the universe teems with mysteries but also with miracles and springtimes.

He wanted to hear the boy him call him "Opa Simon."

But the Voice was as unstoppable as an avalanche during a thaw. And so, crushed between the crude reality of that call and the imagined serenity he would offer Marlene, Keller had come up with a kind of compromise and put it into practice.

He had taken the rifle and gone hunting in the woods, for the Voice. He would kill animals. Blood for blood. A life for a life. Just as it was written.

He had killed much more game than he needed, and for that he felt guilty, but he clung to the illusion that these lives had not been wasted.

Three days earlier, his hunting bag still empty, exasperated by the Voice, made anxious by the approaching darkness that would stop him from sacrificing blood, he had gone as far as the top of the mountain, and there, a few minutes before sunset, surrounded by sharp rocks, shivering with cold, he had seen the silhouette of an ibex against the dying light, a proud animal with a powerful chest and long, curved antlers. He had fired, and the ibex had fallen from the cliff with a thud. He had not collected it. It was too cold for that. But for that day, at least, the blood had been shed.

He told Marlene that a pregnant woman needed fresh meat. He told himself that, too, during daylight hours, as a way of calming himself down and convincing himself that he had not become a

226

menace. He told himself it was the right thing to do. That it was his own will, not the Voice, that was making him hunt. A pregnant woman needed fresh meat if she wanted to give birth to a strong, healthy child. She needed fruit and vegetables as well, so he vowed to go down to the valley and buy some. But he never did.

If he went to the village, he would not be able to shoot, and deep in his heart he knew why the animals had to be killed. This was his compromise: trading animal blood against Marlene's.

He had to protect her. He was no longer delicate young Sim'l, incapable of stopping his father's hand. He was a man, a strong man. The past would not repeat itself.

And so he hunted. Blood in exchange for other blood. A life for a life.

And in fact, the Voice did fall silent after the killings.

For a while, anyway.

69

Captain Carbone had left a message, and two hours later they met in the café on the square, not far from the bus station.

It was a quiet place, with few customers, small tables, background music and a display of cakes. The owner, a fat man who looked like a drunk, was talking to Carbone. He had a wary expression, while Carbone was all smiles. The Trusted Man knocked on the glass window and gestured for them to come outside. You could never be too careful.

Despite the cold weather, the fat man was in his shirtsleeves. He looked the Trusted Man up and down, arms crossed. The Trusted Man did not introduce himself. Carbone obliged: a trusted colleague, a friend.

"Tell us again what you told me earlier."

The fat man did not need to be asked twice. "He was tall. I'm one metre eighty and this guy was almost a head taller than me. Old, maybe sixty. Looking older, if you see what I mean. I see a lot of people here, and trust me, this man had come down from the mountains. A cheapskate."

"Who are we talking about?"

"Your oddity," Carbone said.

The Trusted Man had ordered him to report anything out of the ordinary that might have happened on the day of Wegener's murder, no matter how insignificant. The fat man's story was not the only one. Funny how so many bizarre events could occur in such a sleepy town. On the other hand, even just looking at the clouds you can make out all kinds of shapes.

Carbone had neglected nothing. As soon as his men reported a burglary, a tip-off, a drunken brawl, he would rush to the scene, investigate, ask questions. The Trusted Man was doing the same.

Even though up to now none of his meetings with the captain had led anywhere and the trail was going cold, the Trusted Man knew that looking at the clouds was not always a waste of time.

"For crying out loud, he actually grunted like a pig."

This rekindled his interest. "Who?"

The fat man huffed with annoyance. "Are you listening to me or are you deaf?"

The Trusted Man smiled.

The fat man turned pale. "I . . . mean no offence."

"A tall man, you say. One metre ninety, could we say?"

"It's possible."

"And he scared you."

"Yes, he did."

The Trusted Man raised an eyebrow. The bar owner had biceps like hams and looked like someone who picked fights. "An old man. You were scared of an old man."

"You'd have wet yourself if you'd been there."

"I doubt that."

The fat man was about to retort, but Carbone took hold of his arm to restrain him.

"Tell us everything from the beginning. Calmly."

The old man, dressed in black, had sat at the table. That one. The waiter had immediately seen that he wasn't all there in the head. Because he had taken out bread and speck and started eating. A kind of travel bag like the ones sailors carry. No, not a rucksack. A bag, alright? Just a bag.

"Please go on."

The fat man was becoming incensed. It was a bar, not a damn soup kitchen for retards and the homeless. So the waiter had told him to clear off. Nothing doing. Yes, perhaps he was scared, too. In fact, he really was scared, because he had come back inside and told him to get the rifle he kept under the counter.

"A rifle?"

Just to be on the safe side. There are a lot of weirdos around. But he had not brought it out. After all, it was just an old man, right? And they didn't realise just how crazy he was. He had a knife, with a blade this long. A hunting knife. No, he hadn't used it to threaten him. He had just put it down on the table. Are you even listening to me?

As the café owner talked, the Trusted Man nodded. It all fit together. The bus station. The Wolf. A scary old man.

Once he had what he needed, he left Carbone and the café owner talking and, without saying goodbye, headed for the bus station.

There were not that many buses listed on the timetable as arriving around the time the Wolf had been kicking up all that fuss in the café on the square. They all came from the west. A good sign.

The captain joined him. "What do you think?"

"The picture's becoming clearer."

"That's what I think."

The Trusted Man cocked his head, intrigued. "Really?"

"He's not a professional. A professional doesn't leave traces. There's no way a hitman would pick an argument with a guy like that."

"One more point for me. It was you who mentioned a hitman."

Carbone nodded. "That's true. You were right. And he might have left other clues. Plus, if he took the bus, it means he doesn't own a car."

"A man who came down from the mountains."

"Which tells us . . ."

Far from being annoyed by Carbone's attitude, the Trusted Man cut him some slack. "That Marlene got lost. Or that she changed her mind at the last minute. It's a possibility. Perhaps the clinic business was a diversion."

"Bull's eye."

230

"There's one thing I don't agree with you on, Captain."

"What?"

The Trusted Man took a deep breath of bus-station air saturated with exhaust fumes. "Although he isn't a hitman, I think he *is* a professional. I think he's used to death. You see, if what our friend in the café said is true, then the Wolf didn't attack but merely bared his teeth."

Carbone lit a cigarette. "He growled. He's crazy."

"Pigs are nasty animals. But they're not stupid."

"I still don't follow you."

"I'm saying he bared his teeth because death is something he's familiar with."

"He's used to violence."

"Not to violence. It was a clean, efficient cut, remember? He's used to death."

"Aren't violence and death the same thing?"

The Trusted Man put a hand on Carbone's shoulder. "You stick to using violence, Captain. Leave death to people like me."

He moved a few steps away.

Carbone threw the cigarette he had just lit down on the pavement. "What are my orders? Do you want me to keep looking?"

"Forget about this business."

"What about you?"

"I'll ask around. I'm very good at making friends, you know."

They had reached Carbone's car.

"What about us? Are we friends?"

The Trusted Man studied his face. "Would you like us to be?"

"I'd like to be able to sleep with both eyes shut."

"Who wouldn't like that, Captain?"

Carbone did not know how to respond. He opened the car door.

The Trusted Man put up the collar of his coat. "Give my regards to your wife."

70

Crouching behind a mound, waiting for his prey to sniff the trap, Keller traced a perfect circle in the snow with his gloved index finger.

The world teemed with mysteries. They all had the shape of a perfect circle. That was one of the first lessons *Voter* Luis had taught him.

How does the marmot sleep for months without being sucked into a dream world? What do stars breathe that makes them burn so bright? How, after months of being trapped in ice, does the earth manage to yield fruit in spring?

Mysteries.

And yet every spring burst with crops, the marmot emerged from its sleep and the stars continued to glitter in the dark. Over and over again.

Miracles.

The world was a mystery and a miracle, and the shape of the mystery was a circle. Lissy's incarnations were also a circle. The seasons changed, times changed, but Lissy was always the same. The first Lissy had given birth to a sow a little blacker and a little bigger than herself. The first Lissy had died. The new Lissy had started the circle all over again. Weak, sickly pigs until the final litter, when a female was born, blacker, bigger and hungrier.

A perfect circle.

The first Lissy had asked for just one sacrifice: *Voter* Luis. The second for another one: a traveller, frozen half to death, whom Keller had come across on his way back from the village. Killing him, he had told himself, had almost been an act of pity.

The third Lissy, the first to grow fangs instead of teeth, had asked for three: two poachers Keller had surprised in their sleep in early May and a woman in the autumn of that same year. It was hard to kill a woman. She had begged him to spare her and tried to reason with him. When he had told the woman about the Voice in his head, she had stopped screaming and tried to run away. He had had to run after her. About the men he remembered nothing, not even their faces.

But he did remember his fear when a carabiniere in camouflage clothing had knocked on his door and shown him a picture of the woman who had tried to run away. Her name was Gertrud Kofler. She had gone missing while picking mushrooms, he said. Had he seen her, by any chance? The Voice had told him what to say. It had worked. The carabiniere had asked if he could fill his flask. He had never come back. Keller had been nervous for months after that, and ever since, there had always been a Gertrud in the pigsty below the *maso*. Gertrud the fugitive.

Lissy's fourth incarnation had claimed two lives. The fifth, another three, two of whom had tried to fight back. The sixth, the mother of the Lissy Marlene knew, had been born without fangs but was the first with that kind of albino tuft on top of her head, between her ears. She had wanted just one victim: a doctor who had got lost and knocked at the door of the *maso*, demanding help and looking disgusted when he saw the mess in the *Stube*.

Killing him had been a pleasure.

Meanwhile, the Voice had taught him many ways of throwing investigators off the scent. Keeping items of clothing and leaving them in valleys far from the *maso*. Scattering bullet-ridden shreds of flesh for the sniffer dogs, to suggest a gangland slaying. Keller was no longer afraid of being found out.

The Lissy Marlene knew was the seventh incarnation, the first to be born with two white stripes under her eyes. She was the biggest, blackest and hungriest of them all. So far, she had demanded nineteen sacrifices, and she was not even three years old yet. Lissy was hungry. Lissy was always hungry.

A rustling in the woods.

Keller adjusted the butt of the rifle against his shoulder and kept the barrel trained on the bale of fragrant hay in the middle of the clearing. That was where he had set his trap.

A deer emerged from the bushes and sniffed the air hesitantly. Simon put his finger on the trigger, ready to shoot as soon as the animal came out into the open.

The deer, a beautiful doe, approached the bale of hay, nostrils quivering. Keller waited. The deer snatched a mouthful, its thigh muscles quivering, ready to flee at the slightest sign of danger. A second mouthful, then a third. The animal's breath condensed in little blue clouds. Keller squeezed the trigger.

The deer stepped to the side, at first frightened by the shot, then surprised by the sudden pain in its chest. One last little cloud of breath, and its heart stopped beating. It fell to the ground, dead by the time it hit the snow.

Keller propped the rifle against the mound, took out his knife and began walking down the slope – slowly, because his knee hurt.

Hunting was not a clean business, let alone a sport. The animal had to be gutted as soon as possible to stop the body fluids from poisoning the meat.

It took him a while to reach the spot where the deer lay on its back. As he did so, he thought once more with amazement that the world truly did teem with mysteries.

For instance, how could the deer, lying in its own blood, lift its head towards him, even though his best bullet had hit it right in the heart? How could the deer speak, speak like a human being and not an animal?

234

What Keller saw as he got to the circular clearing in the forest was no longer the deer, its chest torn apart by the bullet, but little Elisabeth propped up on the bale of hay, her hands on her stomach, her little dress stained with blood. Sweet little Elisabeth staring at him with those wide-open eyes of hers, eyes full of mystery and questions. "Why? Why? Why are you doing this to me?"

Keller dropped his knife.

"Why? Why? Why do you want to kill me?"

Keller rubbed his eyes, pressing hard until lights flashed in the darkness behind his closed lids. He opened them again and was astonished to see that Elisabeth was still there, looking at him and asking, "Why? Why? Why do you want to hurt me?"

He went closer.

"I'm hungry," Elisabeth whimpered. "Give me something to eat, Sim'l. Why won't you give me something to eat? I'm so hungry. Please."

Keller looked at the little girl in the blood-stained dress, the blue flames glowing in her eyes, and his shock was swept away.

Just as when *Voter* Luis had grabbed the knife to kill Elisabeth, Keller understood.

The Voice.

The Voice that had been with him all his life belonged to Lissy. It had always been her. She was not up there, at Mutti's side. She had always been at *his* side. Always. She had never abandoned him. He had never been alone.

"Sweet Sim'l," she whispered. "Little Sim'l . . ."

Keller's eyes filled with tears. He kneeled in the snow and took her in his arms. Her hair smelled of hay and sunshine – and blood. He cradled her.

"I'm so hungry, Sim'l. Why won't you give me something to eat?"

He stroked her hair, then moved her face away from his chest in order to reply.

He heard a noise behind him and turned with a start.

He smiled.

Yes, the universe truly did teem with mysteries.

71

His name was Alex and he was a poacher.

Not that he was born that way, as he insisted on saying whenever he got close to someone, usually after the third beer. He was not yet thirty and had never turned down a job in his life. He had been born to get his hands dirty.

But he was not stupid. He was sensible. He knew he was often asked to do things that went beyond legality. Poaching was just one of many examples. He was not proud of it, but when the owner of the sawmill had made him redundant Alex had had to make his principles a little more flexible.

Poaching was a good way of scraping together a few pennies. It was hard work, but he had never been put off by hard work. Of course, life at the sawmill had been something else. Set working hours, a routine as comfortable as a pair of old slippers. You could tell the odd joke, have a laugh. He had liked that job.

Then the Arabs in the Middle East started throwing tantrums, there was a crisis, and he was made redundant.

Staff cuts. The first time he had heard that expression, he had thought of a huge butcher's counter, its tiles spattered with blood, on which Herr Egger, the sawmill owner, had put him and three of his other colleagues to turn them into sausages and fillets. The other three had cried and begged, one of them had turned to the unions, but Alex, realising it was a lost cause, had not been discouraged. He was strong and was not afraid of elbow grease. Plus, unlike his colleagues, he was a bachelor and had no mouths to feed. He had started looking for a new job.

He had to admit it, the past summer had been fun. He had cut hay and repaired roofs: plenty of fresh air, a healthy lifestyle. Best of all had been the month he had spent working in the market. It had been an opportunity to meet a lot of people and watch girls' legs as they walked down the street.

Winter, though, had been another story. No seasonal jobs, no jobs indoors where it was warm. No prospects. His savings had shrunk to almost zero. So he had started smuggling rucksacks full of cigarettes across the border and poaching. Restaurant owners were not interested in where this or that stag came from. Their only concern was to get meat at a reasonable price, and Alex was always prepared to haggle. He enjoyed it. He found it fun.

The actual poaching wasn't bad either, apart from the cold. Sometimes he was so cold he felt like weeping. But not for long. Work was work, and he was born to work hard. Sooner or later, winter would be over and he would go back to working in the market. Pretty girls, jokes, nice things to eat.

Alex had come all the way up here on the trail of a deer. A nice large female. That same deer the old man in black had killed with a shot that had drawn a whistle of admiration from him. A hundred metres, was it? A hundred and fifty?

Alex approached to compliment him, but also to have a chat. He had been wandering alone for hours, and he liked the idea of exchanging a few words with a stranger. He was already holding his flask of grappa, ready to offer it, when he saw the old man in the greatcoat do something truly unusual.

Alex had seen quite a few crazy people in his time, but never one like this.

The old man was hugging the deer, getting his dark clothes smeared with blood. He was rocking it and muttering heaven knows what.

"Hey!" Alex said, emerging from the woods.

The old man turned to him. He had pale eyes, his face was white and he was crying.

"A soft heart, I see," Alex said jokingly. He showed him the small bottle of grappa. "I'm joking. It happens to me, too. I feel sorry for these poor animals. Still, we have to live somehow. I'm Alex. What's your name?"

The old man muttered something.

Alex went closer. "I saw the shot. Where did you learn to shoot like that? Were you in the war? I bet you were. How far was it, two hundred metres? I've never seen a shot like that. Tell me the truth. You're a marksman, aren't you? I didn't catch your name."

The old man laid the carcass of the deer down and traced a circle in the snow with his finger.

"Great. What is it? You're not dumb, are you?"

But then the old man spoke. Strange words, uttered in a tone Alex was unable to interpret. Gentle, yet at the same time menacing. "Lissy is hungry."

Then they both heard her calling.

A young woman emerged from the woods, out of breath.

72

It was the fault of the wind.

After Keller had put his rifle over his shoulder and gone hunting, Marlene prepared the slop for the pigs and went down to the sty. She fed the sows and the boars, then got the silver bowl ready, put on the steel glove and opened the little grille.

Lissy approached. It was the first time she had done that. Usually, this huge black animal would retreat into the shadows as soon as Marlene came in and stay there until she left. But not today.

Puzzled by this unusual behaviour, Marlene kept still, hearing the sow's deep breathing, smiling at her, ready to bolt at the first sign of aggression. Keller had warned her often enough about Lissy. She was dangerous. Never lower your guard. With those fangs ...

The sow stopped less than half a metre away, her fat hips moving like bellows. She turned her head to one side and studied Marlene with her right eye. The pupil narrowed and widened, depending on the swaying of the oil lamp hanging from the beam. The jangling of the little bell around the sow's broad, powerful neck, on the other hand, followed the rhythm of her breathing. Marlene reached out with her steel-covered hand. Lissy snorted but did not move. Marlene bent down a little.

Lissy stood motionless.

Marlene stroked the silky tuft between her ears. Lissy cocked her head towards the steel glove, which was motionless in mid-air. Marlene held her breath.

Lissy licked her fingers.

Marlene reached out with her other hand. She felt the animal's hard bristle beneath her fingertips. She smoothed it until she found the base of her ears, then scratched.

The sow emitted a sound which Marlene could not figure out at first. It was almost as if she were purring. What was it Simon Keller always said?

Sweet Lissy, little Lissy.

The sow shifted to the side, and Marlene pulled her hand away. Lissy flicked her tail, whipping the air, then came back towards her.

"Do you want to be cuddled?"

Lissy grunted.

Marlene giggled and stroked her again. "We're becoming friends, aren't we?"

Lissy opened her jaws, her eyes rolled back and she fell on her side.

Marlene leaped to her feet.

The sow was moving her legs about, kicking. Foam started coming out of her mouth. Her eyes had rolled up in their sockets, her legs stiffened. She was shaking, foaming at the mouth.

"Lissy?"

The sow emitted a frightful moan. She was dying. Marlene ran out and set off for the woods, screaming Simon Keller's name at the top of her voice.

73

It was not because of the deer. Well, partly. But mainly it was because of the woman. Even dressed the way she was, her face flushed from running (or perhaps it was precisely because of her flushed face), Alex was unable to resist. She was his type. Petite, well proportioned, with big blue eyes.

But when he saw her disappear with the strange old man (who the hell was Lissy?) he told himself he had to go after them because of the deer. They had forgotten all about it. It was a waste just leaving it there.

Of course, the idea of heaving it over his shoulder and getting away did cross his mind, but he was no thief. If Alex ever stole anything (he had done it a couple of times), he would always choose people who would not feel the loss very much. He had his moral code. The man and the woman were poor wretches like him. So it was out of the question.

Calling them but getting no response, Alex collected the deer and followed the tracks of the princess and the strange old man. It was not hard to catch up with them.

Alex had seen some dumps in his time, but this one beat them all by a long stretch.

For a moment, he even considered dropping the old man's prey and legging it. The *maso*, surrounded by snow, its timber planks darkened by time and glistening with ice, sent a chill through him such as he had seldom felt before. Honestly. Still, those blue eyes . . .

He did not leave. All because of the girl. He wanted to know her name. Perhaps she was looking for a boyfriend. Never put limitations on Providence. What a laugh that would be. He had come out to catch something to get his teeth into and instead ended up with a girlfriend. Funny how things work out.

Alex dropped the deer at the bottom of the steps leading to the main door of the *maso* and followed the footprints of the old man and the girl round to the back of the house. A small door stood wide open and through it came agitated voices and a nauseating smell.

A pigsty.

"Lissy! Lissy!" the old man was shouting.

Alex looked inside. "Hello there!"

No answer.

Alex went down the steps. The stench was dreadful. Really disgusting, he thought. "Hey, there!"

There was a dim light coming from an oil lamp that hung from a beam. The old man was kneeling in the muck and hugging the head of a big black sow. Alex had never seen such a big sow before. It must weigh at least four hundred kilos. And look at those fangs! And the stripes under its eyes! What kind of creature was this?

Alois, at the sawmill, had told him how, back in the good old days, he had gone boar hunting. Once had been more than enough. Nasty business, he had said. Boars were capable of ripping your guts apart in a second. Alex had thought Alois was exaggerating. He would never think that again.

The strange old man did not seem at all scared. He was shaking the sow and stroking its head, talking to it as if it were a little girl, not a four-hundred-kilo sow.

Crazy, Alex thought. Mad as a hatter.

The girl was in a corner, wringing her hands, white as a ghost. Alex walked up to her. "What's going on?" he said, assuming a knight-in-shining-armour voice.

She did not reply.

The old man turned to her and practically tore a large metal key from his greatcoat. "The cellar. Go. Run. It's a fit, she needs medicine. Directly on your right, next to the stairs. It's a red-and-white box. It says 'sodium pentothal' on it! *Run!*"

The girl did not need to be asked twice. She all but knocked Alex over.

74

Seizing a candle and running to the cellar door, Marlene twice missed the lock.

The air that assaulted her was putrid, worse almost than the pigsty. She lit the candle and went down the steps, counting them as she went. Nine. Just like those leading to the sty. And, just like the sty, the cellar was much larger than she had imagined. It had the same walls of dark brick and smelled of lime and dung.

She saw it immediately. You couldn't miss it.

In the middle of the cellar, almost touching the cobwebbed ceiling, stood a kind of monolith covered with a sheet. It was at least three metres high, almost two metres wide and just as deep. An imposing, enigmatic monolith that seemed to be daring her to take a peek at what was hidden beneath the sheet. Marlene took a step forward.

The sheet was not cloth but leather, leather made dark and shiny by time. Holding the candle out in front of her, she went closer. The leather was covered in tiny notches. By the light of the candle flame, they looked like scales. Marlene shuddered. She hated snakes. Usually, scales would have made her run away.

But the monolith was luring her in, and Marlene stepped forward to take a closer look.

They were not scales (how could they be? there were no snakes as big as that). They were incisions, burned in with a scalding iron or something similar.

Perfect circles.

She reached out, ready to pull off the cover and see what it concealed, but then she stepped on something that squeaked, stopping her in her tracks. She lowered the flame.

Rags. Except that rags did not squeak. With the tip of her boot, she lifted what remained of a check shirt and kicked it aside. Beneath the rags were bones.

The bones of mice, squirrels, marmots. She pushed away some wrapping paper and found more.

Slightly larger ones, like rabbit bones, or light ones, like birds of prey. Stag bones, deer, ibex. Bones scattered all over the floor.

Vulpendingen, she thought.

But that was not what she was here for. Nor was the monolith, although she was immensely curious.

Sodium pentothal, remember?

With difficulty, Marlene looked away. All around her was chaos. Clothes of all sizes thrown in the corners, mostly men's clothes – boots, windcheaters – but women's clothes, too, some reduced to shreds by time and insects. There were shelves, some ramshackle, others reinforced with wooden beams bristling with nails. All sorts of objects were stacked up on these shelves. Chipped cups, broken rucksacks, flasks. And books. Dozens, if not hundreds, of books. On the floor, a pair of small, round glasses glittered in the candlelight. What the hell was a pair of glasses doing here? She did not wonder for long, her attention drawn instead to the skulls hanging on the walls.

They were pig skulls. She counted six of them. Skulls covered in spider's webs, which looked as if they were ready to pounce on her, maul her like—

Stop it.

She saw it on a shelf. A large box with a cross. Sodium pentothal. Red and white, as Keller had said.

Marlene took it from the shelf and turned it over in her hand. A pile of chemical substances, a pile of warnings printed on the outside. Inside, phials.

Anti-epileptic.

Epilepsy? Did pigs suffer from epilepsy? Still she did not go up the steps. With unprecedented violence, a thought took hold of her: *Let that damned sow die.*

Marlene could not do it.

She closed the door behind her, blew out the candle and ran to the pigsty.

75

After they said goodbye, it struck Alex that he had never seen anything like this.

A sow having an epileptic seizure. Fancy that!

It also struck him that those two weren't telling him the whole truth. They had said they were father and daughter, but they didn't look at all alike. They had said Marlene was married and her husband was working in town, but there was no wedding ring on her finger. They had insisted he stay for dinner and then spend the night with them because it was getting dark and it was a long way back to the village, but Alex did not like the idea of spending the night in this place.

He did not like it at all.

There was something in the strange old man's eyes (and in the way he had said "Lissy is hungry") that had sent chills up his spine. And something wasn't quite right with the girl, either.

She seemed to be hiding something, a terrible secret. Alex just wanted a quiet life, and those two reeked of trouble.

They might even be criminals. Not criminals like him. Nasty criminals, wanted for serious stuff. Otherwise, why hide up in a place like this?

There was *nothing* here.

Except for the pigs. And the sow. The epileptic sow. He would probably laugh about this encounter in a few days' time. An epileptic sow, for Christ's sake.

Still . . .

No, they were just a couple of oddballs, and he was nothing but a coward.

He had accepted a small glass of their grappa as a pick-me-up and because it would have been rude to refuse. He had chatted about this and that for ten minutes or so, warming himself in the heated *Stube*, then had wished them luck and left.

Quickly, down through the meadows and into the woods.

It was not until he reached the clearing where the old man had killed the deer with that masterly shot that Alex realised he had left his gloves in the *Stube*. Shit. They were almost new, they were warm and it was bitterly cold out here. What was he thinking?

He stopped. Should he turn back? No way. Was he scared?

Damn right he was.

To hell with the cold, to hell with the *Bau'r*, to hell with the sow. And to hell with the blue-eyed girl. He wasn't going back there.

It was almost dark, the sun casting its last rays, when he heard the noise. A kind of cough above him, behind the rocks. Or maybe just a rolling stone.

In winter? With all that ice?

Alex squinted at the cluster of shadows from where the noise had come. The hairs on the back of his neck were standing on end. As he took his hands out of his pockets, he thought he heard a stifled voice. He grabbed his rifle and put it to his shoulder.

"Who's there?"

He aimed the rifle.

76

Everything was fine with the first three, but not with the fourth. With the fourth Lissy, Keller began to realise that something was not right with the sows. When the fourth had her first fit, foaming at the mouth, eyes rolling up, legs going stiff, he thought he would go mad. It only lasted a minute or two, but to him it felt like an eternity.

The following day, he took his holdall, went down to the village and caught a bus to San Valentino, where there was a vet.

Dr. Kaser – that was his name – listened to his story, then reassured him. It was nothing dangerous. Some animals did suffer from epilepsy. It was rare but it was not unknown. Epilepsy? Keller had never even heard the word.

Dr. Kaser explained that it was a problem with the brain: every so often it would short-circuit. Epileptic fits, he said, were not risky *per se*. Epilepsy was almost never deadly, and the *person* actually suffering the fit did not even remember it. There were two kinds of problems. One was if the sufferer fell and hit his head. The other was if he swallowed his tongue, which might lead to his choking to death.

In any case, the doctor concluded with a broad smile, he had nothing to worry about. "Epilepsy has no effect on the quality of the meat."

"The quality of the meat?"

"If your sow had an epileptic seizure, you could still slaughter it and sell it."

Keller's eyes opened wide. "Slaughter Lissy?"

"Lissy?"

"That's the sow's name."

"I see," Dr. Kaser said, even though he didn't.

"How can she be cured?"

The vet put his hands together on the desk. "You can't cure epilepsy. It's a genetic condition."

"Aren't there drugs?"

The vet laughed. "Of course there are, to keep the condition under control. Not for animals, though."

"But for people, yes?"

"Yes. Epilepsy is a condition that's been known for a long time. People used to say that epileptic seizures were a sign of benevolence on the part of the gods."

"Can you give me these drugs?"

"I'm a vet, not a neurologist."

"Can you give me the name of a neurologist?"

The doctor shook his head in disbelief. "Trust me, not for a pig. You'd be wasting your time."

All the same, Keller insisted so much that Dr. Kaser wrote the name of a drug on a piece of paper. Sodium pentothal.

Keller approached a smuggler. They haggled a little. Keller slaughtered three boars and a sow and sold the meat at market. With the money he made, he bought the phials of sodium pentothal.

They were not enough to provide a cure, but they did keep the seizures under control and avoid serious damage.

Lissy number five and Lissy number six did not need the drug. Lissy number seven, though, had a fit every three months or so. The one that had come on a few hours earlier was the longest to date. He really did think she was going to die, and if that happened, what would he do? He did not want to think about that, so he picked up his pace.

Lissy was hungry. That was all. All he had to do was get her food. Then she would get better. Much better.

251

"Sweet Lissy, little Lissy . . ."

It did not take him long to catch up with Alex, the young poacher whose disappearance would not cause a stir. That was what the Voice had told him. Lissy's Voice.

Nobody will miss him, Sim'l . . .

The Voice was right, as usual.

Keller stopped behind some snow-covered rocks, watching him.

The young man was walking a little crookedly, his hands in his pockets. He was in a rush. Maybe he was scared. For sure, he was cold. Keller slipped the rifle off his shoulder, lay down flat and aimed at the poacher's heart.

Less than seventy metres. He could have hit him with his eyes closed.

"Lissy is . . ."

He did not finish.

His finger failed to obey his command. He tried but it was no use. The rifle remained silent. The hand holding the weapon shook. The barrel of the rifle collided with the heap of snow behind which he was lying. Keller tried to shoot, but he could not pull the trigger.

He ducked down behind the rocks, panting.

He should have felt startled, bewildered. Instead, he felt at peace. Keller thought about Wegener's smile of gratitude when he had killed him in the villa on the Passer. He thought about sledges and eyes carved into the wood. He thought about a little boy with blue eyes and a beauty spot at the end of his smile. He thought about Elisabeth and how she had trembled as her life drained out of her along with all that blood.

Then he thought about Wegener again.

His was the last blood he would ever spill. That death had broken the circle. It was over. He could not kill anymore. He must never do it again. Above all: he did not want to.

Peace.

He closed his eyes, smiling. Peace.

But only for a short while. A very short while.

The Voice screamed in his head. A roar that drew an exclamation from him. *Lissy is hungry, Lissy is hungry.* The Voice wanted blood, wanted it now.

Lissy is hungry. Kill him!

"Opa Simon," he whispered. "Opa Simon."

He heard the young man's voice from down below. "Who's there?"

Keller peered out.

Below him, as the shadows of night turned into darkness, Alex the poacher was aiming his rifle. He was shaking. Keller could see him even at that distance, lurking amid the snow-covered rocks. The young man was shaking. Keller was sorry for him and the fear he was feeling.

All because of him.

Then he thought of the fear of all those he had killed. Some had been lucky: death had caught them unawares, like a black curtain falling, putting an end to all joy and pain. But others had seen it coming. They had known.

And death had not been gentle with them.

Kill him, Sim'l. Please.

Keller hid again.

"I won't do it."

Why, why, why?

Keller counted to a hundred. And then he checked. The young man had gone.

Keller blessed him with a prayer, dug a hole in the snow and laid the poacher's woollen gloves in it. He set fire to them with a match, waited until the wool was burnt to a cinder, then closed the hole and got back on his feet.

The Voice whimpered.

Lissy is hungry.

"Yes," Keller murmured, "I know."

Lissy was hungry, and he would take care of her. Because, even though the circle had closed, Lissy loved Sim'l, and Sim'l loved Lissy, and Lissy had not abandoned him.

Keller would continue to care for her. But he would do it differently. How, he did not know, nor did he know if there was another way. He only knew that he would not kill anymore.

Never again.

77

The following day, Alex sold his rifle and ammunition to a smuggler, who put everything into the boot of his car. He did not give them away, but he did not cheat the man either. The rifle was a good weapon and the smuggler an old acquaintance. They agreed on a fair price. The smuggler asked him why he had decided to quit, and Alex made up an answer off the top of his head. He was going south for a while. He was sick of the cold.

He did not mention the feeling he had experienced as he had aimed the rifle at the darkness. Or the impression he had had, once he had put the weapon back over his shoulder, that God had searched his soul and decided to give him a second chance. Freezing cold, terrified, he had made a vow. If he managed to get back to the village safe and sound, he would change his life.

Selling the rifle was just the first step. He really did go south.

The first year was tough. He did not speak the language well and had to make do with a few pennies for day jobs that sapped all his energy. He slept wherever he could. He spent a week in a shelter where an emaciated-looking guy offered him heroin. Alex refused. He hung on and moved from city to city until he came to a port. He had never seen one before. He liked the coming and going of the passengers, sailors, prostitutes and dockers, the mixture of languages from every part of the world. He decided to stay and look for work.

He met a Dutch sailor who spoke German. They became friends, and the sailor introduced him to a guy who smoked a cigar and spoke too loudly, as if he were slightly deaf. They needed German speakers as waiters on a cruise ship. Was he interested? Yes, he was.

The pay was good, and his life took a new turn.

He was easy-going, fond of a joke, so the customers liked him. On top of that, he discovered he had a talent for singing. Just a few months later, he was noticed by the ship's captain who promoted him to master of ceremonies. He learned a fair number of sentimental songs and would often punctuate his caterwauling with jokes and double entendres that made the dancing couples laugh. It was a life he enjoyed: pretty girls, travel to exotic lands.

He fell in love. He got married and used the money he had saved to open a restaurant. He had children. Never once did he tell anyone about the night he was given a second chance. Still, he often found himself thinking about the old man and the girl.

And the sow.

How he would have ended up without them was anyone's guess. The universe teemed with mysteries and miracles. His whole life, Alex would wonder what the difference was between the two.

78

It was shortly after dawn. Going down to the *Stube*, Marlene found Simon Keller there, his extinguished pipe in his mouth, engrossed in the pages of a frayed Bible open on his lap. When she spoke to him, he was disorientated for a few seconds and did not respond to her greeting at once.

She opened the shutters to let the light in, and they both squinted. She lit the fire and prepared the espresso pot. As she filled it with ground coffee, she asked after Lissy.

"The fit has passed," Keller said.

"It's not the first time it's happened, is it?"

"No," he said, relighting his pipe. "She's had this problem ever since she was a piglet. Lissy needs to be taken care of."

"She couldn't have found a better place or a better *Bau'r*."

Keller gave a strained smile and drummed on the cover of the Bible with his fingers. "There's . . . there's something I have to ask of you."

Marlene put the espresso pot on the fire and sat down opposite him. "Anything you like."

"A period of self-denial."

Keller ran his hand over the back of his neck. He looked worried. He probably was, Marlene thought. But he also seemed confused, as if he were trying to solve a riddle.

"*Voter* Luis used to say that there is always a period of self-denial before a celebration. And that's what I'm asking of you. A period of self-denial." His eyes brought her into focus. "Lissy isn't well," he explained. "The fit is over, but she needs me to stay with her." He looked down at the floor, shrugged and continued, "There could be more fits. It does happen."

"Does that mean we're postponing our departure?" Marlene said, trying to dispel his embarrassment. "No problem. You mustn't fret about it."

"Just a few days' self-denial," Keller hastened to add. "Only a few days."

"Please don't worry, one day more or—"

"Once Lissy's better, I'll take you down to the village and put you on the bus. You need to take care of the baby. You can't do it here, and the more advanced your pregnancy, the harder it will be to go down the mountain. But we'll celebrate before we part" – smiling, he took her hands in his – "because the period of self-denial always comes before a celebration."

Marlene felt her eyes fill with tears. "Not a farewell party, though, alright?"

"Not a farewell party," Simon replied, adding, "Not if you don't want it to be."

Marlene bit her lip. "I'll be back, and when I come I won't be on my own."

She felt his hands squeeze hers tighter. "Opa," he said inadvertently.

"Opa?" Marlene echoed, surprised.

Keller moved away from her, his face flushed. "It's just something silly."

Marlene quickly grabbed his hand. "Opa Simon. Why not?"

Yes, Keller thought, why not?

Then he put on his greatcoat, put the rifle over his shoulder and the Bible into his haversack and went hunting.

The Voice was silent.

79

Nothing, not even the little bell.

Lissy did not show her face for three days.

Marlene paid no attention. She would get up at dawn, make Simon Keller's breakfast, see him off at the door, wait for him to vanish beyond the horizon, then go back to the *Stube*, prepare the pig slop and go and pour it into the trough in the sty.

By now even the females had got used to her presence. The males, as Marlene knew, were less fastidious. And when they smelled the food, they did not stand on ceremony. What did they care if it was Marlene or Simon Keller? They would jump all over one another, biting and grunting, until they had lapped up the last drop of that disgusting stuff.

Marlene would call them by their names. The Doctor, with dark spots under his eyes, never came when she called. Franz was more courteous. He would look up and wag his tail. Kurt, on the other hand, would cock his head. He was funny, with his floppy ears. Gertrud the fugitive had got into the habit of walking up and down the pen as soon as she saw Marlene appear at the top of the stairs. It was a kind of welcome – or maybe just a sign of impatience.

Self-denial. And an obsession. For three days, all Marlene could think about was the cellar and the leather-covered monolith. She was curious, but she was also scared. And fear acted as a trigger to her curiosity.

For three days, the monolith was her first thought when she woke up and the last one before she went to sleep.

For three days, Marlene tried to stifle her curiosity. It was none of her business. There was nothing under the cloth. Some old piece of furniture. Junk.

Did she really want Simon Keller to catch her down there? In the only room under lock and key in the entire *maso*? How would he react to such an intrusion?

There was nothing under that cloth. Nothing.

And yet . . . And yet there was something in that cellar she could only guess at. Something (and this was what finally convinced her to steal Simon Keller's key) she did not *want* to see.

And she had sworn to herself that it would never happen again. No more lies. No more fairy tales.

Right. Precisely.

Lies to avoid facing reality. Marlene was a champion at the sport. Like when she had realised she was pregnant. It had taken her a while to come to terms with the idea. She was about to become a mother. She would give birth to a child. Had she been happy? Radiant? Of course, but only later.

At first, she had spent days acting as if nothing was happening. She had hidden her head under the blankets.

It seemed crazy in retrospect, but that was what she had done. She had tried to erase her child. If you ignore it, then it doesn't exist. But Klaus wanted to live.

He was there. With her.

And he had fought.

Marlene had dreamt about him. A beautiful newborn baby, waving his arms as though he wanted to be picked up. She had woken drenched in sweat, scared but happy, terrified but in seventh heaven. She had cried silently while Wegener slept. And, once she had calmed down, she had vowed: no more lies. Because her entire life was a lie. The Thieving Magpie. The mice in the walls. You're pregnant, she had thought. You're about to become a mother.

A mother doesn't live in fairy-tale land. A mother faces reality. Like Gretel the Brave. Not like Hansel. That whining child Hansel.

A mother does what Gretel the Brave does. She accepts reality and acts on it. Look around, she had told herself. Look at the villa. The cars in the garage. The jewellery.

Look at the photographs of your husband. His arrogant eyes. That cruel streak that never leaves him. His bloodstained hands. Do you really want your child to grow up like that?

To become . . . *Kobold*?

And that was how Marlene had become Marlene the Brave and started plotting the escape that had brought her here. Klaus had taught her to face the world.

On the fourth day of her self-denial period, she stole the key.

80

Simon Keller had four keys jattached to a rusty ring. The one for the cellar was the largest and oldest, made of bronze. But it wasn't hard to steal. Before dawn, feeling both guilty and excited, Marlene had taken it from the rucksack Simon Keller always carried when he went out.

Then she had made breakfast, chatted to Simon Keller once he had woken up, and witnessed his usual morning ritual. The greatcoat done up to his neck, the snowshoes, the rifle over his shoulder. With her heart in her mouth, she had said goodbye to him and watched him vanish over the horizon, expecting him to turn back any minute and ask her for the key that was burning a hole in her pocket.

It had not happened.

She was alone and would be for hours, as usual.

She got down to work. She prepared the pig slop, poured it into the buckets and, defying the cold, went down into the sty. She fed the animals, first the boars, then the females, as usual leaving the silver bowl inside Lissy's grille, and went back to the *Stube*. Without giving herself time to think, she inserted the key in the lock and turned it twice. The door opened wide.

No creaking. Not like the one . . .

Stupid woman.

Marlene turned back, searched until she found a candle and lit it. With that faint flame to guide her, she felt ready. The air of the cellar snatched at her throat when she was only halfway down the steps.

The dirt. The chaos.

The monolith.

The top of the covered object almost touched the ceiling. There were spiders' webs over it, although not many, as if the spiders kept away from it. Marlene huffed impatiently. The fairy-tale world again.

Marlene the Brave would not let herself be intimidated by this … this … *What was it?*

Time to find out.

That was when she heard it. The roar, loud and hollow. A kind of subterranean thunder. Marlene froze and looked around.

Boom.

The thunder had sounded again.

The candle flame swayed from side to side. Marlene was bewildered. She could not locate the origin of the sound – or figure out what was making it.

An earthquake? Impossible.

Boom.

Not thunder, she thought, but the thumping of a gigantic heart. She shuddered.

Boom.

Then an unmistakable squeal.

Lissy.

Marlene almost dropped the candle.

The squeal had come from her right.

Marlene understood now. Nine steps down to the pigsty, nine down to the cellar. The cellar and the sty were part of the same room, divided by a wall.

The wall from where the squeal had come. From where the thumping was coming. The wall to which Marlene now turned, shielding the flame with her hand, barely able to breathe.

The thumps were turning into a rhythmical beat. *Boom. Boom. Boom.*

About half a metre from the ground, there was a small window, protected by metal bars, connecting the cellar and the pigsty.

To reach it, she only needed to take a couple of steps, taking care not to trip over the junk strewn all over the cellar floor. That was where the thunder was coming from.

And a strange glow. It was green, as if covered in mucus, or moss. The light vanished and . . .

Boom.

Marlene bent forward and looked. Behind the bars, Lissy was bleeding, her forehead cracked open, her fangs dripping with blood.

Marlene felt faint.

Lissy withdrew into the darkness, emitted a squeal and charged, hurling her black, menacing form at the barred window with such force and fury that the metal rippled and creaked. She shook her head and rolled her eyes, as if stunned by the impact. But that did not deter her. She withdrew again into the shadows, emitted another long squeal and struck the metal again. Then again, and again. Harder each time. Angrier each time. Spraying blood around her each time.

Darkness. Squealing. Impact.

Boom.

The metal rippled, as if about to give way.

Lissy is hungry, Marlene thought.

Blood spattered her face and she pulled back in disgust, narrowly avoiding a fall. It was a miracle the candle did not go out. The prospect of being plunged into darkness filled her with terror.

On the other side of the window, Lissy was staring at her with hatred. She brought her snout close to the bars, sniffed the air and snorted, squirting blood and mucus. Then she sank her teeth into the metal.

The sharp fangs rasped the iron, which bent under the force of her bite.

Marlene could not stand it anymore. "Please, Lissy, stop it. Stop it."

Lissy obeyed. She threw her one final glance, then withdrew and again hid in the shadows.

Marlene collapsed.

81

Sitting on the floor, in the dirt, shaking, she started to cry, big tears of anguish. Crying did her good. She slowly regained control.

She stopped sobbing.

Lissy was just a sow. Nothing more. It was stupid, really *stupid* to be afraid of Lissy. Lissy was just a sow. A sow . . . But was there anything normal about this sow? No. Definitely not. Even so, Marlene tried to regulate her breathing and, after a while, stopped shaking. She rubbed her face with the sleeve of her sweater to wipe off the blood.

The Lissy she feared belonged to the world of fairy tales. Kobolds, witches, possessed sows. All nonsense. It was time to be Marlene the Brave again.

With a sigh, she got to her feet. She glanced at the barred window, then focused on the monolith. That was what she was here for.

She reached out and pulled off the leather sheet, releasing a little dust – actually, less than she would have expected, but it still made her cough. She half closed her eyes and took a step back.

Once the dust (and the spiders' webs and the dirt) had settled on the floor, Marlene examined what the sheet had been concealing.

Books. Hundreds of them, a perfect stack of books piled one on top of the other, all black and thick as bricks, with the spines facing outwards. A stele of paper and glue. Marlene the Brave brushed the monolith with the tip of her finger. It was cold.

The monolith was like a gigantic version of a children's game. These weren't just any books, they were Bibles. She imagined Simon

Keller carefully stacking all these volumes, with that same concentrated expression he had when carving his wooden animals. She imagined him with his unlit pipe in his mouth, kneeling at first, then balancing on a stepladder, piling the Bibles ever higher. What she could not imagine was the reason he had done this.

Moving gingerly, she described a circle around the mystery. Not a single book was out of place. The monolith stood solid and motionless at the centre of the *maso*.

Marlene left the candle on the shelf, went back upstairs to the *Stube*, brought a chair down with her, placed it in front of the monolith and climbed onto it.

She was petite, much shorter than Simon Keller, who was over one metre ninety, so she could not see the top of the monolith, but with a little effort, stretching her hand, she managed to take a Bible from one of the uppermost layers.

She blew the dust off it, opened it and started to read.

Voter Heini
A.D. 1471–1484

The same handwriting throughout the entire volume. *Voter* Heini had spent thirteen years copying this Bible. In Latin, which he must somehow have known, since the same hand that had transcribed Genesis, Deuteronomy and so on, all the way to Revelation, had added notes in the margin, which Marlene could not decipher, no matter how hard she tried, because the ink had faded.

Amazed, she closed the book and, making sure the edges of the binding and the spine aligned perfectly with those of the Bible next to it, slipped it back where it belonged.

She got down off the chair, moved it to the other side of the monolith and took out a second book. This time, she did not look through it standing up but got off the chair and sat down.

Voter Hannes
A.D. 1056–1063

Marlene remembered the beam in the pigsty and Simon Keller telling her about *Voter* Luis' assertion that the *maso* was much older than the 1333 carved in the timber. Here's the proof, she thought.

Voter Luis had not lied. He might have been a child killer, but the was not a liar. *Voter* Hannes's Bible was almost a thousand years old.

Marlene leafed through it, timidly at first, then with increasing wonder. This particular *Bau'r*, now reduced to dust, had filled his Bible not with notes but with drawings. And he had had a remarkable talent. The insects – grasshoppers, bees, ants and butterflies – that decorated the pages of Exodus, Proverbs, Psalms and Judges were so realistic, they looked as if they were about to leap out and vanish into the darkness of the cellar. Beside Revelation, *Voter* Hannes had drawn a pregnant filly. The whole of Ecclesiastes was framed with vines. St. Paul's Epistles were a veritable treatise on taxidermy. Deer, squirrels, ibex and a thousand other animals.

Perhaps it was *Voter* Hannes who had started the tradition of *Vulpendingen*. Who could say?

Marlene found herself picturing Simon Keller's ancestors spending their days copying their own fathers' Bibles. Copying them and commenting on them, century after century.

How had these *Bau'rn* obtained paper and ink at a time when a book was worth more than the life of a human being? Who had taught them to read and write? Was there an original Bible, a first Keller Bible from which all the others descended? Perhaps a manuscript, Marlene imagined – since the invention of the printing press was far in the future – from which the Kellers had drawn their inspiration. But how had they obtained it?

From whom?

And, most importantly, the most mind-boggling question of them all: why had they done it?

Why?

Out of faith, no doubt. And also to pass the time during those long, terrible winters. Writing and meditating were a good antidote to solitude. Marlene thought about Simon Keller talking to the pigs. Yes, that was it, solitude. She could easily imagine Simon Keller poring over the books for hours on end, trying to transcribe the faded scrawls of past *Voter*. Just as his father and his father's father had done, all the way back through time, as far back as the years of the Flood, she thought, echoing the words Simon Keller had uttered.

Faith. Boredom. Solitude.

Or else it was just a way to feel that your loved ones were still alive, their thoughts surviving in their marginal notes.

Or in their drawings.

Marlene got down off the chair. She looked for and found a wooden box and made sure it was sturdy before putting it under the legs of the chair. She then got up on the chair again and searched among those books that looked less damaged.

Here it was.

Simon

A.D. 1962–1966

Just Simon. Not *Voter* Simon. Because Simon Keller had no wife or children. His would be the last Keller Bible, just as Simon Keller would be the last of his line. Nobody would open Simon Keller's Bible in search of inspiration or comfort. Nobody would repeat his words the way he repeated his father's. The Keller name would die with him.

The thought wrung her heart.

She hesitated, then decided against opening this last Keller Bible. She would have liked to, she was very curious, but she could not do it. Snooping through its pages would make her feel dirty. In a way, this book was even more precious than a personal diary. One day, it would be the only proof of Simon Keller's existence.

Delicately, Marlene put the book back on top of the monolith and got down, feeling sad, determined to leave this place. It had been stupid of her to become so obsessed with the cellar. There was nothing down here that concerned her.

Only solitude.

She grasped the leather sheet, spread it the way she did with bedsheets and covered the monolith. Then she put back the wooden box, stuck the chair under her arm, took the candle and headed for the steps that would take her back up to the *Stube*. Less than two paces from them, she tripped over a king, a boar, three brothers and a shepherd playing a flute.

82

A fragment of pottery, one of the many small wooden boxes, an empty bottle, rags, something like that.

If she had tripped over a fragment of pottery, a bottle or some other everyday object, Marlene would not have thought of the king and the boar, or the drunken, murderous brothers. She would have picked herself up, gone back to the *Stube*, brushed the dust off her clothes and the spiders' webs out of her hair. Then she would have gone and shut the door to the pigsty, which she had just remembered she had left open. Had she simply tripped over, the story of Marlene would have gone something like this: Once upon a time there was a beautiful princess who was saved by a kind *Bau'r*, and they all lived happily ever after.

Instead of which, she instinctively raised her hands to shield her face, so that when she hit the stone steps the impact had no consequence except to make her swear and leave her in the dark. She immediately got up, relit the candle and looked irritably at the spot where she had felt the floor move. She pushed away a tangle of rags and discovered that the floorboards were damaged and rotten. There was a hole, but Marlene's foot had not caught in it. No, she had tripped over something sticking out of it.

A king, a boar and three brothers.

The protagonists of a Grimm fairy tale her mother had never told her and which Marlene had discovered only after she had learned to read. The story had given her nightmares for weeks.

The story was about a king and a boar: a cunning, cruel animal nobody was able to kill, as black and nasty as (Lissy) the devil. The king issued a decree. Whoever killed the vile animal would win the hand of his daughter, the princess.

Three brothers decided to try their luck. After a few lame attempts, two of them, the drunken, wicked brothers, gave up and retreated to an inn to drink and boast about feats they had never accomplished. The third, though, thanks to a magical little man who had given him a very special spear, killed the boar and, overjoyed, ran to show his brothers the fierce animal's carcass.

Needless to say, the two brothers killed him, buried him under a bridge, and carried the dead boar to the king. The eldest brother married the princess and lived happily ever after, enjoying her beauty, the king's wine collection and a good life.

Until a shepherd found a tiny bone under the bridge where the hapless third brother was buried. He carved it into a flute. No sooner did he blow into it than the flute sang a song about a brave man who had vanquished a monster but had then been killed by his brothers. A hero who would now never be able to marry the princess. The shepherd hurried to the king and played his flute for him. The two brothers were sentenced to death.

That was what Marlene had tripped over. A skull. No *Vulpendingen* this time. Not the skull of a wren, or a fox, or a rodent. It was a human skull. And there were teeth marks on that grinning skull, curved teeth wide at the base. Rats? Teeth like fangs. *Lissy.*

Suddenly, it was as if she had *really* begun to see.

The tobacco, for instance. The smell was coming from a large jute sack in a corner. She had briefly glanced at it, then forgotten about it. There was nothing odd about finding tobacco in Simon's cellar. He smoked a pipe and sometimes did not go down to the village for months at a time. It was only natural that he should have a supply. Natural, too, that there should be a pair of boots next to the jute sack.

Right?

Boots are essential for life in the mountains. She had seen them and forgotten about them. But now Marlene the Not So Brave Anymore took a proper look at them. No *Bau'r* of sound mind would wear pointed boots like that. Pointed boots squeeze your toes and cause ingrowing toenails. An ingrowing toenail could be a real problem, it slowed you down, made you clumsy. It could also potentially get infected. Wegener would have called them a city slicker's boots. Pointed boots of glossy leather, maybe snakeskin or crocodile. Cowboy boots. Like Kurt the pig.

"Stop it," she murmured. "Get out of here, get out."

But she could not go. She could not stop herself looking.

Not far from her was what she had at first taken for yet another heap of rags. Actually, they were clothes. Women's clothes. The kind of thing a city woman would wear for an excursion in the mountains. Not cheap clothes. And she thought of Birgit, the sow with the cared-for nails. "A distinguished lady." And what was in that suitcase on top of the broken barrel right in the corner? Didn't it look like a doctor's bag? She remembered the round glasses she had seen the first time she had been in the cellar. A bag and glasses. Maybe a doctor with glasses and the unfriendly look of a know-it-all? Maybe . . . She let out a kind of snort that was also a moan.

She looked down at the floor. What else would she find if she were to take up the floorboards? How many skulls?

She had to get out. She needed air.

She did not go. Not yet. She put the candle down, carefully, so that it would not go out, moved the wooden box, put the chair on top of it, climbed up, pulled the sheet away and took one of the Bibles from the top of the monolith. The only one without a bookmark at the end. The one Simon Keller was still compiling.

And there on the first page were the words:

Simon
A.D. 1971–

It was not finished yet.

She opened it at random and read:

Subsequently, they continued to offer a perennial sacrifice to Lissy, and sacrifices on Lissy days and on all feast days dedicated to Lissy, for all the offerings to Lissy.

Trembling, she skipped a few pages.

"If you are the son of Voter Luis, then go tell these stones to turn into bread for Lissy," but Sim'l answered, "It is written: Lissy will not live on bread alone but on all the flesh the Voice will bring to Sim'l through Lissy's mouth."

The Book of Revelation was a senseless sermon that began with these words:

Revelation of Lissy, which Lissy gave him for Lissy, by Lissy, with Lissy and which Lissy manifested by sending flesh by means of her brother Sim'l. This is a testimony of the word of Lissy and the testimony of . . .

Then nothing more, because this Bible of Simon Keller's was not finished yet. The following pages were blank, and as white as bones.

She hurled it from her, as far as she could.

Madness. Pure madness.

And, through the madness, a logical thought at last. Simon Keller was a murderer. He killed and gave Lissy . . .

"Because Lissy is hungry," Marlene murmured.

274

In a state of shock, she got down off the chair, retrieved the Bible, put it back where it belonged, making sure its spine was aligned with the others, spread the leather sheet over them, blew out the candle and climbed the stairs, numbly, taking the chair with her. She closed the cellar door. She left the chair by the table, feeling herself transfixed by the eyes of the *Vulpendingen*.

She ran her fingers through her hair. Dust, spiders' webs.

"Lissy is hungry," she murmured, putting on her jacket. She left the *Stube*. She left the *maso*.

She went down the steps and breathed in the frosty air. She stopped, buttoned her jacket and stroked her cheek. Then she slapped it. Hard.

"Lissy is hungry!" she cried to the mountains, the snow and the sky.

She started to run.

83

How do you flee when Wrath is unleashed upon the Earth? Where do you flee when the waters of the seas and oceans rise, determined to drown every form of life?

You go higher.

The Keller *maso* was perched above the woods and above the limit of the fields, on a strip strewn with rocks and a few bushes. Above it there was only the perennial snow and the constant movement of the clouds. In order to reach it from the valley, you had to take a kind of mule path which was gradually reduced to a hint of a track covered in brushwood and eventually vanished amid roots, stones and moss. In the winter, when snow erased all points of reference, it was impossible to find a safe way to get to it.

Or get away from it.

All you could do was head downhill and hope. That was what Marlene did.

She crossed the fields, the snow coming halfway up her thighs, struggled towards the woods, where the blanket of snow was less thick and more compact, and plunged into them.

She nearly slipped and fell several times. Miraculously, she did not.

She passed the clearing where Alex the poacher had seen Simon hugging the dead deer. She kept running, scratched by branches, her movements slowed by the snow, her knees and back aching.

She ran as fast as she could, and when her muscles and lungs begged her to stop she put on even more speed. It was only when she got to the heart of the forest that she allowed herself a brief pause and leaned against a centuries-old spruce. For a few minutes, she felt safe beneath its canopy. She had stopped screaming a while ago, but was still unable to think clearly.

Panic in its purest form.

A sound made her jump, perhaps an animal or just the thud of snow falling from a branch. Her heart in her mouth, she looked around. There was nobody to be seen.

She resumed running.

Or almost.

Now that she was deep in the woods, the strain she felt was overwhelming. She had to watch out for tree trunks lying buried in the snow, be watchful at every step to avoid falling into a covered hole, walk around thorny bushes concealed by the whiteness.

She would not have struggled so much if she had brought snowshoes with her. She had not done so because she had acted on instinct. And now she was starting to waste breath and energy.

At one point, she came across fresh footprints and shuddered. She stopped, bent down to examine them and realised they were her own. In her terror and exhaustion, she had been going round in circles.

She didn't lose hope. All she had to do was slow down and take more care.

But it was when she slowed down that she noticed the cold. The sweat froze on her neck and she felt nasty shivers up and down her spine. The cold cleared her head a little. The shivers on her back and neck made her think about the night. And she realised she had left wearing only her jacket. Although it was thick, it would not be warm enough if she were caught out in the open at night. Her fingertips had already turned blue. By nightfall, the temperature would drop even lower.

Minus ten? Minus fifteen? Colder still if the wind rose.

Marlene the Brave told herself she would grit her teeth, get down to the valley and from there head south-west, where, she thought, the village she had driven through in her Mercedes was located. Once she was in the village, she would be safe. She would scream, knock on every door. Someone would help her.

You just have to keep going, she told herself. Resist the cold, the tiredness. You have to, for Klaus's sake.

If she had stayed at the *maso*, Klaus would have died with her. Just like Kurt, Birgit and Gertrud. And heaven knows how many others. Because Lissy was hungry. But Lissy wasn't going to have her or her child. She clung to this idea, and yet she was unable to move.

She was exhausted, numb with cold, no longer scared of what she had found in the cellar but of what awaited her shortly. The night and the cold, which would kill her.

I can't turn back. I can't . . .

And as she wrestled with this dilemma, she heard Simon Keller's voice.

84

"You'll catch your death like this."

Simon Keller was behind her, his black hat pulled down over his head, the rifle over his shoulder. He was carrying a large deer on his back, and was looking at her in surprise.

"Simon Keller . . ." she gasped.

He said nothing.

"I . . . I . . ." Marlene stammered.

He took a step towards her: threatening, perhaps, or perhaps not, she could not tell. But he was clearly expecting an explanation. She had to improvise, and fast, before he put two and two together. She took a deep breath.

You're the Thieving Magpie. Make something up. Or this'll be the place where you die. Where *both of you* die.

"Lissy," Marlene said breathlessly. More out of fear than tiredness.

At last, Simon Keller spoke, a note of alarm in his voice. "Another fit?"

Marlene shook her head. "No. Yes. I mean . . ."

He came closer. Marlene noticed that his greatcoat was undone. She glimpsed the hilt of his hunting knife. There was blood on his trousers. Probably the deer's blood. He reached out his hand and stroked her face. His fingers were warm. "Breathe. How long have you been running?"

"I don't know. I . . ."

"You're frightened."

Yes, damn it. Of course she was.

"And you're cold."

Keller laid the carcass of the deer down in the snow, took off his rucksack and pulled from it a moth-eaten woollen blanket. He put it over Marlene's shoulders and rubbed her. Her blood started circulating again.

"Feeling any better?"

Marlene nodded.

"Tell me about Lissy. Why are you here?"

"Lissy isn't well. She's . . ." Shivering, Marlene pulled the blanket tightly around her, closed her eyes and breathed in. "I was feeding the . . . the kids. Everything was normal. The same as always. I gave Lissy her bowl and she started knocking herself against . . . At the back of her enclosure there's a kind of . . ."

"A little window, yes," Keller said.

"She kept banging her head on it, quite hard. I don't know why, I really don't. I tried to calm her down, but . . . there was blood everywhere and I didn't know what to do. I ran out."

Keller looked at her intently for a moment or two and saw fear in her face. He was touched by it. "You're a good girl, Marlene," he said. "Let's go." He hoisted up the deer. "It's nothing, you'll see. She does this every now and again. I think it's the cage. Maybe I should build a larger one."

Less than an hour later (because he knew all the shortcuts, a fact that filled Marlene with terror) they came within sight of the *maso*. In the midst of all that snow, it was black and reminded Marlene of the monolith in the cellar.

Even so, when Keller turned and gave her an encouraging look, Marlene actually managed to smile.

85

It was after dinner, that same evening. Every now and again she would remember to turn the page. The illustrations in her old edition of Grimm's fairy tales were making her nauseous. Children abducted and eaten, women chopped to pieces, lies, cruelty. She could not take her eyes off one picture in particular. The moment when Gretel the Brave shuts the oven door, killing the witch.

Marlene glanced over at Keller. Sitting on the bench, his injured leg resting on a chair, his pipe clenched between his teeth, he was carving a piece of wood, using a knife with a short, sturdy blade.

He was forming a pig's snout. There were three others standing proudly on the table.

It was only now, after tripping over the king, the boar and the three brothers, that Marlene realised something: since Wegener's death, Keller had been carving nothing but pigs. Large or small, smiling or with their snouts turned down, with corkscrew tails or a crest between the ears. Only pigs.

Toys, he had said. For the boy. Once, he had even added: for my grandson.

He noticed her looking at him and she felt duty bound to point at the little pig taking shape in his hands and say, "It's really lovely, Simon Keller."

"Just an old man's pastime," he said.

Marlene went back to her book. She smoothed the page with the palm of her hand, but did not turn it. There was something hypnotic in that black-and-white drawing.

When they had got back to the *maso*, Keller had gone down to the pigsty alone and stitched Lissy's wound. Upon his return, he had reassured Marlene. Lissy would recover soon. He had thanked her several times for coming to fetch him, but also reprimanded her. The mountain was dangerous. She had been lucky to run into him. She could have got lost, and then what would she have done, on her own, in the dark and the cold? "You must think of the baby. You're a mother now."

So she was, Marlene thought. Marlene the Brave.

Keller had roasted the deer, singing softly as he coated it in oil and oregano after carefully butchering it, and throwing away the scraps. While doing this, he had told her about the times when *Voter* Luis would bring home such delicacies. *Voter* Luis had been a skilful hunter, like most of his ancestors, although this might be one accomplishment in which Simon could surpass him. He was a better hunter. But he would never be a better cook than Mutti. Mutti had been a remarkable cook. For the sake of saying something, Marlene had said she was willing to write down the recipes. It would be a shame if they were forgotten. This had made Keller happy, and he had carried on singing.

When the meal was ready, he had given her the choicest part of the deer, sizzling in aromatic fat, and Marlene had forced herself to eat at least a little. In actual fact, the crisp, tasty meat had made her nauseous.

Luckily, dinner was quickly over.

After washing the pans and dishes, Marlene had curled up by the fire, the Grimm book on her lap, reading, or pretending to read, all the while thinking.

Another illustration: Hansel and Gretel walking home hand in hand. Marlene turned the book towards the firelight and looked closely at the children's faces. They were smiling. The story had ended as well as could have been hoped, so of course they were smiling.

"And they lived happily ever after."

But wasn't there a shadow over their faces?

Had the artist responsible for the illustration wanted to suggest something by the way he had depicted the siblings' eyes? Were they not *too* wide open? *Too* happy? As if what they had seen and done had changed them forever?

Was there not a touch of madness in Hansel and Gretel?

Nobody ever said what had happened to them after that "happily ever after." What had Gretel become as a grown-up? Or Hansel? Did they have nightmares? Had they forgotten the witch? Or was it impossible for them to forget the old hag's screams? And what had they done after the witch had stopped screaming and beating her fists on the inside of the soot-covered oven? Had they jumped for joy or immediately run away?

Had they been horrified by this brutal death? Or had they *enjoyed* it?

Had they killed again after that? Could blood become a compulsion? Was that what had happened to Simon Keller after he had killed *Voter* Luis? Had he lost his mind there and then, or had madness gradually wormed its way into his mind?

Marlene winced. It was too much. Too much all at once. She closed the book, got up, said goodnight to Keller then went to her bedroom and slipped under the blankets.

She thought about Lissy, and about Simon. He was a killer. Maybe because of *Voter* Luis. Maybe because of Elisabeth, who had died in his arms. Or maybe because of both. Maybe the trigger had been the solitude of this place. Or else . . . But did the reason really matter?

He was a killer. She had to focus on one crucial question: What was she going to do? Run away. But this time, prepare, make sure she had food and enough layers of clothing to protect her from the cold.

He's been here for a long time. He knows the mountains. The distance you cover in hours he gets through in minutes.

I was scared. I went round in circles. It won't happen again.

He's faster than you.

No. He's injured. He limps.

Did you see how he carried that deer on his back? He's strong. Much stronger than you.

I can do this.

Would you really gamble with the life of your child?

A sigh. What was she to do?

The answer was not long in coming. She thought about the Grimm story, the black-and-white illustrations.

Shut him in the oven and let him scream.

The force of this thought made her get out of bed, bending forward, her hand pressed to her mouth, until one knee touched the floor. The candle flame flickered but did not go out. If that happened, she would scream, and once she started she was not sure she would be able to stop.

She stood up, holding on to the chest of drawers, opened the window wide and breathed in lungfuls of icy air. Nausea seized her by the throat. Her stomach was churning. The first retch was so violent that she almost hit her chin against the window frame.

Once her stomach had stopped aching, she shut the window and went back to bed, her arm over her eyes.

Shut him in the oven and let him scream.

86

That night, after Marlene had retired to the bedroom, Keller went down into the pigsty, double-locked the little door and took a look at Lissy to make sure she was healing properly.

Lissy was sleeping on her side, her breathing regular. Before stitching her wound, he had given her some sodium pentothal to numb her and stop her from thrashing about. He stroked the white crest and examined the wound. The edges were red, but there was no sign of infection. Good. He tapped her on the muzzle and laughed. Lissy had a thick skull, just like him.

Before curling up next to Lissy, he went to the little window that looked into the cellar and ran his fingers over the metal. Lissy's fangs had scratched it. He could feel the marks with his fingertips. In some places, the metal was almost severed. He would have to replace it. And maybe, as he had said to Marlene, it was time to enlarge Lissy's cage. The boys and girls would have to be sacrificed, but the sow needed more space.

Four hundred kilos crammed into that cubbyhole. No wonder she went crazy.

He sighed and pictured the scene, the sow striking out, biting. An ugly sight. Lissy was not fierce, he thought affectionately, but she could be scary. He could well understand why Marlene had been overcome with panic. She had not lost her head, though, and he admired her for that. Marlene had thought about Lissy's well-being and had gone looking for him. It was a brave act. She had taken a big risk. If she had fallen or got lost . . . The mere thought filled him with horror.

He had decided to sleep down here so that when Lissy woke up, she would find him next to her and know that Sim'l would never abandon her. Because Sim'l loved Lissy and Lissy loved Sim'l. He moved away from the little window, snuggled up next to the sow and was about to put out the light, singing, "Sweet Lissy, little—"

The Voice stopped him from finishing. It had never been so powerful inside his head. A cacophony. The deep voice of *Voter* Luis, a whining voice like Elisabeth's, and grunts that were like bites. It hurt.

Keller lifted both hands to his temples.

She's seen. She'll betray you.

"No, she isn't a bad person."

She's done it before. You know she has. She left marks everywhere.

"You're wrong."

The Voice exploded in laughter so sharp it pierced through his skull.

She knows. She's seen. She knows.

"It's not true, it's impossible."

The Voice grew ingratiating.

She was running away. From me. From us. From you.

"Don't—"

She'll kill you. She'll kill me. She'll leave you on your own.

"You can't—"

She doesn't love you. Nobody loves Sim'l. Only Lissy. Nobody will ever love you the way I love you.

The Voice fell silent.

On all fours, Keller shook his head. "It's not true."

Who loves you as much as I love you, Sim'l? the Voice roared indignantly.

"Opa," Keller muttered. Then, in a louder voice, "Opa!" He leaped to his feet, colliding with Lissy.

That was when the unthinkable happened.

With one bound, Lissy threw herself at him, jaws wide open, eyes like tiny slits, muscles quivering, fangs glistening with saliva. Jerking backwards, Keller fell to one knee and the pain shot through him, clouding his vision. Lissy sank her fangs into air. A hollow sound that silenced the Voice.

Keller stared at Lissy. She met his gaze, a string of saliva hanging from a snout as black as night, fangs glistening in the light of the oil lamp. Motionless.

She lay back down and closed her eyes.

Keller left the sty, closed the little door behind him and fled into the woods.

87

Simon Keller had read all the Bibles of the past *Voter*, some more than once. He had immersed himself in them, searching for an answer. His faith was unshakable, but he was a man, and men are inquisitive. He wanted to discover the nature of the Voice.

After all, the Word itself had been dictated to men of faith by a Voice without face, body or blood. A Voice that would sometimes show compassion, at other times fury, but never explained anything about its nature.

He had discovered a lot. And at the same time, nothing. The Voice remained a miracle and a mystery.

Every time he finished reading one of his ancestor's Bibles, Keller would add it to the stack in the middle of the cellar. He had started doing this for practical reasons, in order not to confuse them – which sometimes happened. Then, once the stack had grown nice and big, he had started using it as a desk. It was on that altar, with a light within reach, that he copied his Bibles and read those of past *Voter*. The more he read the taller the altar grew, until it became unmanageable. He had considered building a second stack of books, but when he saw the shape the pile was taking, he decided to carry on erecting a kind of tall black pillar (he did not know the words "obelisk" or "monolith"), because he liked the idea of his ancestors' words reaching up to heaven from where the Word had come down. Besides, it was as good a way as any other of passing the time. Like making *Vulpendingen* or carving wooden animals.

One day, shortly before Lissy number six had given way to Lissy number seven, he had fallen ill. A sudden downpour of icy rain had caught him unawares when he was outside. By the time he was on his way back to the *maso*, he had already started feeling his temperature rising. Once indoors, he had collapsed on the bed fully dressed. Within a couple of hours, his temperature had turned into a raging fever that made his teeth chatter, made swallowing difficult and filled his slumber with nightmares. In the middle of the night, he had woken with a start and got up.

He had somehow dragged himself down to the cellar, where, in addition to Lissy's drugs, he kept a supply of medicines he used whenever *Kräutermandl* wisdom was at odds with the violence of nature. A few bottles of antibiotics, aspirin and anti-inflammatories. He used them sparingly because they were very expensive, but his fever was so high that he felt he needed them now.

He had descended the nine steps, his weak legs forcing him to lean against the wall, but once he was in the cellar, standing in front of the monolith of Bibles, instead of looking for the medicines, he had an idea and, without querying it, put it into practice. Even though his head was spinning, he climbed onto a wooden box (the same one Marlene would use years later) and placed his hat on top of the stack of Bibles. He tripped as he got down and banged his head, then picked himself up again and stood admiring his achievement.

"*Voter* is back," he said with a laugh.

He took the medicines, forced himself to have a sip of water and went back to bed. By the following morning, his fever had subsided. Once he had recovered, he slaughtered three pigs, used their skins to make leather and adorned it by branding little circles into it. Only then had he gone back down to the cellar to retrieve the hat from the top of the monolith.

The hat was the answer to his quest regarding the Voice.

There was no Voice. No Voice at all.

You're mad, Simon Keller. Like *Voter* Luis. You're simply mad.

He had covered the monolith with the leather sheet, closed the door and put the hat back on his head. The idea that he was mad had never crossed his mind again. Not until Lissy had attacked him and he had fled to the woods. There, in the middle of the night, leaning against a fir tree, chewing poppy seeds to keep the Voice at bay (it kept screaming, *Betrayal! Betrayal!*), Simon Keller began torturing himself again about the nature of the Voice. And thinking again about his father.

He had come to terms with *Voter* Luis' madness decades ago. He understood it. The grief over Mutti's death had been too great: *Voter* Luis had lost his mind and killed Lissy.

Could the same be true of him? What if he, too, were mad? And what if that was the reason he had killed so many people?

You're not mad. You did it because Lissy was hungry.

No, Lissy was just a sow.

Lissy loves you.

Keller felt a pang in his heart. Lissy, the real Lissy, had died years ago. When his father had lost his mind. When he himself still had a chance of a normal life: escaping *Voter* Luis, leaving the *maso*, getting off the mountain, working as a farmhand or becoming a skilled craftsman. A carpenter, maybe. He would have liked that. Sanding beams, making toys, cradles for babies.

It's the child. It's all because of him. He's the reason you've become blind, Sim'l.

Keller tried to take his mind off the clamour of the Voice. It did not exist. It was only in his head.

Who knows? Without the Voice, he might have found himself a wife. A nice girl to joke with and smile at, the way *Voter* Luis had done with Mutti before she died. He would have got married and had children, his own children. Lots of children, in whom he would have seen himself reflected.

Voter *Simon*? the Voice teased.

Keller stood up, furious. "Why not?"

Voter *Simon*. Opa *Simon*, the Voice sang.

"Be quiet!"

But the Voice would not keep quiet.

Lissy's Voice.

Except that Lissy had attacked him.

At this point, Keller had a thought that was even worse than the thought of his being mad.

Lissy was evil. Lissy did not love him. Lissy had never loved him. Lissy had put a chain around his neck and imprisoned him there, in the *maso*, with her. She had forced him to kill again and again.

Even the Voice fell silent at this terrifying thought.

Lissy was not hungry, Keller thought. Lissy was *evil*.

That was when Keller decided that he was mad and that he had to kill the sow.

The idea that Lissy could be evil was worse than madness.

88

Blue flames, he thought.

Opa, he thought.

He felt numb, devastated. Behind him, the first rays of light set the mountain tops ablaze. Ahead of him the *maso*.

He leaned against the door to the pigsty, panting. He had run out of poppy seeds. He waited a few minutes. When he felt ready, he opened the little door, went down the nine steps and slipped the rifle off his shoulder.

He thought of the blue flames rising up to heaven, of a little boy with a beauty spot and blue eyes, reaching out to be picked up because Opa Simon was tall and strong as an ash and no harm could ever come to him when he was in his arms.

Opa.

Keller entered Lissy's cage. He raised the rifle and pointed it at her head. Lissy was asleep. In her slumber, disturbed by the cold air coming in through the open door, she let out a snort. Keller put his finger on the trigger.

Blue flames, he thought.

Opa, he thought.

If *Voter* Luis had realised he was mad, would Elisabeth still be alive?

Yes, probably. He would not have killed her. *Voter* Luis was not an evil man.

Lissy was evil.

He breathed in and out.

His madness had been born with the sow with a mark on her snout and would end with the black, sleeping sow, because Lissy was the eye that offended.

Those had been *Voter* Luis' words, Keller thought, before he plunged the knife into Elisabeth's body.

He hesitated. He begged the Voice to return. Not to reassure him, but because if the Voice spoke it would try and dissuade him, and he would then have proof of its cruelty. He would then find the strength to pull the trigger.

The Voice was silent. Lissy kicked in her sleep and wagged her tail. She woke up. She noticed that he was there and got up. Her curiosity aroused, she sniffed the barrel of the rifle.

Keller lowered the weapon and went back to the *maso*.

89

Marlene found him motionless, staring into the fire. She had never seen flames that colour.

Blue.

Simon Keller turned to her with a faint smile, took a pinch of powder from a pouch and threw it on the fire. The blue became brighter. It turned a deep navy blue.

Kobolds, Marlene thought.

She looked at Simon Keller's face. It was a skull. She shuddered and raised her hand to her belly, protectively.

"We've been doing this forever," the skull muttered.

Marlene said nothing.

Simon Keller stood up. He was still wearing his greatcoat, which was dripping wet. He had been out all night, in the frost. "When someone dies we light a fire like this – blue."

Marlene's heart skipped a beat. "Who's dead?"

"Nobody. Not yet."

Head bowed, he walked out.

90

Shut him in the oven and let him scream.

The *maso* did not have an oven large enough, Marlene the Brave thought, but that did not discourage her. She would manage, somehow.

He walked, he asked questions, he made friends. He listened, even to drunkards, even to beggars sprawling on makeshift beds. He smiled, joked, bought drinks. But, above all, he listened.

And once the Trusted Man had listened sufficiently, once he was certain he had overlooked nothing, he would take his leave, find a secluded spot, get out the map of South Tyrol, carefully spread it and cross things out on it with a red marker. Small towns, bus stations, snack bars, convenience stores and ordinary, isolated houses. All the places where no one had seen either the Vixen or the Wolf. This way, the hiding place would eventually emerge of its own accord. Like an iceberg in an ocean of blood.

That was his method and it had never failed him. All it took was patience and determination, and the Trusted Man had plenty of both.

He was hunched over the map when someone knocked on his car window.

A hairpin bend, a wall of trees, a lay-by. A petrol station: nothing but a concrete cube with a sheet-metal roof and sash windows. No one ever came this way. The snow on the sides of the road had not even turned black. The ice-covered sign said CLOSED. Not a big deal, since it was self-service.

If it had not been for the car with the steamed-up windows, this is what would have happened: they would have filled the tank, had a smoke then driven off at lightning speed to look for a nightclub where they would have got drunk, picked a fight and worked off the toxins of a day spent repeating "Yes, sir." But this car was too enticing: parked in a secluded spot with steamed-up windows with no smoke coming from the exhaust pipe.

Robbing couples was fun.

There was no need even to discuss it. They had done it before. Terrified the couple and emptied their wallets. Easy money was what the beanpole in the passenger seat called it.

The beanpole's name was Markus. Walther was the short one. The names of the other two hardly mattered, they were just big lumps Walther and Markus had been dragging around with them forever, for no particular reason.

Of the four, Walther was the most sober. And the nastiest. He switched off the engine and they got out with scarves across their faces, leaving the doors wide open. Markus picked up a handful of snow and smeared it over the number plate. He checked and gave a sign. They surrounded the parked car. Walther tapped on the window.

The man in the car was alone. A pity: Walther enjoyed it when the girls started screaming. The man was elegantly dressed and had a map spread out on the passenger seat. Maybe he was lost. One thing was for sure: judging by his clothes, his wallet must be nice and full.

This would not be a waste of time.

"Get out."

The man was unperturbed. He did not even look surprised. He was calm, almost relaxed. He raised an eyebrow. "Why?" he said.

Annoyed, Markus slammed his hand down on the roof of the car. Walther tried the handle. It was unlocked. He opened the door and stood aside. "Get out."

The man turned up the collar of his thick jacket and obeyed, calmly, as if he had all the time in the world.

"Wallet."

The man took it out of his trouser pocket, opened it, counted a few banknotes and held them out.

Walther felt the blood pumping in his head. "All of it."

"I still have to fill her up. Surely you don't want to leave me stranded here?"

Markus gave a contemptuous laugh. The other two stepped forward menacingly. They had calluses on their hands and wide shoulders. Peasants and the children of peasants. Usually, their build alone was enough to make anyone with thoughts of being a hero see sense.

Not this time.

The smartly dressed man eyed them up for a second, then smiled at Walther.

That was all Walther was waiting for. He would have to get heavy. He pulled out his flick-knife and clicked open the sharp blade. "You want me to cut you open right here? Right now?"

The man looked around. "Not a bad place."

"He's crazy," one of the big lumps said, shaking his head. There was acne showing above his scarf.

"Do you want them or not?" the man said, waving the banknotes. "I'm starting to get cold."

Walther stepped forward and put the knife to the man's throat, piercing the skin and drawing a drop of blood.

The man did not lose his smile. He did not move either. He sighed. "Alright, then." He emptied his wallet and handed the notes to Walther, who snatched them and put them in his pocket.

This guy was making his blood boil. "I don't like smartarses. Give me the keys. Let's see what you have in the boot."

The man cocked his head. "It's not wise to tempt fate. If you tempt fate you might have to take a test. And you don't look very bright to me."

"If you don't shut up, I'll cut your throat."

One of the big lumps came forward with a grunt. He pushed the man aside, snatched the keys from the ignition and threw them to Markus, who caught them in mid-flight.

The lock of the boot was faulty, and it took a while to open it.

Once he had done it, he took a step back and let out a stifled cry, "Fuck it, Walther!"

"Surprise," the man muttered.

Walther glanced over at his friend, who stood there, staring vacantly into the boot. "What's in it? Money? Is he a smuggler?"

"Fuck, Walther. We're in deep . . ." Markus's voice broke.

Walther had known him all his life. He knew he was not the bravest of souls, but he also knew it was not like him to stammer like this.

"What is it?" Walther repeated. "What's in there?"

"The tools of the trade," the man said, making no attempt to run away, instead putting his hands on Walther's shoulders in a friendly, almost brotherly gesture.

Walther let out a gasp.

"Pressing a blade to the throat of a defenceless man is an irreversible act," the man said in a low voice. "Think carefully about what you're about to do. Do you know what the word 'irreversible' means?"

"Why don't you—"

"Keep still? Shut up?"

"Both."

"Or else?"

"I'll kill you."

"Have you ever done that? Have you ever killed anyone?"

Walther hesitated. Then he said to Markus, "Talk to me, for fuck's sake. What's in there?"

"Guns," was the reply. "I've never seen so many guns in my life." Walther stared open-eyed.

"And now," the man said, "it's time for the test. Are you ready?"

Walther swallowed. "You're crazy."

"Just as I imagined," the man said, taking hold of Walther's wrist and twisting it until it snapped. Then he kicked him in the ankle so that he fell and lay there, face up.

He pointed the knife at his eye. How he had managed to grab it so quickly, nobody ever worked out.

"Now say after me: 'Don't move, boys.'"

"You son of a—" The pain in Walther's wrist made him scream.

"Don't move, boys," the man repeated.

"Keep still," Walther whimpered.

There was no need to say it. None of his friends could have moved a muscle. They were paralysed.

The man threw the knife down in the snow, pulled out a gun and pointed it at Walther's forehead. "Let me tell you a story about an old man and a little boy. It's important. A test, remember? You lads have tempted fate. And fate is a strict teacher. Concentrate. Think. Listen. I want to tell you about an old man and a little boy. Are you listening?"

Walther nodded.

"What about you three?"

The three of them nodded.

"The old man was missing some fingers, because a wolf had eaten them. Can you believe it? A wolf. The little boy liked it when the old man told him about wolves. He would sit on his lap and say, 'Tell me about when you used to go hunting for wolves.' And every time, the man would smile and explain that it was the wolves that would come looking for him and not the other way around. They would come because he owned sheep, and the sheep were the first ones to notice when something was wrong. They would form a circle, with the lambs in the middle and the strongest sheep on the outside. To protect themselves, you see? Then the old man would pick up his double-barrelled rifle and wait. Once he saw those red eyes all around, he knew he was surrounded. Because that's what the wolves did, they blocked every avenue of escape. A bit like you. At that point, the pack would start howling."

The man laughed. Walther shuddered.

"You should have seen that crazy old man. He'd throw his head back and put on the best performance of a wild animal anyone had ever seen. And the little boy would stare and picture the wolves, the sheep, the forest and the night. He'd catch his breath and ask, 'So then you shot them?' 'Of course not,' the old man would reply. 'I had hardly any ammunition left, and there were a lot of them.' He'd stroke the boy's head and say, 'All I could do was pray they weren't too hungry.'"

The man looked at the four of them.

"And here's the test question: What was the old man trying to teach the little boy with his story about the wolves?"

No one answered. Not Walther, not Markus, not the two lumps.

"Don't be shy. The first answer doesn't count."

It was Markus who spoke up. "That it's trouble that comes looking for you and not—"

The shot echoed for a long time. It raised a spray of snow at

Markus's feet. Markus fell to his knees. His trousers were soaked in urine, but he was not hurt.

The man again pointed the gun at Walther's forehead.

"Your turn. But first I want to make something clear. I'm not going to kill you. You'll be the one to decide if you live or die. I'm only the guy who pulls the trigger." He sighed. "These are the two most important seconds of your life. Enjoy them."

Walther heard the crunch of the snow, the wind in the heavily laden branches of the forest, the noise of the motorway a few kilometres away, the chirping of a nightjar, the breathing of hibernating marmots. He heard his own heartbeat and fell in love with that sound.

The man smiled. "Now tell me. What was the old man with the missing fingers trying to teach the little boy?"

Walther ran his tongue over his lips. He stared straight into the man's eyes. "To tell the wolves from the sheep."

93

They helped him fill his car with petrol and returned his money. The Trusted Man shook hands with all of them, even Walther with his broken wrist. Smiling, he glanced at the map and drove off, leaving them behind.

94

It was not the rifle, it was not a knife, it was just a spoon. And she had needed a great deal of courage to steal it.

The rifle was the first thing that had come to mind. Steal it, load it, aim it and pull the trigger. Except that Marlene had never used a firearm and knew she would get only one chance. Fail, and she would end up being fed to the sow.

She had almost immediately dismissed the idea of using a knife. Better make do with a spoon. The disappearance of a spoon would hardly create a stir whereas a missing knife would be another story, and the last thing Marlene wanted was for Simon Keller to be uneasy. A spoon was a spoon, even at the North Pole. It was made of metal, just like a knife. And the metal could be sharpened and turned into a blade. Better to avoid Keller's questions.

Over the past few days, he had started behaving more strangely than usual. He had grown quiet and withdrawn. He spent a lot of time reading the Bible and muttering in such thick *dialekt* that Marlene could not make out what he was saying. He seemed to have no appetite and spent all day outdoors hunting. He always came back with his game bag full, and she had the impression it contained only a small part of whatever he had managed to shoot. His supply of ammunition was diminishing at an alarming rate.

Something else Marlene had noticed in the past few days was that the piglets Keller was carving had changed.

Click, click, click. He carved one piglet after another, as frenetically as if it were an assembly line. Except that now these small wooden figures were somewhat eerie. Their mouths were too big, their smiles too wide, their teeth like fangs. They were evil creatures, and they sent shivers down Marlene's spine.

Ever since the day Marlene had found Keller staring into those blue flames, he had not said a word about Lissy. Nor had he mentioned their leaving. Not that she cared. She had other things on her mind. Studying, planning.

Marlene the Brave had thought of everything.

Using remnants of old fabric, she had made herself a pair of slippers and stuffed the insides of the soles with cotton wool. Taking advantage of Keller's long absences, she had oiled the hinges of the *maso*'s doors. She had drawn a mental map of all the creaking floor-boards and started putting quantities of poppy into Simon's meals. Not enough to make him suspicious, but enough to dull his senses.

And she had stolen the spoon.

It was her weapon. She had sharpened it on the same grindstone Keller used for his hunting knife, so that now it was as sharp as a razor. She had hidden it in her pillowcase, and sleeping with her cheek against it gave her a sense of security. A faint one, but better than nothing. Meanwhile, she tried to follow the usual routine of the *maso*. Cooking meals, housekeeping, putting dry moss under the window frames, making new clothes for Keller, reading Grimm's fairy tales – and feeding the pigs.

Lissy had stopped coming forward. She would watch her, standing motionless at the edge of the shadowed area. That was fine by Marlene.

95

Every evening, before coming home, Simon Keller would go down to the pigsty and ring the little bell. Lissy would approach, and he would slip the rifle off his shoulder and point it at the animal's head.

Blue flames, he would think.

Opa, he would think.

He would think about the bowl of soup Elisabeth would never be able to finish. He would think about *Voter* Luis.

The Voice was silent.

Keller would chew poppy and go up to the *Stube*.

96

Keller noticed that Marlene's belly was growing. Despite the sweaters, the pregnancy had become clearly visible, her stomach softly curved. He could not take his eyes off her.

She considered fetching the spoon and plunging it into his throat, right there and then. She was scared.

That would have been madness, though. Keller was strong. And she was Marlene the Brave, not Marlene the Kamikaze.

Be clever, Marlene. Use your brain.

So she tried to distract him. She joked that she would soon be as fat as Lissy. She asked if *Voter* Luis had left any remedies to treat morning sickness, even though she had not yet had any bouts of it, and if it would not be a good idea to make the front door of the *maso* wider before she got stuck.

Keller did not answer any of her questions, did not smile at her jokes. At one point, he stood up, wild-eyed, and Marlene watched as he gathered all the figurines he had carved and put them in a bag, desperately searching for even the smallest wooden piglet under the bench against the wall, next to the poker, among the firewood.

Finally, hugging herself, she followed him out of the *Stube* into the open air.

She saw him hunched on all fours like a dog, digging a hole in the frozen snow with his bare hands. She saw blood trickling between his fingers, but she said nothing. She was terrified.

Keller emptied the bag into the hole, got laboriously to his feet, putting his weight on his good leg, threw powder in the hole and set it on fire. The blue flames rose high in the air.

Once the flames had died down, Keller took the rifle and shut himself in the pigsty. He stayed there for hours.

At dusk, Marlene heard a shot. Then another and another. She ran to the pigsty and saw Keller come out through the little door. He was crying, and he was bloodstained.

Marlene pretended nothing was wrong. She ate, unable to summon the courage to look at him. She pretended to read, pretended not to hear the chanting emerging from his lips.

"*Opasimonopasimonopa* . . ."

Then she went back to her room. She had made up her mind. Tonight would be *the* night.

97

Then it was just the hours of waiting.

The night.

Seven days after the king, the boar and the attempted escape. Marlene was certain she had not neglected a single detail. All she had to do was act.

She waited for midnight and let it pass. Wegener had once told her that the police liked to kick down doors at around four in the morning because that was when everybody's guard is lowered.

Marlene did not have a watch, but she had calculated the time by the movements of the night sky through the shutters.

The waning moon could be seen between the mountain peaks, looking like a child's drawing. It made her shudder, and she turned her eyes away.

At the appointed hour, she got ready.

Not a sound.

She put on the slippers and took the spoon. She closed the shutters and waited for her eyes to grow accustomed to the darkness. Counting her steps, she went to the door.

It was freezing inside the *maso*: even the moss and the double panes of glass could not keep out the winter cold. And yet Marlene was drenched in sweat. She had never felt so hot in her life. Or so afraid. It took her a few seconds to summon up her courage. The oiled hinges moved without a sound. She had done a good job. She stepped out into the corridor.

One step forward, one to the left. Forward again, then left. A kind of waltz.

Marlene walked down the corridor, focusing on her mental map of the floorboards: which ones creaked, which ones were sturdy. It was like walking in a minefield. The sharpened spoon in her right hand, her left one clenched in a fist. No more fear, no more nausea. She was determined, and she was strong. Marlene the Brave wasn't fighting for her own life. She was doing it for Klaus. Klaus gave her courage.

She needed it.

She stopped outside Keller's bedroom, bent down to the keyhole and peeped in. It was pitch black in there. She pressed her ear to the time-darkened wood. All she heard was the buzzing of her over-excited ears. Good.

He's asleep. Kill him.

She tried the handle, lowered it and pushed. The door opened a few centimetres. It slid on its hinges with the grace of a ballerina. She had done a good job. Not a squeak. She opened it a little more, just enough to listen.

Nothing.

A few more centimetres. She held her breath.

She popped her head around the door and looked in.

In comparison with the corridor, Keller's bedroom was better lit, because he slept with his shutters open. The light of the half-moon was enough to allow her to make out the extinguished candle on the bedside table, a Bible and part of the bed.

The door was now half open. She pushed it some more and took one step forward.

Piled-up blankets, the black hat hanging on the wall.

As silent as a mouse, Marlene tiptoed to Keller's bed. She raised her arm.

She had prepared herself, imagining the scene of the murder: the flesh ripped open, the blood gushing, the screams. Above all, she had prepared herself to have no pity, even though she knew that the memory of what she was about to do would give her nightmares for the rest of her life.

But it did not happen like that. She struck, with all her might, then struck again. The spoon only cut through the sheets and pillows.

Then the voice came. A voice like stone.

98

Simon Keller had killed them. All of them.

He had done it for Marlene. For the child.

He had fired quickly and reloaded even faster. To stop the fear from creeping in. A shot in the back of the neck and they had collapsed on top of each other.

He felt bad about all these deaths. Their screams still echoed in his ears. Their eyes, imploring pity, gave him no peace. That was why he could not sleep, even though his head was spinning as if he had taken too much poppy. He was tired, infinitely tired. His hands, still heavy with pig blood, reminded him of the scale of the massacre, tormenting him.

He got out of bed and looked at the moon over the mountains. He stood because his knee was driving him mad with pain and sitting was torture. The moon did not calm him.

He moved away from the light and leaned against the wall. Lost in the shadows, he started to pray. Even though he knew he was in the right, he could find no peace.

Peace did not come, and nor did sleep.

He stood motionless, praying, waiting for a sign.

The sign came.

The girl. *The betrayal.*

Keller watched as Marlene struck the sheets and pillows. Only then did he open his mouth.

An old song.

The same one Sim'l had sung so many times to sweet little Lissy.

"*Nibble, nibble, little mouse! Who is nibbling at my house?*"

99

Marlene swerved to the side.

Behind her was the menacing form of a man, arms folded, his back to the wall. For a moment, she thought it was *Voter* Luis. She screamed.

But wasted no time.

Marlene the Brave lunged at Keller, who dodged her and grabbed her by the arm, squeezing it hard. The pain forced her to let go of the spoon. It fell to the floor. Marlene felt herself being lifted up. In vain, she struggled.

Keller shook her and sent her thudding into the wall. She felt the vibration of the impact travel down her shoulder to her elbow and then up to her head. She was seeing double.

Keller picked her off the floor and lifted her up once again in his steel grip. "I refused to believe it. I refused."

He shook her again, his face a mask of animal hatred, and flung her to the floor. Her forehead hit the floorboards. A spider's web of white lights whirled in front of her eyes.

Keller took her by the hair and dragged her out of the room. She attempted to struggle free, kicking and trying to sink her nails in the floorboards.

"I refused," he cried as he dragged her towards the stairs. "I refused to believe it."

Klaus!

Marlene crossed her arms over her belly, raised her knees and bent her head, instinctively, to protect Klaus at all costs.

Pain each time she hit a step. Teeth clenched, tears in her eyes.

Her bones did not break.

Keller was still shouting. "She told me! Yes, she told me!"

Marlene mumbled words of apology, words that made no sense.

"I told her it couldn't be true," he went on. "That you weren't a bad person."

They reached the *Stube*.

Keller crouched over her, his breath smelling of poppy. "I was wrong."

Marlene curled up, but he did not hit her.

"I knew it. I knew it."

"Please . . ."

"She never lies," Simon muttered. "Never."

Marlene turned just enough to look him in the eye. "Who?"

He opened the door to the cellar. She tried to crawl away. There was a poker next to the fireplace, which she could have used as a weapon. But her head was spinning and her shoulder throbbed. The violence of Keller's attack had been a real shock. She was slow. Too slow.

"Who?" she said again in a thin voice.

Keller lifted her by the ankle as if she were one of the animals he hunted and killed.

"*Who?*" Marlene cried one last time.

There were nine steps down. She did not hit a single one. She landed straight on the floor, in the dark.

100

It was the smell, the sickly sweet stench that told her where she was even before she opened her eyes. She forced herself to breathe through her mouth, but it was worse: like having a sponge pushed down her throat. Her stomach churned, and she felt as if she were about to vomit. She managed to resist. She even managed not to start screaming. It would have been pointless anyway.

She peered around her. The green light from the little window on her right, which looked into the pigsty, cast shadows over the mess under which the room was buried.

Balls of spiders' nests all over the place. Buckets tipped over, broken boxes.

The *Vulpendingen* bones. And others she did not want to think about.

In the middle, covered by the leather sheet, the monolith. In this strange light, the patterns seemed to move, like the coils of a snake.

On all fours, moving like a crab, Marlene crawled to the little window, keeping her eyes fixed on the monolith, as if it might pounce on her.

The light made her feel better. Marlene peered through. What she saw took her breath away. The carcasses of the pigs. Blood. A massacre.

She retched and looked away.

She huddled close to the window, raised her knees to her chest and hugged them tight. She cried, then stopped, then cried some more.

The pain started all of sudden, at the base of her skull. She felt as if she were being pulled backwards. She slid, unwillingly going along with the force of it, and felt the pain again, even stronger than before, if that were possible.

She tried to resist, and the pain made her scream. Groping, she felt something humid and alive on the other side of the metal bars, something that smelled rotten and wild, yanking her by the hair. She screamed.

Again, she was yanked, and this time her hands and the back of her neck hit the bars. She tried to free herself. The pain increased.

Lissy was strong.

Marlene pulled away with all her strength, feeling her scalp splitting. The sound of tearing was awful. It hurt, but it worked. She fell headlong amid the junk. Panting, she turned.

From the other side of the bars, Lissy was staring at her, a lock of hair in her fangs.

Lissy. The only survivor of the massacre.

Like Abraham, Keller had stopped short of killing his favourite.

The panic ebbed away to be replaced by anger. Marlene approached the window and spat at the animal's snout.

"Fuck off, you bitch!"

Lissy blinked.

I know who you are, sweetie. I know it only too well. And I also know what you're about to become.

Marlene punched the bars. "You don't know anything!"

Lissy did not bat an eyelid. The hair had vanished from her fangs. Marlene did not want to know where it had gone. She slumped to the floor, her hands over her face.

She was losing her mind. What was the point of picking on the sow?

You're food. That's what you are, sweetie. Food for Lissy.

Marlene got to her feet, climbed the nine steps and started beating on the cellar door with her fists. She yelled, thumping and kicking the door. All she got for her pains was scraped knuckles, but at least she had let off steam.

She felt more lucid. Try to think, she told herself. There's a lot of stuff down here. Your luck could change.

She looked through the shelves, knocked over stacks of books, turned clothes and old suitcases upside down. Lifting a leather bag, she heard a metallic sound, and something fell to the floor.

She groped around until she found the origin of the sound: a metal file. It was old, narrow and rusty, but . . .

Lissy grunted.

"Drop dead, you bitch!" Marlene cried, then burst out laughing and only managed to stop by biting her tongue until it bled.

Brandishing the file as if it were a dagger, she imagined stabbing it into Simon Keller's neck. The thought made her feel better.

"Then it'll be your turn," she said, turning towards the window.

She was answered by a bark-like grunt. *Just try.*

She had to get out of here, or she would go mad. She climbed back up to the door, closed one eye and looked through the keyhole. All she saw was darkness, with maybe just the glow of the stove. Marlene inserted the file in the keyhole and started turning it, the way she had seen it done in the thrillers Wegener loved watching. It was madness, but she had nothing to lose. Fortune favours the brave, she told herself.

The brave and (Mamma) the mad.

Twice, she heard an encouraging sound, a *click* that filled her with hope, but twice the file slipped from her fingers. She did not give up. Concentrating hard, hair plastered to her face, she bent over the keyhole, trying once more to click it open.

"Damned bitch. Damned b—"

The file curved in her fingers and broke into two pieces, one of which bounced up. Marlene jumped back. The blade had narrowly missed her eye.

Game over.

Marlene burst into tears.

She was hungry, but mainly she was thirsty. The hunger increased by the hour, but the thirst was worse: it increased by the minute. And the more she tried not to think about it, the more it drove her insane.

The stench in the basement had taken second place. She had got used to it.

Marlene did not know how much time had passed. Hours? Days?

Lissy's grunts filled her with horror and disgust. Every so often, the sow would look through the bars, as if enjoying the show. Marlene had stopped insulting her. She was too thirsty, and it would have been a waste of energy.

She had drifted off to sleep and woken up so many times she had lost count. Once, she thought she heard Simon Keller's voice on the other side of the barred window.

Sweet Lissy, little Lissy.

Marlene had groped her way closer, pressed her face to the bars and seen him. Keller was stroking Lissy's head. Marlene had begged him to let her out. She had cried and screamed. He had not so much as glanced at her. Neither had the sow. Marlene had resigned herself.

Now she thought it must have been a dream.

She was hungry, and she was thirsty. She had stopped begging some time ago.

It was the thirst. The thirst made her delirious. She talked to Lissy. She talked to her parents, mainly to her mother, but also to her dried-up little mouse of a father. She insulted them, then begged their forgiveness.

She talked to Wegener.

The world had shrunk to this stinking room, with Lissy's breathing, grunting and snorting as background to the delirium and the thirst. The terrible thirst.

At the end of the second day (or was it the beginning of the third?), her nostrils started to detect a vague smell of damp. It was a smell that went to her head, and it was torture.

At first, she thought it was a trick of her imagination. The smell was real, though. Marlene sniffed and realised it came from the worst place of all. The window to the pigsty. No, no, no.

She would not go near it. No, never again.

But then she dragged herself to the window, only to turn back. One centimetre, two. Ten. Then back again.

Time dragged on. Her fear subsided.

Marlene spent hours looking at the monolith in the middle of the cellar.

Going back and forth to the window.

Towards the smell of water.

After a while, the thirst obliterated the fear. She crawled, one centimetre at a time. When she reached the window, she pulled herself up into a seated, cross-legged position. Her back was aching and her knuckles, which she had hurt when pounding on the thick wooden door, felt itchy. She kept scratching them, making them bleed. She had tried drinking the blood but it had not helped. She needed water. That was all she asked for. A few drops.

She reached out and ran her fingers over the metal, feeling the marks left by Lissy's fangs. At the point where the metal met the stone, there was humidity. She lifted her fingers to her mouth. The water made her feel dizzy.

She heard a grunt, and pulled away.

You mustn't, you mustn't. You can't, you can't.

Marlene sat there frozen, staring at the drops oozing from the chink in the wall.

The thirst.

She knelt in front of the window and put her lips to it. The dampness had a metallic taste. Her brain exploded with gratitude. She started licking, licking and crying, in gratitude and terror and madness.

She did not stop licking for a second. Not even when she saw Lissy, motionless, staring at her.

103

The Trusted Man's map was covered in red marks. All the places where Marlene *had not* been seen. All the places where the Wolf *had not* been seen.

The red marks multiplied until they were superimposed, one on another. They created a borderline which, as the days and the questions went by, turned into an irregularly shaped patch that looked like the wound from a gunshot fired at point-blank range.

In the middle, surrounded by all that red, was a tiny village, at the entrance to a long, narrow valley surrounded by tall peaks. A village like so many others, with a small church, steps leading up to its entrance, a few houses and an inn.

The Trusted Man arrived there in the evening. And, as usual, he began to make friends. Three old men who liked a good laugh, to be precise.

104

The lights in the inn were still on well past midnight because the well-dressed stranger who had parked his car next to the church never seemed to tire, and he had the cash to buy them drinks.

He was a friendly fellow, even though he had good teeth and not so much as one broken fingernail. A bit too much of a city slicker for their liking, but you never said no to free beer. So they chatted, laughed and told stories.

A man dressed in an old-fashioned black greatcoat, the kind they don't make anymore, which can withstand rain, snow and cold. Do you know him?

Of course we do. We've seen him.

Then they nudged each other and began to snigger. The Trusted Man kept his smile. He raised the beer to his lips and pretended to drink.

"We saw him forty years ago."

And they laughed hysterically.

"Forty years ago?"

"Give or take. They called him *Voter* Luis. A *Bau'r*. A *Kräutermandl*. He was a good man. Peter here can tell you what a good man he was, isn't that so, Peter?"

The old man with the ruddy nose and watery eyes nodded so energetically that he spilled some beer on himself, right on the crotch of his trousers, triggering more laughter.

"He saved my wife. It was in . . . Let me think. Was the war over or not?"

"There's just one problem, stranger," one of the three old men said. "*Voter* Luis died a long time ago. Looks like you're chasing a ghost." And he slapped the table.

The Trusted Man signalled to the barman to bring more beer. "The man I'm looking for is still alive. But it's a beautiful evening and we're all friends. You've made me curious. Are there really ghosts around here?"

The three old men laughed, but not the way they had earlier.

"That's just nonsense."

"I like nonsense."

The old men exchanged looks, and the drunkest of the three, who was also called Peter but unlike the other one had a bloated belly and not a single hair on his head, stroked his thick beard and knocked back his drink.

"They say that towards the end of his life," he said, tapping his own temple, "*Voter* Luis wasn't all there. He went mad and started messing about with fire."

"If you're going to tell it," the other Peter interrupted, "then tell it properly. He wasn't mad, he—"

"Oh, he wasn't, was he?" The third old man muscled in. He had a droopy moustache, like a Viking. "What would you call someone who starts worshipping the devil?"

The Trusted Man raised an eyebrow. "The devil? *Voter* Luis worshipped the devil?"

Fat Peter slammed his hand down on the table. "You see why it's nonsense? *Voter* Luis, may he rest in peace, was a decent man. But after his wife died he became a little . . . strange. That, definitely. I remember it well. And maybe his daughter's death made him more solitary than before. Of course it did. My brother, down in Monguelfo, lost his son. He had an accident while he was taking the hay down the mountain on a sledge – he was crushed, poor boy – and my brother almost lost his mind from grief. It's only natural, don't you think?"

"Except that no one ever found out how *Voter* Luis died," the Viking said suggestively.

Fat Peter snorted. "People die, that's all."

"So where does the ghost come in?"

"I've never believed in ghosts."

"Oh, really?" the other Peter said. "And what about people going missing? You don't believe in that, either?"

"What people?" the Trusted Man asked.

"It's all part of the story," the third old man said, while the two Peters hunched over their glasses. "Because we're all talking about the same story, stranger. And if you want to hear it, you should treat us to something better than this cow's piss."

The Trusted Man did not need to be asked twice. The innkeeper left a bottle of grappa on the table, together with the keys to the inn. "You lock up," he said. "I'm going to bed."

He left.

"*Voter* Luis dies, but his ghost makes people disappear?" the Trusted Man asked, after the first round.

"He makes them disappear. Quite a few people. He kills them, so they say. Not that the rest of us" – he coughed – "really believe that."

"It's just a story."

"It's just a story."

"And where would I find this ghost?"

"In *Voter* Luis' *maso*," fat Peter said. "At the far end of the valley, high above the treeline. A hellish place."

"What's beyond the valley?"

"Mountains. Glaciers. That's what."

"And beyond the glaciers?"

"Austria, obviously," the other Peter replied.

The Trusted Man took out his map with the marks all over it and put it on the table, shifting the empty glasses and the bottle of grappa out of the way. "And no one goes through there?"

The three old men didn't reply.

The Trusted Man smiled. "Smugglers?"

"Who do you think you're talking to?"

"I'll take that as a yes. And do they all come back?"

The Viking toyed with his glass. "A person doesn't always have to come back the same way he went, does he?"

"So is there or isn't there a ghost?"

Fat Peter refilled the Trusted Man's glass. "There certainly are three old men enjoying making fun of a stranger. There's only rocks, snow and death up there in the mountains if you don't know what you're doing. And you're not a mountain man, am I right?"

The Trusted Man spread the map on the dirty table. "No, but I'm curious. Can you show me where *Voter* Luis' house is?"

The Viking stood up. "I'm going to have a pee, and then I'm going home. My wife will be worried."

The other two laughed. No one put a finger on the map.

"Please." The Trusted Man moved the map towards the two Peters.

It was the thinner Peter who pointed a thick finger at the far end of the valley. "Here."

"And where's the area where they say people go missing?"

The first Peter drew a circle large enough to encompass mountain peaks, glaciers and depressions. "More or less here," he muttered.

The Trusted Man examined the map. The image he had formed of the Wolf suddenly vanished. Instead, he pictured a spider. A long-legged spider lying low amid these mountain peaks, surrounded by an invisible web, waiting for a victim: an unfortunate little fly. That explained his familiarity with death. The clean cut to the throat, the indifference, the madness.

Especially the madness.

But not his connection to the Vixen.

"This entire area?"

The two Peters exchanged glances. "More or less."

"It's many, many hectares," the Trusted Man said. "At an altitude of two thousand metres."

"A hellish place."

"Could you be more specific?"

In the meantime, the Viking had come back and sat down, grumbling. "It's a dangerous area, my boy. We had a laugh, a joke. We had fun, didn't we? But that's still a dangerous area. I wouldn't set foot there for love nor money."

"Bullshit," the second Peter said.

"Would you go there?" the Viking said, challenging him.

Both Peters bowed their heads.

The Trusted Man waited. This was the right moment. The moment when the three old men would either continue bullshitting or spill the beans.

The Viking knocked back the remains of his drink. "Listen," he said in a low voice. "Here's the story. Forget about ghosts and all the rest, alright?"

The Trusted Man smiled. "Clean slate."

"*Voter* Luis was a good man. A man of faith. We all know he saved quite a few people before he went mad. His wife died in childbirth, and then a few years later his daughter died. Whenever he came down to the village he'd talk nothing but rubbish. Then he also died and his son was left behind. All the rest, about *Voter* Luis starting to worship the devil, is just nonsense, something to scare the kids."

"And nosey strangers," fat Peter added, pouring himself a drink.

"*Voter* Luis had a son?"

"He's the ghost. He comes down to the village every now and then. Doesn't talk much. He's . . . he's different."

"What does 'different' mean?"

"He wears his father's clothes," the Viking said. "That's why they say he's *Voter* Luis' ghost. But it's just spite."

"What about the people who go missing? Could it be that . . ."

"People disappear here same as anywhere else," the Viking said emphatically. "Some end up in a crevasse, others get killed over a gambling debt. Then there are those who drop everything and move to town without telling anyone. It's just that the loud-mouths always have to have their say. When they say it was the ghost, they're actually blaming the poor fellow. Believe me. I've spoken to him. He's a man of faith, like his father. An eccentric, yes. And a lone wolf, that's for sure. Who on earth could live all alone up there? But" – and here the old man leaned towards the Trusted Man and looked him straight in the eye – "*Voter* Luis' son isn't dangerous. He's got his *maso*, his mountain, and he doesn't want anything else."

"Everybody wants something else," the Trusted Man said with a sneer.

"Not him."

Finally, the second Peter spoke, his eyes swimming in drink. "You're going up there, aren't you, son?"

"Maybe, maybe not."

"It's a dangerous place for a city slicker."

"Appearances can be deceptive."

"You like dancing with the devil, don't you?"

The Trusted Man held out as long as he could, then burst out laughing, tears running down his cheeks. "I'm sorry, I'm sorry, I . . ." He sniffed and tried to catch his breath but could not stop laughing, despite all his efforts. "Please excuse me if I seem rude. It's just that I, too, in a way, was raised by a man of faith and . . ."

He could not go on. He rolled up his shirtsleeves. His arms were covered in burns. The three old men, who had seen many horrors in the war, were taken aback.

The Trusted Man still could not stop that irrepressible laughter. "Please excuse me, really . . ." He took out a handkerchief and wiped his eyes. "The devil . . . I'm really sorry . . . the devil doesn't exist. I know. These scars are my witnesses."

105

Six. Nine. Four. Four.

Another combination for accessing the past. Two things happened in Bolzano on 6 September 1944. The blinding flash of a meteorite lit up the night sky, and a baby was born. A blond little angel with a downturned mouth.

The baby was a little angel, but a sulky little angel. A seraph. He did not laugh and he never cried. A thoughtful child, the doctor told his mother, who was concerned about her otherwise healthy son. And who could blame her?

He had been born during the bombardment (although this was not true: the first bomb fell on Bolzano on the ninth of September, not the sixth; the sixth was the day of the meteorite) and had had to take life seriously from his first breath.

It was a joke, and his mother laughed. Deep down, she thought the doctor was a prize idiot.

The child grew, a self-absorbed boy who did not laugh or cry.

At school, he was top of the class. The teacher never missed an opportunity to praise him in front of schoolmates and colleagues. If he had conformed to the cliché, he would have been hopeless at sports, but this was not the case. He was always in the top three at competitions. He was nimble, accurate and tireless.

His father was very proud of the prizes the boy would bring home, and displayed them in a row, like soldiers, behind the cash register in the family shop in Dodiciville, northwest of Bolzano. Unlike his wife, he was not worried about his son's behaviour. His ancestors were made of strong stuff, heroes who had fought under Andreas Hofer against Napoleon and the French. They certainly weren't people who gave in to their emotions. Besides, he thought the boy looked happy.

And indeed he was.

Until the age of nine, the world of the boy who did not laugh or cry was perfect. Everything around him – cars rushing past over the cobbles, women chatting at the market on Piazza Erbe, the aroma of cakes in the oven, sparrows chirping on the windowsill – was pure illusion. The world would start when he opened his eyes in the morning and sink into darkness as soon as he drifted into sleep. That was why the boy did not laugh or cry. Nothing could touch him because nothing really existed.

Except for him.

He was the only real thing in this perfect world. At least until, aged nine years and six months, he was scratched by a cat.

The boy had reached out to touch it, and the cat had reacted. As simple as that. Except that when the boy pulled his hand away, he was horrified to realise that he could see through it. Overcome with panic, he ran home and looked at himself in the mirror. His suspicions were confirmed. His image was blurred and grainy.

He was disappearing, the way the chalk vanished whenever the caretaker washed the blackboard. Worse still, as the days went by, this process did not stop. On the contrary, it accelerated.

People in the street bumped into him without apologising. Children playing in the courtyard did not invite him to join them. The teacher's eyes drifted from one side of him to the other. He was stung by a bee, and his mother did not notice.

As he disappeared, his thoughts went in bizarre, unexpected directions. He had fantasies so vivid they seemed real: his father in a pool of blood, the sweet girl in knee-high socks who sat next to him in class writhing in flames, his mother blue in the face, strangled.

Unlike the sense of disintegration, which filled him with anxiety, these imaginings were pleasant. And since his anguish was becoming increasingly stifling, the boy clung to these fantasies with all his might.

Until these thoughts gave him an idea for arresting the process of disintegration. No sooner did he conceive it than he felt relief.

How come he had not worked it out sooner?

He lured the stray cat with bacon he had pilfered from the pantry at home, ran it through with a sharpened stick (imagining he was doing this to his mother's stomach, which excited him so much that he almost fainted) and, as he looked into its dying, suffering eyes, he saw his own reflection reappear. By the time the cat breathed its last, the process was complete.

The boy laughed. He laughed for the first time in his life. He laughed with tears in his eyes. He laughed as though the sun had exploded inside his chest. Because when it came down to it, he was the sun.

Nobody noticed anything. Time passed.

Thirteen years after the night of the meteorite, as is customary in good families, the boy was entrusted to the care of a holy man, so that the latter might add a spiritual dimension to his intellectual growth.

The holy man took him with him to the fortress of the Lord: the Vinzentinum, the seminary in Brixen. He taught him to cultivate friendships and feel love towards all creatures, to be sensitive to art and beauty and see talent as a precious gift. He taught him to cook (the boy proved a genuine prodigy, although his father turned his nose up at the prospect of his son as a cook) for the soup kitchen.

Above all, he taught him self-discipline and mercy.

The boy, now a young man, made sure he learned these lessons. Self-discipline allowed him to keep his fantasies of death at bay, although they still haunted him. The excitement of seeing the life draining from the cat's eyes, followed by a violent sense of complete-ness, had a powerful appeal. The temptation to repeat the experience was strong, almost irresistible at times. Perhaps he could kill a dog? Or one of the cows grazing in the fields outside the city? Every so often, he flirted with the idea of killing a human being. What stopped him, besides self-discipline, was the holy man's other teach-ing: mercy.

Mercy, the holy man had explained, helped us to see the world with the eyes of God. That was true. Looking at the world with the eyes of God was like watching a show from the top of a mountain and realising just how unreal everything was. Apart from the person looking and his mercy.

When neither mercy nor self-discipline was able to chase away his death wish, the young man learned to use pain. Feeling a little pain made the desire vanish.

During the long years of study that took him to the verge of qualifying as a schoolteacher, the young man was once again the only real thing in the world.

Until a drunken prostitute mistook him for a priest. Not exactly a huge error. After all, the young man enjoyed going for walks with his mentor, during which the holy man would indulge in digressions about the nature of God. These digressions never failed to fascinate him. He had been struck by one in particular. The Lord is the point from which all trajectories unravel, the holy man said. In His infinite mercy, God traces the life of every one of His creatures. Trajectories no one can avoid.

"Irreversible" was the word he had used.

The woman was no beauty. She was drunk and not soliciting. She was sad, she wanted to confide in somebody, and she had mistaken him for a priest. So she approached him.

His first instinct was to run away. He sensed danger in this woman. Perhaps it was her weary expression, or her strong resemblance to the black-and-white photographs of his mother as a young woman. He did not know.

Still, he did not leave.

They walked through the slumbering town. She told him about her wretched life, and he listened, feeling increasingly uneasy. He kept looking at their shadows cast by the street lights, worried for no apparent reason. Then, all of a sudden, in an alley, the woman pressed her lips to his. Her hands started touching him in places where no woman had ventured before.

Confused, he pulled away from her and, without even thinking, grabbed her by the throat with both hands and squeezed with all his might. He would have killed her, had he not noticed that his hands were starting to disappear. The panic he had felt as a child returned a thousandfold.

He ran away, his legs barely supporting him. He was growing weaker by the minute. He reached the seminary thinking only of pain. Pain would help him.

He found two cans of kerosene in the basement. One was empty, and the other he poured over his arms. The pain of the flames was atrocious. So were his screams, which drew attention. The last images registered by his mind before he lost consciousness were his companions' horrified faces and the holy man's devastated expression as he recited the expulsion ritual. The holy man was performing an exorcism. And for the second time in his life, the young man laughed, genuinely laughed.

Then came the hospital, where, numbed by drugs, he had ample time to meditate. His family, ashamed of his mental illness, disowned him. That was no big deal: he had never really loved them. When he recovered, he noticed that the pain caused by the fire had not halted the disintegration process, but had merely slowed it. So once he was discharged, he went looking for the prostitute.

Instead, he found her pimp, a man with rotting teeth and rank breath, who beat him up. After he had finished, he dragged him to the apartment of a lawyer, a man highly respected in the criminal community, who was called in whenever a dispute had to be settled. The pimp would have accepted compensation, but the young man had no money, and the pimp (who, in his heart, believed he loved the prostitute who had nearly been killed) asked permission to kill him. The lawyer asked to be left alone with the culprit.

They talked.

And, as they talked, the lawyer realised that this young man possessed a rare talent: he felt no emotions. He compensated the pimp from his own pocket and got rid of him. Then he put the young man to the test. He told him about a card sharp who had been cheating the wrong people. The young man found him and killed him. In killing him, he became real again.

The lawyer was impressed with his work. The young man killed cleanly, and had proved to be a real bloodhound. The lawyer told him about a group of people who needed a weapon like him. They were known as the Consortium, and they were capable of showing gratitude. He would be well rewarded for his services.

The young man had no use for any reward. The world belonged to him, it was there for him. He would have refused if it had not been for one word the lawyer used.

"Weapon."

A weapon, the young man thought, dazzled, was just metal that destiny had turned into an instrument of death instead of a hoe or a tin can. A weapon was innocent. The guilty one was the person who pulled the trigger. A weapon looked at the world with eyes full of mercy. A weapon was the point from which irrevocable trajectories unravelled.

So a weapon he became.

They said goodbye at the door. The Viking was the first to leave, stooped against the lashing wind. Then it was the turn of fat Peter, who set off singing a dirty song.

Only the second Peter was still left. Of the three old men at the inn, he was the one who had drunk the most but had remained the most clear-eyed.

"So you were raised by a man of faith, were you?"

"They said he was a holy man."

"But you're not a man of faith."

"No."

The second Peter rubbed his hands to warm them. "You're not a mountain man either, but you want to go up there."

The Trusted Man looked in the direction the second Peter was pointing: the black, gaping mouth of the valley. "That's right."

The second Peter spat on the ground. "You don't believe in the devil, and yet you want to meet him."

A twisted smile appeared on the Trusted Man's face. "You could put it like that."

"And you really expect me to believe you're not a man of faith?"

It was the smell of burning that led him to the *maso*. If the wind had not brought that acrid blast to his nostrils, he would have given up.

He had left early in the morning, wearing the latest fashion in ski suits, padded and windproof, after spending the night preparing the equipment and checking the maps. With a spring in his step, he had entered the valley, heading north.

A few hours later, he had got rid of the skis and put on crampons to go up above where the vegetation ended, trying to avoid being seen (yet feeling like a target at every step). He advanced, hidden by ice-covered rocks, increasing his pace whenever there was nothing to take shelter behind.

Every so often, he would stop, take a sip from his flask and check the map. Then he would take off his rucksack and move his shoulders about to restore circulation. He would drink, catch his breath and resume walking.

The further he went, the scarcer the signs of human presence became. At first, there was the occasional mountain hut with closed shutters, then ruins half buried in the snow and finally nothing.

In the meantime, despite himself, he could not stop thinking about the words of the three old men. Their description of the Spider, *Voter* Luis' son. A man who did not want anything.

They were wrong.

Everybody wanted something. Money, sex. Some wanted revenge, others fame. Most people were content with food, a warm bed and a simple life. But sex, money, fame and food were merely masks concealing the truth.

All men, in the secrecy of their own conscience, knew they were not real. They asked for a faithful companion, a well-paid job, a magnificent castle, but what they yearned for was something that would tear them away from their illusory state. That was why, once they had reached their long-desired goal, they would sink into a painful, dismayed emptiness. They realised they had asked for the wrong thing. They had longed for reality but were terrified by it.

All of them, except one.

The three old men had no way of knowing this, but if there was one person who did not need to ask for anything, it was not the hermit in the black greatcoat, but the Trusted Man.

He did not need to ask for anything because he *was everything*. That was why men were afraid of him and, at the same time, fascinated by him. They sensed that there was something different about him. And they were right. He was real, while they were not. He had realised this years ago.

And yet those words tormented him, and he kept thinking about them all day. He thought of them as he climbed ever higher, increasingly self-absorbed even as he trod the mountain slopes and searched the horizon.

The fading daylight had caught him by surprise, and he was on the verge of turning back. He knew he would not find anything at night, except death from exposure.

And he would indeed have turned back, if it had not been for the smell of burning.

108

The Trusted Man followed the smell, and the smell led him to the *maso* up there on the rocks, outlined against the sunset. But he was not looking either at the sunset or at the *maso*. He was looking at the fire. And in the middle of the fire he saw the Wolf. Or rather, the Spider. He was walking strangely, hunched over, wrapped in his greatcoat, his black hat pulled down over his head.

There was no doubt: it was him.

The hunt was coming to an end.

Luckily for the Trusted Man, the Spider was busy, because if the man had turned, his own life would have been over. The Trusted Man quickly climbed onto a mass of rocks that stood higher than the *maso*. The cold and the fatigue were mere memories. Once he had reached this vantage point, he looked down just in time to see the Spider go back into the house. That did not worry him. From where he was, as long as there was daylight, he had an excellent view.

He took a metal box from his rucksack and set it down on the snow. Then he took off his gloves and breathed on his fingers until he could feel the blood circulating again. The temperature was plummeting. The Trusted Man opened the box and assembled the rifle with quick, efficient gestures.

It was his favourite: a 7.92-calibre Mauser 98k, which seldom missed.

He fitted the Zeiss scope and the silencer, the latter not because he thought he might attract attention – he assumed there was no living soul for kilometres around – but for fear of provoking an avalanche.

He put the box back into the rucksack and pulled out a rolled-up camping mat. He spread it on the snow and lay down on top of it, his left leg straight and his right slightly bent. The perfect position for shooting. He propped the butt on his shoulder and the barrel on the rock, then looked through the scope at the blueish flames the Spider had been stoking.

The Spider had dug a spiral trench around the *maso*, which stood at its very centre. Not satisfied, this strange mountain man had filled it with bundles of firewood, then set them on fire.

A blue fire.

The Trusted Man had seen fires like that before, but natural ones. They called them will-o'-the-wisps. Except that will-o'-the-wisps were the result of dead organisms decomposing, usually in swamps and marshes. Here, there was only ice and rock.

He wondered if the Spider had sprinkled some chemical devilment or other on the firewood. As it was impossible to tell why he had done so, the Trusted Man was not interested. The owner of the café in Merano was right: the Spider was mad. So why bother trying to understand what he was doing?

The Trusted Man emptied his mind. The Zeiss scope framed the door of the *maso*.

Night replaced twilight. The sky was clear, and there was no sign of the moon. Or of the Spider. It was getting colder. Every so often, the Trusted Man would breathe on his fingers, never taking his eyes off the door of the *maso*.

The starlight was reflected in the snow, creating a strange, hypnotic impression in conjunction with the blue flames of the spiral bonfire. The wind rose.

The Trusted Man squinted. He was breathing slowly, counting his heartbeats. He took a bar of chocolate from the pocket of his ski suit and chewed it without tasting it.

The only light in the *maso* came from a small window on the raised ground floor, right next to the door. The Trusted Man assumed it was the *Stube*.

But for the blazing firewood, he would not have waited this long. He would have burst into the house. But if the Spider had set that strange spiral on fire, the Trusted Man thought, he must have done it for a reason. Sooner or later, he would come back outside.

Best to wait, ready to shoot from a distance. It was more certain that way. He was three hundred metres from the *maso*. Even with this wind, it would be difficult for him to miss. He had managed to hit the target in much worse conditions.

Suddenly the door of the *maso* was flung open, and warm light spilled out, followed by the black shadow of the Spider. The Trusted Man blinked. The Spider was carrying more firewood in his arms. He kicked the door shut behind him with his heel and came down the steps.

The Trusted Man did not shoot. He watched as the Spider threw wood where the flames had died down and sprinkled powder on it. The blue glowed even brighter.

The Spider was obviously limping. Was he injured? There had not been any indication of a struggle in Wegener's villa. Maybe he had been in a fight since then. Or previously. Or perhaps the Spider had been born lame. Keeping him in the centre of the scope, the Trusted Man followed the Spider as he went back up the steps.

The Spider opened the door wide. The Trusted Man felt his shoulder muscles relax. The Spider stood out clearly against the light from the *Stube*. The Trusted Man pulled the trigger.

The Spider fell.

109

Marlene had lain curled up by the cellar door for hours, listening to Simon Keller chopping wood, singing and muttering, then to his heavy footsteps going back and forth in the *Stube*. It had occurred to her that he might want to set the *maso* on fire, with them inside it. The prospect had appealed to her. Better to die, even such a terrible death, than remain down here one more minute, one more second. She was going mad.

No, she was already mad, she was sure of it.

She had begun to hear sounds coming from the monolith. The rustling of a faraway, endless forest. The hissing of the wind between sheets of ice. Noises that had turned into voices. Mamma telling her that she would soon become like her: *crazycrazycrazy*, because she had wanted all that *moneymoneymoney* instead of being a shit shoveller, as was written in her stars. And when Simon Keller returned, Mamma had cackled, he would not find any Marlene in the basement. No Marlene the Brave or Marlene the Whore, just a tiny, squeaking little mouse, and then . . .

In an attempt to dismiss all this clamour, Marlene had begun telling herself stories. Out loud, and increasingly louder. Clinging to something that would help her not become like Mamma: *crazycrazycrazy*. Klaus did not deserve a mother like hers.

The voices ceased for a while. Then, as she was drifting to sleep, it was Onkel Fritz's turn.

A cavernous voice, like an ogre's, mumbling obscenities. Because in actual fact, Onkel Fritz had not struck her to punish her for theft.

One thief does not hit another, not even if she has wings and thinks she's a Thieving Magpie. No, Onkel Fritz wanted to tear her clothes off, roll her in the muck and hurt her, hurt her so much.

Because that was what she deserved. She was just a *shit shoveller, shit shoveller, shit shoveller*. And a whore, of course. Her mother had said it, but Onkel Fritz had realised it much earlier.

Hoping Simon Keller would hurry up and kill her, Marlene started to cry. That was when she felt something leap in her belly. Maybe it was her imagination. But no, she had felt it. A small drop of warmth in the midst of the cold she was feeling. Klaus.

The ghosts vanished. The monolith was once again what it was: a heap of old books and nothing else. But not Lissy. Lissy had been watching her constantly through the window, but she was just a sow and would never be able to get past the metal bars into the cellar. She could carry on biting them with those fangs of hers that she had instead of teeth, and perhaps even damage the iron, but the truth was that Lissy was always hungry and a disgusting lump of fat like her would not be able to get through that window in a million years.

This thought gave Marlene strength.

And so, without Mamma's racket, Onkel Fritz's obscenities and Lissy's eyes, Marlene the Brave started to think again. And as she thought, she smiled. And as she smiled, she started searching.

Because Onkel Fritz was right. Marlene the Brave was a shit shoveller. A real shit shoveller. How much of it had she shovelled in her life? Tons. Chicken shit, goat and cow dung. And pig shit. Enough to fill a lorry. Except that the shit was not done with the moment she had left the mountains. She had had to shovel shit after that, too. Even though it did not always stink.

Shit was the smiles that said "Here comes the whore" whenever Wegener introduced her to his associates at some social occasion.

Shit was the tears whenever she heard Wegener give orders over the telephone. Shit was the jewellery, the nail polish, the clothes. Shit was Old Mother Frost. The world was one huge open-air pigsty.

And Marlene knew how to deal with shit.

Seek and ye shall find, she kept muttering. Seek and ye shall find.

110

Cautiously, the Trusted Man got to his feet, pointing the Mauser, still with the Spider in the centre of the scope. He stretched his legs and shook off the snow. He arched his back. His vertebrae cracked.

He began his descent. The wind made his eyes water, but he did not close them even for a second. When he was thirty metres or so from the *maso*, his face paralysed from the cold, he began to feel the waves of heat coming from the Spider's spiral bonfire. He kept going.

He knew the Spider was not dead. He had not shot to kill. If that had been his intention, he would not have taken so many precautions. He had shot to wound.

The Spider and the Vixen. He wanted to know what connected them.

The Spider's knee was in a bad way. There was a pool of blood all around it. The black-clad old man was moaning, his face turned towards the *Stube*. The Trusted Man pressed the barrel of his rifle to the back of his neck.

"Where is she?"

The Spider was about to turn, but the Trusted Man pressed harder, preventing him from doing so.

"The girl. Marlene."

"There's no Marlene here."

"The girl with the sapphires. Where is she?"

The Spider said nothing.

"Hand her over," the Trusted Man said, "and I'll spare your life."

"There's no Marlene here. There's just Lissy."

The Trusted Man frowned. Who was Lissy? What had he missed? "Where?"

"Down there. With my father. And my father's father."

The Trusted Man bit his lip. It was so cold that he felt no pain.

The old man was delirious. Or pretending to be.

"I'm only interested in Marlene. Then I'll let you live."

"With this leg?"

"Where is she?"

Lying there on the ground, the old man was losing a lot of blood.

"Don't faint."

"In the cellar, beneath the *Stube*, there's a door. It's locked."

This made no sense.

"Have you locked her in?"

"Yes."

The Trusted Man searched the old man's pale face. "Did you kill Wegener?"

"Yes."

"Why?"

The old man closed his eyes tight. "Sweet Lissy, little Lissy."

The Trusted Man moved the barrel of the rifle from the back of the old man's neck to the mangled knee and pressed down on the wound.

A terrible grimace on his congested face, the old man cried louder, "Sweet Lissy! Little Lissy! Sweet—"

The Trusted Man fired again. The old man screamed. The chanting ceased.

"It makes no sense. It makes no sense."

The old man turned slowly towards him. Now that the Trusted Man was able to look him in the face, he realised that the old man's pupils were narrow and his eyes watery. He was under the influence of some drug or other.

"The world teems with mysteries."

That statement did not make much sense either.

"The key," the Trusted Man said, on edge now. "You said the door is locked. Give me the key, and I'll make the pain stop."

The old man gave it to him. As soon as the Trusted Man's hand closed over it, the old man grabbed his wrist and pulled the Trusted Man towards him. He did it so quickly that the Trusted Man had no time to react. One moment he was pointing the rifle at the old man, the next he was on the ground, lying on top of him. Eye to eye. The Spider was *strong*.

"It's coming," the old man whispered.

"What is?" the Trusted Man said, surprised.

"The truth."

The Trusted Man felt the blow in his stomach. The world turned upside down. He hit the wall of the *maso*. He saw the old man, wounded but still in possession of incredible physical strength, throw himself to the side, hurtle down the creaky wooden steps and plunge into the darkness. He heard a thud and a stifled scream. Getting up, he grabbed and aimed the Mauser in a single gesture.

At nothing.

The old man had vanished into the shadows.

The Trusted Man hesitated.

The Spider was done for. However strong and stoned, no human being could survive the wound he had inflicted. With one knee out of action and haemorrhaging blood, he was a negligible threat. Certainly not an immediate one. He decided to forget about him.

He would not let him live, of course. The Trusted Man never left witnesses. He would kill Marlene then take care of the old man. It would be child's play following the bloodstains in the snow. First, he had to find the Vixen.

He walked inside.

111

The door opened. The figure outlined against the light was not Simon Keller.

Hiding on the other side of the black monolith, behind an overturned bookcase, her back pressed up against the damp wall, Marlene held her breath.

The man was carrying a rifle over his shoulder.

"Marlene?" the stranger called out.

Marlene made herself small.

"It's over," the voice said. "You can come out."

Marlene did not answer.

The man came down a couple of steps. "I've come to save you. It's over. You're free."

Marlene did not know who this man was, what had happened to Simon Keller, whether it was day or night or whether this encounter was no more than the fruit of her imagination. What she did know was that, for all his tone of concern, the stranger was lying. Being a good shit shoveller, she improvised. She grabbed a blanket and put it over her legs.

"I guess you don't trust me," the voice said. "I wouldn't either if I were in your shoes. You don't know why I'm here. You don't know anything. You've been through a lot, I understand that. How long has he been keeping you a prisoner?"

Another step.

There weren't many left.

"Do you want some answers?" the soothing voice asked. "You

know about the Consortium, don't you? They've sent me. Don't be afraid. The debt has been settled. Wegener's dead. But you already know that, don't you?"

This man knew a great deal. Perhaps too much. Or had she been locked up for so long she couldn't believe it really was over?

"You have the sapphires. Hand them over to me and that's the end of the story. You're still frightened of that man in black, aren't you?"

Marlene stared.

"He's dead," the voice announced.

Simon Keller. Dead. Dead. *Dead.*

"Of course!" the stranger exclaimed, stopping at the bottom of the steps. "It's the rifle. It scares you. You're right. Now the old man's dead, I don't need it anymore. Look."

Standing against the light, the man lowered the rifle, propped it against the wall, stepped away from it and raised his hands in the air. As he leaned to the side, Marlene saw his face. He looked like a famous actor.

He was smiling.

"I'm here," Marlene said in a low voice.

"Come on, let's get out of here. Are you hungry? I saw there's food in the *Stube*. I can make you something to eat. Then you can rest. Maybe we could wait till daylight before going back to town. There's no rush. I'll keep watch."

"I'm chained," Marlene said. "I can't move. He didn't want me to run away."

The stranger looked at the overturned bookcase. Her hiding place. Coming closer, he saw her. She lay curled up on the floor, her legs covered with a moth-eaten blanket.

He came closer still. "Marlene," he said, "it's a pleasure to meet you in person. I've heard so much about you. You're a resourceful girl."

Marlene pushed her hair away from her face and stared at the stranger. He stood there looking at her, hands on hips. He was smiling.

But not with his eyes.

Marlene smiled back.

"They said you were beautiful." He crouched beside her. "But I never imagined you were *this* beautiful."

He was reassuring. Too reassuring. Like the voice of the witch. *Who is nibbling at my house?*

Marlene the Brave made up her mind. "Can you see me?" she said.

"Of course," the Trusted Man said, surprised.

"Good," she said, "because you're not going to see me anymore."

She made a sudden gesture, and a cloud of white dust settled on the Trusted Man's face. Quicklime. Shit shovellers' stuff. It scalds, it burns. And if it gets into your eyes . . .

Nibble, nibble, *nibble*. Quicklime, too, was always hungry. Just like Lissy.

The Trusted Man jerked back, screaming. He banged into a cupboard and knocked it over, causing a whole lot of bric-a-brac to come tumbling down, burying him. He screamed with increasing pain as the quicklime acted on the mucous membranes of his eyes.

Marlene quickly threw herself in the opposite direction.

Out, out, out.

She climbed three steps, stopped, turned back, grabbed the stranger's rifle – by now he was gasping and writhing – and dashed to the door.

The key was still in the lock. She turned it twice.

112

The *Stube* was empty.

No spoons this time. Marlene was brandishing a Mauser, waving it right and left, feeling clumsy and stupid. She'd never seen a rifle like this before. It was a weapon of war, not for hunting like the one Simon Keller had, with barrels one on top of the other, or her father's double-barrelled model.

But it worked the same way, she told herself. Decide who you want to kill and pull the trigger.

She went to the door and saw blood.

The stranger said he had killed Simon Keller. There was blood here, but no sign of Simon. The dead don't go walkabout. It wasn't over.

Where are you? Where are you?

The wind clawed at her face. She came back inside, stood the rifle against the wall and put on her padded jacket. She brushed Simon Keller's rifle with her fingers. She looked at the Mauser. It had a magazine, unlike Simon's rifle. Marlene knew nothing about weapons, but she knew that a magazine contained more bullets than a normal rifle.

More ammunition meant a higher chance of hitting the bull's eye. That was excellent news for someone who had never handled a firearm in her life.

The excellent piece of news is that you're alone. Get out of here. Move!

There was some black bread on the table. There was also water. She could not resist the water. She drank it and took a few bites of the bread. Then she drank some more. All that cold, ice-cold, wonderful water. It tasted so good it almost made her cry.

Still she did not leave. This time, she would do things properly.

There was a Bible on the *Stube*. Marlene tore out the pages, arranged them in an insulating layer around her body and buttoned up her jacket. Then she took some rags and stuffed them down her trousers, around her shins and thighs.

It was cold outside, very cold. She grabbed the Mauser. Ready? Ready.

The broken banister bore witness to the struggle between the stranger and Simon Keller. The fires around the *maso* were like a whisper of madness, terrifying her. She started to run.

Towards safety.

The heat of the flames wafted over her face. She ran past the first circle of the blue spiral. The heat was inviting. She passed the second circle and stopped.

It was too cold, much too cold. What she was doing was pure madness. She would never survive out there, beyond the fire. Paper could not withstand frost. Who was she kidding? Death was waiting for her further down the mountain.

For her and for Klaus. He was not even born yet, and already he was condemned. By his own mother.

No, stop talking nonsense. If you go ahead, you'll die. If you keep still, you'll die. There's only one thing to do.

Find Simon Keller and finish him off.

Spend the night in the *Stube*. Eat. Rest. Wait for dawn. Go down the mountain.

Forget.

But not before setting fire to the *maso* and the stranger inside.

Shut him in the oven and let him *scream*. To hell with everything and everybody.

Then she heard it.

The jingling.

113

The Trusted Man's fingers found something. Slimy stone and metal. Panting, he rubbed his fingertips on it. A small window with metal bars. The stone was damp and warm to the touch.

His eyes had turned into burning embers. But the stone was damp. He needed water to rinse his eyes before the quicklime damaged the corneas and left him blind. He would make do with the few drops oozing from the stone.

He knelt below the window. He wiped his hands on his ski suit, resisting the impulse to rub his eyelids. His eyes were hurting a lot. It could have been worse, he thought, if the quicklime had hit him right in the middle of his eyes. But luckily, that had not happened. Plus, he was real. He could feel the pain but would not be overwhelmed by it. And death was reserved for illusions.

Only a small amount of the handful of quicklime Marlene had thrown had ended up in his eyes. Much more of it was on his face. His face was burning, too, because of the sweat, but fortunately not as much as his eyes. He might end up scarred, and that could be a problem in the future. A disfigured man attracts attention. But he would deal with that in due course.

Once he had finished wiping his hands on the wind-resistant fabric, he pressed them against the cellar wall, wet them, and put them on his eyelids. He forced himself to keep his eyes open. The pain was excruciating. He pulled his hands away, cursed, spat on the floor, took deep breaths. He calmed down. He rubbed his fingers again and laid them on his face, determined this time to withstand the pain. He repeated the procedure three more times, then tried looking around.

The world was shrouded in white mist but he could still see. Not enough, though. He put his hands on his eyes and rubbed, then did so again. The haze cleared, enough to allow him to get back into action. He took a flick-knife out of his pocket, pressed the button and heard the familiar mechanical click. Twenty centimetres of Swedish steel. A good blade.

There was a terrible stench of pigs. The window was square, sixty centimetres by sixty. With a little push, he would be able to use it as a way out. He beat on the frame with the blade of the flick-knife. It was sturdy, but he did not lose heart. Clicking his tongue, he wedged the point of the blade between the metal and the mortar, trying to lever it out. The metal was solid, but the mortar was old and yielded.

He sat down Native American–style and began scraping patiently. Every so often, he would use the flick-knife as a lever.

The grille began to give way in several places. This almost made him forget the pain in his eyes. His left eye in particular worried him. It was certainly damaged.

As the window was about to yield, he thought he heard a wheezing sound.

A voice saying, "Sweet Lissy. Little Lissy."

114

Lissy.

Marlene heard her coming. The bitch. She picked up the rifle and propped it on her shoulder. The wind drowned the sound of the little bell, and the crackling of the firewood did not help.

Should she aim right or left?

A squat, shadowy figure behind the flames, straight ahead of her. Marlene pulled the trigger. The rifle came to life. There was an explosion and, at the same time, a pain in her shoulder.

The Mauser recoiled, hitting her chin. Stunned, Marlene slipped backwards and fell. She shook her head, got to her feet and checked.

No sow, only the flames.

She picked up the rifle again. She had to reload it, but how?

There was a lever on one side, and Marlene remembered the gangster films Wegener liked so much. Pull and push. Or push and pull. One of the two. She pushed and pulled. Then pulled and pushed. There was a metallic clang. Just like in the films.

The rifle was cocked. At least she hoped so.

She wedged the butt of the Mauser in the hollow of her shoulder, which was throbbing like an abscessed tooth. She put a hand on the breech, thinking about the way the rifle had bounced out of her hands and trying to calculate the recoil as best she could.

"Okay."

One step. Head tilted, muscles tense, finger on the trigger. She jumped over a strip of fire where the flames had burned away the fuel, creating a gap. The fire lapped at her hair but nothing happened except that there was a slight smell of burning. Otherwise, there was only the wind and the cold.

And the little bell, somewhere close by, to her left.

Marlene turned and fired. The bullet vanished in the dark. Her shoulder protested. But at least the rifle stayed where it was. Pull and push. The clang. Rifle cocked. How many bullets were left? She had no way of knowing. Shit.

The little bell. Lissy. *Behind* her. Damn her, she was fast.

Marlene turned and fired. The shot faded in the darkness.

Pull and push. Pray there was still something to shoot with.

Where are you? Where are you?

A particularly strong gust of wind moved the fire in her direction. This time, Marlene did not just smell burning, she also felt the heat. She let go of the rifle and threw herself in the snow with a sob. She looked up and there she was.

The bitch.

Lissy.

Black against a blue background. With the fire behind her. Wagging her little tail. Four hundred kilos of black.

Her crest moved twice, left and right, as if she were denying something.

No way, sweetie. You're not getting out of here. No way.

The white stripes under her eyelids were glowing like exclamation marks charged with menace. Her fangs were dripping with saliva. Because Lissy was hungry, Marlene thought.

She was always hungry.

The sow emitted a couple of snorts through her nostrils, which then turned into clouds of condensation. She took a couple of steps forward, holding Marlene transfixed with her eyes. You're food, those nasty little eyes said. Food for Lissy.

Marlene reached out for the rifle.

Lissy froze. Legs quivering, head turned to the side to get a better look at her.

Slowly, Marlene brought the Mauser closer. Slowly, she got up on one knee. Slowly, she put the rifle to her shoulder. Slowly, she closed one eye and aimed.

Slowly, she put her index finger on the trigger.

Lissy lowered her head, bending it towards the snow, baring her fangs at her.

Lissy *screamed*, and charged.

The little bell rang wildly.

Lissy advanced, head down, sending up snow and ice with her trotters, her powerful muscles rippling like demons under her black coat, steam billowing from her nostrils, her sharp, curved fangs ready to rip Marlene open.

Don't shoot.

She didn't.

Let her come closer.

Fifteen metres.

Without slowing down, Lissy raised her snout to the stars and screamed again.

The barrel of the Mauser shook.

Ten metres.

Fangs like the blades of a plough.

Nine metres. Eight.

Getting closer and closer.

Marlene felt the ground being battered by Lissy as she ran. She felt the vibrations of this black, evil mass coming towards her.

Now!

The firing pin clicked on empty. She had run out of ammunition. She closed her eyes and dropped the rifle, prepared to feel the full weight of Lissy. The impact. Her bones groaning and breaking beneath Lissy's fury. Fangs sinking into her flesh. The pain. The suffering. And death.

356

She apologised to Klaus.

She could feel the sow's breath, but there was no impact, no pain, no blood. Nothing but the sound of the little bell. Marlene opened her eyes.

Blue flames. The dark. The wind.

No Lissy.

Just the prints of her trotters in the snow, coming to within a metre of her, then changing course and vanishing behind the curtain of fire. Marlene put her hand on her heart. She thought she could feel it beating through the fabric of her jacket and the pages from the Bible. She was still alive.

Why?

115

With what little strength he had left, Simon Keller opened the door in the grille and let Lissy out of her cage and out of the sty.

Maybe the cold would kill her, but ice was more merciful than hunger.

Alone now, he felt that his end had come and that death lay curled up at his feet. Tired as he was, he could not quite make it out. But he knew it was there.

Death was not cold.

He had always imagined it to be ice cold, ever since he had first encountered it, when *Voter* Luis had introduced it to him years earlier. A long time had passed since then, and they had become friends. He had glimpsed it whenever he killed.

And now death was here for him.

"I thought you were cold," he said.

Death did not reply.

He pressed down on the floor with his hands and dragged himself to Lissy's bed in the dark corner. He realised he was smeared with shit and felt sorry about that. The clothes Marlene had made for him were beautiful, the most beautiful he had ever owned.

But now he was dying and nothing mattered. He smiled and death smiled with him.

"You can read my thoughts, can't you?"

Yes, it could.

Death came closer, leaned over him and planted a soft kiss on his forehead. Keller could smell its breath. It was like the aroma of freshly cut hay. He closed his eyes and saw it.

A lush meadow. Tall, ripe grass bending in a light breeze as pleasant as a flowing stream in summer. There was a tree in the middle of the meadow. Somebody was hiding behind it.

But the breeze made him open his eyes again.

It was not the breeze, it was death. Death was kneeling next to him, close to him.

"What is this place?" he asked.

There was no answer.

With a caress, death closed his eyes. It put its hand on his heart and the beating grew fainter. And for this he was grateful.

The tree was an ash, proud and strong. Keller felt small beside it, which made him happy.

He approached, wanting to know who was hiding behind the trunk.

A voice called him.

Sim'l.

She had not changed despite all these years. He hugged her.

"Lissy," Sim'l said, smelling the aroma of cut hay in the little girl's hair.

She stood aside and handed him a little wooden pig. The pig was smiling. The little girl pointed at the light, and Simon wished he could go there.

"Push harder," he told death.

Death did not obey. It withdrew.

Keller nodded and coughed. Death did not obey anybody. It was wilful. It would come before its time and then vanish if it was called.

He had to be patient.

The meadows. The trees.

The light.

Elisabeth took him by the hand and led him beyond the ash tree. Keller was sorry because he felt that the ash tree loved him. It had always loved him. All that light.

Then death disappeared, and Lissy vanished.

Keller was back in the pigsty.

And he was no longer alone.

116

"You scared her off," Keller said in a tone of regret.

Holding the knife, the Trusted Man looked around. There was nobody there. "Who?" he asked.

"Lissy," Keller replied with a sad smile. "You made her run away. But she'll be back soon. She's never left, you know. She's always been here. With me."

He let his eyes drift around the pigsty. Death was here somewhere. It was waiting for the stranger to leave so that it could come back and take him to Elisabeth. All Keller wanted was to see the meadows again. And the light. All that light.

All the Trusted Man could see were the carcasses of dead pigs, a wooden pen and a lantern hanging from a dark beam. The light from the lantern made his one good eye sting. He rubbed it. It hurt. The other one had gone. Nothing but quicklime.

He lowered the flick-knife and shook his head. "You're mad."

Keller focused on him, and the Trusted Man realised that death would soon take him.

"I used to think that, too," Keller said, panting. "But Lissy's not mean. She's never lied to me. It's not an illusion. Lissy is real. Lissy has always been with me. She's never abandoned me. And she never will."

With difficulty, he slipped his hand inside his waistcoat and pulled out a little bell, which he shook three times. He could not manage a fourth. Even that tiny little bell was too heavy for him. It slipped from his fingers and fell in the muck. The silvery jingling faded away.

Nothing happened. Nobody came. It was just the two of them. The Trusted Man remembered the words of one of the old men at the inn. He had said that *Voter* Luis' son was a man of faith, just like the holy man who had taught him to see the world through eyes full of mercy. But they were both just men. And men wished for illusions. Consolation.

And it was with eyes full of mercy that the Trusted Man went close to Keller, pointing the flick-knife, and whispered, "Do you want me to bring her to you? Is that what you want?"

Keller raised his arm with difficulty and pointed to a spot behind him, behind the ash tree, on the hill.

Lissy was beautiful. Barefoot in the meadow.

Lissy was holding out the little wooden pig. The little pig was smiling.

And the light. There was all that light.

The Trusted Man did not see the light, but he heard jingling. He turned abruptly.

She was there.

Up there on the threshold. Up there on the hill.

"Lissy," Keller called.

Lissy, the Trusted Man thought. Lissy was a sow. A large, nasty black sow.

Lissy lowered her head and charged. She came down the steps like an avalanche and hurled herself at the Trusted Man. Before he was knocked down he instinctively struck out at her, plunging the knife into the thick layer of fat around her body, but it was as if she didn't even feel it. The impact broke the Trusted Man's femur. The blade stayed there, sticking out of the sow's hide. Lissy raised her snout, and the Trusted Man felt himself being lifted, practically to the ceiling.

He remained suspended in mid-air for a few seconds, then fell to the floor, face down, screaming.

Lissy came crashing into his back, skewering him and making

him roll against the male pigs' pen. He turned and raised his hand to shield himself from a second attack. Lissy tore off three of his fingers with a single bite. The Trusted Man saw his blood spurt, watched it form a perfect arc then fall to the stone floor – and disappear.

The pigsty, the dead pigs, the wooden pen, the metal bars, the window, the shit, the dying *Bau'r*, everything was disappearing, erased like chalk on a blackboard. The Trusted Man looked into the sow's eyes and saw a terrible, infinite hunger in them. What he did not see in them was his reflection. Or the world's.

Only Lissy was real.

She lowered her head to split his stomach open with her sharp fangs, but Keller's voice stopped her.

"Sweet Lissy, little Lissy."

Lissy turned to the *Bau'r*, and the Trusted Man saw him ring the little bell. He saw Lissy approach the *Bau'r*. He saw her lower her head and lick his face. He saw him stroke the sow's bloodied snout and heard him repeat these words: "Sweet Lissy."

The sow rubbed her muzzle against the old man's face.

"Little Lissy."

The sow started to cry.

The Trusted Man opened his mouth, then closed it again. He started laughing. It was madness. Sheer madness. What he had seen in the sow's eyes did not matter. She was just a sow. He was a weapon. He was the only solid thing in the world.

He *was* the world.

He crawled towards the steps. Towards the darkness outside. He dragged himself up the first step. His broken femur radiated unbearable pain as it hit the steps, much worse than his hand. But the Trusted Man blessed the pain. The pain allowed him to feel the steps, to see his own hands as he climbed. He kept telling himself he was a weapon. He looked at the world through eyes full of mercy. He must not forget that. No.

The second step. The third. The Trusted Man pressed his torn hand against the stone. He banged his femur. He wanted to feel pain.

He looked up. Not far to go. He had only to keep dragging himself. Get to the door. And overtake Marlene.

Even though she was translucent, the Trusted Man recognised her. The raven-black hair, the beauty spot, the eyes glowing like embers. Marlene pointed the old man's rifle at him.

The Trusted Man raised his mutilated hand. "I . . . I beg you."

Marlene took a deep breath and lowered the barrel of the rifle.

The Trusted Man took another step forward. The step was as soft as mud, but he was not. He was real. He was solid. The sow was an illusion, the *Bau'r* was an illusion, the girl was an illusion. Illusions that existed because he existed. That was why the void into which the world was rushing would never engulf him. That was why the girl would do whatever he asked her.

Without him everything would vanish.

"Drop the rifle," the Trusted Man commanded.

Marlene let it drop.

Just three more steps.

Clear. Perfect.

Two.

"Now help me," the Trusted Man said, reaching out to her with his good hand.

Marlene looked at him. She looked right through him. Her eyes were cold.

She closed the door and locked it.

The door vanished.

The Trusted Man was now floating in a void, distraught. He was no longer a weapon. He was a man again, the most frightened of men. His perfect world was a perfect fiction. The Trusted Man was frightened of everything.

He no longer had arms or legs. Or a head. All that was left

was panic. And what would happen when panic, too, vanished?

In the void, the Trusted Man heard Keller's voice and clung to it.

"Lissy. Sweet Lissy. Little . . ."

The pain returned. So did the door and the pigsty. Just a bare outline. Opaque. But solid, real.

He begged the old man to continue, he begged death to grant him just enough life to chant a little longer. To become solid again. But instead, death approached Simon Keller and took his heart in its hand. Gently. Like *Voter* Luis when he lifted him up to show him the nests on the branches of the trees. Death blew, and Simon Keller's heart stopped beating.

The *Bau'r* breathed his last.

The Trusted Man heard that faint link disappear, and once again he was panting in the dark. Then, with what little strength he had left, he looked for a way to cheat death.

"Lissy," he said. "Little Lissy."

A sound emerged from the void. A little bell ringing.

"Sweet Lissy."

And Lissy came.

117

1984

The sea's undertow is a lullaby. The woman sitting on the shore is beautiful. She looks older than her thirty-two years, but she's beautiful. Nobody can deny that.

She is especially beautiful as she watches the little girl building sandcastles. She taught her to. She's her daughter and her whole world.

The little girl also has black hair and is also very beautiful. You can tell they are mother and daughter. They have the same smile.

The little girl speaks Spanish and knows only a few words of German. *Mutti* is her favourite. But she only uses it when they are alone together.

The little girl's name is Astrid, but to everyone here she's Estrella. Estrella is a beautiful name.

Marlene does not mind the fact that the little girl cannot speak German or Italian. Or that she has no interest in her mother's country.

Estrella will never go back to those mountains.

She and Carlos have sworn that. Astrid must never know anything about her birth. About Herr Wegener, about Simon Keller. Nothing. Carlos knows the whole story. Marlene loves him and could never have lied to him. She really does love him. Carlos is a patient, gentle man. He met this stranger with a heavily scarred soul and made her laugh and fall in love. His love brought her back to life. Carlos also loves Estrella. He says she's a gift. She truly is. For both of them.

There is only one thing Carlos does not know: a memory Marlene is trying to erase. She will finally manage it, a year or two from now. The moment when the midwife had placed the raven-haired baby in her lap and asked her what she wanted to call it. Klaus, Marlene had replied.

Klaus. But Klaus is a boy's name.

The midwife had smiled. "It's a girl. A lovely girl."

Marlene had looked. Yes, a girl.

"I'll call her Astrid. Like a star."

She had said Astrid. But it was another name she had thought of.

118

It was lovely off-piste. The fresh snow, the whole of nature just for them. That was how they met, in the mountains. Except that now she has a broken ankle (although he says it's just a nasty sprain) and the idea of fresh snow and nature all for themselves is no longer so romantic.

Snow, nature. And no emergency services.

He is not discouraged, he's not like that. He lifts her over his shoulder and starts retracing his steps, following the ski trail. She's a heavy load, but he knows he can make it. He's fit, and it's just another adventure to tell your friends about, nothing more.

Except that then it starts to snow. Well, of course it does. They are in the mountains, and it is late November. The weather forecaster was not talking nonsense. And that is a problem. There's too much snow. The tracks are like Hansel and Gretel's breadcrumbs: they are disappearing.

The trees all look the same. The snowfall turns into a blizzard. Then it is dark. And cold. The cold bites at your muscles and your voice becomes hoarse. But there is nobody about. Only nature, just for them.

They do not realise how scared they are until a man emerges from out of the blizzard. He is blind in one eye, but he has a beautiful smile. Just like a Hollywood actor.

He looks like an old man, especially because of the greatcoat he is wearing, but he cannot be that old, judging from how easily he puts the girl over his shoulder.

Lucky for them, because the young man's at the end of his tether.

The older man points to the top of the mountain. Up there is the house of *Voter* Simon, he says, a man of faith. They can wait there for the blizzard to pass, and in the meantime he will give them something warm.

I was hungry and you gave me food.

Thus it is written.

The young man can barely hear him; he walks right behind him and cannot stop thanking him.

In the wind, the older man walks and starts chanting.

119

"Sweet Lissy, little Lissy."

Acknowledgments

Thank you to Piergiorgio Nicolazzini, tireless workaholic, and Luca Briasco, because unstoppable is the least one can say about him. To Francesco Colombo, who always knows the right word. To Severino Cesari, spiritual father of these pages, to Paolo Repetti, Rosella Postorino, Raffaella Baiocchi, and the entire Einaudi family. Thank you to the *Kräutermandl*, *Voter* and *Bau'rn* who have shared their knowledge with me without asking for anything in return, and to Aldo Gorfer, whose works are an unequalled source of inspiration. Thank you to Hermann Tamanini, gentleman and man of medicine. Thank you to Robert Gorreri for his record-breaking advice. Thank you to Luis for his patience, to Maurizio Girardi because the second one was better than the first, and to Michele Melani, sparring partner, talented man and friend.

Last but not least, thank you to Alessandra, steady at the helm when I go "to the other side."

LUCA D'ANDREA was born in 1979 in Bolzano, Italy. *Beneath the Mountain*, his first novel, was translated into thirty-five languages and was a bestseller across Europe. *Sanctuary* was the winner of the 2017 Scerbanenco Award.

HOWARD CURTIS is an award-winning translator of Italian and French literature. His translations include works by Georges Simenon, Gianrico Carofiglio and Marco Malvaldi.

KATHERINE GREGOR is a literary translator and writer who has also been an EFL teacher, a theatrical agent, a press agent and a theatre director.

ALSO BY LUCA D'ANDREA

BENEATH THE MOUNTAIN
A NOVEL

".... D'Andrea's story sweeps away the reader in an avalanche of life-threatening revelations that make Beneath the Mountain a complete success as a debut thriller."
—*New York Journal of Books*

In Luca D'Andrea's atmospheric and brilliant thriller, set in a small mountain community in the majestic Italian Dolomites, an outsider must uncover the truth about a triple murder that has gone unsolved for thirty years. Completely engrossing and deeply atmospheric, *Beneath The Mountain* is a thriller par excellence.